This book is dedicated to the memory of
Chris Altemara and Race Godsen,
who taught me that I am capable of doing anything.

"They prefer their meals alive and terrified, for fear is their favorite sauce."

—Donald G. Firesmith, Demons on the Dalton

"Keep away. The sow is mine."

—William Peter Blatty, The Exorcist

"And when He came to the other side into the country of the Gadarenes, two demon-possessed men confronted Him as they were coming out of the tombs. They were so extremely violent that no one could pass by that way. And they cried out, saying, 'What business do You have with us, Son of God? Have You come here to torment us before the time?' Now there was a herd of many pigs feeding at a distance from them. And the demons begged Him, saying, 'If You are going to cast us out, send us into the herd of pigs.' And He said to them, 'Go!'"

—Matthew 8:28-32

ONE

Though his eyes were closed, and he was no longer on the inside of the old run-down shack, the face still taunted him, etched into the back of his eyelids, glaring into his soul with black, lifeless eyes. He again gasped for breath as the acrid smell crept out of the doorway, following him into the overgrown garden. The odor wrapped its invisible arms around him from behind, cloaking him with its essence, squeezing him in a bear hug he could not escape from. His attempt to evade the smell by putting more distance between himself and the shed proved pointless; it had already found its way into the fibers of his clothes and made itself a new home.

How did he end up here tonight? There was no plan for this. Of course, a police officer needed to prepare for anything, but in Cumberland Springs "anything" never amounted to much more than a speeding ticket or a cat stuck in a tree. He never imagined he would one day stare into the eyes of a living nightmare. Eyes that eagerly pulled at him, tempting him to fall into a hideous world of darkness and dread.

Just moments ago Glen Crawford's life was simple, not completely boring, yet by no means bold... Vanilla. Just the way he liked it. The rest of the world could continue to spiral out of control—as it appeared to be doing through the eyes of evening cable news—as long as it left Glen, his family, and his tranquil town of Cumberland Springs in peace. He had always imagined someday the madness would discover this place. A place where people were happy and kind and still respected and trusted each other. It would see simple folks in this tight-knit community living peaceful lives, enjoying quiet days together, and it would say, "*This cannot stand!*" It would then ascend on their gentle existence, slither through the well-maintained streets and picket fences searching for the innocent, looking to deface and destroy the simple life which so many here have worked a lifetime to achieve. The world outside would indeed creep in one day, and tonight in Glen Crawford's mind, that day may have just arrived.

He thought about his wife, Vicki, at home in bed, how beautiful she must look right now curled up under their warm oversized comforter and how much he adored her. How could he describe what he'd just seen? He couldn't hide it, she'd see right through him the second her eyes met with his.

Get your shit together, Crawford! He thought, shaking his head, attempting to snap himself back into reality.

"Are you going to be alright, Glen," Mrs. Rolley said, touching his arm.

He looked down at the small gray-haired woman and smiled. Her concerned voice brought him out of his thoughts and back to the moment. Behind her the potting shed loomed against the night sky, its dark opening reminding him of what lay in the shadows just beyond the doorway. Another shiver poked at the underside of his skin.

At around 9:30 this evening, when Glen got into his police cruiser after a late-night lunch break at Nana's Diner, he noticed a thin sheen of frost had formed on the car's windshield. It was a subtle sign that Pennsylvania weather was about to throw its first punches of the year. Being the Chief of Police meant that when the mess came, he was sure to be waist-deep in car wrecks, stranded motorists, and a full buffet of other emergencies the snow season brought to the table. A frosted windshield on a cold November evening was a sure indicator of what would soon come this way.

He exhaled a long sigh when he saw the frost expelling a cloud of condensation in the air. He thought about getting out to scrape the glass, then vetoed the idea. The only thing he had planned for the remaining few hours of his shift was to sit at his favorite speed trap along Route 31 and listen to an audiobook. A few extra minutes in Nana's parking lot, while the defroster worked on the glass, wouldn't matter much.

Several chilling moments passed before a subtle warmth began trickling through the defroster vents. It would be another ten minutes or so before the windshield cleared enough to see through safely. He had the time.

"Car 01, dispatch, over." The staticky words of the station dispatcher crackled through the police radio speakers. A squelch of feedback followed her voice.

Glen reached for the mic and pressed the side button. "Car 01, over."

"Be advised of a 10-66, Suspicious Person, reported at 414 Township RD #4. Over."

Suspicious Person? Glen didn't think he'd ever received *that* call before. There were no suspicious people here. In most places in America, a call like this wouldn't give pause to a police officer. But here? There were no strangers in Cumberland Springs. Residents promptly deposed every new arrival visiting Cumberland Springs. All information ascertained by these innocent depositions—covertly disguised as small talk—quickly passed along the various wires and communication avenues throughout the rest of the community, thus removing the stigma of *stranger* and allowing the newcomer to conduct their business free of scrutiny. Glen couldn't remember the last time he'd even heard the word *stranger* used around here, if he'd ever heard it at all. The tourists never lingered long on their way through to the ski resort 15 miles up Route 31. Maybe a stop for gas and a bite to eat at Nana's, but they never stuck around for more than an hour. A *stranger* was something altogether uncommon.

And she said Township Road #4. There were only three houses out there. One was for sale, the other had been vacant for several years, and the third was... "Was that Mrs. Rolley who called in? Over."

"Yes, Chief, it was. Over."

"Shit," Glen said without activating the mic.

"She said a strange man is sleeping in the garden shed behind her house. Over."

Glen stared at the frozen windshield, contemplating what he had just heard. *A stranger in Mrs. Rolley's garden shed?* It took him a few seconds to realize it, but he was smiling. He had to think about it, though, this odd grin on his face. Where did that come from? As his thoughts dug deeper through the catalog of reasons, he came up with two: First, had he been so bored with life lately and so void of excitement that the thought of confronting a person unknown had awakened his sense of adventure? Could this be a fugitive on the run? A bank robber? Someone on the FBI's most-wanted list? Those were all possibilities. Of course, it could also be a drunk from town who stumbled out there to sleep one off, and she simply didn't recognize him (the most plausible explanation). The second reason for this unexpected grin—and probably the real reason— was that he knew the old garden shed on Mrs. Rolley's property and knew it well. Glen spent most of his childhood summers playing in that shed with her sons, Michael and Lucas. When the dispatcher mentioned the shed, a flood of memories washed over him. He could feel hot July sun on his skin and heard the laughter of the two best friends he'd ever had, cracking jokes and wrestling with each other on freshly cut grass. The garden shed was their clubhouse and the center of the universe for those few unforgettable years, the years mostly everyone has and reflects upon often when adult life isn't going well (what we wouldn't give to go back just for one day). Glen now understood the smile on his face, and he embraced it like an old friend.

"Chief? Over."

The voice harshly snapped him back to the present. "Yeah Lindsay, I'm on my way out there now. Over."

The frost had melted away in two oval patterns close to the dashboard. Not full visibility, but there was enough space to see through if he leaned forward. Glen had pulled people over in the past for doing this very thing, but they weren't on official police business.

When he arrived at Mrs. Rolley's home moments later, she was on the porch, arms crossed, face stern, like a century standing guard. "He hasn't come out of there yet, or made any attempt to," she said as Glen approached from the walkway. In her right hand, she held the grip of a nickel-plated revolver, which may have been a .38. Even though she was a small-framed woman in her late sixties who couldn't have weighed more than a hundred pounds, she clearly wasn't afraid to take on anyone who trespassed against her.

Glen smiled and tried not to sound condescending. "I'll handle this, Mrs. Rolley. I think it's safe for you to put your gun back in the house."

She looked down at the pistol in her hand and laughed. "My home defense. You know I'm out here all by myself, Glen." She hugged him and kissed his cheek as he joined her on the porch. "You don't visit me enough."

"You don't visit me at all," he said and rustled her hair.

"You know I don't get out much."

"Well you should," Glen said. "It's not good to spend so much time by yourself. You'll get weird."

Mrs. Rolley was alone out here on this dark stretch of Township Road #4. Her dear husband Jim of forty-seven years exited ground level while sitting in his favorite La-Z-Boy by way of a cardiac arrest in the middle of Monday Night Football—Steelers vs. Ravens—five years ago. The entire community felt the loss when Jim Rolley passed. He had devoted his life to serving the people of Cumberland Springs by organizing events, attending church, belonging to the Masons, Lions, Rotary… If there was an event going on in this town, Jim Rolley had probably put it together.

Her eldest son Michael worked as a history teacher and lived in Florida, around St. Augustine. No one ever understood why Michael had moved clear down there. He could make the same living much closer to home, plus he'd had no family issues to speak of that would have pushed him to move that far. People stopped asking about him a few years ago, assuming he just didn't feel at home in Cumberland Springs anymore.

And then there was Lucas, the Rolley's youngest son. One of the saddest stories in local history. Most accepted the *"Natural Causes"* theory as the truth and have lived with it all these years. But there are those who never could digest that explanation, choosing to believe something more sinister was in play. Whatever the case, they found Lucas Rolley dead in Charlie Matin's barn on a hot August night in 1984 at the tender age of eleven. Mrs. Rolley tries her best not to think about it, and most folks have the decency not to bring it up.

She did as Glen had asked and went into the house to stow the pistol back in the nightstand beside her bed. As soon as she was inside, Glen proceeded around the back of the house to the garden shed.

The house, a well built two-story cape cod, sat on the front side of seven acres. Mr. Rolley had poured a cement walkway years ago from the front porch to the mailbox and pull-off where Glen's patrol car sat now. Two large silver maple trees stood on each side of the walk close to the road. Luckily, the power lines were across the road, so they didn't have to worry about the utility company butchering their beautiful trees.

Township Road #4 rolled past the front of the place but rarely saw much traffic. There were only two other residences out this way, and one of them had been empty for the last fifteen years. It was a nice secluded place, but a little too far removed for a widow living alone. And definitely too far out of town for someone to wander out here aimlessly.

The garden shed seemed way more dilapidated than it did when Glen was a kid, leaning to the left and looking like it could collapse if you were to even slightly lean against it. The wooden slats that made up the exterior walls were sun-faded, split, and barely holding onto the frame. A garden that had once surrounded the shed was now a fenced-in courtyard of tall grass, briars, and various other iron weeds. Luckily, the old brick path leading from the house into the garden was enough to keep the weeds at bay, giving Glen clear access to the structure.

With each step closer, his mind opened doors to memories he hadn't experienced in years, filling his heart with a warmth he happily embraced on this cold November evening. To Glen, this run-down old shack would forever be the clubhouse of the *Cumberland Springs Adventure Society*; the base of operations where he, Michael, and Lucas would plan out the expeditions they'd undertake throughout the town and surrounding areas. Like the caves on Indian Hill that moonshiners had once stored their secret inventory in during prohibition, or the empty Walton Foundry, which had closed down in the 1960s, or the brick coke oven's that once refined coal into coke and creosote oil for the steel mills of Pittsburgh and had dotted the hills throughout the region—none of which had been operational since the great depression of the 1930s. This area of Braddock County was vastly populated with natural caves, old railroad tunnels, and abandoned structures from industries that had long since moved on and left their skeletal remains, offering a virtual treasure map for adventure-seeking young boys to challenge their imaginations and pique their curiosities. Sadly, it was one of those adventures that had led Lucas out to Charlie Martin's barn alone the night he died.

But now was not the time to revisit the past. An unknown individual apparently lay behind the door in front of him, and only God knew his intentions. Glen needed to focus. After all, if this was a homicidal maniac on the FBI's most-wanted list, he didn't want to get caught with his flag out in the wind.

The door seemed to fall open and almost slip away from its rusty hinges. When it hit the side of the shed, it made a sound like wooden boards being thrown onto a pile. Glen meant to shine his long-handled flashlight into the entrance as the door came open, but something knocked him back and almost brought to his knees. It wasn't a solid force throwing him backward, but a wall of horrific, vile odor, like the lid of a septic tank being flung open in his face. He had instinctively taken a deep breath as the door opened and millions of tiny stench molecules flooded his lungs as he inhaled, shocking his throat and sinuses. Suddenly all he could muster were quick gasps as his body tried to block any more of the repugnant filth from getting into his lungs.

"I forgot to tell you about that," Mrs. Rolley said from behind him. "He must have been shitting up a storm in there."

Glen pushed past her to put some distance between himself

and the potting shed. He was going to be sick if he didn't get clean air into his lungs immediately. A raging river of shit had now washed away the childhood memories he'd so fondly recollected before opening that door.

"Want me to get you a towel to hold over your nose?" Mrs. Rolley called out. Glen was bent over in the middle of the weed-choked garden, trying to force as much air into his lungs as he could fit. He held up one hand and waved it, letting her know that he just needed a minute. In reality, a minute would not help at all; it would take a lifetime to wash this smell from his memory.

Mrs. Rolley went into the house and came back a few moments later with a damp dishtowel. "You'll have to hold this over your face when you go in there."

He took the towel and wiped his face. It had a fresh linen smell, plus it was cool and damp. On this cold November evening, Glen Crawford was sweating as if it were the middle of July.

He continued taking deep breaths and looking back at the door to the shed which still looked like it could fall off its hinges at any second. He had to find out who was trespassing in there. It was his job, but the thought of having that disgusting odor pass through his nostrils again made his stomach convulse.

After a few hard moments of contemplation, Glen gained as much composure as his constitution would allow. He held up his flashlight, put the towel over his nose and mouth, and boldly trekked back to the shed. The towel worked well to his surprise, allowing him to breathe enough to at least peek his head through the entrance. The sight on the other side of the doorway, however, was one he would try—and fail—to forget for the rest of his life.

The shed had changed little since the last time he had been inside, some thirty-odd years ago. Rusty shovels and assorted gardening tools hung on pegs along the walls. The workbench Mr. Rolley had built himself remained intact, still covered with dozens of orange, terra-cotta pots. The motorless reel mower that

Glen, Michael, and Lucas attempted to cut grass with—never successfully—stood rusting away in the far corner. Also leaning in the far corner by the mower was a long rectangular sign with red child-like hand-painted letters. It read: CUMBERLAND SPRINGS ADVENTURE SOCIETY. The place looked as if it were still the summer of 1984, and the Society was about to meet to prepare for their next adventure. The only thing strange and out of place was a mass of something in the middle of the dirt floor.

Glen focused the flashlight beam, trying to determine what he was looking at. He knew there was supposed to be a man in here, but this seemed like nothing more than an old tarp with maybe a few tools under it. He shined the beam around the room again. There was no sign of a man. The guy couldn't be hiding under the tarp; the bulge didn't look big enough to conceal a human being. He assumed the trespasser must have run off after Mrs. Rolley discovered him. Although, what about that stench? There were no piles of feces in the room that he could see from the flashlight beam. The only place left to look would be under the tarp, and if the guy had left a giant pile as a gift for letting him stay in her shed, Glen had no interest in opening it.

"I guess he took off," he said as he backed out of the doorway. His voice muffled through the towel held firmly to his face.

"What are you talking about, Glen?" Mrs. Rolley said. "He's right there behind you!"

Glen spun around quickly toward the open door. He dropped the towel from his face while reaching for his sidearm. "*Where?*" He shouted. The room looked the same as it had seconds before.

"Right there!" Mrs. Rolley exclaimed. She was pointing at the tarp on the floor in the center of the shed.

Glen removed his hand from his weapon, then picked up the dish towel and put it back over his face. "There's no one under there; I can tell from here just by looking at the shape of it. Whoever you stumbled upon has run off. I'll look around the property to make sure he's not still lurking around. I'll bet he's long gone by now."

"You're not listening to me, young man!" She scolded him. "I found him under that tarp. I hadn't been out here since Jim died, but I had a few boxes that needed storing, so I figured I'd put them in this old shed. The smell was so bad I thought I was going to keel over right as I opened the door. When I lifted the tarp... well... You just have a look for yourself."

Glen looked into Mrs. Rolley's eyes. The woman wasn't lying, though he'd never known her to do such a thing, anyway. There was only one thing left to do, and he wasn't at all excited about it.

Like ripping off a band-aid, he grabbed one corner of the dirty canvas tarp and flung it out of the way, exposing the hidden object underneath. The sight made him gasp in shock and back away as quickly as his body would allow. Mrs. Rolley wasn't mistaken. There was a person under there, but a person by definition only. This thing didn't look like any human being Glen had ever seen.

Loose wrinkled skin hung over bones like worn curtains on a bent rod. He couldn't have weighed more than 80 pounds—Glen could tell it was a *he* because all he was wearing was a torn t-shirt; the man was completely naked from the waist down. The body lay curled in the fetal position over a bed of excrement—now explaining the source of the smell. His flesh was pallid and covered in sores of various shapes and sizes. The fingernails and toenails, which were black, chipped, and rotted, hadn't been clipped back in quite a while, and a few of them torn off. One eye rested halfway open, exposing a deep black, fully dilated pupil, while the other, also black and dilated, bulged partially out of the socket. There was nothing even remotely resembling life behind the gaze of either eye. Glen wasn't a medical examiner or a paramedic but felt strongly enough to say to himself, *This fucker is dead!*

He stepped back out of the shed and headed to his patrol car. For the first time in his life, he felt faint.

TWO

The solid darkness of the man's bulging eye grew more and more revolting as it gazed out into nothing. It didn't seem possible that life ever could have existed behind this black marble in the sunken socket. If the eye is the window to the soul, as they say, that part of him looked as though someone had viciously ripped it out. *If this thing winks at me, I'll run screaming like a twelve-year-old girl*, Glen Thought. But it didn't wink. It didn't flicker, move, or twitch. It only remained still and black and lifeless.

Glen didn't realize it at first, but he had been in a sort of mild trance, staring into the dark gaze of this thing on the ground in front of him. After a moment or two, he closed his eyes, shook his head, and ran his hands down his face to refresh himself. Things of this nature rarely bothered him—all part of the job. But up to this point, the job had never dumped a half decimated corpse into the middle of his favorite childhood hangout.

At first glance, there didn't appear to be any wounds, save for the myriad of open sores and chipped fingernails. The medical examiner could determine a cause of death in more detail after his exam, or autopsy if he deemed one to be necessary. Glen's opinion currently leaned toward death due to self-neglect. Maybe he was a junkie who somehow stumbled his way into Mrs. Rolley's shed, passed out, then took his final journey to the great beyond out here. An occurrence so rare in Cumberland Springs that he couldn't recall a similar instance. Except maybe for the time when Harold Ransier went missing overnight, and they found his body in the cemetery, frozen to a bench near his wife's grave. Harold didn't have a very pleasant look on his face that frosty January morning, but it was nothing compared to the face staring up at Glen tonight.

The towel he'd been holding over his nose and mouth had helped a bit with the smell, but it wouldn't work well enough for him to stay in the shed much longer. As he stepped out of the doorway to get some air, he noticed three men approaching through the weed-choked garden. The first was Larry Gilmore, one of his officers; the other two were paramedics.

"Who called the medics?" Glen asked.

Larry shrugged his shoulders. "I guess Lindsay did?"

"I did," Mrs. Rolley spoke up through the rag she held across her face.

Glen smiled with a hint of sarcasm. "Thank you, dear, you're very helpful."

As they continued toward the shed, the repugnant odor tickled their nostrils lightly. The three adult faces looked puzzled at first, then became increasingly more repulsed with each step closer. Larry slowed to a stop, as did the medics behind him, about 15 feet from where Glen stood. None of them spoke. They stared, confused, waiting for him to explain this horrifying scent that was filtering into their senses.

Glen's voice muffled through the white towel held against his nose and mouth. "Trust me guys, it's worse than you think."

"Hang on a second," one medic said. He turned and headed back around the house to the ambulance parked out front. A few moments later he returned with a small can of white paste. He took a generous dab on his finger, spread it under his nose, then passed the can around to everyone else. The rest of the men followed his lead, and miraculously the smell of fresh pine masked the terrible odor.

The three congregated around Glen at the doorway of the potting shed like football players waiting for instructions from their coach. A look of hesitation and concern showing on all of their faces, resembling an almost childlike fear of an unknown nightmare that could lurk behind the door of a dark closet. Glen paused for a few seconds—mostly for dramatic effect. "Before you head in there, I want you to know that it's pretty bad. No, it's more than that, it's flat out disgusting! There's an emaciated body on the floor that's been lying in a pile of his own shit for God knows how long. I know we're all trained to deal with

15

things like this, but sometimes reality can throw you back on your heels. This one has definitely tossed me back on mine."

Each man nodded in acknowledgment.

Glen stepped out of the way, fully exposing the dark opening of the structure. The two medics looked at each other as if playing a silent game of rock, paper, scissors; neither emerging as the victor. Finally, Glen handed his long-handled flashlight to the taller of the two, silently choosing who would be the first through the door. The medic took the baton with a visible amount of apprehension, turned the light on, and slowly passed through the entrance. His partner followed closely behind. After a minute or two of dead quiet, Glen heard the rustle of the canvas tarp. *"Jesus Christ!"*

Larry jumped as he heard the shout. "Is it that bad in there, Glen?" His boyish face and concerned expression reminded Glen of his son, Ryan, when he gets scared. Ryan didn't like to admit it as he was cruising into his teenage years, but an open closet door in a dark bedroom still scared the crap out of him.

"Hell, Larry," Glen said. "Other than a few of the car accidents I've responded to in the past, this is top of the list." He put a hand on Larry's shoulder. "The area is secure, and the medics can handle getting him out. You don't have to go in there if you don't want to."

The young officer swallowed a mouth full of pasty dry saliva and looked past Glen at the doorway. He had only been a member of the Cumberland Springs Police Department for six months now, and although he'd seen a few gruesome training films, he had not responded to a situation like this up close. He and Glen both knew it was time.

Larry was another one of those lifelong Cumberland Springs residences—the ones who could trace their family back over a hundred years and were proud to run down their genealogy with anyone who'd give them a minute to do it. Each generation never moved farther than a block away from the last, and all seemed to share the same traits: community servants; church on Sunday at First Baptist; volunteers at every cookout, barbecue, street fair, fireman's parade, church bazaar, pumpkin festival and 4th of July picnic this town could think up. At twenty-two years of age, Larry was growing right on course into the man his family and everyone else who knew him imagined he would be.

When the young man chose the law enforcement field, he understood it would entail more than just parking tickets and speed traps, but up to this point in his career, that's all there had been. Well, there was that bar fight between Nester Wade and Jim Phillips last month at Stoney's which he attempted—and failed—to break up. That one landed him a sizable ink blotch covering the left half of his face for the better part of a week. The two respectable citizens were putting on such a good show in the parking lot that no one in the crowd wanted to stop the main event. Larry had been patrolling the midnight shift when he happened upon a large cheering crowd in the gravel lot of Old Stoney's Tavern on Route 31. When he tried to get in the middle of the two gladiators, one of them—probably Nester, but he couldn't be sure—cold-cocked him and laid him flat out. After the dust cleared and everyone had scattered, Glen went by their homes and brought the two men to the station to face charges.

The scene inside of the old potting shed tonight, however, was going to leave a mark on Larry that would last much longer than the shiner he received from fight night at Stoney's.

THREE

Ronnie Miller stood at the dark entrance of the broken down potting shed, contemplating his next step. The flashlight Officer Crawford had given him cast a brighter than average beam, but not enough to see much from his position. The darkness seemed to swallow the light and digest it before it could illuminate anything inside.

This kind of apprehension at an incident scene felt strange to Ronnie. After all, it was just a simple body pickup; what could go wrong? But there was something in Officer Crawford's eyes telling Ronnie that there was much more going on inside this small room than Crawford's words let on. This perception made the hair on the back of Ronnie's neck stand and dance.

The stare of the other three men began drilling a hole into the back of Ronnie's head. He had to get moving. One deep breath, a silent countdown from three, and he set off to the races, breaking through the darkness, crushing his fear like an aluminum can. The sudden burst of confidence surprised him. He felt bold and empowered. The boost of courage and excitement put a large self-assuring smile on his face. The smile faded as quickly as it had emerged.

After his valiant charge across the threshold, Ronnie focused the flashlight beam on the faded gray tarp in the center of the room. At first, it didn't seem possible that a human being was at rest under there; the shape was way too small, no larger than a bag of mulch or sack of fertilizer. But that's where Officer Crawford said to look. He stepped around to the other side of the tarp, grabbed one of the loose corners, and with a quick pull, yanked it off of the object, letting canvas material fall beside him with the flare of a matador's cape.

Initially, he had a hard time understanding what he was looking at. The exposed figure had human features, but its condition was so extreme that it seemed artificial, almost comical. Ronnie thought of the full-size plastic skeletons his ex-wife used to decorate their front porch with on Halloween—the older trick or treaters found them funny, but they put a pretty good scare into the toddlers. He stared at the figure for a moment by the light of the shaky flashlight beam. It didn't take long to realize that this was not a plastic Halloween decoration. A sensation coursed through Ronnie's entire body, letting him know that fight-or-flight mechanisms were engaging. He attempted to fall back on his training to remain calm—find a happy thought, cycle through baseball stats, list his favorite movies. But the harder he tried to send his mind to a better place, the more his emotions worked to force him back into the moment. Finally, all calming efforts failed, leaving him to the mercy of a pure gut reaction: "JESUS CHRIST!"

"Hey! Take it easy," his partner, Devon, spoke up from behind him. "You can't blow your stack like that at a scene."

Ronnie turned and shined the flashlight beam into Devon's face. Devon was in business mode, stern and serious. He must have found that happy place Ronnie had failed to locate a moment ago.

"I'm sorry," Ronnie said, tilting his head down. "I got caught off guard."

"Yeah, I can see that. Try not to lose your shit here; we have a job to do." Devon took the flashlight from Ronnie's hand and walked around the body, examining it from all sides, but staying a safe distance from the fecal mattress it rested upon. He shook his head in revulsion, not taking his eyes off of it. "We're about to get dirty."

Ronnie volunteered to run back to the ambulance for the battery-powered emergency lights, leaving his partner alone with the body. The two cops outside seemed content to stay out there. Devon could have gone to work on the body right away, but with only the thin beam from one flashlight, he was sure his hand would end up in something nasty.

Devon was the shorter of the two men at five-foot-ten, but he was much stronger and more experienced in handling traumatic situations than his partner. He'd spent two years in the Iraq War as a Marine Corps Medic—on-the-job training that prepared him for anything life could throw his way. His build was lean and mean, a result of a highly motivated personal training regimen that started the second his feet hit the floor each morning.

In stark contrast to Devon, Ronnie stood tall and lanky. Six-foot-four and skin and bones. Not by his own doing, he consumed at least three to four thousand calories per day from the time he was a teenager. They said he had one of those fast-burning metabolisms, kind of like a rabbit. He was also very good at his job, though not as stern about it as his partner.

Devon could see cracks of light coming from Mrs. Rolley's back porch spotlights peeking through the wooden slat walls, which were nothing more than barn siding, probably reused from a structure that had long ago fallen down. Shining the flashlight around the room, he mostly saw rusted tools, metal fence posts, rolls of garden fence, broken pots, and several other nondescript items that hadn't seen use in years. Something in the corner, among the rusted metal and faded wooden handles, caught his eye. Leaning next to an old blade push mower was a long rectangular sign with peeling red letters. Devon walked over to where the sign had rested for probably decades. He picked it up and wiped away countless layers of dust with his left hand. After several swipes, he could make out a hand-painted phrase: "Cumberland Springs Adventure Society." It had to have been painted by a child; the lettering almost looked like something from a cartoon. The sign appeared to be so old, Devon imagined whoever painted the letters was likely a grandfather by now.

A loud crashing noise came from behind, causing him to drop the sign. It was Ronnie, bringing the work light tripod through the doorway. The old dilapidated door had finally let loose from its hinges and fell to the ground. Devon thought the entire building was crumbling down around him. "What are you trying to do, level the place?" He scolded Ronnie.

"I can't help that the fucking door fell off! I barely bumped it!" Ronnie snapped back. Devon didn't reply. There was no sense in having a disagreement in front of two police officers and the shit covered corpse.

Ronnie worked on setting up the lights while Devon figured out how to get the body prepped and ready to move. Both men knew this was going to be a nightmare of an extraction. Not only did they have to deal with the cramped space of the old shed, but excrement covered the subject of tonight's event from head to foot. Devon considered getting the bright yellow raincoats from the back of the ambulance. At least they could rinse those off quickly after moving the patient. The denim EMS jackets they currently wore would take forever to clean if any of this guy's matter ended up on them. There was also the gurney; they'd have to wrap it in plastic before they could use it to transport the body. It didn't matter how many precautions they took tonight though, Devon and Ronnie both knew they'd be going home with shit on them somewhere.

After a few moments of blind fumbling and colorful cursing, Ronnie finally got the work lights in place. He hit the switch, and the shed flooded with bright fluorescent light. It was cold and made the room resemble the inside of a refrigerator. Now that the light fully illuminated the body, both men could see how unusual and disturbing the situation actually was.

Devon went to work right away, being as cautious as he could to avoid the mess. He wrapped a blood pressure cuff around its left arm, which was so thin that the cuff went around three times before it was secure enough to fill with air. Even though the guy looked as dead as a rat in a three-day-old trap, policy dictated they check all vital signs at the scene before transporting a body. There was no room for error. He squeezed the little black ball attached to the cuff several times filling it full of air, then opened up the release valve to let off the pressure. As he expected, the needle on the circular gauge did not move. Next, he held the end of his stethoscope to the arm below the cuff to listen for a pulse. There was no sound. As far as he could tell at this stage, the man was dead.

Devon looked up at Ronnie and shook his head solemnly.

Ronnie acknowledged and lowered his eyes. Officer Crawford's initial assessment of the body was correct. The man who came to rest under an old tarp in the potting shed of an elderly widow was indeed deceased. Devon rose to his feet and stood next to Ronnie.

"Raincoats?" Ronnie said.

Devon let out a slight laugh. "I was thinking the same thing a few minutes ago."

"I'll Radio Ed to bring them up. He shouldn't be exempt from getting his hands dirty," Ronnie was talking about Ed Martin, the ambulance driver. Ed had been bitching about his back for months now, so he pretty much stayed in the truck during every call, eating chips and smoking cigarettes.

"*What the—*" Devon exclaimed suddenly. The two words came out slow and soft. He was looking at the body. "Did you hear that?"

Ronnie stared at the body as well. "I heard something."

"Tell me what you heard," Devon said.

"Ok, well…" Ronnie seemed to be at a loss for words, something that was unusual for him.

Devon interrupted Ronnie's stammer. "I heard a gasp."

"Yeah, I thought I heard that too," Ronnie said. "But couldn't that just be the corpse expelling gas?"

Devon's eyes opened as wide as his lids would allow. "Not if the chest is moving up and down."

Both medics stared in shock, accompanied by a tinge of fear as they witnessed the same impossibility. The body on the floor, which looked to be dead by all appearances, seemed to breathe. Nothing else on it moved, only a subtle rise and fall of the rib cage. It wasn't doing that a minute ago, but neither could deny that it was happening now.

FOUR

"Officer Crawford?" a medic called out from inside the garden shed. The voice lacked any vestige of confidence.

Glen turned and headed into the shed. He didn't ask Larry to follow, leaving that choice up to him. Kneeling on either side of the body, doing their best not to genuflect in the mess surrounding it, were two very confused paramedics. A blood pressure sleeve squeezed the body's left arm and the shorter medic held a stethoscope to its chest. The taller medic stood up and approached the Chief. He shook his head and looked back at the scene on the floor. The young man's mouth was open, but he couldn't seem to speak.

Glen gave him a rigid look. "Do you have something to say, Ronnie?" It was easy for Glen to be stern with Ronnie; he had gone to High School with the kid's mother and had known his family for as long as he could remember.

"Well... yeah, but I really don't know how to say it."

"Spit it out," Glen said. He was becoming curt, not so much because of Ronnie's behavior—he understood the situation would cause everyone to be off their rails a bit—but because he was over this night already. Getting the body out of here so he could fill out his report, burn his clothes, go home, and take a two-day shower was all Glen wanted to do. Plus, he imagined he'd have some type of nightmare trigger from that shit smell for the rest of his life, a thought that didn't sit well with him at the moment.

"He's not dead," Ronnie said.

Glen heard a gagging sound blurt out from behind him. Larry had taken a peek over his shoulder into the shack, now he was stumbling around Mrs. Rolley's garden, bent over, dropping the contents of his stomach.

"You didn't say what I think you just said?" Glen asked.

"Yes, Chief. I'm saying he's not dead. We've got a faint

23

pulse and extremely low blood pressure. Plus, he just started breathing on his own.

"The fucker has rigor mortis! I tried to move his arm. He's as stiff as that statue of General Braddock in the center of town!" Glen realized he was yelling for no reason, other than being unable to control his disbelief.

"We're going to wrap the stretcher in plastic, then get him to the ambulance. I can't imagine he'll even survive the trip to Memorial," Ronnie said, lowering his eyes.

A tinge of guilt crept into Glen's heart for reacting so strongly to the news. Even if the guy put himself in this condition, he was still a human being who deserved care and respect. Who knows, maybe he didn't do this to himself? The possibility existed that someone put him here. Perhaps they wanted him out of the picture, found a quiet spot, then left him for dead. Glen shivered at the thought. Those things happen in other parts of the world, not in Cumberland Springs.

He entered the shed once more to watch over the medics, mostly out of morbid curiosity. The white paste under his nose had worn off, allowing putrid odor to penetrate his sinuses once again. The emergency floodlights set up by the medics cast deceptively eerie shadows around every part of the room. As his eyes scanned the walls and corners, they came to rest on the old sign with the red-painted letters. Thirty years ago, the Cumberland Springs Adventure Society, with all their weird tales and mysteries, could have never imagined an event like this, especially in their own private clubhouse!

FIVE

The over-sized yellow raincoats made a crackling sound as Ronnie and Devon put them on, the distinctive sound of vinyl sticking to itself. After suiting up, they wrapped the gurney in clear plastic—more crackling—while the two police officers stood by and supervised. There wasn't much the officers could do—or wanted to do—to help at this point.

"If we don't clean this guy before loading him, we're never going to make it to Memorial without throwing up," Ronnie said. There was probably a protocol written somewhere for instances such as this; neither of them could think of it now.

Using the disposable shop towels that were stashed in the emergency bag in the back of the ambulance, they did the best they could at cleaning the body before carefully loading him onto the stretcher, hoping to ease the odor that would ride along in the back with them.

The patient was so light that one of them could have easily lifted him without a struggle. But the Chief of police watching over them, there was no room for error; if they were to accidentally drop the poor bastard, it would definitely make it into the police report. Neither of his arms or legs moved as they lifted his fragile body onto the stretcher. He remained grotesquely locked in the fetal position, staring at them with its dark bulging eye as they did their work.

"Are you sure your equipment is working right?" Officer Crawford said as they wheeled the stretcher past him. "This guy looks as dead as Abe Lincoln!" Both medics paused and glared at the Chief with slight contempt. Glen could tell the men were disturbed, so he decided not to push them any further.

Ed Martin sat his fat ass comfortably on the back bumper of the ambulance, smoking a cigarette while Ronnie and Devon struggled to push the gurney down the backside of Mrs. Rolley's house. The concrete pavers Mr. Rolley had put in some time back in the 1970s were cracked, broken, and bulging, making navigating the stretcher almost impossible. Ed took another deep drag from his smoke, not paying much attention to his fellow medics.

"A little help would be nice," Ronnie yelled down. Ed mumbled something in reply, pointing to his back. He was a good sixty pounds overweight and about as useful as a dried-up milk cow. The only time you could get Ed Martin moving was when it was time to clock out for the shift change. Accompanying his overweight frame was a greasy dark head of hair and a very outdated Fu Manchu mustache. Ed often boasted about how, "Chicks love '*the tache*,'" but no one had ever actually seen him with a woman.

After a few harrowing moments navigating the gurney over the misshapen sidewalk and one near spill, Ronnie and Devon arrived at the back of the ambulance with the man who they had now named John Doe—cliche but calling him *"the body"* as the Chief had been doing seemed a little morbid. Ed stood up and flicked his cigarette butt into Mrs. Rolley's front lawn. "That thing stinks! I hope you're going to clean it off before you load it in here."

"That *thing* is a human being, Ed," Devon scolded. "He's a living human being."

Ed stepped closer to the gurney for a curious look. "That don't look like no livin' human being to me. Are you sure you checked him out, right?"

"Just get in the fucking truck and shut up, Ed!" Ronnie snapped.

With one solid heave from the back, the wheels folded under, and the gurney slid smoothly into the ambulance. Ronnie and Devon jumped in behind it and slammed the doors shut.

Cold antiseptic light illuminated the back of the ambulance, eliminating all shadows and fully exposing the medics to a better understanding of what they were dealing with. John Doe's condition in this new light shocked them even more than before. Both men looked at each other over the body in unified disbelief at what they were seeing.

John Doe's flesh had no color to it at all, only a cold, pale gray tone that mostly resembled elephant skin. His mouth was open enough to show chipped and broken teeth, which pulled away from the gum line, and also had no color. Devon shined a light inside Doe's mouth for a closer look and found a repulsive black tongue with no trace of moisture. The sores covering the body were open, seeping, and severely infected. There were traces of parasitism in the open wounds, but neither of the two wanted to think about such a thing right now.

Ronnie spread a sheet out over John Doe's body and pulled it up to his neck. It would be easier to ride out the rest of the trip if they didn't have to look at this nightmare any longer.

"Do I need to hit the lights?" Ed said as he lumbered into the driver's seat.

"I don't think that's necessary," Ronnie said.

They radioed the hospital and received instructions from the E.R. Doctor: Start an IV drip and keep the patient stable during transport. There were no further instructions.

"This goddamn truck is going to smell for a month!" Ed said from the front cab. Ronnie and Devon didn't acknowledge him.

They had been on the road for only a few minutes when Ronnie noticed his partner looking strange. He couldn't put his finger on it precisely, but his demeanor seemed off. His face was becoming pale, he was sweating, and he was nervously looking around the cab.

"Hey buddy, you okay?" Ronnie said. "Devon? You okay?"

Devon didn't answer. He continued looking around and becoming more intense. His breathing was labored as if he'd just run a forty-yard dash. Ronnie knew his partner had been a corpsman in the Marine Corps during the Iraq War and had seen some very extreme events. Perhaps tonight's situation had triggered something in him?

"Devon, you need to chill out," Ronnie said as he reached to put his hand on Devon's shoulder. "You look like you're about to freak."

"There's something in here with us!" Devon said in a voice just above a whisper. He sounded terrified.

Ronnie stared at him over John Doe's body. Devon was still looking around the cab in every direction, pale-faced and sweating. "Yes, Devon, that *something* is a *someone* and we're taking him to the hospital."

"Not him!" Devon scolded. "Can't you feel it? There's something in here with us!"

"Dev, you're flipping. Once we get to Memorial, maybe you should chill in the coffee shop for a while."

Devon became even more intense. His eyes looked twice their normal size and like they could burst from their sockets at any moment. He kept turning his head in all directions, like he was trying to focus on something that was flying around the back of the ambulance.

This change in his partner made Ronnie nervous, not because he saw whatever Devon claimed to see, but because he needed him to stay focused and professional, from the incident scene to the hospital. Their jobs—and a life—depended on it.

Devon lost control completely. He swatted Ronnie's hand as he reached out to calm him. Devon began screaming, "My God! *It's* here! Don't you see? Right here!" He jumped toward the back, and Ronnie instinctively lunged after him, stopping him before he could open the door. There was hardly any room for this wrestling match to take place in the ambulance's compartment. As they struggled, both men fell across the gurney onto John Doe.

"What the hell are you assholes doing back there?" Ed called out from the front.

"Stop the truck, Ed!" Ronnie yelled. He was doing his best to restrain his panicking partner, but Devon wasn't an easy one to hold down. "Stop the fucking truck!"

"We're pulling up the drive to the hospital now. Just hang on a second."

"We don't have a sec…"

Devon caught Ronnie right between the eyes with a hard

elbow. Ronnie saw stars, lost the grip he had on Devon's shoulders, and flew backward, landing face to face on top of John Doe. He jumped up quickly and reached back for Devon. It was too late. The back door was open, and all he could see was the silhouette of his partner running into the darkness. He was screaming as he ran.

SIX

Weather in this part of Pennsylvania during November is highly unpredictable, which is in stark contrast to the other eleven months. Seasons change with almost clock-like regularity around here, and one can accurately predict temperatures with the simple purchase of a Farmer's Almanac, but when it comes to the eleventh month on the calendar, all bets are off. Many of the older residences have superstitions as to why November is so erratic. Bill Harper, a local usually found wasting time and hanging around Lachance Hardware on Saturday afternoons, says it's because of an Indian curse. He believes they're pissed off about the first Thanksgiving, and they want us all to remember that we'd have never made it through that winter if it hadn't been for them. Lisa Allen's grandmother, Lizzy, says the crazy weather has something to do with a murdered girl from back in the mid-1800s. She went missing around this time of year. The girl's spirit apparently comes back and stirs things up for a month. She doesn't have much of a theory as to why. Then there are the scientific types who talk about wind patterns and low-pressure systems caused by the Appalachian Mountains that surround Cumberland Springs. Whatever the case, it mattered little to Danielle Cunningham right now as she stood outside of the hospital emergency room entrance, attempting to light a cigarette. The wind almost seemed to laugh in her ear every time she sparked her disposable lighter.

She knew she shouldn't be smoking. The head ER nurse is supposed to set an example, not only to the nurses and staff but to the patients as well. Also, years of nursing school and training gave her an extensive knowledge of what those evil things were doing to her body. But then there were nights like this. Late shift at a small-town hospital. Doldrums, monotony, tedium… smoking herself to death seemed like a way better alternative than dying of boredom.

Finally, she got her head low and away from the wind enough for the plastic lighter to torch up a small flickering flame. A tiny portion of the tip of her Marlboro caught on before the flame petered out. Danielle puffed in and out in rapid succession, trying to get the cigarette to a full blaze. She was strangely excited when it finally caught all the way, knowing that thousands of toxins were about to rush through her lungs. She didn't care. The rich flavor and rush of nicotine made it all worth it.

Danielle squinted her eyes into the wind as a vehicle approached from the bottom of the hill. It was the ambulance that radioed about fifteen minutes ago. She had hoped for enough time to enjoy a smoke before they got here. Perhaps if she could have gotten it lit sooner? She was about to toss her cigarette and prepare by the door when she noticed the vehicle was driving erratically; it seemed to swerve and rock back and forth. Before reaching the awning of the ER entrance, the back door flew open, and a man jumped out. He stumbled a bit, then took off running down the hill. He was yelling something she couldn't quite make out as he ran. A second or two after, the ambulance stopped, and another paramedic jumped out of the back. He chased the first one for about fifty feet, then stopped and ran back up to the vehicle. She recognized the second one; it was Ronnie Miller, a friend who she'd grown up with since grade school.

"Give me a hand with this, Ed," Ronnie shouted.

A heavy-set man in a medic uniform came out of the driver's side door. "I told you I have a bad back!" He yelled. Danielle couldn't believe that someone would actually grow a Fu Manchu mustache in this day in age.

She ran to the back of the ambulance and helped Ronnie unload the gurney. "What was that all about?" She asked. Ronnie didn't answer.

Together, they pulled the gurney out, letting the wheels automatically spring from underneath. Danielle stopped dead in her tracks when it rolled completely out, and she was face to face with the patient for the first time. She covered her open mouth to keep from gasping at the sight.

"*Come on!* Let's get him inside," Ronnie snapped at her.

Danielle and Ronnie pushed the gurney up to the automatic doors at the ER entrance. Another nurse and an orderly took the patient from them and rolled him the rest of the way inside. Danielle stood and watched as they navigated through the corridor and into the emergency room. "What the hell is going on here?" She said, but Ronnie had disappeared. She turned around and saw him getting into the passenger seat of the ambulance. A second later it was rushing back down the hill.

Most nights at Cumberland Springs Memorial were quiet and uneventful. There was the occasional car accident that could stir things up, but mostly, the ER would only populate with chest pains, high fevers, and stomach issues. Tonight seemed to be a new one for the books. A half-crazed paramedic running out into the middle of the night and a horrible-looking poster child from Night of the Living Dead strapped to a stretcher. Could it get any stranger than this?

Chapter 2

ONE

The midnight shift at Cumberland Springs Memorial Hospital was supposed to be relatively light. At least that's what the board of hospital administrators said when they reduced the staff by half from 11:00 PM to 7:00 AM. Men and women in well-dressed business attire, sitting around a giant burled mahogany boardroom table, brainstorming, shooting out ideas, throwing suggestions against the wall to see what sticks, making the hard choices. *With fewer people awake between eleven and seven, wouldn't there be a significant reduction of emergencies? This hospital should have no trouble operating the midnight shift with fewer personnel. Can't we just have our nurses do a little extra work and pull more weight so the hospital can make the budget and still hit our profit goals? Sure,* Lauren Rivers thought as she walked across the cold parking lot to the hospital entrance. *Shouldn't we also have administrators who have a damn clue?* This internal conversation arose in her every time midnight week came around. Thankfully, she only had to deal with this shift one week out of the month, but it was always a rocky hill to start up.

From the top of one of the larger hills surrounding the valley, the ever-menacing structure known as Cumberland Springs Memorial Hospital seemed to glare down at the town below. The highland it rested upon had lovingly been given the name, "Mount Deathmore" by a few local tavern rats several years ago. For some reason—which is still a subject of debate today—the name stuck.

The state of Pennsylvania had slated the monolithic structure for construction in 1938 and finished just a few months before the Empire of Japan picked a fight with the wrong kid on the playground in late 1941. For a lot of the local boys returning home from overseas in those first few years of WWII, this place would be their first stop on a long road to recovery.

On the way up the winding road—HOSPITAL TRAFFIC

ONLY, the red and white reflective sign read—it would be hard not to notice the ever-present wind, which has haunted this hilltop for as long as anyone can remember. Even on calm summer days when the valley below is as stagnant as a tomb, the wind at the top of Hospital Drive remains active, annoying, and irritating. A doctor who had lost several of his favorite hats to this constant breeze while crossing the parking lot was the one who gave it the name, Stella. He took the name from his first wife's mother, a woman who wouldn't stop bellowing no matter how hard anyone tried to get in a word. When the mother-in-law died a few years ago from a heart attack, he swore he could still hear her bitching even after she had flatlined.

Something had pissed off Stella tonight; she assaulted Lauren with a cold gust to the face as soon as she stepped out of her car. The malicious wind relentlessly tugged at her jacket and spat small pellets of snow all over her as she hurried from the parking lot to the employee entrance. A cruel taunting, like a pack of kids getting off a school bus and tormenting one child until he runs all the way home in tears, leaving him with terrible memories that he'll carry for the rest of his life.

The heavy steel door Lauren needed to open to get inside the employee entrance seemed like it weighed a ton and a half with Stella pushing against it. She struggled. It was as though Stella was trying to keep Lauren out, to stop her from walking into something she might regret. Finally, with all the strength she could muster, she opened a small slit wide enough to struggle and slide herself through to the other side. The door slammed shut from behind once she had squirmed her way through, shoving her forward and causing an explosive bang that rumbled through the long corridor in front of her. "Jesus!" she said aloud. Her voice echoed.

As she walked past the Emergency Room on her way to the employee lockers, she noticed it didn't seem busy at all tonight. She had walked this corridor on rare occasions and seen utter mayhem on the other side of the plate-glass window—usually because of a car accident. But the traffic tonight seemed light; a good indicator that the rest of the asylum might be somewhat calm.

When Lauren approached the hallway between the ER and locker room, the smell hit hard. Antiseptic. It was like walking into a cinderblock wall dowsed in Clorox. This invisible barrier acted as a prophetic voice, reminding you that you had arrived at work, no turning back, no calling out sick, you had crossed the boundary; the rest of your time tonight belonged to the sick, injured, dying, or dead. She felt an immediate change within... heightened focus, alertness, concentration. Her thoughts about being at home with Clay, or Thanksgiving dinner this week at Grandmother's house—Lauren would make broccoli casserole and green beans as usual—had to be shelved away for the rest of the night. The patients were all that mattered now.

On the third floor ICU ward, Lisa Wyndham sat at the nurse's station, early as usual. She had a face that looked like it had never known worry, not a blemish or wrinkle on it anywhere. Lauren swore the girl must have gone to cosmetology school before becoming a nurse because her hair and make-up were about as perfect as any magazine model. She'd often get a laugh at the doctors, orderlies, or any other guy—or girl for that matter —who fumbled past the nurses' station, captivated by Lisa's delightful features.

Six nights! The thought kept rolling through her mind like a loose marble in a glass bowl. Lauren rarely dreaded coming to work, but tonight something was different. The air felt off, almost unsettling. Of course, the midnight shift wasn't her idea of a good time, but most often she endured and pushed through without letting it wear on her. *Something isn't right.* It started earlier in the evening when she and Clay finished dinner and were relaxing on the couch. A feeling came over her, somewhere on the spectrum between mild depression and dread. It wasn't incredibly overwhelming, just unsettling enough to make her take notice, like a cold boney finger lightly poking at her rib cage. Maybe the feeling had to do with knowing that her husband was snuggled up in their nice warm bed on this chilly November night while she was out saving lives and caring for the sick? It first came on while they were having dinner, lasting only for a minute. Then it passed through her again in the shower as she was getting ready for work. It shot through her once more while sitting behind the wheel of her car in the hospital parking lot. Nothing extreme, but noticeable enough unsettle her. Whatever this feeling was, she had to shelve it if she was going to get through the shift.

Next month would mark Lauren's third year as an ICU nurse at Cumberland Springs Memorial. Recruited right out of nursing school, Lauren moved up the chain quickly. There was never any doubt that she was cut out for the job. Her entire family were lifelong members of the local Country Club along with many of the doctors on staff here, she had volunteered as a nurse's assistant during summer breaks while still in high school, and her grandmother was also a nurse in this same ICU until she retired ten years ago. Now grandmother's picture and an engraved plaque that reads, "Sharon Snyder, 40 years of dedicated service," graces the wall just outside of the elevator. Lauren smiles every time she walks by the photo. It was as though the hospital had a job waiting for her since the day she was born in it.

"Your hair looks nice tonight," Lisa said, as Lauren came around the U-shaped nurse's station and sat down behind a computer. She looked over and smiled. Whether her hair looked nice or not, Lisa always had a compliment waiting for her when she came on duty. The flatteries weren't sarcastic or shallow; Lisa genuinely had pleasant things to say to everyone.

"Thanks, Dear," Lauren said. "Compliments of Stella. She's a real bitch tonight!"

"Ha! She did a number on my hair too. It took me ten minutes in the bathroom to get it halfway presentable."

Lauren looked at Lisa, sarcastically. Her hair was immaculate as usual. "Did you have an enjoyable weekend?"

"I did!" Lisa said with her characteristically excitable voice. "Ted and I went up to Bedford Village on Saturday and spent the day going through the antique shops. He bought me several pieces of glassware I've started collecting."

"So, when are you and old Teddy going to seal the deal? You've only been dating for three years," Lauren said.

"We talk about it. He travels a lot for work, and I work shifts, so our schedules don't match up very well."

"Yeah, I can see how that would be difficult," Lauren said while looking at her computer screen. "Oh! What's this?"

"I saw that," Lisa answered, looking over at Lauren's screen. "I haven't been in to check on him yet. Looks like he came in earlier this evening."

"Have we ever had a John Doe come through here?" Lauren asked while reading through his medical chart. It took her a few minutes to read the whole thing. "The chart says he's terminal?"

Lisa looked down and nodded.

Lauren began reading from the chart aloud: "Engorged liver, kidney failure, pancreatitis, swelling of the brain, extreme dehydration . . . I can't imagine he's going to be with us very long."

"I'm assuming this is a result of substance abuse," Lisa said, sounding like a first-grade teacher telling a student that their poor grade comes from poor study habits.

Lauren had seen dozens of terminal cases before, but this one piqued her curiosity. "I'm going to make my first rounds of the night. I see he's not being administered anything but fluids, so I'll check on him last."

"Take your time, he's not going anywhere," Lisa said.

TWO

There were seven patients total in the ICU tonight: Two recovering from major surgeries, a car accident that seriously injured two teenagers, Mrs. Randell, who has now had her third heart attack this year (she's blaming her neighbor and his "*shit-hound*" dog for causing her to have what she refers to as, *heart hiccups)*, Mr. Jacobs, a ninety-five-year-old man who recently started bleeding uncontrollably from his ass, and John Doe.

While attending to each patient, Lauren was every bit as focused as always, but as she walked from one room to the next, her mind became more fixated on John Doe. How would he look? How serious was his condition? She couldn't imagine what made her think about him so much. She'd cared for hundreds of patients since becoming a nurse, so why should this one be any different? Maybe it had to do with the enigma of who he was. She had received no information on who had discovered him, or where, so perhaps her mind had become attached to solving the mystery. Miss Marple, deducing the facts, forming a hypothesis, and unlocking the secret between the pages.

As she approached John Doe's room, she tried to clear her head and focus on the procedures at hand. Suddenly, the strange feeling from earlier this evening hit her once again, even harder than before. It was dread, so overwhelming that it felt like two icy hands on her shoulders, blocking her from entering the room. She paused outside the door and put her hand on the wall to steady herself. Lauren wasn't prone to anxiety, in fact, she couldn't recall ever having an attack like this. Her heart raced. She began to sweat. A chill went through her entire body, pushing thousands of goosebumps to the surface of her skin, which was now becoming pale. *Deep breaths,* she told herself. *In and out, in and out.* She had said those same words to patients more times than she could count, but never thought she'd be speaking them to herself. She looked over at the nurse's station, which was a good fifteen feet away, and thought about calling Lisa to help her. Lisa was staring down at one of the computer monitors. As she tried to speak, another horrific realization came over her: she wasn't breathing! Gasping and mouthing Lisa's name, she clung to the plastic handrail which ran the length of every hallway in the building. The room spun, and darkness closed in from the corners of her eyes. Fear gripped her throat and squeezed. She stood, paralyzed. Her mind didn't have time to diagnose what was happening. It was now her survival instinct that had taken over her thoughts, telling her, screaming at her: BREATHE!

As quickly as it came, it vanished as if nothing had happened. Lauren regained her breath, maintained her balance, and felt warmth return to her skin. Her breathing was rapid, and her heart still pounded in her chest. But at least those systems were working. For a moment, her memory opened up to a time when her grandfather had taken her fishing at Shawnee Lake, and she'd caught her first sunfish. She held the scaly creature in her hands while staring into its face. The eyes bulged, gills flapped restlessly, and mouth opened and closed in a constant rhythm. It was funny to her then, watching this thing go through these strange actions she'd never seen before. Now, as she caught her breath and began coming back to life, she realized what her prize catch had gone through that day.

Like a toddler leaving the security of their parent's hand to take those first uncertain steps, she released the handrail and slowly headed toward the nurse's station. Her legs still shaking, but stable enough to get her to the desk. Lisa didn't look up from her screen when Lauren sat down beside her. "What did you think of John Doe?"

Lauren didn't respond. She was still trying to assess what had just happened.

"Hey," Lisa said, looking over at her. "What about Doe?"

"What? Oh, yeah. I haven't looked in on him yet."

"And you're waiting for?"

"Just give me a second, alright?" Lauren snapped. She picked up a water bottle from the desk and drank so fast that some of it spilled from each side of her mouth and ran down her cheeks.

"Lauren, what's wrong? I've never seen you like this."

"I'll be okay. I just need a minute." She said, then continued drinking until the bottle was empty.

Lisa didn't press the issue, and Lauren didn't elaborate. In the three years they had worked together, the two of them grew to understand when to leave space. Lisa could feel that this was one of those times.

Lauren took a deep breath, composed herself, then stood up and stared at the door to room 337. John Doe was in there, clinging to what ounce of life he had left, and it was her job to attend to him while he was still among the living. She wasn't a superstitious person at all, never had been, but here she stood, scared out of her mind to enter a room with a patient who couldn't talk, move, or even blink his eyes. She had seen people die while doctors tried to resuscitate them, walked in on them as they faded off in their sleep, and held hands with a few as they said their last words and drifted away. There was no rational reason for her to have such a feeling of foreboding now.

"This is ridiculous!" She muttered under her breath and stormed out of the nurse's station. Without the slightest pause, she reached the open door of room 337 and crossed the threshold, pushing her way through the air that had held her back moments before. This time there was no resistance, causing her to almost tumble into the room. She caught her balance at the foot of the bed. In front of her lay the thing that had been causing her this terrible, menacing fear. Here was John Doe, looking nothing at all like the image her imagination had sketched for her. Her mind, beguiled by the mystery of who this man might be, had created its own demonic character; a bit of something pulled from every childhood fear she'd ever had. In her vision, he was a giant, hulking monster who would most likely spring to life and drag her under the bed, then gnaw at her flesh with its chipped and yellowed teeth. That image was the farthest thing from the man she faced now.

Robert Ferencz

THREE

John Doe lay motionless and nearly lifeless. He was still breathing on his own but very shallow, just enough to make the blanket over his chest barely rise and fall. His mouth rested open, exposing bare gums and chipped and broken teeth. His head slightly cocked to the left, one eye half-open, the other bulging and swollen. A fully dilated pupil showed nothing but blackness in the bulging eye. It stared off into space. He was tiny, in his current state couldn't have weighed over ninety pounds. He had thin, dark hair and a week or two worth of stubble on his sunken face. Lauren figured he was an addict of some sort, the type you see in those series of mug shot photos—the first time they get arrested using meth they look to be about twenty-eight years old, one year later they look around ninety. John Doe appeared to be in his nineties right now, but in actuality was probably nowhere near that age.

Her childhood fears about ghouls and monsters had all faded, allowing the compassionate nurse to take over and go to work. She applied the blood pressure cuff to his arm, which she had to wrap around three times to get it to stay on before she could pump it up. His heart rate was faint and steady, but his blood pressure registered as low as a person can get before crashing. As the body is shutting down, the heart does everything it can to keep itself alive until the last possible second—unless you are Mrs. Randall from the next room over, who gets *heart hick-ups* from her neighbor's *shit-hound dog!* His IV bag would be good for a few more hours, and the pain medication administered automatically through that port. Her role would only be to check in on him to see if he was still among the living, or if he hadn't spasmed off the bed in one last triumphant muscle twitch. As of Monday, November 21st, 1:35 A.M., John Doe still resided among the living.

Lauren pulled the med cart over by the bed; it held various

medications and things along with a laptop secured to the shelf on top. She signed into the computer and began typing her notes about her first visit with John Doe. While logging in her comments, she noticed an odor coming from somewhere in the room, something she'd never smelled in this hospital before. It wasn't coming from the patient, that she could be sure of, this was emanating from all around her. Subtle at first, but growing stronger by the second, enveloping her from all sides. It was acrid, almost chemical, yet still organic. She had to think back to her chemistry classes in high school and college. That smell was in the back part of her mind somewhere. What was it? After a few seconds, a memory jarred loose of Mr. Bolton's 11th-grade chem class. One of his demonstrations had gone haywire, caught fire, and the entire school smelled like rotten eggs for two weeks. Sulfur! That was it, sulfur. As she looked around the room to see where the foulness could be coming from, another strange anomaly occurred: the room seemed oddly darker than it was moments ago, however the lights hadn't changed. It was almost as if too much power was being used somewhere else, causing excessive load on the room. The temperature also felt colder. Considerably colder by about ten degrees or so.

Lauren wanted out of here. These strange occurrences and the anxiety attack she'd had earlier were enough. She closed the screen on the laptop and pushed the cart forward, walking faster than its wheels wanted to go, almost tipping the whole thing over. The hall lights were so bright she had to squint her eyes when she came through the doorway. She almost ran into Lisa, who was leaving the room next-door—Mrs. Randell must have been ringing the buzzer again.

"Can you call maintenance and tell them there's a strange smell in 337, and the lights are going all wonky?" Lauren said, not acknowledging their near collision. "I'm going to the cafeteria for a cup of coffee."

"I thought you didn't drink coffee?" Lisa asked.

Lauren kept walking.

FOUR

The hospital cafeteria never closed. 24/7, 365, Sundays, holidays, Easter, Kwanzaa, whatever, there was always someone on duty making sure the coffee was hot and the food... average. At 10:00 PM they would cut the lights over half of the room to conserve electricity, which strangely gave the place a cozy, almost cafe feel. Mrs. Stover manned the station tonight. She had been a cafeteria lady at Cumberland Memorial since the Vietnam War ended. Seven years ago they had brought her husband into the ER after he'd blown an aneurysm on the left side of his brain while cutting the grass at the American Legion. She ran from the lunch counter in her hairnet and apron all the way to the ER but didn't get to say her last goodbye. He departed from this side of the veil before she even made it off the fourth floor. As strong as most people are from that generation, she was right back to work the day after they closed the lid on her husband and hadn't missed a day since.

She seemed to prefer the night shift now that Mr. Stover had gone on. Evenings were quiet and allowed her to complete all the cafeteria duties relatively uninterrupted at the beginning of the shift. The rest of the night belonged to her, giving her the quiet time to delve into the fictional worlds of her favorite authors. Stephen King, of course, was her first writer of choice, but she also enjoyed the stories of Dean Koontz, Anne Rice, Shirley Jackson, and various other artists of the macabre. An eager predilection bubbled behind her eyes for anything that could send a cold shiver up the spine on a dark late night. Mr. Stover never understood his wife's fascination with *the spooky shit,* as he called it, but he tolerated her interest just the same, chalking it up to another one of her amusing quirks.

Lauren came in and went straight to the counter where the cafeteria veteran sat, her nose in a book. The book jacket had a dilapidated old house on it with a full moon in the background.

"Is the coffee hot, Mrs. Stover?" She asked.

The gray-haired woman looked up from her novel over a pair of Foster Grants. "You don't drink coffee, Lauren." She said in a mentoring, grandmotherly tone. "Is everything ok tonight?"

Lauren smiled at her concern; it was genuine, and it warmed her heart. "Tonight is my first midnight shift of the week. I guess I'm just having trouble getting into a rhythm." That was the best excuse she could summon on short notice, trying delicately not to get into a discussion about the evening's events. She'd often had enjoyable conversations with Mrs. Stover over a myriad of topics: the weather, life and death, family, marriage, and anything else two women from different generations could discuss. Lauren found value in the wisdom of people who grew up in the eras of the past. She felt she gained a better perspective on her own life from their experiences. Mrs. Stover knew what life was like before television, before cell phones, before it was common for every family to have at least one car. She had even known what it was like to grow up in a house with three brothers, two sisters, and no indoor plumbing. She had learned how to make due, get by, do without and not complain—tenets that were a lost art to most these days.

"Caffeine is going to throw that rhythm off even more for someone who never drinks it." She put the book down and got up from her seat. "How about if I make a pot of decaf?"

"Ok, Mrs. Stover. You're so sweet."

"I look out for my girls." She said with an endearing smile, then got to work on her self-appointed task.

The windows in the cafeteria which overlooked the parking lot were frosting over. On the other side of the double-paned glass, amid the eternal climate conflict, winter was pushing fall out of the way like a football player shouldering a tackling dummy down the practice field. Sometimes fall could resist its frosty rival and hang around for a few extra weeks, giving way to mild temperatures, but that wouldn't be the case this year. Winter had a full head of steam and no intention of being delayed. Even though it was warm in the room, looking out at the cold, snow-dusted parking lot gave Lauren a fierce chill. She pulled her sweater close around her neck. As if sensing someone at the window, Stella blew a puff of leaves against the glass, causing Lauren to jump.

"Anything interesting out there tonight?" A voice came from behind. It was Danielle Cunningham, sitting at one of the round tables with a cup of black coffee and a small bowl of carrot sticks in front of her. Lauren must have walked right by her when she approached the lunch counter. Danielle, an ER nurse, had started her career at Cumberland Springs Memorial a few years before Lauren. Several doctors had tried their charms and stature to get her into the sack, but all had crashed and burned. She was beautiful indeed, with a slim, athletic figure, black hair, and large brown eyes, but she was also very well-grounded; it would take qualities much deeper than money and influence to have a chance with Danielle. What those qualities were, not even she knew the answer to that.

Lauren smiled, slightly embarrassed. "I didn't see you there, Danielle."

"I know," she replied. "You looked like you were in a daze when you walked in."

Lauren pulled out a chair and took a seat at Danielle's table. "Are you on midnight shift this week too?"

"Yeah, I got pulled into working for Lynn Steiner all week. I guess she had an out-of-town emergency." She took a sip of black liquid from a mug that had an illustration of Winnie the Pooh holding Piglet's hand on the front of it. "I'm sure she's just off banging that new guy she's been ho-ing around with lately. What about you?"

Lauren frowned. "This is my first of the week. Five more to go."

"I feel your pain. My regular midnight rotation starts next week. I'll be lucky if I ever get my sleep schedule back on track after these next two weeks." Danielle pushed the bowl of carrots toward Lauren in a silent offering. She took one without hesitation. The two had known each other since high school when Danielle was a senior and Lauren a sophomore. Danielle had dated Lauren's older brother, Kenny, for six months of that school year. The budding romance had crashed hard when Kenny diverted his interest to a cheerleader named Alicia Murray, who didn't mind showing just the right touch of ass cheek out of the bottom of her frayed denim shorts. Danielle never fully got over him. "What's going on with you? You look a little distant."

Lauren didn't answer. She just stared into the bowl of carrots, expressionless. She wasn't sure there was an answer. Her mind drifted back to the feelings of dread and anxiety she had experienced moments ago in John Doe's room. The cold, the darkness, the acrid smell. How could she even describe these things? Surely if she confided in others, they would all say she had imagined things. It's easy for people to brush off occurrences like this as imagination; it negates the responsibility of helping someone deal with an issue that might be more complicated than they are equipped to process. Then there's the ever condescending, *"Maybe you're coming down with something."* And the prescription, *"Drink some water, take a couple of ibuprofen and lie down for a bit, you'll be fine."* But in room 337 it was all around her, behind her, in front of her, and at one point she swore it had even gone through her. It studied and observed her. In a very subtle yet disturbing way—the more she thought this over—it violated her! She knew what she had felt, and no one could explain it away with their simple analysis. The more her mind attempted to find a rational explanation, the further from reality it took her. As she continued to replay the event, all possibilities ended on the same path with the same conclusion: there was a *presence* in that room.

"Would you girls like some company?" Mrs. Stover said, approaching the table with a cup of decaf in one hand for Lauren and a pot of regular in the other to warm up Danielle's Pooh mug.

Lauren broke off from her stare at the bowl of carrots and looked up at Mrs. Stover. "Please, sit down, your company is always welcome." Danielle got up and pulled out the other chair for her.

Mrs. Stover sat down at the table and poured her own cup of regular from the pot. "What are we chatting about this evening, ladies?"

Danielle chimed in immediately. "We're discussing why Miss Lauren here is looking so distant and out of sorts tonight."

Lauren looked at Danielle and shook her head. "I'm fine. There's nothing to be concerned about." Her tone was sweet but carried just a hint of annoyance.

"You do look troubled, dear." Mrs. Stover said. "But, if you don't want to discuss what's bothering you, we should respect that."

Casually, Lauren took a sip from the mug Mrs. Stover brought for her. The sour look on her face made the other two women laugh. She hated coffee and probably hadn't even tasted it since she'd sipped from her grandfather's mug when she was still a child. And this tasted just like the sip she'd had that day: bitter and harsh. She pushed the cup away, watching the dark liquid splash against the sides, spilling a drop over the lip and down the white outer surface. The other two realized Lauren wasn't amused, so they contained their laughter the best they could.

After a few seconds of quiet Lauren said, "Danielle, were you on duty when they brought the John Doe in tonight?"

Danielle was taking a sip from her mug. "Mmm-Hmm."

"Did you notice anything strange about him?"

"You mean other than that he was in the worst state of degeneration I've ever seen?"

"Oh, my!" Mrs. Stover chimed in.

"Yeah," Lauren said. "Past his condition, I mean, did you feel anything strange about him? Was there something just, I don't know, wrong about him?"

Danielle looked up at the ceiling and thought for a second or two. "Ya know, it wasn't so much the John Doe; I've seen emaciated patients like him before. The strange thing was with a paramedic who brought him in. I think the guy's name is Devon or something. While the ambulance was still pulling up, he jumped right out of the back of it and took off running down the hill, screaming at the top of his lungs. The other medic, Ronnie Miller, chased after him but gave up after a few seconds. He wouldn't tell me what was going on. It was quite a commotion, let me tell ya." She raised her mug for another sip. "I guess you could consider that something strange."

"Sure sounds strange to me," Mrs. Stover said. "Where did they find this John Doe?"

Danielle looked over at Mrs. Stover. "I couldn't tell you for sure. We did a preliminary exam, then sent him right over to ICU. I didn't ask much about him. I had forgotten about him until Lauren brought it up just now."

"Is he still alive, Lauren?" Mrs. Stover asked. "Lauren?"

"Huh? Oh, yeah, he's still alive. At least he was fifteen minutes ago." Her mind was back in the room with John Doe and the feeling that had engulfed her as she stood over his atrophic body. How could anyone do this to themselves? He'd purged himself of any vestige of vitality. Could life be so terrible that a person would give up all hope and destroy their body to the point of complete decimation? She had learned a little about substance abuse issues in college but had never experienced it in her life. It was difficult for her to relate to people destroying themselves like it appeared that John Doe had done. For Lauren, life had a purpose; it was a gift given by God, and a chance to grow and learn, an opportunity to become someone who could make a difference in the world and change the lives of others. Her brain could not compute why a person would throw away such a precious gift. As a nurse, though, she had no choice but to distance herself from the patient's actions or motives. Her job was to heal, not to judge.

"Is something going on with him in the ICU?" Danielle asked.

"Well, yes, and no. I can't say it's John Doe; he hasn't moved, and his condition is the same. I'm just uneasy around him and can't figure out why."

"I can't say you're the only one to have that feeling. You should have seen that paramedic." Danielle said. "He was acting like he saw the devil."

"My goodness girls, who is this person?" Mrs. Stover asked.

"I know the police know that we have him," Danielle said. "I'm sure there will be more clarity about him tomorrow." She looked at Lauren. "Are you going to get through the night with him up there?"

"Oh, of course. I'm not that far out of sorts, just having a strange night. I'm sure it's only me getting inside my own head."

"Try not to think about him, dear, you'll work yourself up into a tizzy." Mrs. Stover said.

Lauren smiled and touched the woman's hand in a thankful gesture. "I better get back to work. Thank you for the coffee, Mrs. Stover, I'm sorry I didn't finish it."

"Don't you worry about that, Lauren. Just focus on getting through the rest of the night."

FIVE

Lauren made it through the rest of the shift with no further issues, although her mind never stopped wandering back to room 337. She was at home now, where the sanctuary of a warm bed welcomed her like a dear old friend. Home felt good. The problems she faced while out in the world seemed to melt away as soon as she made it home.

Ten minutes after nestling into bed with Clay, his alarm went off, sending a shrill scream through the air. John Doe was immediately back in her mind.

Chapter 3

ONE

The thought of going over to Cumberland Springs Memorial to see that shriveled up zombie again had been wearing on Glen's mind all day. It was at the top of his list of things to do, yet somehow kept falling further towards the bottom. Logging in parking tickets, cleaning up his office, checking the oil in the police cruiser. Anything was better than looking into the face of that *thing* again.

Apparently, the guy must have made it through the night, because no one from the hospital had called to report his passing. Of course, he could have died, and they hadn't gotten around to informing him yet. A hope he'd secretly carried all day. If the poor shit had bought the farm in the night, Glen could pass off retrieving his fingerprints to the coroner, saving him from having to touch those cold, bony digits, and the worn leather skin which covered them.

Nothing had never affected him like this before, and this apprehension over such a simple task gave him concern. Had being a cop in a town where hardly anything ever happened made him soft, or was there more to all of this? He couldn't deny that there was an air in the potting shed last night—other than the shit smell—that seemed to burrow into his mind and give off a low-pitched scream, something living on the same frequency as a hunch, an instinct, or a bad feeling.

This is bullshit!

He pushed the receptionist button on the desk phone with the end of the pencil he'd been gnashing between his teeth all afternoon. "Hey Lindsy, have there been any calls?"

"None since the last time you asked me, ten minutes ago," she replied. Glen could hear her chewing gum over the speaker as she talked.

"Nothing from the hospital?"

"Nothing from anyone," she said. "It's been quiet all day."

"Would you call the hospital for me and inquire about the condition of the John Doe we found last night?"

"You found a John Doe?" She said, surprised.

"I'll tell you about it later. Can you make that call for me?"

He leaned back in his chair and stared at the ceiling. The tiles up there were original to the building's construction back in the 1950s, probably full of asbestos. Glen didn't want to think about that, though it was a more appealing thought than what he had dealt with last night.

It took five minutes for Lindsay to buzz his phone. "They have him in the ICU, Chief. The front desk couldn't tell me anything more."

"Ok. Thanks, Lindsy."

It was almost four in the afternoon. There was going to have to be some movement on the issue today, whether Glen liked it or not. Procrastinating would not get this person identified, or help him figure out how the guy found his way to Mrs. Rolley's garden shed. He'd have to retrieve John Doe's fingerprints himself. The responsibility was his and his alone. Putting it off on another officer would be a sign of weakness, and Glen balked at the thought of looking weak.

Because of the practice of Daylight Savings Time, the sun had all but left the horizon by the time Glen arrived at the top of Hospital Drive, though there was still enough light in the sky to cast a red and purple hue against the approaching darkness. The view of the town from up here along with the brilliant colors still hanging in the autumn sky gave him an excuse to spend a few more moments in the patrol car before going into the hospital.

As he sat looking out at the sky and his town below, he felt a tinge of anger. What kind of person crawls into an old woman's garden shed to wither away and die? And not just any woman, but one whom he regarded as a second mother to him. Another thought emerged that angered him even more: what if someone placed him in there? Who could do such a thing? The possibility existed that others were involved in this situation and could still be in the area. His area! He couldn't procrastinate any further. It was time to figure this thing out and put it to bed.

TWO

Glen entered the hospital through the lobby and spoke with the girl at the reception desk. Misty Lawson, a young lady who came from one of the more well-known families in the area. She directed him to the ICU with a pleasant smile, full of bright white teeth.

A nurse walking the floor of the ICU showed him where to find John Doe. The look on her face was as apprehensive as his. He'd been to the ICU a few times in the past, mostly to check in on car accident victims and their families. Oddly enough, the place seemed to have a warm feeling to it. Even though the patients here were facing some of the most extreme circumstances of their lives, the nurses and staff had a way of keeping things calm and somewhat pleasant. That feeling didn't exist in room 337.

They had him cleaned and covered up to the chest with a sheet. The thing still didn't seem alive, or even real for that matter. But the medical personnel involved had verified that he was indeed an actual person, still clinging to life on his own. Looking at him now for the second time, Glen struggled to believe it. The pale gray skin, which looked more like rotted leather; the open bulging eye staring off into nothing; the sunken face, crooked mouth, and broken teeth. He stood at the foot of the bed watching this creature struggle to take in what little breath it could to survive and was more repulsed now than when he'd first pulled the tarp off of it last night.

"Quite a sad situation, isn't it?" A voice came from behind.

Glen turned, startled, and saw a distinguished, grey-haired man in a white frock standing in the doorway. It took him a second to recognize that it was Dr. Bradley, a man he'd known since he was a kid. The doctor continued into the room and stood with Glen at the foot of the bed. "I can't say I've ever seen a person in such a state of degradation and still holding on like this." He picked up the clipboard hanging from the end of the bed and began writing on it. "Were you the one who found him, Glen?"

"Mrs. Rolley found him in her garden shed."

"Charlotte Rolley? How did he end up clear out at her place?" Dr. Bradley asked.

"I don't know," Glen said. "Given his condition, do you think he could have got out there on his own?"

Dr. Bradley took off his glasses and looked at Glen. "He's emaciated. I'd assume by his condition that if he did make it out there on his own, he'd have to have been there for weeks."

Glen shook his head. "Mrs. Rolley said she was in the potting shed three days ago and he wasn't there then."

Dr. Bradley walked over to the door and closed it. "Well, for what it's worth, I'll give you my professional opinion. And remember, I'm not a forensic pathologist, just an old country doctor. We ran a myriad of tests to determine what caused him to deteriorate to this state, and what we found was startling, to say the least. There are no drugs in his system at all. We tested for every other disease that attacks the body in this manner (cancer, hepatitis, aids, etc...) and found nothing. We sent rush samples to Infectious Diseases in Pittsburgh, just to be sure we aren't looking at something exotic. Nothing; not even a cold. The only cause we can point to is extreme dehydration. And when I say extreme, I'm not using the word lightly. It's as if every cell in his body has been drained." The doctor looked back at John Doe. "Honestly, I couldn't tell you how he's alive right now. It's beyond anything I've ever seen, or even studied for that matter."

Glen stared at the body under the sheet. It was dead still for several moments, and then the chest gently rose to take a faint breath and exhale. He was now facing the serious possibility that someone had dropped this person off at Mrs. Rolley's place and could still be somewhere in the area. Glen was going to have to get to work immediately on finding out who John Doe was. He'd also have his officers check around town for anyone who looked out of place. Then there would be the calls and visits from concerned citizens who would want answers—bodies don't just turn up in Cumberland Springs.

Dr. Bradley patted Glen on the back, breaking him out of his thoughts. "If you need anything from me, Glen, let me know. And if I receive anything else back from his pathology, I'll get in touch with you right away."

"Thank you, Dr. Bradley," Glen said, his voice sounding distant.

THREE

The overhead fluorescent lights suspended throughout the corridor of the ICU ward made the entire area feel cold and uninviting tonight. Lauren hadn't noticed this effect in the past, but as she stepped out of the elevator and proceeded toward the nurse's station, she felt as if she were walking through a giant refrigerator. She had experienced quite a bit of discomfort with her environment lately. The unwelcoming tint of the lights seemed to enhance that effect.

Lisa had already started the first rounds before Lauren made it onto the ward. It was a tremendous relief to see that she wouldn't have to visit the patients first. Spending most of the day with her mind on last night's events made her dread these first rounds. At least now she would have a few hours to get into a rhythm, to get her head straight before having to face that thing laying in room 337.

She had asked Lisa last night if she noticed anything strange when it was her turn to check on John Doe. Any odd noises? Smells? Cold spots around the room? Lisa had nothing to report, though she gave a disconcerting look. If Lisa would have come out pale white, cold, and clammy—screaming—it would have provided at least some validity to Lauren's experience. But when she emerged from the room, pushing the med cart with that almost constant smile on her face, it was evident that nothing had happened. If something had occurred, she did a hell of a job of keeping it to herself.

I hope he's dead! Lauren thought as she sat behind her computer screen. The thought was shocking. She abruptly shook her head, trying to rattle the terrible thing loose from her mind and onto the table where she could smash it like an insect and sweep it into the trash can. She wasn't accustomed to having those kinds of ideas. Lauren Rivers was a girl who had never wished harm on anyone or anything. It scared her that such a thought even *could* enter her mind. She began to self-analyze, figure out what drove her to have such an idea. Maybe it was merely compassion; hoping he'd passed on and was now at peace, no longer dealing with the pain of this life anymore—in a much better place, said old ladies who attend funerals as often as they attend Saturday evening Bingo games. But she knew herself better than that, and she knew her reason for wanting him gone was purely a selfish one. Fear drove her thoughts tonight. Fear of John Doe and the presence she had felt in the room with him. A fear which had changed her general perception of life.

Lisa emerged from one of the rooms after checking on a patient. "Hi Lauren," she said while pushing the med cart past the nurse's station. Her voice sounded like an eternally charming Disney Princess character. "You're a little late tonight?"

Lauren looked up from the computer. She was reading John Doe's patient file, which stated that he had not died today and was still residing—caramelized—in the room across the hall. "I know. I don't have an excuse either. I'm just running behind. Thank you for doing the first rounds."

"Oh, it's no problem." She could tell her tardiness didn't remotely bother Lisa. There seemed to be no bottom to the well of cheer this woman drank from.

Lisa pushed the med cart toward John Doe's room. A heightened focus came over Lauren as she watched her fellow nurse step inside. Her mindset had changed. At first, she'd been hoping her partner would have an experience similar to hers, and she could at least regain some confidence back in her sanity. However, if that were the case, it would mean the door had opened for some other type of explanation: an otherworldly explanation. That was not something Lauren was prepared to handle right now. It would be much better if nothing happened to Lisa in there, then Lauren could chalk last night up to nerves or stress, and that would be the end of it. Doe would take his dirt nap soon enough, and she could bury the memory of this disturbing event in the cold ground with him.

Less than ten seconds passed when Lisa came walking back

out. A shot of adrenaline coursed through Lauren's system. Was it happening? "Before I forget," Lisa said. "Mrs. Randell wants to see you when you have a minute. She wouldn't tell me why, just that she had something important to share with you and only you."

Lauren took a deep breath and let it out with a sigh. "Ok, I'll get over to see her in a minute." She patiently waited as Lisa went back into 337. Five minutes passed, which felt more like an hour. Her eyes glued to the door. It was like staring at the lid of a Jack-in-the-box while a demented child slowly turned the crank, laughing as the tension grew thicker and thicker. Lisa was in there with Doe—shriveled and clinging to every breath of life—and the thing that had skulked around her last night. But tonight there were no sounds, no movements, no odors. There were no signs at all to show anything out of the ordinary was happening. Lauren knew Lisa was not in there alone with a dying patient. There was something with her, watching, hovering, looming. Part of her wanted to rush in and warn Lisa, push her out of the way in case the vileness had attempted to accost her. But how ridiculous would she look if nothing was happening? How could she explain her dash of heroics if there was nothing to save her from? Finally, Lisa came through the doorway with her usual pleasant smile. "I guess I'm crazy," Lauren mumbled.

"Were you talking to me, Lauren?"

"Huh? Oh, no, just muttering to myself."

"That's no good to do in public. People might think you're crazy," Lisa said and winked with a smile. "You should go see Mrs. Randell soon. She told me she will not sleep until she has a word with you."

"Yeah, Mrs. Randell, ok." Lauren got up from her chair and sighed. She glared at the doorway to 337 for several moments. Finally, she shook her head and walked across the hall to see Mrs. Randell.

FOUR

"Ah, it's so good to see you!" The woman said as Lauren walked into the room.

"Well, it's very nice to see you too, Mrs. Randell." Lauren pulled a chair closer to the hospital bed. Mrs. Randell immediately reached for Lauren's hand as she sat down. She had the soft, thin skin of a woman in her mid-eighties, almost like that of a newborn. Lauren could tell that her touch made Mrs. Randell happy and a bit more relaxed. She instinctively checked the IV port in the old woman's arm just to make sure it was secure.

"I've needed to talk to you." She said, looking over at the door. "All these other nurses treat me like a child when I tell them things, especially that one out there now... Lisa! She just smiles and tells me to close my eyes and get some rest. They don't *listen!* You're the only one who hears me when I talk. You don't patronize me."

Lauren smiled, still holding Mrs. Randell's hand, hoping to keep her calm. "I'm always interested in what you have to say."

"I know you are, dear. I can't tell you how much I appreciate that." She looked at the doorway again, then back at Lauren. "I'm going to tell you something, and I don't want you to have me taken up to the *Nut Ward* because of it. Do you hear me?"

"Of course. You know I wouldn't do that, Mrs. Randell." Lauren said.

The woman's face became very focused. She squeezed Lauren's hand tighter. "There's something unusual going on in the room on the other side of that wall."

Lauren looked at the wall where Mrs. Randell's finger pointed. This woman, whom she'd known for most of her life, was as serious as the heart attack that landed her here. She could be slightly eccentric, everyone in Cumberland Springs knew that, but there was something in her tone tonight that voiced genuine concern. "What makes you say that?" Lauren asked.

"I'm hearing voices coming from in there." She leaned forward, off of her pillow. "I've been hospitalized enough times to know how doctors and nurses sound when they're in a room with a patient, and this ain't anything like that." Lauren could feel a tremble in the woman's hand. "These voices sound awful. Threatening. I can't make out what they're saying, but I can just tell by the tone that they are not good. I told the orderly I thought someone was in the room over there, saying nasty things. He checked and said there wasn't anyone in there except the patient, and the guy is in a coma." Mrs. Randell's heart rate monitor rose.

"Ok, stay calm, Mrs. Randell. You can't get excited like this after just having a heart procedure." Lauren said. The resident heart surgeon had shoved a fourth stint in the old woman's ticker just yesterday morning. They had put the other three in her ticker over the last several years.

"That's not all. Sometimes the voices laugh, but not in a light-hearted way. They sound malicious." She took a deep breath and let it out slowly. The heart-rate monitor responded by going down a few BPM. "And here's the part where you'll think I should be up in the Nut Ward. A few minutes before I hear the voices, I get an icy chill all over my body."

Lauren's eyes grew large as she hung on every word the old woman spoke. She couldn't tell if the trembling was coming from her hands or Mrs. Randell's. Lauren knew who was laying in the bed on the other side of that wall. The events being described to her now didn't seem far-fetched at all. Oddly enough, she felt relief. Her mind had not left the plane of reality for an alternate one. Another human being sharing the same type of experience indeed corroborated that she hadn't lost her mind. But how in the world could she feel relief over such a thing? Events like these happened in ghost stories and horror movies. Fiction, not fact. Entertainment. The stories that Mrs. Stover was probably sitting in the cafeteria reading right this very minute. Lauren was a rational, grounded human being. There was no room in her life for things that go bump in the night.

"I'm going to be here all night, Mrs. Randell, if you hear anything coming from that room I want you to buzz me right away. I'll make sure I answer your call and not Lisa." Lauren patted the woman's hand. "And no, I don't think you're crazy, so don't worry about the *nut ward* just yet." Lauren got up and started toward the door.

"What do you think it was?" Mrs. Randell asked.

Lauren stopped at the doorway and turned. She couldn't think of anything to say.

FIVE

Lauren paused for a moment in the hallway as two thoughts converged in her head. The first thought: walk past his room and don't look. Don't give it a second glance. Make it to the nurse's station, sit down behind that big ass computer monitor, and put it all out of mind. The second thought seemed like a bolder approach: face the fear. Walk directly into the room, stand at the foot of the bed, look into John Doe's one dilated bulging eye, let him and anything else skulking around in there know that she didn't believe, and was not afraid. The two ideas bounced back and forth in her head like a girl's high school volleyball game. How easy it would be to steer clear of the whole thing, maybe even pass off her rounds later to Lisa and avoid the problem altogether; Lisa wouldn't care. But as Robert Frost so articulately said: *"I chose the road less traveled, and that has made all the difference."* She stood at the door of Room 337, hashing out this internal struggle, and realized that if anyone were looking at her right now, they would certainly think she'd lost her mind.

The decision came to her suddenly, and she acted without hesitation. Lauren took a deep breath and stepped across the threshold, barging her way into the room, reminding her of a Black Friday shopper at the 6:00 A.M. opening of a Wal-Mart. She giggled to herself at the thought, though her light-hearted moment quickly died when she saw what lay in front of her.

John Doe lay comatose, looking almost exactly as he did last night; pallid, frail, and emaciated, surely mere hours away from death. But he was not alone. Leaning over him from the left side of the bed stood a dark, menacing shape. The shape took on a somewhat semi-transparent, human form, but much bigger than a man. Lauren gasped. It became aware of her and stood fully erect. Even though it had no features or color, she could feel it looking directly at her. Paralysis overtook her, and her throat became numb. What little breath came through her vocal cords would not make a sound. Her feet felt as if they were cast in cement and anchored to the floor. Both eyes dried as she could not blink. At this moment, she was utterly helpless. The black mass looming before her remained perfectly still while it stared her down from just a few feet away. The smell had also returned —the sulfuric, rotten egg odor she had experienced last night— except tonight it was more pungent and sickening.

From somewhere deep inside, a voice—either her conscience or the proverbial heart; the ever-present voice of reason and empathy—told her she was looking into the face of true evil. There was nothing in this form but malice and disgust. It hated her! She felt it despising her presence and wanting to spew its bile at her. Nothing in her life to this point had ever made her feel this awful. The entity in front of her spoke no words, nor made any gestures. It somehow telepathically transferred emotion, and the emotion was unsullied unadulterated hatred.

She didn't know where it came from, but after a few moments of being tortured by these terrible feelings of sadness, shame, and fear, Lauren got mad. Anger rose from her heart, giving her the strength to break the hold this thing had on her. She felt lighter, stronger, and unafraid. She realized it could not control her if she didn't allow it. Her voice returned. She finally said aloud the word she had been trying to speak through the course of this entire event: *"No!"*

It was gone. Lauren stood alone at the foot of the bed, looking toward the space where the darkness had taunted her from less than a second ago. It had departed faster than the blink of an eye. She wasn't sure the event had even taken place. Of course, it had, there was no doubting that, but it ended so quickly. The entire experience seemed surreal.

Lauren couldn't stay in the room with Doe for another second. This was all becoming too much for her to handle. As she returned to the nurse's station, she noticed that the light was blinking for room 339. Mrs. Randell's was calling.

SIX

Lisa was walking across the hall from the nurse's station toward the direction of Mrs. Randell's room. "No!" Lauren shouted. It was the second time in a matter of minutes she had yelled that word, in that tone. Lisa stopped in mid-stride, confused. "I'll check on Mrs. Randell!" For the first time in as long as she had known Lisa, the girl actually looked annoyed. "I didn't mean to yell, I'm sorry. I promised her I would check in on her if she rang the buzzer." Lisa said nothing as she headed back to the nurse's station, but Lauren could tell she was chafed.

"It was here! It was just here! I *goddamn* felt it!" Mrs. Randell shouted as Lauren entered the room. Her heart-rate monitor had just hit the magic number, kicking off a sharp, alert sound and filling the room with a sense of urgency.

"Mrs. Randell, calm down, please!" Lauren sat in the chair beside the bed and held her hand again, trying to relax her. "You can't get so excited."

"It was just…"

"Before you say another word, I want you to take three deep breaths, and let each one out slowly. We'll talk after you do that and your heart rate goes down." She listened to the instructions like a child in grade school obeying a teacher. Lauren rubbed her hand gently and somewhere between Mrs. Randell's second and third deep breath, the heart-rate monitor stopped squawking.

"I smelled it first this time—that nasty, rotten egg smell— just after you left my room. It was so pungent! You had to have smelled it."

Lauren looked into Mrs. Randell's eyes. She couldn't lie to her, and if she said nothing, it would be the same as lying. She knew the smell; she knew it the moment the woman described it to her earlier. It was present in 337 last night, and again moments ago. Surely Lisa had noticed it. If it was powerful enough to present itself on the other side of a cinderblock wall into Mrs.

Randell's room, it had to have been present in the hall near the nurse's station. "I need you to take a few moments to calm yourself down a little more, Mrs. Randell. Can you do that for me?"

"You're not going to brush this off, are you?"

"No, I'm not. I believe you. I need to check on something for a minute, then I'll come back. Take a few more deep breaths and get that heart-rate down," Lauren said in a nurturing tone. "I'll be right back."

Mrs. Randell leaned back against her pillow and continued her slow breathing as instructed. Most patients didn't like to listen to Lauren's nursing instructions, thinking they knew their own bodies better than some young girl who was hardly over drinking age, but Mrs. Randell was compliant.

She watched the woman breathe for a few moments, making sure she was calming down, then headed back to the nurse's station. Lisa was logging patient information into a computer. Lauren sat beside her, staring for several moments, not knowing what to say. Lisa didn't look up from the monitor, although she knew Lauren was watching her. Finally, she said: "Is something on your mind?"

Lauren opened her mouth to speak but quickly closed it. She did not know how she was going to word the question she had come here to ask. *Have you noticed any ominous, dark shapes roaming the halls lately? Heard any strange noises? Did ya happen to notice the smell of rotten eggs floating around the ICU?* There was no way to bring it up without sounding like an idiot—unless she was speaking to one of those groups who hunt for ghosts on late-night cable TV. She supposed the best way to address the situation would be to generalize. "Have you noticed anything unusual around here these last few days?"

Lisa didn't look away from the computer screen as she said: "Just you, showing up late for work and acting like a nervous wreck." She leaned back in her chair, then swiveled it to face Lauren. "Why don't you just come out and say what's on your mind?"

"Because what's on my mind doesn't make much sense." Her statement left an uncomfortable silence between the two of them. "Either I'm losing my mind, or, well—"

"Well, what?" Lisa said.

Lauren realized she was too far into the conversation to back out without Lisa pressing her on the issue. And she was a terrible liar, so that option wasn't on the table either. It seemed to her the only thing left to do was to let truth fly and accept the outcome. "Have you had any strange feelings when you go into Room 337?"

Lisa focused her gaze intently on Lauren as she considered the question. "John Doe is terminal. What strange things could possibly be going on in his room?"

Her tone was surprising. She was used to Lisa sounding like the voice of a Miss America contestant, dribbling out an answer as to how we can achieve world peace if only everyone would *Just stop hating and just start loving.* Now there was a hint of irritation in her inflection. "Never mind, it's just me; nothing you need to concern yourself with." She got up and headed back to the room where Mrs. Randell was hopefully still doing her breathing exercises.

"Lauren, if something is bugging you, spit it out," Lisa said.

Lauren heard the statement but didn't acknowledge it as she kept walking.

SEVEN

Mrs. Randell had probably stopped her breathing exercises the moment Lauren left the room moments earlier, but her heart rate was back to a safe number, and she seemed to be much more relaxed. She smiled as Lauren came through the doorway. "You couldn't be sweeter to me if you were my own granddaughter."

"And why is that, Mrs. Randell?"

"You came back. I wouldn't have blamed you if you'd have walked off and left the crazy old lady in here to fall asleep. But you came back." Her smile was enormous and endearing. Mrs. Randell had lived with heart issues for several years. She'd even gone through two open-heart surgeries before this last attack. But as she would put it, *"My ticker's ready to check out, but I'm not!"* Her body might have been thin and frail, but her spirit could still handle anyone or anything. Especially her neighbor's damn *shit-hound dog!*

Lauren took her seat next to the bed and again held the woman's soft, wrinkled hand. She couldn't help but reflect on the events taking place in the ICU since John Doe entered the picture. Why had she and Mrs. Randell been the only people who noticed the strange occurrences surrounding him? Lisa was completely oblivious to any of it. No, there was someone else. There was a name that came up during her conversation with Danielle last night in the cafeteria. A paramedic who had brought Doe in had some sort of episode outside. *What was his name?* Danielle said he had jumped out of the ambulance and took off running down the hill. *Was it Denny? No! Shit!* "What the heck was that guy's na…"

"Are you talking to me, Lauren?" Mrs. Randell asked. Lauren hadn't realized that she had conducted her internal inquiry aloud.

"Huh? Oh, I'm sorry, I was just thinking out loud." She softly patted Mrs. Randell's hand. "You're not alone in this, Mrs.

Randell. I've been experiencing some of the same things you're describing to me." She looked at the floor and shook her head. "I can't even begin to explain what's happening. I've been thinking it's all in my head, but now you're seeing and feeling the same things. I can't dismiss it."

"So you don't think I'm crazy?"

Lauren laughed. "Well, at least not with this situation."

Mrs. Randell smiled. "What are we going to do about all of this?"

"You won't be doing anything except resting and getting your strength back. If you feel uncomfortable or anxious, ring the buzzer, and I'll come right back. And you can tell me about anything you see or hear or feel without worrying that I'll think you're crazy."

"Will you tell me if anything else happens?"

Lauren thought about the question for a moment. These experiences had terrified her over the last two days. To share that with a woman recovering from a massive heart attack, causing her unnecessary stress, would be irresponsible. On the other hand, she detested lying, especially to someone as sweet as Mrs. Randell. "How about if I just say, for now, if I see something you should know about, I'll tell you right away?"

The answer didn't completely satisfy Mrs. Randell, but she knew there wasn't a choice.

Lauren sat with her for several minutes until she could feel her drifting off to sleep, then quietly left the room. Lisa was just coming back from a coffee break. "Everything ok in there?" Lisa said.

"Yeah, she's just nervous and needed someone to listen to her. I need to take a quick break.

EIGHT

The ER was relatively calm tonight. There were a few patients in need of emergency attention, but there didn't look to be anything severely pressing at hand. Lauren observed through the large plate-glass window which looked in on the ER from the hallway to the staff locker room. She walked by this window at the start of every shift and had always wondered what purpose it served. Why would they put a giant window between a staff hallway and the ER? Perhaps it was there so the personnel starting their shifts could get a dose of reality on their way to work, a way of saying, *Look at what you'll be dealing with tonight.* Or maybe it was just a poor design decision by the architect. They built the place back in the 1930s; God only knows what those people were thinking back then. Right now, Lauren used the window to see if Danielle Cunningham was working. She didn't want to barge in and ask for her if the whole ER staff was amid severe trauma. So for her, the strange window in question *did* serve a purpose.

Danielle was on duty tonight, standing at the admission desk talking to the red-headed secretary whom no one liked. Lauren went around to the double doors that led into the room. "Hey girl," Danielle said as she saw Lauren approaching. "What brings you down to the torture chamber?"

"Are you busy? I need a minute."

Danielle looked around and surveyed the status of the ER. "Sure, I have a minute."

They walked through a set of glass doors and into the main lobby of the hospital. The room was spacious and well-lit with a very high—possibly twenty feet high—ceiling. A fair amount of budget money went into the layout and decor here, making it a main focal point of the hospital. It was the first room you would see upon entering for your visit—unless you came in via emergency assistance. A large stone fountain sat in the center, garnished with various types of greenery and brilliantly colored flowers. Portraits of prominent doctors dating from the present and back to the hospital's opening hung from every wall. A fifteen-foot Christmas tree towered in one corner, which maintenance hadn't got around to decorating yet. The entrance to the gift shop and coffee shop were next to each other along the wall across from the main doors. During the day the lobby bustled with visitors coming to comfort friends and relatives who were temporary residents of Cumberland Springs Memorial, but at this hour—2:30 AM—the room was desolate.

Lauren stood quietly, looking at the floor. After a minute Danielle broke the silence. "So…"

Lauren snapped out of her trance. The high ceiling and large open expanse of the room gave an echo when Lauren said, "I wanted to ask you about that paramedic you mentioned last night. What happened to him again?"

Danielle stared at Lauren with a blank look while her mind struggled to retrieve the information. *What did happen? Something happened… What was it?* The ER can be a wild, hectic place. Events blend; it's hard sometimes to recall one thing in particular at a moment's notice. Danielle's mind wasn't coming up with the answer. "Paramedic?" She said, shrugging her shoulders.

"The one that brought in the John Doe! The one who freaked out!"

"Yeah, speaking of freaking out—" Danielle said, sarcastically.

Lauren didn't realize she was yelling until Danielle's comment brought her back to reality. "I'm so sorry. I didn't mean to sound snappy," she said.

Danielle smiled. She could tell something was bothering her friend, but also got the feeling it would be best if she didn't press her about it. "Oh yeah, the kid who got all panicky and ran out of the ambulance last night. What do you want to know about him?"

"What was his name? I need to talk with him about

something."

"Are you a psychologist now?" Danielle said. She cut off the humor when she saw the unamused look on Lauren's face. "I think his name was Devon. Ronnie Miller was the other medic with him last night. He just brought a patient in about 10 minutes ago."

Lauren perked up quickly. "Was Devon with him?"

"No, he had a different medic with him tonight, one I've never seen before." Danielle looked over at the doorway to the coffee shop and slowly began walking in that direction. "In fact, I think they might be sitting in there right now. Ah, yep, they're in there. Do you want to talk to Ronnie?"

Lauren eagerly agreed.

The overwhelmingly wonderful aroma of coffee is noticeable immediately upon entering the hospital lobby, but closer to the shop entrance, the smell becomes an intoxicating drug that must be had at any price—hence the $5 to $8 price tag on a thirty cent latte with a phony Italian name on it. This little shop was a pretty good knockoff of Starbucks: Art Deco decor, light jazz playing in the background, strange European sounding names for every item on the menu, Wi-Fi. But it was a place where people could relax and interact, and that served a valuable purpose. Somewhere during the twentieth century, a group of brilliant intellects decided that coffee should be the beverage of choice to bring the minds of the world together. Discussing art, music, literature, poetry, politics, and any other relevant topic of the day needed a beverage to unify. Alcohol had always been the drink of choice, but its effects clouded judgment and tamped down reason. As rational human beings realized the problem with alcohol, it became apparent that they would need a new beverage to congregate over. Coffee easily became that great unifier.

Two men who looked to be in their late-twenties sat at a table with plastic mugs in front of them. Both dressed in blue Cumberland Springs paramedic uniforms. One man smiled a giant toothy grin as Danielle walked into the room, the other paid her no attention and kept his face in a newspaper. It was apparent that Danielle was more than just an acquaintance to the smiling medic; she had a flirtatious confidence in her step as she approached him, and he ate it up. "Working hard tonight, Ronnie?" Danielle said with a smile. She put both hands on the table in front of him and bent over, exposing her cleavage.

"Very hard," he replied, staring at her breasts and grinning even larger.

Lauren could tell this flirtation was just getting started, and she didn't have time to stand here while these two stoked each other's hormones all night. She loudly cleared her throat. There was nothing discrete about it.

Danielle stood up straight, and the flirtation seemed to break. "Where's that other medic, Devon, the one who was with you last night?" She said.

"Why are you interested in him?"

"Maybe I was wondering why he flipped out. You have to admit, that was pretty random."

"Is he in trouble for it?"

"Not that I know of," Danielle said. "We were just thinking about him."

"This information seems valuable to you. What do I get in return?" His grin became playfully sinister.

"Maybe you should ask yourself what you won't be getting if you don't tell me," Danielle said. She bent over the table once more in front of him; the flirtation ritual had resumed.

"*Jesus Christ!*" Lauren exclaimed. "I don't have time for this crap tonight! Where the hell is he?"

Danielle, Ronnie, and the other medic—Bob might have been the name on his jacket—were all startled at Lauren's outburst.

Lauren paced nervously as Danielle and the two medics stared at her. They were still determining whether to be offended or concerned over being scolded. She didn't care about how they felt. There were much bigger issues weighing on her mind tonight.

For the last two days, the only thing she'd been able to focus on was that unidentified scarecrow lying in Room 337 and the presence surrounding him. A thought which had just occurred to her this evening kept rolling through her mind. *Was there more than one?* She had seen the shape tonight, the dark shadow that loomed over him, then stared her down as it became aware of her. But that situation differed greatly from what she had experienced last night. It was all around her then, circling her from every direction. The only way she could process this feeling in real terms was to imagine being in the middle of a circle of people, all of whom were scolding her and viciously taunting her. Was it possible that she was dealing with several entities instead of just the one?

"He called off work tonight," Ronnie Miller spoke up. "In fact, he said he'd be out the rest of the week."

Lauren snapped out of her thoughts and came back to the present. "Did he say why he couldn't come to work?"

"He didn't," Ronnie answered.

Danielle was still a little miffed at being yelled at, but her curiosity flared over this new mystery. "What was his problem last night?"

Ronnie looked down at his coffee and swirled it around for a second or two. He seemed apprehensive to talk about it. "Devon is… sensitive. I guess that's how I would say it. He has a hard time separating his emotions from the patients."

"How so?" Lauren asked.

"Well, I don't know if I have the right words to describe it. He kind of get's emotionally involved in what the patients are going through. And don't tell anyone I said this, he'd kill me if he found out, but sometimes—most times—he cries after we drop patients here at the ER. Especially over the critical ones." Ronnie took a sip of his coffee. He didn't seem like he wanted to elaborate further.

"But last night wasn't just emotion over a dying patient," Danielle said. "He was in a full-blown panic."

"Yeah, I know," Ronnie said. "It was that damnedest thing. I never saw him get like *that* before, and I've known him all my life. I don't question him about these outbursts, the guy was a combat medic in Iraq and saw some serious shit, so if he's working through issues, it's not for me to interfere."

"What happened after he took off last night?" Lauren questioned. "After his... episode?"

Ronnie looked down at his coffee again. He was becoming nervous.

"Oh, come on, chickenshit," Danielle said bluntly and pushed his arm. She wasn't one to hide her outspoken personality. "Don't hold back on us now." She seemed almost as involved in this story as Lauren by this point.

Ronnie looked up from his coffee. Some of it had spilled over the rim of the mug when Danielle shoved him. "Look, I don't want to talk about the guy behind his back. Maybe he's going through something that none of us understand and he just had an episode. I don't like to gossip."

Lauren needed to know what happened, and she couldn't wait any longer. Something surrounding John Doe had made Devon lose control last night. She was going to have to get this information out of Ronnie tonight, there was no doubt about it, even if it meant sharing something she didn't want anyone to know.

Lauren pulled up a chair and sat at the table across from Ronnie. She reached out and touched his arm sincerely. "I'm having some issues surrounding this patient as well. I don't want to go into all the details, but if you could tell me what happened with Devon when you two picked the guy up, well, maybe that would give me some clarity about my own situation." She looked down, and her voice became very soft and sullen. "I've been having a rough couple of days."

NINE

The room was quiet for several moments. Lauren, Danielle, and Bob—or whatever his name was—stared at Ronnie as he fidgeted with his coffee cup. "A woman stumbled across this John Doe guy last night in her garden shed," Ronnie said. "I guess she went in there to store some boxes or something when she found him. I imagine she took quite a shock," he said, laughing. No one laughed with him.

"The call came in that the police had found a dead body and needed a pickup for the morgue, and he sure as hell looked dead when we got there. I imagine he doesn't look much better now," Ronnie laughed, but again, no one laughed with him. "When we checked his vitals, there was nothing. So of course we figured that was it. Then the fucker took a breath; scared the living shit right out of me! I would have sworn at first glance he was a stiff. Man, was I wrong. Procedure dictated we keep him stable and get him up here ASA*F*P." Ronnie looked at Lauren. "I guess he's up on your floor now?"

"Yes, he's in the ICU," Lauren answered.

"I can't imagine how he's still holding on," Ronnie said.

"So when did Devon freak out?" Danielle chimed in.

"In the ambulance. He suddenly got real cold and started shaking all over, uncontrollably. Then he couldn't breathe. I tried to calm him down and deal with the patient, but that was just about impossible. So I focused on trying to get Devon straight. He kept saying, *Can't you smell it? It's here again!* The only thing I smelled was John Doe, who had been laying in a pile of his own shit for God knows how long. Devon believed there was something else in the wagon with us. That's when he jumped out of the back." Ronnie took a sip from his plastic cup. "I didn't see or smell whatever it was he was going on about, but I didn't think he was making it up either; the guy was terrified."

"Well, his behavior didn't go unnoticed," Danielle said. "But no one said anything to me about it today. I guess it just blew over."

Ronnie looked relieved. "That's good to hear. I'd hate for Devon to get in trouble over this. He's a really great guy." He drank the remaining swig of his coffee. "Did you say something like this happened to you too, Lauren?"

Lauren barely heard Ronnie's question. She was still analyzing and piecing together how Devon's issue coincided with hers. These events were well beyond anything a sane person would consider logical. Nevertheless, another person was seeing, smelling, and feeling the same unnatural thing she had experienced for the last two nights. A strange sort of relief came over her, knowing she was not alone. Mrs. Randell and Devon: two other people whom she had not shared her ordeal with but were having similar experiences of their own. In a court of law, two witnesses corroborating these kinds of details to a story could send a person to death row.

"I have to get back to the ICU," Lauren said. "I've been on break way too long." She left the room in a hurry without exchanging pleasantries with Danielle or the two medics. They all watched her leave. No one said anything.

Chapter 4

ONE

Before crawling into bed, Lauren had set her alarm clock for 10:00 AM, an act that mattered little now as she stared at the ceiling of her bedroom, wide awake and pissed off about it. Getting two hours of sleep wouldn't have been much anyway, maybe only enough to get the battery levels back up to around 40 percent, if that. Unfortunately, she'd gotten used to not sleeping this week.

Her responsibilities for Thanksgiving dinner were the same every year: green bean casserole, broccoli casserole, pumpkin pies, and cranberry sauce. The lack of sleep and everything going on at work had put her drastically behind schedule. She'd hoped to wake up early enough to finish preparing it all before having to leave for Grandmothers by 1:00 PM. Even though she had been making these same dishes—which were her great grandmother's recipes—since she was fifteen-years-old, today they would be a much harder task to accomplish.

Twenty minutes until the alarm would explode in her ear. There was no sense in trying to fall asleep now, waking up after only a few moments of sleep would just make her more miserable throughout the day. Yes, it would benefit her to bite the bullet and jump out of bed right now—rip the Bandaid off and get it over with—but she couldn't bring herself to pull down the blankets. The fabric seemed to come alive and hold her to the bed where it kept her warm and perfectly safe from the world outside. Maybe a countdown from ten. A launch sequence to catapult her off the pad and into orbit. 10… 9… 8…

Before she could complete the sequence, a gust of cold air hit her backside, sending a shiver through her entire body. Clay had gotten out of bed to use the bathroom with his usual bullish lack of grace. As if the cold air wasn't bad enough, she now had to listen to him piss with the bathroom door open. It sounded like someone dumping a bucket of water into a deep well.

"Why can't you ever close that door?" She yelled.

Clay responded with a slight laugh.

She threw the covers back and sprung out of bed to end the procrastinating for good. No more stalling. The floor was so cold that she almost jumped right back under the blanket. The jolt was much more effective at waking her up than any cup of coffee. Stress hormones surged through her veins, making her dread what the rest of the day might have in store. The nightmare seemed to continue.

The kitchen was also cold, as was the rest of the house. In a drafty old Victorian in the middle of a remodel, turning down the furnace at night was a must. It would take a good fifteen minutes to get the place up to a comfortable temperature.

Thankfully, Clay had gone to the store the day before with the list she had given him. All the ingredients were at her disposal, so she could get her recipes off and running quickly. She had put her own spin on great grandmother's pumpkin pie recipe, which made it more of a pumpkin cheesecake. The family took notice that it wasn't exactly like great grandmother's, but it came out so magnificent that no one complained. She came from a very traditional brood who strictly carried on their recipes and customs year to year with little to no alterations. However, no one could honestly deny Lauren's pumpkin pie had been worth the adjustment.

She began working on the tasks at hand, hoping her mind wouldn't wander back to the hospital and the man convalescing in room 337. It was no use. No matter how hard she tried to stay focused on baking, the image of John Doe flashed behind her eyelids each time she blinked. His half-open mouth and missing teeth; the black eye staring off at whatever; the pale gray skin, looking like rough leather. It wasn't only today that she suffered through these images; they had been cycling through her mind ever since the first night she'd seen him. And, if the visions of Doe weren't hard enough to deal with, there was also the thing— or things—lurking around him. She would never have imagined these things in the physical world. *Shadow figures? How could that even exist?* And the feelings that shook her to the core: anxiety, dread, helplessness. Nothing had ever made her feel this terrible. The harder she tried to block it out, the more her mind drifted back to what took place in that room. Fear ran its boney fingers over her again, and she noticed her hands shaking as she attempted to grease a pie pan. Anxiety was bubbling to the surface again, and Lauren was powerless against it.

"How's the baking going, baby?" Clay said from behind her.

Lauren screamed and dropped the metal pie pan onto the hardwood floor. It wobbled like a spinning quarter. "Fuck! Clay!"

"What?" Clay shouted back. Her reaction had startled him as much as he'd startled her. "I just came out to see how my wife was doing."

Lauren let out an annoyed sigh as she picked up the pan. "I'm fine. Just tired."

"Just cranky is more like it."

"Can you go watch TV or something, please? I need to get this finished."

"Are you making your pumpkin cheesecake?" He was wringing his hands and smiling.

"It's Thanksgiving, Clay. What do you think I'm making?"

His smile grew wider and he couldn't contain himself from giggling.

Lauren shook her head and laughed. "You're hopeless, Clay Rivers." She pointed toward the living room. "Now out!"

Even though the jolt had been annoying at first, Clay had taken her mind off of John Doe long enough for her to get back to baking and actually focus on it. The anxiety peacefully subsided to a simmer instead of a rolling boil. As she continued her work, she thought of how lucky she was to have a husband she loved and was there to help her through any situation, whether he realized he was helping or not.

TWO

Ronnie Miller couldn't take it anymore. The time for action was now. There was no way around it. For the last three days, he'd been going to work asking about his partner and getting no answers. *His wife says he's sick.* The guy hadn't missed a day of work since he started with Cumberland Springs E.M.S.. Now suddenly he's out for three days straight? *Bullshit!* Ronnie knew Devon better than that. Something happened to him in the ambulance the other night that affected his friend more than he'd initially thought. He needed to get to the bottom of it. Now!

The house looks cold, Ronnie thought as he exited his car and proceeded up the sidewalk to the front door. He'd been to this house more times than he could count since he and Devon became friends in elementary school, but had never known the place to give off a vibe like this. It was the first time the little two-story cape cod with the white clapboard siding and sharply pitched roof made him feel unwelcome. There wasn't anything tangible like the weather or an odor giving him this feeling of unpleasantness, something just seemed off.

"I already told you people, he's sick," Devon's wife said, standing in the archway of the front door, wearing the stern face of a drill sergeant. She did not attempt to disguise her frustration.

"Linda, don't give me this crap. Where is he? I know you *and* Devon better than you think."

She stared at Ronnie, trying to keep up her guard. He could tell right away by her red, puffy eyes and nose that she'd been crying. As he stared at her without speaking, tears formed in her eyes, and her lips quivered. She looked at the sky and blinked as rapidly as she could, trying to keep them at bay.

Ronnie reached out to hug her. He hadn't made it a full step in her direction before she grabbed onto him, buried her face in his chest, and spilled out a flood of emotion. "It's happening again."

Ronnie didn't know how to answer. He thought he knew Devon better than most—better than anyone. The only time the two were ever apart for long was when Devon joined the Marine Corps. If something was happening *again*, he should have been familiar with it.

"Where is he now, Linda?"

"He's in the basement. But he won't let you in. He has both doors locked."

Ronnie pulled a tissue from his coat pocket and handed it to her. Linda's emotional outburst didn't last long. It only took a minute for her to calm down and regain control.

"I don't understand what you meant by, *it's happening again.* What's happening again?"

She wiped her eyes with the tissue and began toward the door. "I shouldn't have said anything, Ronnie. Just forget about it."

"Well, no, I'm not going to forget about it. You guys are my friends. I'd like to think if there was a problem, I could help somehow."

"There's nothing you can do right now," Linda said. "When he gets like this, he has to work through it on his own."

These statements seemed so foreign to Ronnie. *It's happening again. When he gets like this... Gets like what?* Devon wasn't some co-worker or a guy he met for an occasional beer. The two were practically brothers. They knew everything about each other. When Devon rolled his truck over while messing around one late night in Bobby Orr's cow pasture, it was Ronnie who rushed to help him out of the mess. In eleventh grade when Ronnie's girlfriend, Lynn Anderson, didn't have a period for two weeks and he thought for sure he'd knocked her up, it was Devon who kept him from going off the deep end—it wouldn't have been Ronnie's kid, anyway; she was also nailing two other guys on the football team (go Tigers!). There were countless other situations they'd helped each other out with over the years as well. Either of the two would be hard-pressed to recall a circumstance they didn't share.

Linda went into the house and closed the door behind her. Ronnie stood for several moments staring at the front door. The house Linda and Devon lived in was Devon's parent's home, which he inherited when his mother passed away a few years ago. His father had died when he was a Junior in high school. Ronnie had spent an endless amount of time hanging out with Devon in this house, especially in the basement, which they had set up like a crude living room with an old couch, coffee table, and TV. Even with the furniture, though, it still didn't amount to much more than a dingy basement. But hallowed ground to the two of them and would remain a shrine to their friendship for the rest of their days.

There was, however, a secret way in through an old cast iron coal chute door on the backside of the foundation. When they built the house in the 1930s, coal furnaces were the most common system of heating; every basement had a small room with an iron door to shovel the black rocks through from the outside. There hadn't been coal in there since they updated the furnace to natural gas in the 1960s, so the room had become a storage closet. Devon and Ronnie found it to be the perfect passage to sneak into the house if they were out too late and didn't want to get busted by Devon's mother.

Just as he suspected, the iron door was still there, attached to the cinder block foundation. It looked a hell of a lot smaller than he remembered from when he was in high school. The last time he'd squeezed through there, he was probably around nineteen-years-old, and 140 pounds. Ten years and twenty pounds later didn't leave Ronnie a lot of confidence in this idea. The thing looked rusted shut anyhow. He probably wouldn't even be able to get it open.

That wasn't the case. Two quick tugs and a loud metallic groan and the door popped straight up, almost knocking him backward.

The square opening was two-and-a-half feet wide and the same distance high. The drop into the coal room itself was probably about six feet, *if* he could even get himself through the door. He had to base that measurement on memory alone because only darkness awaited him beyond the opening.

He headed back to the car to get a flashlight. Linda peeked through the curtain in the kitchen window but closed it quickly when she saw him walking back toward the house. Her behavior continued to puzzle him, making him more resolved than ever in his quest for answers.

The flashlight beam illuminated an empty room. He'd remembered that Devon's mother had stored a lot of plastic storage bins in there some years ago, but they must have cleared them out after she passed away. His last excuse to abandon the mission now gone. It was time to squeeze his ass through the opening and try not to break an ankle, or something worse.

He strategized that the best way to enter would be feet first and backward. When his torso cleared the entrance, he could use his elbows and hands to lower down into the room slowly. To his surprise, this approach seemed to work. The opening was tight once his legs were inside, but he was squeezing in fine. When his butt had made it through, he could feel the gravity of the room pulling at him. The distance to the floor must have been farther than he'd estimated because as his chest passed the opening, his feet had still not touched the ground.

"What the hell are you doing?" A voice came from somewhere inside the room. He lost his grip and dropped the remaining seven or eight inches. The momentum caused him to fall backward onto his ass.

A bare lightbulb overhead came on. Devon stood at the other end of the small room with his arms crossed.

Ronnie looked up at him from the floor, clapping 50-year-old coal soot off of his hands. "Apparently making a fool of myself."

Devon said nothing, nor did he change the unamused look on his face. After a few seconds, he turned and left the room.

That was cold, Ronnie thought. His friend should have at least laughed at how ridiculous he looked, sneaking through a dirty coal chute and falling to the floor like an idiot. There was no reaction. His response was blank, as if he saw no humor at the moment at all.

There hadn't been coal in this room for years, but Ronnie's hands still ended up coated in black dust. He brushed himself off, then went out into the main part of the basement.

Devon sat on the couch staring at a small television, which was the same one that had been here when they were young. Amazing that the thing still worked. The two had spent countless hours in front of that thing, watching MTV, playing video games, and wasting time. The Super Nintendo game system was actually still sitting in a box on the floor next to the old footlocker the TV sat upon. Could that thing even work anymore?

"So, what's wrong with you?" Ronnie said, not being at all hesitant or cautious.

There were several prescription bottles on the small coffee table, along with four or five empty beer bottles. Devon reached for one of the medicine bottles, shook out two blue pills, then swallowed them down with a slug of beer. "You shouldn't have come here, Ronnie." He slouched back into the worn fabric of the couch with a beer in hand. "It's not a good time."

"Yeah, well, I call bullshit!" Ronnie walked over to an old refrigerator in the corner and grabbed two beers out of it. The room—as with most basements—had become a repository for old appliances, storage boxes, racks of outdated clothes, and various other things one means to donate or dump but never gets around to doing.

Ronnie plopped down on the couch next to Devon, handed him a fresh beer, and opened the other for himself. "Let's hear it. What's up?"

Devon opened his beer but didn't answer. He didn't even acknowledge being asked the question.

"I'm not playing a game with you today, dude. Spill it!"

Still no reply or reaction.

Ronnie reached forward and picked up one of the pill bottles. "You're popping Xanax?"

Devon didn't respond.

Slouching back into the couch next to his friend, Ronnie took a long swallow of his beer. "Well, I have nothing to do today. What's on TV?" He grabbed the remote off of Devon's lap and started flipping channels, being as annoying as he could. "Oh, look! Martha Stewart. I hope she's baking today. I hate when she does a full episode about sewing, that gets redundant."

His attempt to crack the shell of Devon's somber mood had worked. His friend could no longer hold back the smile that was boiling its way to the surface. They both broke out in laughter. In an instant, Devon was Devon again.

During their twenty years of friendship, they had learned exactly how to handle each other. After breaking the ice, you let it settle. Don't push or the hole will freeze over again. Give it time, and the issue will see its way to the surface.

Ronnie flipped the channels around for a few minutes, then found the Thanksgiving Day NFL game of Pittsburgh vs. Dallas. It only took about five minutes before both of them were cheering for the Steelers and acting as if nothing was ever wrong. As the game went on into the second quarter, the smell of turkey baking in the oven drifted down the stairs and enhanced the mood even further. They were laughing and cheering and analyzing football plays and being the friends they had always been. The thought of bringing up the subject of Devon's problem kept entering Ronnie's mind, but he didn't want to risk sending his friend back into the darkness again. It was much better to enjoy the game and enjoy the friendship; to have a day that would leave both of them smiling for a while.

"I saw it again the other night," Devon said, out of the blue.

Ronnie sat quietly, looking at Devon. It was at the surface now. He needed to listen and let it fester out on its own. He grabbed the TV remote and lowered the volume.

THREE

Vicki Crawford's turkey and stuffing were the best in Cumberland Springs, second to none, and no one in their right frame of mind could contest it. Thanksgiving and Christmas were the only occasions she would make the famed dish, causing those annually invited a year's worth of anticipation. The secret to the stuffing—which wasn't much of a secret; she told practically the entire town how she made it—were walnuts, dried berries, and a unique blend of seasonings which were all mixed together with dried Italian bread crumbs. The mixture then carefully inserted into the turkey's ass to flavor the bird while it cooked. When the turkey breast hit an internal temperature of 170 degrees, she'd remove all the stuffing from the cavity, spread it out on a baking sheet, and put it back in the oven for ten more minutes, just to add the slightest hint of crust. As the first decadent bite hits the mouth, all the flavors and joy of the fall season explode throughout the senses, causing intensely pleasurable reactions from everyone partaking in this well-prepared feast.

Glen was still sleeping as the aromas from the kitchen crept upstairs and made their way under the crack of the bedroom door. What a way to wake up. Not to the usual shrill scream of his alarm clock, but to the soft, gentle fragrance of his favorite holiday meal. He lay in bed, staring at the ceiling for several moments, taking in deep inhales through his nostrils and smiling wider with every exhale. He knew it was going to be a great day with his family and friends, full of love and laughter and the most enjoyable food he'd ever known. Could life get any better than this?

After he and Vicki had married fifteen years ago, they offered to have both his and her parents over for their first Thanksgiving together. Glen's mother, slightly taken aback—this holiday had always been her time to shine—but she conceded just this once to welcome her new daughter-in-law into the family. After that first inaugural dinner, everyone unanimously agreed that young Mrs. Vicki Crawford knew her way around a turkey, and this honor now belonged to her. Glen's mother got over it within about three years, or so everyone thinks.

Glen had a brilliant idea while enjoying this moment of comfort in his warm bed. Today would be about family and friends only. No discussions about work, politics, celebrities, or anyone or anything that did not directly pertain to the people gathered in his home today. Happy thoughts and pleasant conversations. Anything else would be off the table and out of the question. If anyone attempted to bring up a subject outside of this realm—especially politics, he truly loathed politics—he would politely guide them back in by changing the subject to something positive. *They'll thank me for this*, he laughed to himself.

The alarm clock next to the bed read, 12:32 PM. Glen rarely slept this late unless he had worked the midnight shift the night before, but that wasn't his shift yesterday, and he was in bed well before 10:00 PM.

The dream. What was it?

He sat up in bed, puzzled. Something had made him restless throughout the night. He thought it was a dream, but couldn't remember. He recalled getting out of bed several times to check on the house and his son and daughter. What had unsettled him? The feeling hadn't come from a vision or anything he could see in his mind, but more from a sense of anxiety. There was a problem with the protective fabric blanketing his home and family; a tear had occurred. Something sinister had slithered through the newly exposed fissure.

John Doe!

God! He did not want to have the image of that shit covered scarecrow anywhere near his mind today. But he was a cop, and cops don't leave their work at the office. No matter how hard they try to keep it there, it always attaches itself to them like a blood-sucking leech, draining them of joy and optimism until all that's left is apathy and a sour scowl that rests upon their faces even in the happiest of moments. Though crime was almost nonexistent in his town, there were still things that followed him home. The face of John Doe had a good chance of being a permanent etching on his memory, never letting him forget that fateful moment when he pulled off the burlap tarp and his world had changed forever.

Glen got out of bed and hurried down the stairs, barefoot, wearing only red flannel pajama bottoms. His wife stood in the kitchen working at the stove. She had on the fluffy white robe he had given her for Christmas last year. Her long dark hair was messy and driving him wild. She was unaware that her husband was leaning against the archway, adoring her. He often admired Vicki when she wasn't looking. Her petite figure, fair complexion, and slightly larger than average breasts awakened his libido every time laid eyes on her. Then there were the dozen or so freckles across the bridge of her nose and tops of her cheeks. This woman had her husband wrapped entirely around her finger, which he did not mind one bit.

"What are you doing?" Vicki said as she caught her husband staring.

Glen snapped out of his trance. He approached her and put his arms around her waist from behind. "I'm checking out my hot wife. Do you have a problem with that?"

She turned around in his arms to face him. "I certainly don't, Chief."

They began kissing and giggling. Both became instantly aroused. Glen's hands wandered over his wife's body, and she could feel the bulge in his pajamas grow and poke at her waist, causing the kissing to intensify. Time didn't seem to matter; they became increasingly more focused on one another, forgetting the world around them and surrendering to the moment. Their breathing escalated in unison while their tongues explored each other's open mouths. They looked at one another and smiled, giving the green light that it was time to run upstairs to the bedroom, lock the door and—

"Brandon won't let me watch the Thanksgiving parade on TV!" A small voice came from behind.

Glen turned away to hide the pole that was now turning his pajama bottoms into a full circus tent. Vicki fixed her robe and tried her best not to look flustered.

In the kitchen's archway stood their eight-year-old daughter, Sarah. She was still in her flannel nightgown. The rich dark hair she'd inherited from her mother's DNA pulled back in a ponytail.

"Honey, you have a TV in your room," Vicki said. "Go watch it upstairs."

"I want to see the floats on the big screen! Brandon's watching The Avengers again for the twentieth time."

"She has a point," Glen interjected. "Snoopy does look better on the big screen."

Sarah was daddy's little girl. She had a way of getting Glen on her side just by being her adorable self. But make no mistake, when the cuteness approach didn't yield her desired result, she was not opposed to throwing down a full-blown tantrum.

"Come watch it with me, daddy," she said and took Glen by the hand.

"Daddy needs to go take a shower and get dressed," Vicki said. "Tell Brandon I said to go clean up his room and get dressed as well. You can watch the parade after you're dressed and ready for company. We have people coming over today and I will not have my family looking like a pack of wild heathens." She had become General George Patton, directing tanks and barking out orders before the Battle of the Bulge.

Sarah could tell mom meant business. She didn't put up a rebuttal. She left the kitchen and relayed Vicki's orders to her older brother, who was lying on the couch in the family room watching his favorite superheroes save the world. Her shrill voice echoed through the house as Brandon ignored her.

"Want to jump in the shower with me?" Glen whispered to his wife. "I'll scrub your back, among other things."

"The window of opportunity is closed, Chief," Vicki said.

"You'll have to dress yourself today. And go make sure those kids of ours are doing what I told them to do."

Glen kissed his wife on the forehead. The smell of the turkey in the oven and the sound of his kids bantering in the other room gave him a warm smile. These were the moments in life he cherished the most. He would do his best to absorb the day and hold on to these memories forever.

FOUR

Lauren and Clay arrived at her grandparent's house just as Grandmother uncovered and organized the day's feast on the large mahogany buffet table which she'd had since 1951. Lauren received *the look* from Grandmother as she rushed to get her pies and green bean casserole onto the table with all the other items. Grandmother didn't like tardiness. She promptly served dinner at 2:00 PM every year regardless of rain, shine, traffic, or violent act of nature. Excuses not accepted. If you were late, dinner went on without you, and you'd have to eat yours cold while everyone else chattered on around you, which was akin to a child receiving punishment in front of an entire 4th-grade classroom.

Clay bypassed everyone's greetings and went straight to Lauren's grandmother. He kissed her on the cheek and gave her a loving hug. "Sorry we're late, Gram. It's my fault." He looked at Lauren and winked, accepting his husband points.

"Oh, don't worry, sweetie," Grandmother said. "I'm just happy you're here."

Lauren shook her head and laughed. Her grandmother adored Clay, and he took full advantage of it.

The food was spectacular, as always. Each relative bringing the same assigned dish year after year, made from Grandmother's recipe book, handed down from her mother, and her mother before her. Keeping these traditions alive was important to Lauren's family. She knew there would come a day when the recipe book would get passed down to her and she would be the one responsible for upholding them; a task she proudly accepted.

Reverend Allen had been coming to Thanksgiving dinner for the last three years, ever since his wife had passed away from breast cancer. He gave a beautiful, heartfelt blessing before the meal, bringing a tear to more than a few eyes. It seemed official whenever a preacher presided over the blessing, rather than just a family member who Grandmother had guilted into the assignment.

Throughout dinner, the conversations ran over the usual catalog of family subjects: Who's getting married, who's pregnant, who died, how the nieces and nephews and little cousins are doing in school, who are arguing or mad at each other. Lauren did her best to take it all in and engage with everyone, though she struggled to keep up. She heard them speaking and tried hard to focus, but all the words seemed to run together into a giant chaotic bowl of Alphabet Soup, spelling out phrased which made no sense.

After everyone had finished eating more than they imagined they could, it was time for the men to adjourn to Pop's den to watch football and suck on beer bottles. Another of those traditions that seemed to endure forever. As soon as Pop got up from the dinner table, the rest of the men followed like a herd of sheep, a few of them almost falling over each other. Cousin Fielding, however, liked to stay back and gossip with the ladies. *That boy should come out of the closet any day now.* Some of the uncles would snicker with each other over their beers.

Lauren had used the restroom, then wandered into her grandparent's sunroom. A large glass enclosure added onto the house when Pop retired, full of plants and a pleasant seating area with a couch and two chairs. The floor tile was a rustic slate that made you feel as though you were walking on stone. The room created a small scale tropical retreat, even on the coldest days of winter.

She'd just needed to get away for a bit. A quick five minutes of rest to recharge and clear her head.

Plopping down onto the couch felt too good to be true. The oversized cushions were so soft they seemed to pull Lauren in like giant warm arms, making her feel as though she could stay here for hours, letting the couch absorb all of her anxieties like an enormous sea sponge.

She tried her best not to fall asleep. The effort was futile. With each attempt to open her eyes, the lids became a weight that was too much to bear. The darkness felt wonderful. The background noise of men cheering football and women and Cousin Fielding gossiping in the kitchen faded farther into the distance with each passing second. Soon all she could hear was the sound of her breath getting deeper and slower. She was crossing over into a state of pure relaxation. Lauren surrendered and allowed sleep to take her.

An image flashed through her mind for a mere split second, shocking her back to reality and causing her to gasp aloud. John Doe's face. She grabbed her chest and felt her heart pounding against the back of her ribcage, a feeling she had been experiencing far too much this week.

"I hope I didn't startle you, sweetie," Grandmother said as she entered the sunroom.

Lauren took a few seconds to focus. "Oh," she said, sitting up. "I must have dozed off."

Grandmother sat next to her on the couch and held her hand. This woman had an unyielding intuition about others, especially those in her immediate family. It was a skill developed over a lifetime of being a nurse, mother, and grandmother. She had genuine empathy for those around her, giving her the ability to sense when there was a problem with someone she cared about. There was no hiding an issue from this woman. "You look out of sorts today."

Lauren's eyes lowered, and she looked away.

"Tell me what's wrong," Grandmother said, her light blue eyes sparkling through her wire-rimmed glasses.

"I think I'm just having a rough midnight shift this week. You know what that's like."

Grandmother laughed and shook her head. "Oh, I sure do. They try to tell you that the midnight shift is less stressful. That's bullshit!"

Lauren smiled. The woman was never afraid to tell it like it is.

"You can't let it get to you, sweetheart. Nursing is a job that few people can do. You have to be kind and sincere on the one hand, yet tough and heartless on the other. Then you're expected to come home from your shift and leave the day behind." She squeezed Lauren's hand a little tighter, but still gently. "Only the right person can balance it all out... a gentle *bitch!*"

They laughed with each other for several moments.

"So what's bothering you?" Grandmother asked. "Admin, staff, or patient?"

"If I told you, you'd think I needed to spend a week in the *Nut Ward*."

"Honey, I was a nurse in that same hospital on that same floor for forty-five years. There's nothing you're dealing with that I haven't already seen."

"Yeah, I guess your right," Lauren said. "But I'm not sure if my problem is physical or psychological."

Grandmother said nothing. She didn't have to. The look on her softly wrinkled face was one which Lauren had seen time and time again and knew exactly what it meant: *Start talking.*

Lauren took a deep breath, then began. She told Grandmother everything that had happened with her John Doe patient this week, from his condition and the circumstances surrounding his arrival, to what she had felt upon entering his room. The fear and anxiety, dread, hopelessness, and even anger. Feelings she couldn't recall ever having in the past. She then described the other more physical experiences. The horrible odor of rotten eggs and decaying animals; the darkness which didn't come from dim lights, but felt like an actual substance of matter; the shadow figure.

Grandmother didn't change her expression or break eye contact. She focused intently on every word as her granddaughter's incredible story unfolded.

When Lauren finished talking, her eyes were glassy, and her cheeks had become red. The emotion of the story had come to the surface. She let out an insecure laugh and wiped her left eye before a tear could break loose.

She looked at Grandmother, expecting her to say something, but Grandmother remained silent. Her eyes were still on Lauren but seemed to stare through her as if her mind had gone some place else.

They had held hands throughout the entire conversation. Suddenly, she felt Grandmother's hands trembling. Subtle at first, then growing more intense with each passing second. The faraway look in her eyes and the trembling frightened Lauren.

"Are you ok?" She said, gently shaking Grandmother's hand.

It took a moment before she finally came around. "Oh. Yes, I'm fine, dear."

Lauren studied her, as a nurse instinctively does when someone looks ill. She turned her hand over and checked her pulse with two fingers. "Your heart rate is up."

Grandmother looked down at Lauren's fingers on her wrist. "Yes, I imagine it is."

"What's that supposed to mean?"

Grandmother looked around the room, not making eye contact with Lauren. "It means that you're not crazy, and neither am I."

"No one could ever accuse you of being crazy. You're the most grounded woman I've ever known."

Grandmother laughed. "Stay here." She got up from the couch and left the room. In a few minutes, she returned with what appeared to be an old scrapbook.

She sat next to Lauren and began leafing through the pages. The book looked ancient with its yellowish faded cover and worn fraying edges. It smelled musty, as old books often do. Roughly taped to the interior pages were newspaper clippings, some with grainy black and white photos, others with only bold headlines and long columns of text. As Grandmother turned the pages looking for one, in particular, Lauren caught glimpses of a few headlines. 4 KILLED IN FIERY CRASH; TEEN DROWNS IN SWIMMING ACCIDENT; 3 DIE IN MINE EXPLOSION. The subject matter of this macabre scrapbook shocked her profoundly. She'd never known her grandmother to have an interest in such things.

Grandmother stopped on a page close to the middle of the

book. She gasped slightly and placed her hand on her chest. Lauren nudged closer and saw the photo of a stout, angry-looking man with a flat-top crew cut looking back at her. He appeared to be in his mid to late thirties. His expression was cold and visceral, like an animal about to stock an unsuspecting prey.

Both women sat captivated in fear by the photo, neither able to speak. Lauren could not pry her eyes away from the image, no matter how hard she tried.

Finally, Grandmother spoke up. "This is Harlan Wallace, the most evil, despicable creature I've ever been in the presence of." Her words were monotone and void of emotion.

FIVE

The football game had just started to get exciting. Both the Steelers and Cowboys were launching dazzling aerial assaults against each other and racking up huge scores, making the game an all-out nail-biter. Devon should have been on the edge of his seat, clutching his Terrible Towel and screaming at the TV, but now he seemed to be somewhere else, some place cold and dark; a place as far from the comfort of the basement couch as he could get.

"What did you see the other night, Dev?" Ronnie asked. "In the ambulance. You said you saw something." He turned the sound all the way down on the TV.

Devon held his beer bottle up and studied the foaming liquid swirling around inside. On TV the Steelers were mounting a tremendous drive that would almost certainly end in a score, putting them in the lead with only seconds remaining on the clock. Devon had no interest at all. He only stared at his bottle, making the liquid churn at a slow even pace. His love for the Steelers was legendary, so it was far out of character for him not to be going crazy at a moment like this.

Ronnie touched Devon's arm and pushed it down slowly to take his focus off of the bottle. "Hey buddy, tell me what's wrong." He took the bottle out of Devon's hand and set it on the table. Devon didn't resist.

"I'm fucked up, Ronnie."

"Did you drink too much? Take too many pills?"

"No, that's not it. My head is just fucked!" Devon leaned forward and buried his face in his hands. He sobbed.

Ronnie put his hand on Devon's back. "You're not fucked up. Everybody has rough times, it doesn't mean there's something wrong with you."

Devon sat back and wiped his eyes with his t-shirt. "You don't know what I've been through, what I've seen."

Ronnie sat still, concerned. "You can talk to me, buddy. You know that, right?"

Devon grabbed the beer bottle and gulped down the rest of it. "I've never even told Linda this," he said as he stared into the empty bottle.

Ronnie sat back and prepared to listen. He grabbed the remote and turned off the TV, just as Pittsburgh was getting ready to score. The two sat in silence for a while until Devon built up the strength to start.

"I don't know what they showed on the news during the Iraq War; I saw little of the footage. There were a lot of news crews trying to latch on to us before we'd head out on patrols, but we kept them away from forward operations, mostly. Fucking dip-shit reporters in their L.L. Bean safari outfits," Devon said. He had just put a Camel in his mouth and lit the tip with a silver Zippo lighter. The lighter had a beautiful military crest on it, with a sword over a blue shield and a few letters at the bottom.

Devon continued: "I saw some pretty messed up shit over there. Stuff I didn't know people could do to each other. We see movies and video games with people getting blown away all the time, but when you see the real thing, dude, it's a whole different monster.

"I was a medic in the 3rd Battalion/1st Marines during the second battle of Fallujah, Operation Phantom Fury. The military said it was some of the heaviest urban combat U.S. Marines have been involved in since the Battle of Hué City, Vietnam, 1968. I never imagined I would see anything like that in all my life." He took a long drag off of the cigarette. Ash fell from the tip as it shook in his lips.

"We'd had a couple of intense skirmishes right off the bat. In the first three days of Ops I had twelve men die in my hands while I tried to patch them up. Twelve! The first few got to me, ya know, the look in their eyes, the fear. If they were knocked out and just died as I worked on them, that was fine, but if they were wide awake and fully aware… damn! There is nothing worse than watching a guy whose blown full of holes crying out to God or his mother. The mother thing surprised me. I heard that a lot.

"Sometimes I'd be working on a wounded Marine and I swear I'd see myself staring back up at me. It was the weirdest thing. Like a premonition, or some supernatural crap. Really freaked me the fuck out. But I'd shake it off and do my job because that's all I was there to do.

"After the first Battle of Fallujah, the Iraqi interim government wanted to hold on to the city with their own security force and no coalition help, which was fucking stupid. Those assholes couldn't fix a flat tire, let alone defend a city. So they built up defenses and stockpiled weapons that we gave them for a year, then lost it all to the insurgents in the snap of a finger. When we came back to take control of the city again, the insurgency was heavily armed and dug in like rats.

"These insurgents were absolute evil. They did things to the people of that city that I don't even think animals could do to each other. No regard for humanity at all." Devon paused and looked up at the basement rafters. His eyes had filled with tears and were about to spill over.

"Dev, you don't have to go on, man," Ronnie said. "If you don't want to tell me the rest, it's ok."

Devon sniffed hard to keep his nose from running and let out a slight laugh. "When I finish, you can tell me if I'm crazy or not."

Ronnie shook his head in agreement.

"Heading into this one city block," Devon continued. "We came under serious heavy fire, probably the most we'd seen since the start of the siege. Fucking grenades going off, rockets, machine gunfire. Two of these assholes even came at us wearing bomb vests and tried to blow us up with them. Bomb vests! What kind of psycho does it take to do that? We capped them way before they penetrated our position. Both of them blew to pieces. Some of our guys cheered.

"After the suicide bombers were toast, I looked up ahead and saw this one rag head herding about a dozen children into the street. As soon as they knew we saw this, five more of them got behind the kids and started firing at us, using the children as human shields." Devon lit up another Camel with the silver Zippo. Ronnie could read the letters on it when Devon tossed it on the table face up. Under the crest, it read: "Tip of the Sword."

"How are you supposed to shoot back over fucking kids?" Devon said, shaking his head. He inhaled another long hit off of his smoke. "We hunkered down real quick, there was nothing else we could do. They fired at us long enough so they could get out of the street. I saw them grab up the kids and head into a building about a hundred yards back from where they were shooting at us. We let it play out for a little over ten minutes. Maybe it was because of all the shooting and because my ears were spent, but the quiet in those ten minutes was almost supernatural. I felt like something heavy had fallen over the battlefield. Like an invisible blanket laid over us. But this thing wasn't warm and comforting, no, sir. I had a feeling of dread like I had never known before.

"During that quiet time, we were able to get two snipers on a rooftop to put eyes on the insurgent's position. Three of the bastards tried to sneak out of the building and the snipers put two of them down. The third took a hit, went down, but crawled back into the building. I caught a quick glimpse of him from my position. I could tell by the blue turban on his head that he was the one who ushered the kids into the street and started this shit storm in the first place. And then the shit really hit the fan."

Devon got up and went to the refrigerator.

Ronnie stared at the pack of Camels sitting on the small coffee table next to the Zippo lighter. He hadn't smoked a cigarette since he was in high school and hadn't had the urge to since then. But he was nervous now. The look that had come over his friend and the sober way in which he told the story got to him. He grabbed the pack and shook one out.

"I can't remember the last time I saw you smoke," Devon said as he came back to the couch. He handed Ronnie a fresh beer and opened a new one for himself. "Am I freaking you out?"

"You've always freaked me out," Ronnie said sarcastically as he lit the cigarette. He coughed as the first puff hit his throat.

"I probably shouldn't tell you the rest of this," Devon said. "It was the worst day of my life, I don't need to lay that on you."

"When we became friends as kids, I signed on for all of it, good or bad."

Devon sat back on the couch. Seeing Ronnie struggle to keep from getting sick lightened his mood.

"We had the visual of six insurgents going into the building with those kids. Two confirmed kills and one wounded, leaving three healthy fighters and one gimp. Our Captain radioed in for a tactical strategy, but command said to wait for further instruction. Then, after a few more minutes of quiet, it happened."

SIX

"Command, be advised that we have eyes on six Ali Babas who just entered a Haji Shop on the North-West side of Sector H. They have a group of eight or more children they're using as human shields. Request tactical order." Captain Bender released the button on the mic, waited for a response, and stared intensely at the building 500 yards ahead of his position. The rest of his Marines, positioned behind him, held a unified gaze as they pointed their weapons in the same direction.

"3rd Platoon, stand by," the radio voice squawked back.

Captain Bender was calm and squared away. Tension had risen throughout the rest of 3rd Platoon over the current situation, but Bender remained unaffected. His composure unwavering. In the thick of combat with bullets flying, explosions going off in all directions, and men screaming, Captain Bender never lost his stability.

There were fifteen men currently in 3rd Platoon on this day, led by Captain George Bender of Greensboro, NC. Six engagements with enemy combatants within the last week had left the platoon short by twelve men. Seven of them now Battle Field Angels.

The duty they pulled this morning was to be a short in and out recon patrol, back by lunch. But as with most assignments in Fallujah, back by lunch didn't necessarily mean today's lunch. After insertion into the South-East section of town, the objective was to gather intelligence on an airstrike that took place several hours before, then head to the North-East section to rendezvous with members of 2nd Platoon and wait for a joint extraction. Along the way they encountered several pockets of resistance, resulting in four intense firefights. 3rd Platoon had eliminated 16 enemy combatants while only taking one casualty, Private Thomas Wilson, who took a load of shrapnel to the shoulder. He was still on his feet though, not hindering the group from keeping to the schedule.

They hunkered down behind the rubble of a half blown out building on the south side of the street. A large pile of bricks and wooden beams mixed in with an old burned up Toyota truck provided the perfect cover for the men to keep safe and still see the building the insurgents had ducked into.

Lieutenant Cook made his way slowly and cautiously over to Captain Bender's position. "Any word from Command, Cap?" He whispered.

Bender shook his head, keeping his eyes locked on the building.

"What about our snipers?"

"Waxed two, wounded one. The wounded one crawled back in the building."

"So we're dealing with three, possibly four combatants inside?"

"Good math, Cook," the Captain said, still glaring at the building.

The early afternoon sun beat down upon 3rd Platoon without mercy. Temperatures in the shade were 110 degrees if not higher; in the sun it could have easily been 15 degrees hotter. The men did their best to keep it together and stay focused, but the climate didn't help their effort. It was like the enemy had an ally who followed them everywhere.

Private Devon Harris had taken cover behind the flatbed of the burned-out pickup truck at the edge of the rubble pile, toward the back of the platoon. It was important for the medic to keep to the rear and out of immediate danger—although he had fired his weapon in almost every engagement the group had encountered. From his vantage point, he could see his entire platoon, and the position of the two snipers on the roof of the building across the street. Everyone remained frozen in place. The street dead calm and quiet. Too quiet.

Nothing was happening. Usually, once the enemy position became known, either the squad would engage or call in a close support airstrike from a group of Apache helicopters. This long of a wait put all the men on edge, including Devon.

Devon knew that water consumption would become an issue within the hour. The men had to stay hydrated in this heat, but there was only so much water they could carry on a mission. If the group didn't get moving to the extraction point soon, the effects of dehydration would set in, causing a whole new litany of problems. He hated to bother the Captain, but it was his duty to look after the wellbeing of the men. If they didn't get moving within the next five minutes, he was going to have to make the boss aware of the situation.

A shocking sound cut through the silence, causing all the men of 3rd platoon to jump. It was the sound of gunfire. But it didn't burst out through the air as usual. Something rang different with these shots. They were muffled. There were a lot of them. They sounded like a bag of popcorn popping in a microwave just as all the kernels finally erupt in unison. And the shots weren't directed at the Marines of 3rd Platoon either. They didn't seem like they were going anywhere. Then silence.

No one moved. They all held tight to their positions with weapons fixed on the market building. Safeties off. Fingers resting on triggers.

Two minutes of silence passed. The tension was a heavy lead weight pressing down on everyone's shoulders. No one could move—or hardly breathe, for that matter—as they tried to process what was happening.

More gunfire erupted, this time loud in the open air, and coming from much closer. The snipers were opening up. Their shots exploded through the calm afternoon from the roof of the building across from the market. The hail of shots lasted for less than ten seconds, then silence returned.

"Snipers report," Captain Bender commanded into the radio after the echo of the last shot had faded into the atmosphere.

Silence.

The Captain took a deep breath and let it out slowly. The mic in his hand, close to his lips. He did not move or speak.

Lieutenant Cook put his hand on Bender's shoulder. "Cap?"

"Snipers report!" Bender shouted. He shook the mic in front of his lips as a mixture of frustration and saliva bellowed into it.

The radio suddenly screeched and a young man's voice came through. "Three more Hajis down, sir. They attempted an exit from a side door into the adjacent alley."

Captain Bender let out a deep breath. A look of pride for his men came across his face. "Is the threat neutralized?"

"Five are down and out, one crawled back inside after taking a lower chest hit."

"You mean a gut shot," Bender said jokingly into the mic. They trained Snipers to hit center mass at the chest; missing the kill spot would bring a fair amount of harassing after the mission.

"My statement stands, sir."

The men around the Captain all laughed.

"We're coming to sweep the building, keep up the cover," Captain Bender said. He looked back at Lieutenant Cook. "Fuck tactical command, I'm not waiting for those assholes to check with a team of lawyers before we make a move. We're going in."

Lieutenant Cook motioned for the platoon to gather behind him. Everyone kept silent as they interpreted his hand signals. Within seconds, the Marines filed out from behind the rubble pile in a tactical formation and headed for the building.

SEVEN

"We tucked in behind the Lieutenant and slowly advanced toward the market," Devon said. "The snipers were still covering overhead, so I felt a little more at ease. Being a medic, I had to stay toward the back of the group, but I still had a weapon and engaged the enemy every time we were attacked. I was supposed to stay in the rear till someone went down.

"When we got to the market, eight Marines busted in like only Marines can do: safeties off, balls out! I expected to hear a firefight, but there was nothing, just dead calm. We'd done a bunch of these house to house raids and in every instance, there was a lot of shooting and even more screaming. Not this time, though, just an eerie silence.

"In about ten seconds, three Marines filed back out of the building. The third one hit the ground and puked everywhere. The Captain and a few more Marines went inside, then I heard his thick southern accent screaming my name. He sounded more pissed off than a buzzing hornet's nest.

"I ran up to the door. Two more Marines came out looking pale and sick, pushing their way past the rest of us and into the street. The Captain came out next and stopped in front of me at the doorway. He just stared into my eyes. I don't think he knew what to say, which terrified me. He nodded for me to go inside, then walked past me into the crowd of other Marines who had not yet been into the building.

"I knew exactly what I was going to see before I even crossed that threshold. And my hunch was right." Devon bent forward, putting his face in his hands. "Those worthless pieces of shit had blown away all of those little kids." He broke down and sobbed in agony.

Ronnie sat still and silent next to Devon, almost unable to comprehend the weight of the story. He had watched news reports and learned about horrible tragedies that had taken place throughout history, but he'd never known someone personally who'd been this close to anything like that. How could a person cope with witnessing that level of depravity? He wanted to reach out and hold Devon, or say something to comfort him. He wanted to be the friend who knew exactly what to say or do at a time like this. But he could only sit quietly in a mild state of shock.

Minutes passed as Devon cried and Ronnie watched. After a while, Devon was able to slowly calm himself down. He wiped the tears away from his eyes with the palms of his hands.

"Something else happened in that room," Devon said through the tears and sniffling.

Ronnie couldn't imagine how this story could get any worse.

They—the proverbial *they*—say a person grows up fast after joining the military. One day you turn eighteen, graduate high school, have a bunch of parties, and enjoy the last days of a carefree life, and the next day a deranged drill instructor is screaming in your face as you do more push-ups in the mud than you ever thought were possible. These are the kids who come back to town after a few months of basic training looking fit, trim, and serious as a heart attack. There is a distinct look in their eye. They may have had anxieties or uncertainties before they took up this grand adventure to serve, but now they look hard, cold, and invincible. Fear replaced with courage; doubt replaced with ambition; apathy replaced with motivation. They have a glow that only a proud few can exude. And then the moment comes when their country asks them to put that taxpayer-funded training to use in some shit-splat part of the world that not one person from their hometown can even pronounce. To witness depravity on a scale that human beings cannot measure because the acts themselves are too far outside of the realm of human understanding. Do they grow up or do they regress? Do they revel in misery every day, straining themselves and those around them, or do they bury it deep down inside? Whatever the case, they have grown up fast, and they have now realized that this whole "adult" thing isn't as good as the brochure said it would be.

Devon drank some more beer, lit a cigarette—adding another link to what seemed like an endless chain of smoking—and composed himself. "Do you want me to stop?"

"Only if you want to, bro," Ronnie said.

"There's a lot more to this story, I'd like to get it out, and I think you're probably the only person I could ever tell this to. The V.A. shrink had all the info about that day from the D.O.D. Report and wanted me to talk about it with him. I couldn't. I know he's educated and all, but sometimes this kind of thing just needs to boil to the surface on its own. They were probably worried about PTSD or something. Besides, if I would have told them what I'm about to tell you, they would have locked me up in a psych ward. I'm sure of it."

"Okay," Ronnie said. "Let me hear it."

Devon smiled. He was proud of the friendship he and Ronnie had cultivated over the years; it was something he cherished most in his life.

"I went into the room and started checking to see if any of the kids were still alive. None of them were.

"Of course the question of, *why*, kept rolling through all of our heads. It wasn't until weeks later that we found out they were all kids from a tribe hated by this group of insurgents. They had stolen the children from a nearby village and were keeping them in Fallujah to use for shielding their escape. Cutting them down as they did was just brutal savagery. There was no reason or purpose for it unless it was maybe some deranged scare tactic. I don't know.

"Then I saw him, the insurgent with the blue turban who got plugged by our snipers, laid up against a wall, covered in blood. I went up to him and noticed that he was still alive, but just barely. His breath shallow and quick and his pupils fully dilated, a sure sign that death was coming. I squatted down next to him to check his pulse, then I heard the voice of Captain Bender from behind me. 'You will *not* give that fucker one single American aspirin. Am I clear?' I was definitely clear. No one argued with Captain

Bender… ever!

"One of the Marines standing beside the Captain wanted to put a round in the guy's head to finish him off. Bender told him not to waste the ammo. Then he looked at me and said, 'Finish up in here and make sure that dirtbag departs in a timely fashion. We're heading out in ten.' Then everyone left me in the room alone with eight dead kids and one dying asshole.

"The insurgent had no chance, his blood pressure was on the floor, and I could barely find a pulse. There was so much blood puddled around him, he couldn't have had much more left in his body.

"Then I felt something. The only way I can explain this to you in real terms would be to say that I felt the presence of others. It was like several people were suddenly standing throughout the room, kind of wandering around. This was the most unnatural feeling I have ever experienced.

"There was a smell that sprung up out of nowhere, as if someone had just opened a carton of rotten eggs. It was so disgusting that I felt a gag welling up in my throat.

"It was the middle of the afternoon and there had been plenty of light in the room just a moment ago, but now everything seemed darker. It wasn't like a light being turned off, but more like a blackness slowly filtering inside. And with the darkness, the odor became more intense than I could bear.

"That's when I saw it!" Devon's hands were shaking violently now, almost as if he were having a mild seizure. His face became pale and sweat ran down his temples. The collar and underarms of his olive green T-shirt darkened with perspiration.

Ronnie became nervous that his friend was going to have another vicious panic episode. He didn't want Devon to go through something like that again. He needed to calm him down. "Let's give the conversation a rest for a bit, Dev. I don't like how this is affecting you. Maybe we should come back to it later."

Devon looked at Ronnie, his face stone cold. "I saw the devil."

Ronnie stared at his friend, mouth open, unable to fully

comprehend what he had just heard.

"I mean it, Ronnie," Devon said. "It was the devil himself."

Still baffled by the statement, Ronnie couldn't help but ask, "What are you talking about?"

"I saw a giant black mass appear among other shadow figures in the middle of the room. It floated right past me and when it did, I felt what I can only describe as despair and hopelessness. I froze in place. I couldn't blink, couldn't even breathe! The shape seemed sort of human, but way bigger than any man I've ever seen. And it was pure blackness; the absolute absence of light or color. At that moment I had an understanding that I was looking at something we are not meant to see."

"Holy shit!" Ronnie said. He was on the edge of his seat and absorbed by the story.

"I know," Devon said. "This is beyond amazing." He shook out the last cigarette of the pack and crumpled up the wrapper.

"What did you do?" Ronnie said.

"Are you kidding me? I didn't do shit! I just stood there in shock like a little kid staring at the boogeyman." Devon looked at the floor and took a long drag off of his Camel. "What happened next, though, that's the real kicker!

"That thing floated over to the dying insurgent on the floor and lingered over him. Even though the guy was unconscious and had dilated pupils, his face changed to the most terrified look I had ever seen on a human being. The room became ice cold. The darkness seemed to fill every corner, and the environment felt like being wrapped in a blanket of static electricity—if that's even possible. And then it was over, just like that. No more shadows, no more darkness, no more foul odor. Everything had lifted as if it had never even happened.

"I stood in shock, almost in a trance, I guess. My mind couldn't process what I had just witnessed. I don't know how long I was standing there. It was Captain Bender's voice yelling from outside, 'Is that fucker dead yet?' that snapped me out of it. I checked for vitals on the insurgent. He was dead. But that look on his face was still there like a name etched into a gravestone;

absolute horror!"

Devon crushed out his cigarette. "There hasn't been a day since that moment when I haven't thought of the experience. It pops into my head at any random moment: when I'm brushing my teeth; working on a patient; watching TV; making love to my wife… it's always there, looking over my shoulder, waiting for me to almost be happy, then it jumps out and say's, '*Hey, remember me? The experience that fucked up your life… FOREVER!*'

"You want to know why I freaked out in the ambulance the other night?" Devon said. He laughed, almost maniacally. "That fucking shadow thing that I saw in Iraq was in the truck with us!"

"Don't! Don't you dare!" Ronnie shouted. "I was in that wagon with you. There was just you, me, Ed upfront, and the John Doe we picked up. No shadow people were hovering around us. Don't you fucking dare go schizophrenic on me!"

"I saw it, Ronnie."

"No, you *didn't*!"

"It was in there with us."

"NO!" Ronnie pounded his fist on the small coffee table, rattling the ashtray and empty beer bottles.

"Look, I don't know why I saw it and you didn't. None of the other Marines in my unit saw anything either that day. Maybe I'm just sensitive to this kind of shit. I don't know. But that thing was in the ambulance with us and it was watching the guy on the stretcher. It had no interest in you or me at all."

"Ok," Ronnie said as he stood up. "You know I love you like a brother, always have. I'm glad you got this shit off your chest, and I'm honored that you chose me to open up to. But this story stays right here in this basement, and it stays between the two of us. You're a hero, Devon. I will not have the people of this town thinking of you as the crazy war vet for the rest of your life. If you let this story get out, it'll spread through Cumberland Springs like a brush fire."

"Yeah, I guess I can see your point."

"If you ever need to talk about this or anything else, you call me and I'll be here in minutes. I'll even crawl in through the *goddamn* coal door again if you want me to. But we're keeping this stuff down here, between the two of us. Agreed?"

Devon stood up and gave Ronnie a powerful hug and even let out a few more tears. "I agree, buddy, we'll keep it down here, locked in the basement."

They ascended the basement stairs together, which led into a kitchen full of the pleasant aroma of Thanksgiving Day. Linda had just finished preparing the small table in the corner with three place settings. She looked to be in a much better mood than when Ronnie had first arrived.

EIGHT

"Welcome," Glen said as he opened the front door. Larry Gilmore stood on the landing, which Glen's wife had festively decorated with pumpkins, cornstalks, and artificial leaves—enough leaves were blowing around the yard already, Lord only knows why she had to add the fake ones. Larry was holding a bottle of red wine. He wasn't wearing his police uniform this afternoon, he'd have that on later when he went in for tonight's midnight shift. Today he sported a comfortable pair of Levis and a dark green outdoorsman style shirt.

Standing next to Larry, holding a freshly baked pie of some sort, was his lovely girlfriend, Darla. She too wore a comfortable, outdoorsy style outfit—blue jeans and a feminine flannel sweater. They looked like they had just sprung out of a clothing ad from Field and Stream Magazine.

Glen Hugged them both and ushered them into the house where they were again welcomed with warm hugs from his wife, Vickie.

As Glen stood watching his wife dote over the young couple, the doorbell rang again. This time it was his mother and father, both standing in the doorway with adoring smiles on their faces. "There's our boy," Glen's mother exclaimed. She hugged him tightly and kissed his cheek, then took out a Kleenex and wiped her lipstick off of his face. His father handed him a six-pack of Budweiser and patted him on the shoulder as he stepped past and into the house.

Glen stayed on the porch to greet the next arrivals, who were coming up the walkway. They were Vicki's parents, Jim and Pattie, followed by Vicki's sister, Lynn, and her husband Ted along with their two young boys. He greeted them all with hugs, handshakes, and pats on the head. Inside he could hear the loud exclamations of a family greeting each other and preparing for another warm, traditional Thanksgiving. He took a deep breath of the crisp fall air and made it a point to ingest all the sights, sounds, and smells around him so far today. It was a day of great joy with family and friends; he sought to relish every moment.

Vicki, her mother and sister, Glen's mother, and Darla were busily fluttering around the kitchen, unwrapping the covered dishes they'd all brought, and getting the last minute items in and out of the oven. Glen offered his help, but as usual, the ladies directed him to go into the den with the guys and stay out of their way. He did as instructed.

With the women hustling around the kitchen, the men cheering on a football game in the den, and the children running throughout the halls upstairs, the house brimmed over with excitement. Glen again paused in the middle of it all to absorb the moment and commit it to permanent memory. He kept these memories filed away in the recesses of his mind to pull back out at later dates when he needed something to put a smile on his face.

Within a half-hour of everyone's arrival, Vicki rang the dinner bell—a small, antique brass bell that had belonged to her great-grandmother. The sound filled the house with a pleasant tinkling which seemed to possess the power to make mouths water.

Everyone filed into the kitchen, filled their dishes with all the food they could handle from the buffet, then stood by their respective seats at the dining room table, waiting for all to get situated. Even the children resisted the powerful urge to steal a bite from their plates.

"Well, son," Glen's father said after all were in place. "You're the man of the house; you do the honors."

Glen smiled and bowed his head. The room became reverently silent. "Dear Heavenly Father, we thank You for this day and the opportunity You have given us to come together as a family to give thanks for the blessings You have bestowed upon all of our lives. We thank You for the meal we are about to share and the fellowship we are about to exchange. We thank You for the prosperity You've allowed us to enjoy, along with the health

You've helped us maintain. But most of all, Lord, we thank You for the love in our hearts, which You have taught us through the lessons we've learned from each other. Please continue to bless us throughout the rest of our lives and help us live out our remaining days in peace. We ask this in the name of our Savior, Jesus Christ. Ame…"

The loud digital screech of a cell phone screamed over Glen's voice. No one acknowledged the clamor. It was, of course, a common dignity to shut your phone off during dinner, especially Thanksgiving. Someone must have just forgotten. Then the culprit emerged. Larry had his hand in his shirt pocket, trying to silence the little monster without bringing it to the surface. His face red with embarrassment and his girlfriend looking away as if to say, "I do not know this person next to me!"

Larry failed to silence the phone, so he hurried off into the den where he could take care of the issue in private. It was a small indiscretion. No one—other than Darla—begrudged him for it.

Knives and forks clinked against the china dishes, and a chorus of, "Mmmm's and Aaaa's," created a lovely holiday symphony, pleasant to everyone's ears. Glen had taken his first bite of turkey, heaped with the perfect amount of dressing and gravy. He worked diligently to put this first bite together, making sure it was equally balanced with the exact proportions so that it wouldn't overload his tastebuds and would give him that exhilaration he looked forward to every year. His effort paid off. The food melted in his mouth, sending a rush of intense joy throughout his entire system. He almost shed a tear.

As Glen sat with his eyes closed, reveling in the flavors and sounds surrounding him, he felt a tug on his shoulder and someone close to his cheek. He snapped out of his moment and saw Larry bending over to whisper in his ear.

"Chief, I need to see you in the den," Larry said. He sounded nervous.

"Really?" Glen replied.

"Yeah, Chief, right now."

Glen got up from the table, still chewing on the only bite he'd taken from his favorite meal of all time, and followed Larry toward the den. His father looked at him with concern as the two left the room.

Glen waited until they were safely out of earshot. "Larry, you of all people know how I feel about Thanksgiving…"

"Chief, there's a big problem," Larry said, his voice sounding nervous.

"Is the station on fire?"

"Well, no, but…"

"Is the town on fire?"

"No, sir."

"Is anyone in imminent danger?"

"Um, not exactly, but…"

Glen held up his hand to stop Larry from talking. "Then it can wait until after we have all finished eating." He turned to the room.

"There's an FBI agent at the station, tearing through your office."

The statement stopped Glen in his tracks.

"That was Lindsy on the phone. I had my ringer off, but she pushed an emergency call through. Here," Larry said, handing his cell phone to Glen. "She's still on the line."

Glen grabbed the phone. "Lindsy, what's going on?"

The young girl's voice on the other end of the line sounded frantic. "Chief, this guy in a suit showed up, flashed an FBI badge, and asked for you. When I told him you were unavailable today, he just walked into your office and started going through your desk and filing cabinet."

"Is he still in there right now?"

"Yeah," she said, sounding more nervous.

"Put him on the phone!"

Glen could hear a few muffled phrases being exchanged, then Lindsy was back on the line. "He said for you to…"

"To what?"

"He said for you to get your ass down here right now! I'm sorry, Chief, that's just what he said."

Glen handed the phone back to Larry and stormed out of the den. His calm, festive mood quickly replaced with anger, bordering on rage. Someone had strolled into town—his town—out of nowhere and began barking out orders to him and his staff. This was something he could not abide.

Vicki approached her husband as he stood in the foyer, putting on his coat. "This looks serious, honey; what's going on?"

"I'm sorry, babe, there's a problem at the station and I have to resolve it. I'll do my best to get back here as soon as I can."

"Do you want to take a plate of food for Lindsy?" Vickie asked.

"Um, give it to Larry to bring to her; he's coming down in a bit. I told him to finish his dinner and relax for a while."

"I love you," she said, wrapping her arms around his neck and holding him tightly. If he hadn't been so frustrated, this would have been another moment he would have loved to absorb into memory.

NINE

Lauren and her grandmother sat in silence, staring at the angry face of the man in the faded newspaper photo. It was as if his eyes held both of them in a trance. Yes, the face in the grainy image was that of a human being; the physiognomy was all accounted for—eyes, ears, nose, mouth—but it lacked that certain indescribable thing that makes one a human being. There was no humanity looking back at them.

Finally, Lauren turned her head. "I can't look at this creepy thing anymore. Why on earth would you keep such a picture? In fact, why do you even have a book like this in the first place?"

"These people were all admitted to the intensive care unit and died while I was there," Grandmother answered. "I was very sensitive to the pain they and their families had gone through during these moments, so I put this scrapbook together for myself to remember them. Sometimes I feel drawn to open this book and pray for each of them. I guess I feel a connection because I was with them during their final moments. In some of these cases, I was the only one there when they departed, holding their hand so they wouldn't die alone."

Her level of empathy resonated with Lauren. She'd always known what a kind and caring soul her grandmother was, but she hadn't realized it ran so deep. At this moment, she felt more love for the woman than she ever had before.

But then there was the hideous-looking man. Hadn't she said he was the evilest creature she'd ever been in the presence of? How could she have compassion for a person like that? Lauren had to ask, "What about this man, Harlan Wallace? You said he was evil? Why are you keeping his picture with these other people?"

Grandmother placed her hand over his image and closed her eyes. "He's in here for a particular reason, dear: to remind me that evil does exist, in this world and beyond."

Lauren slowly pushed her grandmother's hand aside so she could see the article that accompanied the photo. The headline read: DERANGED MAN KILLS FAMILY OF FOUR!

"It happened in 1964," Grandmother said. "I was twenty-two-years-old and had only been working in the ICU for three months." She starred out of one of the many windows in the sunroom for several moments before speaking again. "This man —this horrible man—had been trying to abduct a little girl from her home when her father discovered him breaking in. Wallace was much stronger than the girl's father and also carried a hunting knife. He killed the father quickly, then went on a brutal rampage throughout the rest of the house, stabbing the mother and two daughters to death. The twelve-year-old son, who had run upstairs and grabbed his daddy's shotgun, had ultimately stopped him. The boy shot Wallace twice at close range, once in the stomach and once in the pelvis."

Grandmother put on her glasses and scanned through the article with her finger until she came to a sentence close to the end. She read it aloud: "Wallace died at 1:46 AM in the Intensive Care Unit at Cumberland Springs Memorial Hospital." She took her glasses off and leaned back, again staring out the window.

"You were there when he died, weren't you?" Lauren asked.

"I was," Grandmother replied, her voice cloudy and cold.

Lauren, fascinated by the story but concerned for Grandmother's feelings, didn't want to push her to elaborate further. She could tell by the change in her demeanor that this event had bothered Grandmother on a much deeper level. It wouldn't serve either of them right now to keep mulling over it.

Grandmother finally spoke up in that same solemn voice. "I watched him die, and I watched them take him."

"You watched *who* take him? Are you talking about the orderlies? The Coroner?"

"No. I wish it were that simple," Grandmother said. "What I

saw that night changed me forever.

"I had just started my shift the night they brought Wallace in. I know they worked on him in the ER for a few hours, but the best they could do was get him stabilized. The buckshot tore holes in just about every major organ. I don't know how he even made it through the ambulance ride.

"It was a circus downstairs with police and reporters running all over the place. I didn't go down to see, but I heard all about it. One nurse came by and said, 'Did you hear there's a murderer downstairs? He got shot by a *kid!*' As you already know, not much happens in Cumberland Springs, so an event like this set everyone's hair on fire.

"Myself and two other nurses were on the midnight shift that night. Doctor Ernest came by a few hours into the shift to tell us they would be bringing Wallace up to our floor shortly. All three of us got the creeps!

"I went into the empty room to prep it for the incoming patient. I had only been in there for a minute or two before they rolled him in. One thing that struck me as peculiar: they had both of his wrists handcuffed to the bed rails. The guy was barely clinging to life; there was no way he was going to get up and cause any trouble. It must have been a police procedure or something. I don't know why, but I never forgot those handcuffs.

"After the doctor and orderlies had left, the other two ICU nurses came in, and the three of us just stood at the foot of the bed, staring at him. I don't think any of us knew what to say. He was so big! I mean, he really looked like a monster lying under the sheet. When you see someone like that up close, knowing what they've done, it's hard to comprehend. I knew he was a person, but he had taken on a very unnatural appearance. It was ghastly to look at. I had to get out of there, and so did the other two nurses. I think the three of us shivered in unison as we rushed to the door. I stopped at the doorway, though, because I thought I heard him mumbling something. When I turned around, I saw his eyes were open and looking at me. Then in a low grumbling voice, he said, '*Zlo.*' I do not know what that meant, and I didn't care to ask him. I left the room even more chilled than before."

Lauren crossed her arms and felt a shiver run down her spine. This story and her current experience with John Doe was becoming too much for her to handle. There had to be an end to all of this somewhere in her near future. Hopefully, she could bury the memory of this week deep down in her mind, far enough that it would fade off into a forgotten blur—unlike her grandmother, who had carried her experience with her for almost half a century.

Grandmother continued: "It was well after midnight, and everything had been quiet for a few hours. I was alone at the desk—one nurse went on break, the other had to use the restroom—when I heard the heart monitor spike in Wallace's room. It happened a few times, then went back to normal. I didn't want to go in there with no one else on the floor with me, but that monitor wouldn't stop spiking. Finally, I bit the bullet and went in alone.

"I could tell he was about to go. His heart would stop, then kick in again, then stop again. The only thing I could do was wait. They had put a 'Do Not Revive' order on him. There would be no resuscitation efforts, so I stood at the foot of his bed—silent—and watched.

"That's when I noticed something strange happening in the room."

Grandmother closed the scrapbook and gently set it on the coffee table in front of them. She reached for Lauren's hand and gripped it. "The darkness, the shadows, the horrible smell, everything you're going through with your John Doe patient, I had experienced that night in 1964 in the ICU room with Harlan Wallace. I saw it all, just the way you described your experience with your patient now."

Lauren was astounded. She didn't know whether to be relieved or even more afraid. On the one hand, knowing another person—especially someone she trusted and respected above anyone else—had had a similar experience made her feel like she hadn't imagined this whole thing after all. On the other hand, though, the possibility that something like this could exist in the world filled her with even deeper anxiety.

"I don't want to discuss this anymore," Grandmother said. "It's upsetting both of us. I will say one more thing, however: Harlan Wallace was evil; no question about it! I believe something came for him that night from a place we're not supposed to know about and took him back with it. I don't know why I saw it, or why you're seeing it now, and I don't want to know. Perhaps we're sensitive to things like this. But if you're seeing it now with your patient, I'd bet dimes to dollars he's a bad person."

As hard as Lauren tried to control her emotions, the effort went in vain. She put her face in her hands and cried. "I just don't know what to do," she said.

"I don't think you have to do anything," Grandmother replied. "He's about to die any moment now, isn't he? Why don't you take a day or two off?"

"Would you?" Lauren said.

"Before that event took place with Wallace, I would have said, no. I'd have thought that nothing could bother me enough to keep me from doing my job. But having had that experience once, I can tell you I never want to have it again." Grandmother took a deep breath and let it out in a sigh. "So my answer is, yes. I would take a few days off until that man is deceased and carted out of Cumberland Springs Memorial for good."

"I'm so sorry, ladies," a voice came from behind them, "I couldn't help but overhear some of your conversation as I was walking past from the restroom." Reverend Allen stood in the doorway to the sunroom. His face very apologetic, and as sincere as always. His gray hair and distinguishing features added to his soft charm. "Are you having a problem with a patient at the hospital?"

"Oh, Reverend," Grandmother said. "It's nothing; just a John Doe whose about to pass away in the ICU."

"You both seem upset," he said.

Lauren spoke up. "It's a sad situation, Reverend."

"Has anyone been in to pray over him?"

The two women looked at each other. "Well," Lauren said finally. "No. No one has been in to see him. They don't even know who he is yet."

"And you say he's about to pass?"

"Yes."

Reverend Allen lowered his eyes in empathy. "Do you think there would be any objections if I were to stop by the hospital on my way home this evening to say a few prayers?"

"I can't imagine that being a problem," Lauren said. "You're always up there looking in on patients. The staff knows you pretty well."

"Well then, I'll meet John Doe on my way home and put in a few good words for him with my Boss." He smiled and looked down at the coffee table. "Is that an old scrapbook of family photos?"

Grandmother grabbed the book and held it to her chest with both arms crossed. "It's more of a collection of Personal Curiosities, one might say. Nothing you'd be interested in seeing."

TEN

Glen didn't bother taking the time to change into his police uniform before heading to the station. There was no need to bother. He planned to head into the office, tear this so-called FBI agent a new asshole, then be back home at his dining room table with his family and friends before they even started dessert. Quick and painless.

When he pulled up in front of the station, he right away noticed a black sedan with government plates sitting boldly in his parking space. The sign in front of the spot clearly stated, "Reserved for Chief of Police." The car looked like a giant shiny black middle finger, waving at Glen and laughing. His already elevated annoyance level climbed a few more notches toward its peak.

The municipal building, which housed the police station, magistrate's office, town records, and a small public library, was just like every other building in Cumberland Springs: old. Built in 1957 and well maintained ever since. County funds had been available several times over the years to construct a new facility, but the councilmen and other town officials always felt a soft spot for the old nostalgic building. They used the money for improvements and upgrades, of course—getting all the asbestos and lead paint out of there was a big one—but for the most part, everyone was happy with their quaint little municipal building, nestled comfortably in the south-east corner of the town square.

As Glen got out of his car, he waved to the members of the Elks Lodge and Women's Rotary Club, who were in the center of the town square, putting the finishing touches on the twenty-foot tall Christmas tree for tonight's lighting ceremony. In a few hours, the square would be full of people, singing and laughing and enjoying the tradition of kicking off the Christmas season together. The sight lightened Glen's mood a bit. He thought back through all the years his parents had brought him to this

Robert Ferencz

ceremony when he was a kid, and to the years he'd been sharing the event with his own wife and children. Growing up and continuing to live in a small town rich with traditions was another blessing he didn't take for granted.

"Looks like you got a real important fella in there today, Chief?" Bill Davis asked. He was an older gentleman in a blue flannel jacket and matching cap. He'd broken away from the decorating crew to do a little reconnaissance. A strange black car parked in front of the police station on Thanksgiving day was sure to spark the curiosity of such a close-knit bunch. "Those are government plates, aren't they?"

"Yeah, Bill," Glen replied. "He's an FBI agent."

"Something the matter here?" Bill asked. His look was both of concern and excitement.

"Nope. Nothing to worry about, buddy. Just some paperwork kind of stuff."

"On Thanksgiving Day?"

Glen put his arm around Bill and began walking him back toward the decorating crew. "The tree's looking great!" He shouted to the group. "I can't wait to see it tonight."

Everyone waved and smiled. Bill Davis reluctantly rejoined his decorating crew with nothing interesting to report.

Inside the station, Lindsy was standing in front of her desk with her arms crossed, looking angry and nervous. Her blond hair pulled back in a ponytail. She was twenty-five, but with her hair like this, she appeared more like a sixteen-year-old. She looked at Glen as he walked in and nodded over her shoulder. Glen walked past her into his office.

"Well, I hope my office has been accommodating enough for you," Glen said sarcastically to the tall man in the suit who was sitting at his desk. "Can I get you a cup of coffee, perhaps?"

"Are you Chief Crawford?" The man asked as he got up from behind the desk. Glen could see that several of his files were out and scattered around the top of his desk.

"Yeah. Now, who the hell are you?"

The man pulled out his FBI credentials from his inside suit

jacket pocket and flipped them open in front of Glen's face, but looked past him as he did it. "I'm Special Agent Brandon Ward, Pittsburgh field office. I need to see all of your files on the unidentified man you have in your custody."

Agent Ward stood at least six-foot-five. He appeared young but looked as though he'd been through a great deal of stress. By his slim-cut physique and stern facial features, it also seemed like he had spent some time in the military. The tight haircut added to that assumption.

"I don't have anyone in custody," Glen said. He didn't conceal his frustration.

"You sent fingerprints from an unidentified man to the FBI print database, did you not?"

"Yes, I did," Glen replied.

"Where is that man?"

Glen took in a deep breath, trying to remain calm, and let it out with a sigh. "If he's still alive, he's in the ICU at Cumberland Springs Memorial."

Agent Ward briskly stepped past Glen and into the lobby. "Take me there now."

"You want to tell me what the fuck…" Glen started, but the agent had already rushed out the main door of the building.

Instead of following directly, Glen went back into his office and straightened up the files Agent Ward had scattered across his desk. Lindsy came in after a few moments. "He seems pretty uptight, huh?"

"Yeah, I'd say," Glen replied.

"What are you going to do?"

"Well," he said as he started putting the files back into the cabinet. "I guess I'm going to run him over to the hospital to see that John Doe. But I think I'll let him cool off a minute before I do."

Lindsy laughed. "Do you want a cup of coffee to go, Chief?"

"Sure, that would be great. Thanks!"

Glen smiled as he walked out of the municipal building, sipping his coffee from a travel mug. Bill Davis had once again left the decorating party on a recon mission and had Agent Ward cornered. It didn't look like he was able to garner much information, though. The Agent only stared at him with a stern, solemn face.

"I guess I'm driving?" Glen asked.

Agent Ward didn't answer as he opened the passenger side door of Glen's police cruiser and got in.

This is going to be a fun ride, Glen thought as he got into the car.

ELEVEN

Reverend Allen felt blessed to have been invited to Thanksgiving dinner for the last three years by Lauren's family. Their traditions were warm and comforting, and just the sort of atmosphere he'd needed since the death of his wife.

He'd spent a challenging and painful two years standing by helpless as Mary Ann's body slowly succumbed to cancer. First, the diagnosis and treatment options, followed by the success rates and stories of other people who had triumphed over the same disease—*10 years cancer-free,* the woman in the poster yelled while skydiving. Next came the sickness; her body reacting violently to the chemo they relentlessly poured through her veins. If that wasn't bad enough, there were those damned glimmers of hope the doctors would offer, telling the good Reverend that the treatments appeared to be having an effect. That wasn't the case. The doctor's optimism only amounted to a swift kick in the balls. But the cherry on top of this whole fucked up mess was the constant, unrelenting stream of prayer. For two solid years, he begged God to spare his beloved. *You can't take her from me! I will give You everything I have! Please, let me take her place! I NEED HER!*

Mrs. Mary Ann Allen, age fifty-two, of Schellsburg, PA, died on a snowy December morning in a small hospital room at Cumberland Springs Memorial. Reverend Allen had gone down to the chapel to have a word with his Boss during Mary's actual departure, so he missed holding her hand at that last moment; a regret which has haunted him from that day on.

It would be a lie to say that those two years of pain and sorrow didn't shake Reverend Allen's faith. For six months after Mary Ann's death, the church congregation could tell he was only phoning it in; there was no *hutzpah* behind the message. But they stuck by him every Sunday, without waiver. It was this showing of solidarity and compassion that finally brought him back around and helped to strengthen his faith once more. Even though there was a part of him missing now, buried in the cold earth out in Round Hill Cemetery, he would go on, filling in the missing part with the love of a community who needed him.

During the drive over to the hospital, his thoughts were on the unidentified man in the ICU. He honestly didn't mean to eavesdrop on the conversation between Lauren and her grandmother, but when he heard the two ladies discussing an evil presence surrounding a patient, his ears perked up. He was, after all, *in the business.* If something malevolent was indeed surrounding someone—though he didn't fully believe that—it was his job to offer prayers. Put in a good word with the Big Guy.

Driving up the hill to the hospital, he couldn't help but notice how foreboding the structure appeared, like a castle from a piece of gothic fiction. The architecture surely was something to admire, but seemed somewhat out of place in the modern world. Then again, this town took pride in keeping things nostalgic.

"Good evening, Reverend," the girl at the reception desk said with a smile. "What brings you out tonight?" The staff at the hospital was well acquainted with Reverend Allen from his weekly visits to sick patients. He'd become as much of a regular face as anyone who worked here.

"I'm here to call on a patient in the ICU. An unknown man brought in a few days ago?"

"Oh," she said, breaking eye contact and looking down at her desk. "You're here to see our John Doe."

Reverend Allen took immediate notice of her change in disposition. "Is there something I should know about him?"

The girl smiled once again. "No, there's been a few rumors going around, but nothing more than that."

"Ok," he said. "I know my way up there. I'll find the room from one of the nurses on the ward."

The halls were much quieter tonight than usual. The Reverend passed a handful of staff on his way to the elevator, but not the normal calamity of busy medical professionals. He thought perhaps the emptiness had to do with the holiday.

The polite nurse at her station on the ICU ward directed him to room 337. On his way over to the door, he noticed that Mrs. Randall, one of his parishioners, was in the room next to John Doe. He made a mental note to stop in and visit with her on his way out if she was awake.

He stood at the foot of John Doe's bed and starred for quite a while, in shock at the man's condition. As hard as he tried, he could not resist thinking back to the way his wife looked during her last days. She hadn't been as bad as the man lying here in front of him tonight, but still emaciated to where he almost couldn't recognize her.

God loved us, that he was sure of, but why then did we have to suffer like this? The world is such a beautiful place, brimming with wonder and amazement and love; why are His children made to endure such horrible circumstances? He didn't believe suffering was a punishment for sin—he couldn't recall a single indiscretion of Mary Ann's—so there had to be some other reason for it.

During his deep contemplation, the voice of his conscience—the voice he considered to be that of God—spoke up, reminding him that his job wasn't to understand or contemplate, it was to ease the suffering of others. That's what he was called upon to do, and what he'd signed on for.

Reverend Allen smiled in acknowledgment, then pulled up a chair close to the dying man's left side. He opened his worn, leather-bound bible to Romans 6:23 and read: "For the wages of sin is death, but the gift of God is eternal life through Jesus Christ our Lord and Savior."

Reverend Allen's head snapped back violently as a hot, shooting pain flashed through his mouth and jaw. For a brief moment, he saw only darkness and stars. He'd been in enough fistfights as a kid growing up in Pittsburgh to understand precisely what had just happened: He'd been punched square in the mouth.

He recovered from the hit and got his bearings back within a few seconds, then scanned the room to see who the culprit could have been. It surely wasn't John Doe. Even if the guy could move, he'd could never muster up the strength to deliver a wallop like that.

His fighting instincts kicked in quickly. Yes, he was a man of God, sworn to a life of peace, but someone taking a cheap shot at him like that was going to have some explaining to do.

Suddenly the room went dark, as if a black fog had rolled in. An odor appeared out of nowhere, causing the reverend to lose his breath and gag. Something grabbed his wrists, pinning him to the chair. He sat paralyzed with fear. As he struggled to move, he noticed an enormous black shape materialize in front of him. It was as high as the room's twelve-foot ceiling. Other dark shapes formed around the bigger one and closed in on him quickly. They began hitting him over every part of his body with what felt like punches, slaps, and even kicks. Abruptly, something lifted him out of his chair, raised him all the way to the ceiling, and suspended him there for several seconds before dropping him to the floor. The pain from the fall felt as though thunder and lighting were physically inside his body, exploding in bright flashes and earth-shattering explosions. Lying in the fetal position, he felt a myriad of blows continuing all over his body. The only thing he could do was cover his face and curl up as tight as possible. As he struggled, something pulled his hands away from his face and began viciously scratching his cheeks, scalp, forehead, and neck. He even felt claws scrape over his eyelids. During this savage melee, he heard what sounded like strange high-pitched voices, speaking hastily and taunting him. The attack was horrific and seemed only to be gaining momentum. He wanted to cry out to God, but couldn't gather his thoughts to do so. The only thought he could put together was that today would be the day Reverend Paul Allen would meet his Maker.

TWELVE

"Would you care to bring me up to speed as to why this John Doe is so important that you needed to pull me away from my family during Thanksgiving dinner?" Glen asked Agent Ward. He received no reply. The Agent focused on his phone, which steadily went off from the moment they got in the car.

The hospital was a short ten-minute drive from the police station but seemed like an eternity for Glen in the company of this prick. He couldn't get even the most basic of pleasantries out of him.

"Look, buddy," Glen finally said, his patience worn thin. "Give me some kind of answer, or I'm going to drop you off right here on the side of the road, head back to dinner with my family, and not give a shit where you end up."

Agent Ward didn't look up from his phone. After a few seconds of silence, he said, "His name is Hanson Parker."

It wasn't much, but at least it was a start. "And? What has Hanson Parker done?"

"He killed eleven children, that we know of; possibly more."

That was not the answer Glen had expected to receive. For a moment, he almost could not drive. The shock of Agent Ward's statement seemed to cause actual pain to course through his body. Finally, he said, "Is this alleged or factual?"

"Factual."

"*Holy shit!*" Glen said in a dry whisper.

Agent Ward continued reading from his phone. He was receiving several texts and phone calls. The messages he read, the calls he ignored. Glen realized the weight of the situation and decided not to press the man any further.

He parked the cruiser in a spot reserved for police, close to the front entrance. The two men entered the building and headed for the elevator. The receptionist didn't question their purpose. As the steel elevator doors closed, Agent Ward turned off his phone completely, then pulled out his sidearm and checked the round in the chamber.

"*Whoa!*" Glen exclaimed. "You don't need that. The freaking guy is catatonic; he can't even move. In fact, he might not be alive at all right now. I haven't checked in with the hospital about him today, so for all I know he's probably already croaked!"

The agent holstered his weapon, then fixed his suit jacket around it, not acknowledging Glen.

All Glen could think about now was how badly he wanted to be back in his nice warm house, with a fire burning in the fireplace and his family sitting around in the den, laughing and enjoying each other. The best he could hope for now to save his Thanksgiving would be a late-night turkey sandwich—a thought that added a slight touch of warmth to his heart.

The elevator doors opened at floor number three: the ICU ward. The two men stepped out, turned left, and began walking down the corridor toward the nurse's station. They immediately noticed a commotion up ahead of them, just past the desk. It sounded like a half-crazed gorilla trashing one of the rooms and a person screaming bloody murder. Suddenly, before they could take another step, a tall man flew out of the doorway of the room caddy-corner from the nurse's station and smacked into the wall across the hall. He appeared badly hurt, but still attempted to crawl away from the room as fast as he could.

Two nurses hurried out from behind their station to help the man as he struggled to drag himself along the floor. Glen ran to assist. When he got to the group, he saw that the man was Reverend Allen, pastor of his church. Agent Ward rushed past them all, without giving their situation a second glance, and charged into the room recently vacated by the Reverend.

"Don't let him go in there!" Reverend Allen screamed from the floor, pointing at the doorway. "The devil is in there!"

Glen looked back at the open door. There didn't seem to be anymore commotion coming from inside. The silence sent an uneasy jolt through him.

A nurse ran to the phone at the ICU desk and began frantically making a call.

"Get me out of here, Glen!" The Reverend exclaimed as he clung to Glen's jacket with two white-knuckled fists. His eyes were as wide as silver dollars. Blood seeped from wounds that looked like the claw marks of a wild animal. Some gashes were small, others could have come from a bear, but each wound was in a pattern of three, making him think there actually could be a wild animal on the loose. "It wants me dead!"

"Ok Reverend," Glen said, as he looked at the open doorway. "We'll get you out of here."

THIRTEEN

As Glen slowly approached the door to room 337, he put his hand on his sidearm but did not pull it. When he peaked his head inside, the scene astounded him.

Two chairs lay on the floor, one of them smashed to splinters, the other's foam padding ripped out and strewn about the room. A nurse's cart lay tipped over and the various syringes, pill cups, and medications housed in the cart scattered everywhere. The laptop computer which sits atop the cart was also on the floor and broken into pieces. Blood spattered the walls, chairs, and floor—presumably from Reverend Allen. On one wall there was an imprint of blood in the shape of the reverend's face. The scene reminded Glen of a bar fight that he'd broken up once at Stony's Tavern.

Standing at the foot of the bed, staring down at John Doe—who seemed to have been untouched by the melee—was Agent Ward. He had his hands on his hips and looked to be in deep contemplation. He didn't appear at all bothered by the condition of the room or the strangeness of the situation.

Glen looked around to see if who—or what—had caused this destruction was still in here. He found no trace of anyone other than Doe and Ward.

"Is this your guy?" Glen asked while examining what could have been claw marks, scratched into the padding of one of the broken chairs.

Agent Ward let out a deep breath. "If this is the man you fingerprinted, then yes." He pulled up a photo on his phone and held it out over John Doe's head. "But I can't tell by looking at him. This thing in the bed here looks like a horror movie prop."

The agent pulled out a pair of handcuffs, fastened one end to John Doe's wrist and the other end to the bed rail.

"Do you think he's going somewhere?" Glen asked.

"No, but I'm not taking any chances."

Two hospital security guards came through the door, both astonished by the state of the room.

Agent Ward turned and headed into the hall. "Show me where you found him." His voice was still cold and lacking emotion.

Glen stood still for a moment, taking in the strangeness of the situation. Someone trashed this room and beat the hell out of his preacher. What kind of deranged person could do such a thing? And how did this lunatic get past them without being seen? The room had a window, but it wasn't functional. He'd seen the Reverend thrown through the doorway with his own eyes; that had to have come from inside.

The devil is in there!

Glen instructed one of the security guards to stay on the ICU floor and keep an eye out for anyone who appeared as if they may have just been in a fight, or looked even remotely out of place. He told the other guard to patrol the rest of the hospital. He then made a call to Larry Gilmore and Paul Sanders, two of his other officers, and told them to get to the hospital immediately.

They took Reverend Allen to the Emergency Room to attend to his injuries. As Glen headed in that direction, Agent Ward stopped him in the hall. "Chief, I need to see the place where you found Mr. Parker."

"Mr. Parker?"

"Your John Doe," Agent Ward replied quickly. He seemed annoyed.

"I'm sorry, but I've got a nutcase who just beat up a preacher running loose in this hospital. I can't leave right now." Glen pushed past the agent and headed for the elevator. Ward followed him.

Inside of the elevator, Agent Ward reached past Glen and hit the stop button on the control panel. Glen gave him a disconcerting look.

"I've been chasing this asshole for ten years," Ward said. "This ends tonight!"

"You got him already, chained to a bed," Glen said. "Why don't you go babysit him?"

"It's not that simple," The agent replied. "I need all the facts to complete the investigation. Parker—John Doe—just showing up in your town out of the blue like this leaves too many unanswered questions."

"Well, of course, I can appreciate your conviction, but right now I have a problem that needs my attention. If you'd like to assist me in finding the idiot who beat up my pastor, I'd welcome the help. I'm sure he's still in the building somewhere." Glen hit the button to restart the elevator. "The sooner we get him in custody, the sooner I can help you with your investigation."

The two men stood in silence for the rest of the elevator ride.

Chapter 5

ONE

She had tried to get in a quick nap before work. The effort was futile. All Lauren could see when she closed her eyes were faces, horrible faces that sent shivers of fear down her spine. The main one, of course, John Doe. His half-open eye, glaring at her from an expressionless face, staring into her soul. Though motionless, he'd appeared to be asking—nearly begging—for something. *I can't help you,* ran through her semi-conscious mind. *Please, just pass on!* As if his image wasn't disturbing enough, a new face appeared beneath her eyelids now, one from a grainy newspaper photo. The rage behind the man's eyes showing through the faded years of the picture as if he were still alive today and focusing his anger directly at her. Harlan Wallace. She wished Grandmother had never introduced him to her memory.

Clay had done his best to convince her to take the night off. He could see his wife struggling to get through the week. "Stay home tonight, babe. Relax on the couch with me." The gesture was sweet. She politely declined. Lauren had never missed a day of work since starting at Cumberland Springs Memorial, and she wasn't about to now. What kind of nurse would she be if she couldn't handle a touch of stress?

Sitting in her car in the parking lot, staring up at the foreboding outline of the hospital against the night sky as it waited for her to step inside, she prayed. She had always been a spiritual person, raised in the church and active in her faith; praying wasn't an unusual exercise by any means. Tonight's prayer, however, was undoubtedly out of the ordinary. Lauren asked God to remove another human being from the earth. To ease the suffering of a man who had no chance of coming back to life or living without agony. Praying to ease someone else's pain by dying wasn't the part that scared her, though. The fear came from knowing she wanted him gone so she would no longer have to deal with the man and the thing which had attached itself to him. Her prayer was a selfish one. She had never known herself to think that way, but she merely wanted this ordeal to be over, for her and for John Doe. By the end of the prayer, she'd asked God to forgive her for praying it in the first place.

Once on the ICU ward, she noticed a strangeness about the place. The entire floor seemed out of sorts. Orderlies were pushing cleaning carts around, hospital administrators were talking with the two nurses from the 3-11 shift and one of the security guards, and various other staff members were milling around who rarely visited this floor. It was clear something had happened.

She continued walking toward the nurse's station engaging none of the new personnel. Lisa sat at the desk, looking at Lauren with wide eyes as she approached. She was bursting at the seams to tell her something.

"Come here! Sit down!" Lisa commanded in an excited whisper.

Lauren quickly took a seat next to her. "What the hell is—"

"You will not believe what happened during the 3-11 shift tonight!"

"Okay," Lauren said. "Spill it."

"Do you know Reverend Allen from First Baptist Church?" Lisa said. Her eyes were as wide as they could get.

"Of course I know him," Lauren said. "I just had Thanksgiving dinner with him this afternoon."

"Oh? Well, I guess he came in to pray for our John Doe, and someone beat the living heck out of him, right there in Doe's room." Lisa looked around, then back at Lauren. "They're still looking for whoever did it!" She whispered.

Lauren stared at Lisa with her mouth open in shock. For the first time, she honestly contemplated taking a sick day and going home. This entire situation was officially now too much for her to bear.

"Is the Reverend okay?" Lauren said.

"They have him down in the Emergency Room right n—"

Before Lisa could finish her sentence, Lauren was up and heading down the hall. On her way to the elevator, she frantically tried to decide whether she was going to the ER to see Reverend Allen, or to her car and straight the hell out of this place. Tears welled up in her eyes. She'd finally come to her last straw with the whole mess. Now a man she adored and looked up to was the victim of a brutal attack, and she knew exactly who—or what—was responsible.

The elevator doors opened on the first floor. Lauren stepped out and stared straight ahead. To her right, the corridor leading to the parking lot. Ahead of her, the doors to the ER. During her few moments of contemplation, an image flashed through her mind of Reverend Allen smiling at his parishioners at a Sunday evening potluck dinner. The decision became obvious.

"What business do you have on this floor, miss?" The tall, official-looking man in the dark suit said as Lauren entered the Emergency Room. "State your business."

"Business? I'm a nurse here. That's my business!"

"Are you part of the ER personnel?"

Looking up into the tall man's eyes, Lauren could tell he was indeed an authority figure, but how much authority he wielded was unclear. "I'm part of the staff at this hospital. My business is to check on a patient."

"What's the name of your patient?"

Letting out an exaggerated sigh, she said, "Reverend Paul Allen."

"I'm sorry, miss," the tall man said. "But Mr. Allen is not available at this time."

"Calm down, Ward." A voice came from behind. It was Chief Glen Crawford. "When I said I needed your help, I didn't mean you could intimidate people. Go help with the search."

The tall man walked away frustrated. Before going through the ER doors, he turned back toward the Chief and pointed to his watch, then left the room.

"That guy's intense," Lauren said.

"Ha! Ya think?" Glen replied. "I've been dealing with him all day."

"Chief, what happened to Reverend Allen?"

Glen let out a sigh, looked down, and shook his head. "I don't know, Lauren, we've been trying to figure that out. It appears someone attacked him while he was visiting a patient."

"John Doe?"

"Yes, that's the patient." Glen looked over at the room where a doctor and two nurses attended to the Reverend. "You work here, so I'm sure it's ok if you see him, but I don't think he's up for any visitors just yet. They told me I could interview him after they get him patched up."

"I see," she said, frowning. "I better get back to work then."

"Oh, and if you see anyone suspicious—anyone at all—call the front desk immediately. We're still looking for whoever did this," the Chief said.

Lauren agreed, but knew it wasn't a man they needed to be on the lookout for.

TWO

A nurse came out of the examining room occupied by
Reverend Allen. She approached Glen with a half-hearted smile.
He was sitting on a very uncomfortable metal chair with a fake
leather green cushion, listening to his stomach growl, and
thinking about the turkey sandwich he planned to make when he
got home. "Doctor Barnhart is finishing up with the Reverend
now," she said. "You can speak with him, but he is still agitated.
Please be gentle."

Glen stood up and walked over to the doorway of Exam
Room 11. Reverend Allen sat on the examining table with his
feet hanging over the edge, while the doctor put the finishing
touches on a wrapping that went around his midsection. It looked
like they had the poor guy covered in bandages from head to
foot.

"Somebody did a pretty big number on you, didn't they,
Reverend?" Glen said, trying to lighten the mood.

The reverend looked up. It was apparent from the darkness in
his eyes that the fear hadn't subsided in him at all. In fact, he
seemed even more afraid than when Glen first found him in the
hall of the ICU, as if the incident had time to settle into his mind
and intensify his anxiety.

"I'll give you a few minutes alone with him, Chief, before we
move him upstairs," Doctor Barnhart said. "We're going to keep
him overnight for observation, to be safe. He's still very shaken."

Glen pulled up a stool next to the exam table. "Well,
Reverend, what happened?"

"Glen, I swear to you, the devil is in that room! I saw him,
along with his minions!"

Glen let out a deep sigh. "The devil? That's who did this to
you?"

"Yes!"

"A red-faced man with horns, a tail, hoofed feet, and a

pitchfork kicked your ass tonight? That's who I'm supposed to be looking for?"

Reverend Allen sat quietly, staring at Glen, his eyes filling with tears.

"Alright, let's go from the beginning. What brought you to the hospital tonight?"

The Reverend wiped his eyes on the hospital gown he now wore, trying to gain his composure. "I came to pray over the unidentified man in the ICU. I'd overheard Lauren Rivers talking about him with her grandmother at dinner today and I felt compelled to call on him on behalf of the Lord."

"Was anyone in the room when you entered?"

"No, just the man in the bed."

"Did you notice anyone suspicious or out of place on the ICU ward before you went in the room?" Glen asked.

"No."

"How about anyone unusual from the time you got out of your car until you got to the ICU floor?"

"No one. The hospital was silent this evening."

Glen situated himself more comfortably on the stool. "Okay, what happened after you went into the room?"

The Reverend sat quietly for several moments, trying to calm his mind and gather his thoughts. "His condition astonished me when I first saw him. I'd never seen anyone in such a deteriorated state yet still alive. As I stood gazing at him, I could swear I'd heard what sounded like muffled voices coming from around the room. There was no one in there but myself and the man in the bed, so I brushed it off as background noise from out in the hallway.

"After a moment or two, I sat beside the bed and took out my bible. I read from the Book of Romans, and that's when it happened. Something punched me in the mouth, knocking my head back and almost throwing me out of the seat. I tried to get up, but a force had pinned my arms to the chair. The room went dark and suddenly a giant, looming shadow—the shadow of the devil—appeared in front of me, along with several smaller ones.

Within seconds, they set upon me and began pummeling me relentlessly. I believe I blacked out during the beating; a lot of it is fuzzy at the moment. I do remember flying into the hall where you found me."

"This makes a little more sense now," Glen said. "You say the room went dark, and a shadow appeared? To me, it sounds like someone shut the light off then attacked you in the darkness. You were looking down at your bible when they entered the room, so you couldn't get a good look at them when the lights went out, hence the shadow figure."

"That's not how it happened at all, Glen. No one walked into the room! This thing manifested out of the air!"

Glen sighed again. "You didn't see a face?"

"There was no face, just a huge black, semi-human shaped void."

"How tall was this figure, in terms of feet? Six foot? Maybe six-five?"

"No," the Reverend said, shaking his head. "It was way bigger than that. However high the ceiling is in that room."

Glen shook his head. "Here's what I think: Someone reached in and turned out the light while you had your attention focused on your bible. When they came into the room, the light from the hallway behind them cast an oversized shadow on the wall which is what you looked at first. The smaller figure you described was the actual person who attacked you."

Glen gently placed his hand on the reverend's arm to settle him. "I understand you're upset, and I don't blame you. A person who would attack an unsuspecting man—a preacher none the less—is a lunatic. We're going to keep looking until we find him. In the meantime, I want you to think of anyone who might have it out for you. Have you pissed anyone off lately?"

"Of course I haven't!" Reverend Allen had become angry. He knew what he saw, and Glen was trivializing it with his theory. "God, give me patience!"

Glen stood up. "They're keeping you overnight, so I'm going to have one of the security guards stay outside of your room until we find whoever did this. Try to get some rest, Reverend."

He could tell his pastor—and friend—was angry. But really, Glen's theory of a man attacking the Reverend in a dark room made a lot more sense than the devil appearing and whipping the shit out of him. How could he put out an A.P.B. for a red-faced fellow with horns and a little black goatee?

When he left the exam room, Agent Ward was walking toward him through the corridor. "We have the security camera footage queued up."

"Does it show anything interesting?" Glen asked.

Agent Ward stared at Glen for a second or two, then said, "Come with me, Chief."

As they stepped into the corridor outside of the ER, Larry Gilmore approached. The young officer was walking quickly and appeared flustered. He had something in his left hand.

"You won't believe this, Chief," Larry said, slightly out of breath.

"If you're planning on telling me you saw the devil, I don't want to hear it," Glen said.

Larry stood staring at Glen for several moments.

"Alright," Glen finally said. "What is it?"

"I had just checked out the room where the attack took place. I swear there was no one in there except, well, you know, the guy in the bed. When I walked out into the hall, I had my back to the room, and then I felt something hit me in the back of the head, hard. I turned around, but there was no one there." Larry ran a hand over his face to refresh himself. "This was on the floor next to my feet."

Glen took the object Larry was holding. It was a very worn, leather-bound book. When he turned it over, he saw three large, parallel scratches which were cut deep into the cover, slicing through the words "Holy Bible." He was not a man who spooked easily, but between the story, he'd just heard from Reverend Allen and the evidence in his hands now, Glen felt a chill run down his spine.

"Ok, Larry," Glen said. "Put this in an evidence bag and stick it in your patrol car for now."

THREE

Much of the commotion had died down over the last few hours, and things in the ICU seemed to get back to a somewhat normal pace. Lauren felt more comfortable than she had all week, probably because there was now a police officer patrolling the halls of her floor.

As she started the 1:00 AM rounds, she noticed the patient load was light tonight; another reason for her to feel more relaxed. If things could continue on this path for the rest of the shift, she'd be fine. When 8:00 AM rolled around, she'd punch the time clock and have the next three days off. This break couldn't come soon enough.

The police officer escorted Lauren into John Doe's room when it was time to check on him. Were they worried that something terrible might happen to her in there? Were the nurses in danger of being attacked like Reverend Allen was? She knew what was going on in that room. Whatever this thing is that's attached itself to John Doe didn't like the Reverend praying for him. That must have pissed it off. Well, there would be no prayers coming from Lauren tonight. They could go back to hell for all she cared, and they could take that half-dead carcass lying in there with them. She was tired of stressing over the whole mess.

She jotted down the numbers from the machine Doe was hooked up to in her nurse's log, checked his IV—without actually touching it—then scuttled past the cop and out of the room. By the numbers, she couldn't see how Doe was still alive. There were probably hospice cases like this where the patient hung on for much longer than expected, but John Doe had to be a record of some sort.

They hadn't moved Mrs. Randall out of the ICU yet. Lauren quietly walked into her room, hoping she would be asleep, but found her wide awake, staring at the doorway. "You should be sleeping," Lauren said in a kind voice.

"Really?" Mrs. Randall said. "How could a person possibly sleep in a place like this? It's like a war zone around here."

Lauren laughed and pulled up a chair next to her bed. She checked her IV port and took a blood pressure reading.

"I heard all the commotion earlier," Mrs. Randall said. "People running, yelling… it was crazy!"

"Yeah, I heard about that. It all happened before my shift started."

"You know what it was, don't you?"

Lauren let out a deep breath. "I believe someone had a disagreement with Reverend Allen."

"Disagreement? Are you kidding me? You know exactly what happened in that room tonight!"

"Don't get excited, Mrs. Randell."

"I saw the Reverend walk past my door and I heard him ask the nurse at the desk which room was John Doe's. I can tell you cold as kraut, as soon as he stepped in there, that horrible smell came up and this whole place got dark. A few seconds later, all hell broke loose. It sounded like a pack of alley cats fighting over a chicken bone."

Lauren held Mrs. Randell's hand and gently massaged it. "I believe you," she said. "I also believe this is all about to be over shortly."

"Oh?"

"Yes, I do. Call it a hunch, but I have that feeling." Lauren patted Mrs. Randell's hand. "Besides, you're going to be getting out of here soon, and you won't have to worry about the creepy things going on around here."

"Well, I'm still going to worry about you, sweetie, you're like a daughter to me."

Lauren smiled as she thought of Mrs. Randall's kind words. She left the room feeling almost normal again.

FOUR

Agent Ward ushered Glen into the control room where Harold Anthony, head of hospital security, sat in an office chair behind a bank of flat-screen monitors. The room was vast, full of computers and server racks with thousands of different colored cables plugged into each of them. Glen imagined if he pulled out one of these wires, alarms, and red flashing sirens would go off. He didn't test the theory.

"Hey there, Chief," Harold said as he stood up to shake hands with Glen. "Quite a mess going on here tonight."

"It looks that way, Harry," Glen said. He and Harold had known each other for years.

"I can't imagine who would have a beef against Reverend Allen? He's such a nice fella."

"Yes, he is," Glen agreed.

"Do you have the security footage from the ICU ward cued up?" Agent Ward interjected, making no effort to conceal his discomposure.

"Huh? Oh yeah, I got it all set up." Harold looked at Glen. His demeanor had changed from jovial to uncertainty. "I don't know what you're going to make of this, Chief. It sure is a head-scratcher."

Harold retook his seat at the oversized desk and began typing what appeared to be log-in and password information. Three large flat-screen monitors loomed over them from above the desk like a TV setup found in a sports bar. When Harold finished typing, the screens filled with images from different camera angles in the ICU ward. The first monitor on the far right covered the main corridor from the elevator to the nurse's station. The second screen, in the middle of the three, showed a view from behind the nurse's station, which encompassed the central part of the floor and several rooms. The third projected the view from the far end of the corridor. With all three angles covered, it should have been easy to deduce what happened to Reverend.

"Ok," Harold said. "The screen on the right is camera one. In a few seconds, you'll see Reverend Allen step out of the elevator and head toward the nurse's station… there he is. Now, camera two shows him talking with the nurse for a minute before he heads across the hall to room 337. Camera three, on the left monitor here, shows a portion of the inside of the room. That camera is positioned behind the nurse's station, looking across the hall; it shows the room in question. You can even see some of the inside from this angle. You can't see the Reverend after he goes all the way in the room, but keep watching."

Glen gazed at the monitor, waiting for something to happen. There was no activity for at least two minutes. Suddenly, a shock he never expected coursed through his system. Out of nowhere, Reverend Allen flew into the wall to the left of the open door, inside the room, about four feet up, then fell to the floor. He crawled away from the wall and lay in the fetal position, clearly in pain. Glen gasped and took a step back as the next event flashed before his eyes. The Reverend abruptly levitated to the ceiling and was held there with his arms and legs stretched out. There was no sign of anyone holding him up, but there he was, pinned to the ceiling like a poster. Without warning, he dropped the full twelve feet to the floor, landing on his face and chest. And whatever had raised him up there wasn't finished. Something lifted him again, held him in mid-air for a moment, then hurled him out of the room with incredible force. He hit the wall across the corridor and landed on the floor. Within seconds, Glen, Agent Ward, and the ICU nurse entered the view.

Harold and Agent Ward stared quietly at Glen, studying his reaction. Though he had jumped a few times during the video, for the most part, he kept decent composure.

"How many security guards work here altogether?" Glen asked Harold.

"Well, there's me and two others working tonight, and I got two more who are off till tomorrow."

"Call them in right now," Glen said. "I want everyone you

have patrolling this place tonight. I'm leaving my two officers here as well. I'll be back in about an hour." Glen walked to the door of the control room, then turned towards Agent Ward. "Are you coming or not?"

FIVE

During the car ride from the hospital to Mrs. Rolley's place, Agent Ward's demeanor was as solemn as it had been since he rolled into town. He played with his phone, stared out the window, adjusted his tie several times. Not remotely interested in conversing with Glen. And at this point, Glen didn't care. He was too busy trying to internalize what he'd seen on the hospital security footage. But what the hell had he seen?

There was no one in that room.

He'd thought perhaps a camera glitch. But could a camera glitch explain away levitation? Reverend Allen was pinned to the ceiling and held up there for at least ten seconds, which was not possible. In the physical world, people cannot defy gravity at will. And it went farther than levitation; something forced him up there.

John Doe was not responsible for this. Not in a million years. A man who is nothing more than a vegetable, rotting away at the bottom of a produce cart, did not raise Reverend Allen to the ceiling. Yet, the Reverend now lay in a hospital bed, battered, bruised, and terrified. And there was even security footage to prove the event.

Glen looked over at Agent Ward, who was motionless, staring straight ahead. He knows something. He's not entirely upfront about this John Doe/Hanson Parker fellow. Yes, he said the man was a child killer, but there's more going on between these two than he's letting on. Glen decided not to press the issue until they arrived at the spot where he had found Doe. But after that, it was time for Ward to talk.

"Mrs. Rolley is in Florida with her son for Thanksgiving," Glen said as he parked the police cruiser in front of the house. Agent Ward did not reply.

The two men got out. Glen opened the trunk, retrieved two long handle flashlights, and handed one to Agent Ward. They

158

then proceeded around to the back of the house.

The acrid smell of feces still present as they approached the potting shed, but not nearly as horrible as the night he'd found the body. He didn't think they would need nose protection.

"She found him in here," Glen said, standing by the open door. "He was curled up under a tarp."

Ward shined his flashlight into the dark opening and proceeded inside without hesitation.

His indifferent attitude continued to piss Glen off. He'd been around these types before—the ones who take their job more seriously than a heart attack—and hadn't usually been too bothered by them. But today, Special Agent Ward was in Cumberland Springs, not Pittsburgh. Yes, he brought the weight of federal jurisdiction with him, but out here in Braddock County, people were a little nicer to each other. Call it professional courtesy. Glen didn't plan on taking much more of Ward's bullshit tonight.

He gave the agent a few moments alone in the shed to look around and get his own perspective. When he finally went inside, he found Ward standing in the middle of the room with his arms crossed, looking down at the spot where they had discovered John Doe three nights ago. The agent's face, expressionless. Glen stood beside him but did not speak.

As motionless as a statue guarding a crypt in an ancient cemetery, Agent Ward did not wavier from his cold stance. Glen had thought about speaking up a few times, then felt that maybe he should keep his mouth shut. Something looked off about the guy. It was as if he was attempting to control emotion, working desperately to keep it stowed inside. But what emotion? At first, Glen thought perhaps anger or rage, though there were also hints of sorrow and anguish mixed in as well. Or was he was merely reading too much into this? After all, the guy was only just standing there, still and silent.

"It's not supposed to end like this," Agent Ward finally said.

Glen looked at him, almost surprised that the man had actually spoken. He'd half expected him to turn and rudely walk out of the room without saying a word like he'd done to Glen all day. His speech was unexpected. Was he finally going to open up?

"How is it supposed to end?" Glen said.

Ward looked at him but did not speak. It was hard to tell in the dim light, but Glen thought the man's eyes were glossing over. Possibly tears welling up.

"I'm sorry," Glen said. "I don't mean to push you on the subj —"

"I didn't get my chance at him! He's getting off too easy!"

Now it was Glen who stood silent and expressionless.

Ward walked around the room, examining the various tools and gardening implements, being careful not to touch anything. He stopped at the old sign leaning in the corner and shined his flashlight over the faded, chipped letters. Tilting his head to see it better, he read aloud, "Cumberland Springs Adventure Society?"

Glen let out a laugh. "We're always looking for new members if you're interested."

Ward looked at him and smiled. For a fleeting moment, the two men shared the feelings of childhood. Reality, however, as cold and icy as midnight in January, quickly snapped them both back into place.

"I've been after Hanson Parker for a long time," Ward said. "Actually had the bastard in custody twice. They let him go both times." He continued walking around the room, looking over the contents.

"How long *have* you been chasing him?" Glen asked.

"I picked up the case eleven years ago, about a year after he killed, Katie." Ward lowered his eyes. "She was my niece."

Glen didn't know what to say. The coldness Agent Ward had given off all day now seemed to have purpose. "I'm very sorry. I can't imagine."

"She was ten-years-old. The doctors told my sister the cause of death was Cardiomyopathy. Otherwise known as, *dying of fright.*"

Glen stood quietly, trying to internalize what he'd just heard, and not doing a good job of it.

"You're going to ask me how Parker scared my niece to death." Agent Ward said.

"Well, forgive me, but this is intriguing."

Agent Ward stepped past Glen and out of the shed into the cold evening air. Glen was happy to follow him and get away from the lingering odor still inside. He followed Ward to the front porch of Mrs. Rolley's house. Ward took a seat on the steps, pulled out a new pack of cigarettes, unwrapped them, and lit one. Glen hadn't noticed the smell of tobacco on him when they were together in the car. His smoking came as another surprise for the evening.

"Cardiomyopathy: a sudden and extreme release of stress hormones which causes the heart to go into shock." Ward took a long drag from his cigarette. He didn't seem to enjoy it.

"Again, forgive me, but, what did Hanson Parker do to 'scare' your niece to death?"

"I don't know."

Glen had no response. Ward didn't know how Parker scared his niece to death? It seemed highly unusual for an FBI agent to have so few facts about a person he'd been chasing for the last eleven years.

"It was in July, eleven years ago. Katie went missing for three days. We found her at the Whites Creek recreational area, which was the last place anyone saw her. Someone placed her body under a stack of rental canoes. Her arms folded neatly over her chest.

"You don't have to ask, because I already know what you're thinking. It's the same thing I've been hearing since I presented Hanson Parker as a suspect. How was he involved? Where's my proof?"

"Well, you have to admit..."

"Remember when I said we had him in custody twice, but they let him go?"

"Yeah."

"Both times he turned himself in to the Pennsylvania State

Police, claiming he was responsible for the deaths of dozens of children, spanning several decades. Both times they committed him to a state psychiatric facility. His claims were outrageous and eventually shrugged off as mental illness. The first time he spent six months in an institution before being released. The second, he was in for a little over a month."

"Did he offer any evidence other than his confessions?" Glen asked.

Ward took another hit from his cigarette, then coughed as he flicked it into the front yard. "He claimed he was being coerced to abduct the kids, then hand them over to another individual who committed the crimes. Parker would then return the body close to where he abducted them, out of respect for the family."

"Ok, I'm pretty much just a small-town cop without a criminology or psychology background," Glen said. "The only investigations I have to do around here are figuring out who toilet papers the trees around the town square at Halloween. But I have to ask: isn't there *any* physical evidence? DNA, footprints, fingerprints?"

Agent Ward shook his head. "Nothing." He let out a long sigh. "I haven't been able to find a District Attorney willing to bring a case with the only evidence being a confession from someone mentally unstable. Plus, every doctor who has examined him has concurred that he's delusional."

"But you're certain he's responsible? What makes you so committed to Parker as the suspect?"

Ward stood up and walked around Mrs. Rolley's front porch. He took a seat on one of the wooden chairs placed next to a small matching table. Glen followed and sat in the adjacent chair.

"He claimed to have been responsible for the deaths of close to thirty children but gave no information on names, dates, or locations. The ambiguity of his statements was why many other investigators shrugged him off as a suspect. Just another lunatic looking to be relevant."

"But you didn't take to that theory?" Glen asked.

"Not a chance. No, sir.

"Sis had called me right away when Katie disappeared. They were having a picnic at Whites Creek with a few other families. A lot of children were playing by the creek and in the nearby wooded area all day. One kid approached my sister and said they had lost track of Katie while playing hide and seek in the woods. The parents searched for several hours before calling the police. When it started getting dark, Sis panicked. She called me at around 11:30 PM after the local police had already searched for over three hours. Of course, I came right away. I also brought six other FBI agents with me, highly trained in this sort of thing.

"We turned over every inch of a ten-mile radius for three days straight without producing a single clue. Then suddenly, she was just there. A state trooper helping with the search found her under a stack of rental canoes. She looked like she was asleep, but she was gone."

Glen didn't want to interrupt Ward's story. He could tell the man had experienced a great deal of pain over the ordeal.

Agent Ward continued: "The State Police headed up the investigation. I was told by my Assistant Director to let them handle it; the FBI saw no reason to get involved, as there was no initial evidence of foul play. However, their conclusions didn't add up for me. If I was an outside investigator looking at this case purely on paper, without knowing the victim or family, I could have easily concurred with their theory. But I knew this child! Something in my gut told me they were incorrect.

"There was no arguing the medical examiner's findings. She had died as a result of Cardiomyopathy; the proof was solid. The issue I had was with the theory of what caused her such a scare that her heart went into shock. The coroner attributed the fright to her coming into contact with a large spider or snake while hiding under the canoe rack. Knowing Katie as I did, I don't think there was ever a time when I didn't see her picking up spiders, snakes, lizards, or any other slithering thing she could find. The girl was fascinated with bugs and critters. If she crawled under that rack of canoes and ran into a spider, she wouldn't have thought twice about picking it up and carrying it around all day.

"There was no other evidence to warrant further investigation, so I had to let it rest. Until the day I got the call that someone had claimed responsibility for her death." Ward stood up and walked to the porch railing. He looked out over the dark front yard. "The State Police called my office and said they had a man in custody claiming responsibility for the deaths of several children. He didn't give any names, but he described some of them. One was a ten or eleven-year-old blonde girl that he had placed under a stack of canoes at Whites Creek."

SIX

The chaos which had echoed throughout the halls of Cumberland Springs Memorial earlier in the evening had eased slightly, but not by much. Police and security guards patrolled every floor, giving the place an uneasy, almost prison lockdown atmosphere. The staff continued their jobs—as professional people do—but their uneasiness hung in the air like a fog bank, waiting to drop at any moment. The lunatic who attacked Reverend Allen was still on the loose, and most likely still in the hospital, a reality that weighed heavily on everyone's mind tonight.

The ICU continued to run efficiently, with Lauren and Lisa keeping to their procedures. They did their best to focus on work, and not discuss what had happened earlier with Reverend Allen —who, though heavily sedated, was still in a state of shock. Officer Gilmore from the Cumberland Springs PD patrolled the floor and even supervised when it was time to check in on John Doe. It put their mind at ease a little. His boss had instructed him to monitor all comings and goings from room 337. No one could enter the room without his direct supervision.

By 2:15 AM Lauren had completed her rounds, and all the ICU patients slept quietly in their rooms. She thought this would be a good time to go on lunch break. Grandmother had made her take a healthy plate of leftovers from Thanksgiving dinner earlier, and she was very much looking forward to it.

Mrs. Stover looked up from the book she was reading to greet Lauren as she walked into the dimly lit cafeteria. The room was empty and somewhat eerie.

"Don't they have anyone here to watch over you?" Lauren asked. "You shouldn't be in here all by yourself tonight."

"Oh, I'm fine, dear. One of the security guards pops in every fifteen minutes to check on me."

Lauren walked around to the giant refrigerator behind the

counter where she had stored her lunch. She put the container in the microwave, and within seconds the entire room smelled like Grandmother's kitchen.

"Smells like you had a nice Thanksgiving," Danielle Cunningham said as she entered the cafeteria. "If I even look at another piece of turkey, I'm going to be sick!"

"Overeat today?" Mrs. Stover asked.

"No, the entire family is in town. I helped my mother cook and prep three turkeys over the last two days. I'm over it!" Danielle went to the coffeepot and poured herself a full mug.

Mrs. Stover pulled up a seat at the round table with the other two girls. "Were either of you here this evening during Reverend Allen's attack?"

"I came in after it happened," Lauren said.

"I was here when they brought him to the ER," Danielle said. "Somebody did a number on him. Not only was his body in terrible shape, but the poor guy was so terrified! I've never seen a person's eyes that big."

"Someone told me he said the devil attacked him," Mrs. Stover said.

Danielle let out a short laugh. "I actually heard him say that, several times."

"Yeah, but he's a preacher," Lauren said. "Of course he's going to equate an event like that with something biblical."

The three women jumped in their chairs as thunder cracked loudly outside the window. They laughed at the coincidence of its perfect timing with their conversation.

"Think God's trying to tell us something?" Mrs. Stover said, staring at the window.

A hard rain began, carried by a wind that thrashed droplets against the windows like a bullwhip. More flashes of lightning and rolling thunder accompanied the shower.

"So, whatever happened with your John Doe patient, Lauren?" Mrs. Stover asked.

Lauren finished chewing her mouthful of turkey breast. "He's still up there. In fact, that's the room where Reverend Allen was attacked."

"I thought that guy was a vegetable?" Danielle asked.

"Yeah, he is. He couldn't be the one who did it. Somebody had to have been hiding in there, waiting for the Reverend."

"That's just despicable!" Mrs. Stover said.

"The worst part is this asshole could still be in the hospital somewhere," Danielle said.

Lauren sighed. "I'm going to try not to think about it. I've had enough stressing me out lately."

Lightning bolted directly outside of the windows, and an explosion of thunder cracked less than a second behind it. The building shook from the concussion while the lights flickered three times. Danielle and Lauren took that as a cue to cut their breaks short. They both hurried back to their stations.

SEVEN

The November evening had become even more chilling as a sudden wind picked up out of nowhere. The weather forecast for the Thanksgiving holiday said nothing about wind or rain in the area, yet evidence of a storm brewed in the air. The impending weather didn't seem severely threatening at the moment, so Glen didn't feel compelled to move his conversation with Agent Ward to a safer location. Mrs. Rolley's front porch would be fine for now.

As Ward progressed with his story, Glen could see the emotional toll the ordeal had taken on the man surfacing. He thought of his own children. What if something like this were to happen to his son or daughter? He couldn't imagine the loss and what it would do to him. The devastation. How does a parent cope with life after losing a child? When God gives us the gift of children, He is, in essence, saying He believes in us enough to protect and raise them, putting our needs—even our lives—aside for them. Glen suddenly felt a strong, heart sinking urge to be at home protecting his family.

Ward leaned against the porch railing and attempted to light another cigarette. It became apparent that he was not a seasoned smoker as he struggled to get the tip to flame up. Finally, he gave up and threw the unlit cigarette into the yard.

"So, Hanson Parker had confessed to killing a girl who resembled your niece, but didn't offer any evidence?" Glen asked.

"When I got there to interview him, they had already transferred him to the hospital for a psychiatric evaluation," Ward said. "It was obvious to the State Police that he was mentally unstable."

"Did you see him at all?"

"Not at this point. But I saw the video recording from the interview room," Ward said.

"What did you think of him from the recording?"

"For starters, he was just a scrawny little fuck. Somewhere in his mid to late forties, with greasy dark hair and a face that hadn't seen a razor in a few weeks. Very unimpressive. He didn't seem strong enough to abduct an eleven-year-old without a struggle."

"What changed your mind about him?" Glen asked.

Ward inhaled a deep breath of cool autumn air. "During the police interview, Parker had three severe emotional outbursts. After the second eruption, a State Trooper came into the room and handcuffed him to the table. He kept saying, '*It's all my fault!*' Then he switched gears and placed the blame on someone he called, Zlo.

"At first I thought he was a nutcase, out to catch a few minutes of fame. From his ranting and screaming, it was clear he needed mental help, and this story of his nothing more than a fabricated to garner attention. But then he described my niece. He gave details about her that no one could have known just by what they'd seen on the news. Things about her voice and the words she used. He said she had called him a 'Meanster.' That was a word that Katie and I made up to describe bullies in her class. I'd heard no one use that term before or since. It was part of our playful dialog we had together, not shared with anyone else. I was shocked when I heard him say it. And by the way, he described her, it was very plausible to me that he could have been with her. The use of one made up word certainly wasn't enough evidence to hang him with, but it was enough for me to change my opinion about my niece's death."

Tree branches began clicking together as the wind became more aggressive. The sound the air made blowing through the distant hills created a roar of background white noise through the hollow. The temperature also continued to drop making it uncomfortable to sit in the open air of Mrs. Rolley's porch.

"I began an investigation into Hanson Parker, mainly on my own time." Agent Ward said. "The FBI didn't see enough evidence to open a case, though I tried like hell to convince them. The evidence was crystal clear to me: every kid Parker claimed he was responsible for died of cardiomyopathy. That's a very rare way for a healthy child to die. My superiors at the Bureau simply wrote him off as a nut, and they felt I was pushing the case because of my niece. The directors looked at the medical reports from all the names Parker mentioned, but agreed with the conclusions on the reports: Natural Causes."

Agent Ward sat back down in the wooden chair across from Glen. "The irony of this whole mess is that the first death happened in 1984, right here in Cumberland Springs."

Glen stared at Ward as he tried to internalize what he had just heard. A child's death in 1984 in this town? That would have been... "I don't want to hear any more of this!" Glen exclaimed as he got up from his seat and headed for the porch steps. He stopped as if hitting a brick wall when he heard the agent's voice again.

"The boy's name was, Lucas Rolley," Ward said.

That name had crossed Glen's mind at least once per day, if not more, for the last thirty-some years. When he was alone in his thoughts; reading a novel in his study; watching his children play. The smallest trigger could have him thinking about Lucas, the best friend he'd ever lost. Hearing his name as part of a murder investigation sent his blood to boiling.

"Lucas died of natural causes," Glen said. "The kid had a heart murmur from birth, and when he was ten-years-old, it killed him. There was no foul play involved. I've looked over those old records a dozen times."

"Chief, these kids all died of heart attacks."

Glen was becoming furious. His friend died one night when they were kids because his ticker was defective. No one questioned it.

"Ok, Ward," Glen said smugly. "Connect Hanson Parker to Lucas Rolley for me."

Agent Ward leaned forward, resting his elbows on his knees. "On 18 July 1984, Cumberland Springs Chief of Police, Jim Harris, ran a check on a suspicious white Ford panel van,

Virginia plate: DGE-8923. The check determined that the van was registered to an Alice Carter of Winchester Virginia, nothing outstanding. In later years, several more requests from different precincts in various states requested checks for the same vehicle and plate number. The FBI logged the checks into the bureau's central database, which is used to spot patterns and habits. After a few years, a pattern emerged, which is undeniable. In every city where a police officer requested a check on this van, a child had disappeared and turned up dead after three days.

"Upon further investigation, I uncovered the van is registered to a false name. The only Alice Carter from Winchester, VA died in 1859. On a side note, I discovered a newspaper article on microfilm at the Winchester public library about an eleven-year-old girl named Alice Carter, who went missing for three days in 1859 and was found dead in a ravine less than a mile from her home. A doctor determined her death to be of natural causes.

"The day after your police Chief ran the plate on the suspicious van, Lucas Rolley disappeared and was found deceased three days later. In Hanson Parker's confession statement, he claimed the first child he took was playing alone in a barn at night. Where was Lucas Rolley found?"

Glen looked at the floor. "In Charlie Martin's barn."

"Was he missing for three days?"

Glen didn't answer.

"The only thing I can conclude is that Parker was probably dying and knew it. Maybe he came back here after all these years for closure. I imagine he stalked Lucas for a while before making the abduction. He could have known this house, and that old shed back there and made this his final act."

A churning began in Glen's stomach. He was about to be sick. The thought of him and his closest friends being stalked by a predator during the most innocent and enjoyable time of their lives sent his constitution to the floor. Dizziness overtook him. He needed to sit down.

Breathing deeply for a few moments as he sat on the porch steps, he kept the nausea contained. "What about this other person he claimed was involved? Did you ever find him?"

"Zlo? He doesn't exist as far as I'm aware," Ward said. "The psychiatric evaluations stated that Hanson Parker may have a dissociative personality disorder, but they never had enough time with him to make a complete diagnosis. If I had to speculate, I'd say this person came out of his imagination."

"Even if Parker made him up, how did he claim he was involved?" Glen asked.

"Parker alleged Zlo was in control. He said the guy would direct him to find a child of a certain age, abduct them, then leave them at a remote location. He didn't know what Zlo did to them while they were with him, but three days later he'd come back to pick up the body, then drop it close to the abduction site. His reason for returning the body was for the family's sake, so they could have closure. The whole thing is very sick!"

Lightning flashed throughout the sky, and the rumble of thunder began bubbling in the distance. The wind intensified, carrying drops of precipitation and fallen leaves onto the porch. Swirling at Glen's feet, the leaves made a scratching sound as they danced across the wooden floorboards.

There was nothing more to say or ask. Glen had heard enough. Ward seemed to believe and stand behind his story with conviction. But for Glen to change his opinion about a tragedy that had stuck with him since the day it happened, he was going to need more than a crazy story from a man he'd just met a few hours ago.

"I need to get back to the hospital to see if they figured out who beat up my preacher," Glen said.

EIGHT

The lights in the elevator flickered on and off twice as it traveled to the ICU floor. Lauren rushed out before the doors had opened entirely in fear of being trapped in that dark metal box for the rest of the night.

The hospital had plenty of emergency power in place for occasions such as this. State codes dictated it had to run independently from the power grid for no less than forty-eight hours. She'd hoped that plan wasn't about to be tested.

Lauren criticized herself for being so stubborn. Why couldn't she have listened to Grandmother's advice today? Would it have been so bad to take a sick day? People do it all the time. No, it wasn't something she was in the habit of doing, but look at the position coming to work placed her in tonight: John Doe is still alive, meaning whatever terrible thing attached to him is here as well; a horrible storm is menacing the building from outside, threatening to kill the power; there's a maniac who attacked a preacher possibly hiding in any crevice or dark shadow he can find, waiting to pounce on whoever stumbles upon him. If there were ever a time to take a sick day, this would have been it.

Lisa was not at the nurse's station when Lauren approached. She was most likely attending to a patient. The police officer who had patrolled the floor all night was also nowhere to be found. She stood alone in the hall, developing a chill. Except for the rumbling storm outside, the ward felt eerily quiet. Dreadful.

Everything was getting to her. An entire week of stress, loss of sleep, events surrounding a patient which one could only describe as *paranormal*. She couldn't remember a more trying time in her life. Luckily for her, tonight would be the last night of this arduous stretch. She was off for the next three days. Lauren decided right here in the hall—with no one around to witness it —that she would not be coming back to work until that skeleton in 337 was dead and his carcass carted out of the building. She would call in everyday next week to check, and if John Doe still clung to life, Lauren Rivers would gladly take a personal day. She'd take a *goddamn* leave of absence if she had to. She'd grow fucking tomatoes for a living if that thing was still here when she ran out of personal time. After tonight, she would deal with John Doe no more. Fact!

As she stood in the hall, ranting to herself about not dealing with this crap anymore, a chilling sound pierced the air. It was a sound she had heard many times, and one which immediately sent her into business mode. A heart monitor attached to a patient in one room flatlined, sending out a shrill alert signal. It only lasted for a few seconds, as the patient's heart must have started again on its own. She looked around to see which room it came from, but couldn't tell directly. Then the alarm sounded once more, and it came from room 337. This was it. John Doe was finally leaving, departing for the great beyond. Upon Doe's arrival at the hospital earlier in the week, Dr. Bolton had placed a Do Not Resuscitate order on him. There would be no crash cart, no emergency personnel rushing in to save him. He would depart peacefully once and for all. Not a moment too soon, as far as she was concerned.

Someone had to go in there, though. Lauren looked around for Lisa, but she was still nowhere to be found. The monitor couldn't ring off the hook all night; it would disturb the entire floor. There was no way around it, Lauren had to do it. *How fitting!* All she had to do was walk in there, shut the screaming monitor off and leave. She didn't need to look at him. There would be nothing to see anyway, just his emaciated corpse staring up at her with that one open, dilated, soulless eye. Couldn't anyone have closed that thing this week? A doctor? Another nurse? Surely everyone here noticed that bulging black marble staring off into space?

Get it over with, she thought. *Rip that band-aid off and get back to life as usual.* Could it be that simple, though? Next week, when John Doe would be nothing more than a terrible memory, would life return to normal? She was concerned that something had changed in her. She'd been exposed to knowledge that humans aren't supposed to have. The veil lifted, enough for her to see further past our own reality than we should. Lauren knew in her heart that nothing would ever be *normal* again.

The alarm stopped on its own once more as she entered the room. She had only made it two steps inside when the monitor went silent. Doe's body was in the last stages of the dying process. As she looked at the man lying in front of her, Lauren felt something she hadn't felt since first laying eyes on him. No matter what he had done throughout his life that led him to end up in this state, he was still a human being, and a child of God deserved compassion. She felt sorry for the awful things she had thought about him. It was very out of sorts for her to have been so selfish, wanting the man to die so she'd no longer have to deal with him.

Lauren lowered her head, closed her eyes, and began a silent prayer. She asked the Lord to forgive her for the thoughts she'd had about Doe since the day they met. She asked that He forgive this man for any—

Something knocked her to the floor. It was as if an immense pressure grabbed her shoulders and forced her down. She let out a quick scream as her knees hit the ground and the palms of her hands smacked against the cold tile. She stayed in the position on all fours, afraid to twitch even a finger. The weight had lifted as quickly as it came upon her, but she maintained her stance, almost unwillingly.

Thunder burst overhead, shaking the old hospital from its roof to its foundation. The lights went out, leaving her in pitch blackness on the floor of the room she'd been in constant fear of all week. She couldn't imagine herself in a worse position.

Within seconds—which felt like an eternity—the emergency floodlights kicked on. The building was supposed to have full backup power that would last a few days, but apparently, the generator needed a certain amount of coaxing to get fired up and running.

Finally, she found the strength and fortitude to get back to her feet. As she rose, the already dim emergency light seemed to go almost completely dark. She knew what was happening, though, she'd been through this situation before in this room.

Darkness slowly crept in as if it were a living creature, blanketing and stifling the room. The air became thin, lacking oxygen. Lauren found it harder and harder to breathe. Out of the consuming darkness appeared many shadows in roughly shaped human forms. It looked as though the darkness was an actual doorway that they were using to gain access to our world.

They quickly surrounded her and spoke in low, maniacal tones. They taunted her. Hissed at her. Called her terrible names. The voices, filled with malice and hatred, were relentless. They loathed Lauren. She'd never felt such anguish.

Without warning, she felt the terrible sensation of being scratched across the back. The image of rusty barbed wire raked over bare skin flashed through her mind. The scratches tore through her blue hospital scrubs and gouged deep into her skin. Warm blood immediately leaked from the wound and trickled down to her lower back.

Paralyzed with fear, and unable to scream, Lauren felt that there would be no escape from this torment; this was to be her end. A cold, dark room, purged of all humanity, replaced with misery, pain, and corruption. A place forsaken. There was no love here, no caring, no honesty. The room had become a void where nothing good could exist.

But *she* was a child of God. She'd given her soul over to Jesus Christ on more than one fine Sunday morning at the First Baptist Church of Cumberland Springs. If the teachings were correct, these foul things had no dominion over her. She belonged to the Lord. Her soul spoken for and nothing from the blackness could harm her. These things were a grim joke. Nothing more than a lie created to cause fear and panic. *Fuck* them and whoever sent them here.

Lauren clasped her hands together and squeezed as tightly as she could. She closed her eyes and began reciting the Lord's prayer as boldly and loudly as her voice would allow.

Thunder again cracked fiercely overhead. The building shook as though a boulder hurled out of a catapult from an invading heathen army had smashed into its walls. Lauren's voice rose as her confidence grew, knowing that God would protect her from anything that could come through the darkness. She smiled when a stream of tears rolled down her cheeks. Her heart burst with joy as she felt the love of the Lord surround her, protecting her and pushing back the evil. Her body became warm as His loving embrace shrouded her. She prayed louder and louder still.

She became aware of an enormous, solid black figure standing in front of her. It was human-shaped, but as tall as the ceiling. Lauren looked directly up into its face—or where a face should have been—and continued praying. It stood in front of her for a moment, not doing anything. It seemed to analyze her. Finally, the figure bent down, putting what may have been its face directly in front of hers. There were no eyes, nose, or mouth... nothing but darkness. A complete void.

Standing face to face with unimaginable evil, Lauren should have been terrified. She was sure it had only the worst intentions, yet she had no fear. Staring directly into the darkness, as bold and empowered as she had ever been, Lauren knew in her heart that there was nothing this thing could do to her.

A puff of rank smelling air blew into her nostrils. It must have opened its mouth, releasing the stench of a thousand sewers into the environment. It let out a low, rumbling growl, then merely said one word: *"Leave!"*

NINE

The storm relentlessly pounded the old stones and bricks, which made up the early twentieth-century architecture of Cumberland Springs Memorial Hospital. To those inside, it felt like the building was under siege from a medieval foreign invader. At any moment the foe would assault the castle walls and pour inside to wreak havoc upon those who opposed them.

It was highly irregular to experience thunderstorms in Braddock County this late in November. Spring and summer, of course, these things were to be expected, but in late fall, snow was on everyone's mind, not thunder and lightning. The last time a late-season storm hit the area was clear back in 1986. There's still a pretty big scorch mark on the municipal water tower where a bolt of lightning cracked off of its side. The county codes department came by shortly after to properly ground the structure, ensuring that nothing like that wouldn't happen again.

The last thunderbolt to burst near the hospital knocked out the power completely. The backup generator kicked on for a few seconds, then promptly sputtered to a halt. This happened three or four more times within the first five minutes of the outage, causing the lights to flash between the full strength bulbs and the emergency floodlights. The effect intensified the chaos as staff members hurried through the halls, trying to keep the place operational.

As calmly as she could, Lauren exited room 337 and headed toward the nurses' station. Lisa stood at the desk trying to get the phone working, with little success. Lauren gave little thought to the surrounding disarray, she was still in shock over what had taken place in John Doe's room moments ago. Were human beings even capable of processing such intense situations? She had looked into the face of evil and stood her ground. This wasn't an overblown bully she had taken a stand against; it was evil, in its purest form. But she wasn't afraid, even now.

Eventually, the gravity of the event would sink in someday, but for the time being, Lauren remained temperate.

Lisa tapped the phone receiver over and over, trying to get a signal. The attempt yielded nothing. She seemed uncharacteristically nervous. "I can't get a hold of anyone!"

Lauren heard her speak but didn't process the words.

"Did you hear me?" Lisa asked, her voice demanding.

"Yes, I heard you, Lisa," Lauren said. "There's a storm going on outside, I'm sure that's the reason the phones are down. Is there an emergency?"

"The lights keep going on and off!"

"Again, there's a storm," Lauren said. "These things can happen—"

An explosion of thunder and lightning went off overhead, shaking the entire hospital. All the lights went out, even the emergency floods, causing total blackness.

Lisa screamed.

TEN

The old hospital sat in ominous darkness. Everyone who wasn't laying in a bed remained perfectly still, paralyzed by fear. Patients called out from their rooms for help or reassurance, hoping everything would be alright soon. The staff did not meet their pleas. No one dared to make a move.

In room 514, Mr. McMullen—scheduled to have a tumor removed from his abdomen in the morning—moaned and cried out like a child looking for a lost parent. Jimmy Moniak, the eleven-year-old who had crashed his bicycle flying down the Yankee Bumps trail, breaking his left wrist and rupturing his spleen, shared the room with Mr. McMullen. He told the old man to, *"Quit being such a baby!"*

May Withers sat in a delivery room with her legs spread wide open, preparing to give birth to her first. Her water broke all over the place just seconds after the lights went down. With her husband rummaging for a snack at the vending machines and the attending nurse out looking for the doctor, she imagined she'd be popping this kid out on her own tonight.

After an eternity—actually less than five minutes—a loud pop, then a sputter came from the generator outside. The lights flickered several times before finally hitting full strength and remaining lit. A collective sigh of relief and a few low cheers echoed the halls.

Lauren and Lisa took action without hesitation, checking on patients and making sure all ICU equipment was functioning properly.

As Lisa walked toward Mrs. Randell's room to check on her, Lauren stopped her at the door. "Let me check on this one, you go ahead and get the next room," she said, knowing full well that the next room housed John Doe. Lisa looked at her strangely for a moment, then moved on without challenging.

Mrs. Randell was sitting up in bed, anxious and motioning

for Lauren to hurry into the room. "I know it was here again!" She called out. "That *goddamn* thing was over there, I just know it!"

"Please keep your voice down, Mrs. Randell," Lauren said. "And try to stay calm."

"You can't ask me to stay calm when Armageddon is breaking loose here!"

Lauren took a deep breath as she tried to think of a way to settle Mrs. Randell down. "You're not going to have any more issues with the patient next-door. It's over."

"Over?" The woman asked, sounding like a child looking for reassurance.

"Yes, Mrs. Randell," Lauren said. "I think this mess is over." She took another deep breath and stared at the wall separating the two rooms. "Please don't ask me how I know, because I'm not sure how I do. I just know that it is if that makes any sense."

Mrs. Randell laid back against the hospital bed and also stared at the wall across from her. "You know what, Lauren? I think you may just be right. I feel like something has changed here. I can't put my finger on it, but there is a change in the air tonight; a positive change."

The air was different, there was no denying it. After all, she had gone through this week, and the terrifying ordeal which had happened only moments ago, Lauren felt as if it had all gone away. Like a black cloud had rolled passed and now the sun was back to brighten the world once more.

A sound came from the room next door, not a scream, but still an exclamation of shock. Lauren knew it was Lisa, in the room with John Doe. "I'll be back in a little while to check on you, Mrs. Randall. Please get some rest," Lauren said as she left the room.

She stopped at the threshold of Room 337, but the apprehension she'd felt all week was strangely missing. Maybe her mind hadn't fully processed what she had faced in there. All week the thought of crossing through that doorway had terrified Lauren, yet now it felt as if the barrier no longer existed. She had no reservations at all about going inside. The only thing stopping her was her own curiosity as to why she was no longer afraid.

As Lauren boldly stepped into the room, she saw Lisa standing at the foot of the bed with her handheld over her mouth. The woman looked to be in shock. "Lisa?" She asked, touching her shoulder. "What's wrong?" Lisa didn't respond. She just stared down at the bed, eyes wide, hands trembling.

Lauren moved her gaze from her coworker to the man lying in the bed before her; the man who no one seemed to know anything about; the man who had caused her more fear than she'd ever known; the man she would no longer fear, and would no longer allow to be a part of her life.

At first, she couldn't tell what she was looking at. This didn't seem to be the same person she'd checked on so many times this week. For the duration of their time together, John Doe had not moved or changed at all. His appearance remained exact for four straight nights. However, what she looked upon now was something shockingly different, and a sight that would burn into her memory for the rest of her days.

John Doe *had* moved. His arms stretched out in front of his face in a defensive position, as if he were attempting to protect himself from being struck. His legs—still under the bed sheet—had buckled up toward his chest, putting him in a sort of twisted fetal position. And his face, which had been expressionless since his arrival, had contorted to a look of unimaginable terror. John Doe was frozen in this stance and as dead as Julius Caesar.

Lisa stared in shock at the grotesque image in front of them, but Lauren remained calm. She finally understood what had happened here and had come to terms with it. This was an evil man. John Doe had most likely done things during his life which decent people could never imagine. And at the end of it all, something came to take him to a place where a person like him belonged. For some reason, which she would never understand, she'd received a glimpse of that side of reality. She didn't question why she was shown these things, or why God would even let this happen. It was part of *her* journey; that's what she took away from the experience. There was a lesson here somewhere, and someday she might come to understand. Or perhaps she would never know. But it didn't matter. She felt God wanted her to see this, and His will was not for her to question.

She put her arm around Lisa and guided her out of the room. Neither of them spoke as they walked to the nurse's station.

ELEVEN

Ronnie's smile was as wide as it could get when Devon said, "I'll see you at work tonight, buddy." He'd been able to get through to his friend and help him get back on track. There was no way he'd ever be able to understand the stress that Devon went through during the war and the way it would surface throughout his life by even the smallest of triggers, but he could be there for him, just as he had since they were eleven-year-old kids. He would always be there for him.

As the night shift went on, Ronnie and Devon sat at the ambulance station, waiting for calls to come in. Ed Martin, the driver, slept on the small sofa in front of the tiny television which no one ever watched. He would awaken from his snore-fest every half hour to smoke a cigarette, then go back to sawing logs. If it weren't for his brother-in-law on the city council, Ed Martin would not be employed.

At 4:10 A.M., a call came in from dispatch. Local resident, Don Finley, was having chest pains… again. His wife called in a panic. "Hurry! My Donnie! Please hurry!" Mrs. Finley demanded. Don Finley had chest pains four or five times a year and had them for as long as anyone could remember. Usually, the ER doctor would check him over, give him a couple of aspirins, then send him home within the hour. And even though the Finley's lived less than a mile from the hospital, they would always insist on a ride in the ambulance. It was entirely possible that Mrs. Finley liked the attention of the flashing lights and commotion in front of her house. It gave her something to talk about the next day, though none of the neighbors even asked about it anymore.

Devon walked over and kicked the sofa. "Get up, Ed. We have a call."

Ed didn't open his eyes or attempt to move. He just grunted and said, "Please don't tell me it's the fucking Finley's."

Devon laughed. "Come on, let's go."

When they arrived, the scene was the same as every other time they came to this house. Mrs. Finley in her red terry-cloth robe and hair in night rollers, nervous and yelling at the medics. "Please hurry! You have to help my Donnie!" And Mr. Finley sitting on the couch in his tighty whities underwear and undershirt, breathing heavily and holding his chest like something was actually going wrong behind his ribcage. Odds were that this was nothing more than anxiety—brought about by his wife, no doubt—but their insurance paid for the ride, so the medics dutifully ran through the procedures as usual.

Ed pulled the ambulance up to the ER doors at Cumberland Memorial, and Ronnie and Devon wheeled the patient out of the back. They didn't bother to check his vitals during the short ride over; it would have been pointless.

"Not feeling well, Mr. Finley?" Danielle Cunningham said as she came out of the ER to assist in the transfer. She had attended to Don Finley several times in the past. Seeing him getting wheeled out of the ambulance was no surprise.

After they passed off the patient, Ronnie said, "Let's grab a coffee in the shop."

"I want to go back to the station and lay down," Ed said from inside the cab of the ambulance.

"I wasn't asking you, Ed," Ronnie said. "You're probably so tired because you ate a whole fucking turkey today."

"I could just leave your asses here!"

Devon walked over to the open window of the cab. "Ed, we're going to go inside for a coffee. If you feel you need to leave us and finish the rest of the shift without medics, you're more than welcome to do so. But if a call comes in and you're by yourself, well, that won't look good for you, even if your brother-in-law is a councilman."

Ed put the ambulance in gear and pulled away. For a moment, Devon thought he actually might leave them, but then he turned into a reserved parking space and got out of the cab. The Navy blue E.M.S. uniform Ed wore was so tight that every button and stitch held at its limit. He grumbled under his breath as he walked toward the lobby entrance.

"I'll catch up with you in a minute," Devon said to Ronnie as they walked through the main entrance. The enticing aroma coming from the open coffee shop door made the lobby feel warm and welcoming. More of the Christmas decorations were up as well, very festive. Devon headed off down the main corridor before Ronnie could ask where he was going. He was still in good spirits and seemed to be on a mission, so Ronnie didn't question him.

Something weighed heavily on Devon's mind tonight, and there was one particular place in this hospital where he could go to let it out.

There is a phrase military people are familiar with, and one which most will agree is an accurate statement: There are no atheists in foxholes. When those moments of extreme stress occur, especially in a combat zone, a soldier is trained to focus on the mission and the men in his company. But when the bullets and shrapnel hit too close, the one they rely upon the most is God.

Further down the main corridor, Devon came to the room he'd intended to visit. There was a double wooden door, which was open, and two vases with flower arrangements on each side of the entrance. A wooden plaque to the right had a single word in the center in script lettering: Chapel. The atmosphere surrounding the area was quiet and peaceful. It was as if anyone walking past instinctually knew to lower their voices out of respect.

Devon sat in the second pew from the back. There was a tall man in a suit sitting a few rows up. He could tell this person was grieving, so he tried his best not to disturb him.

With his head bowed, Devon took a deep breath and thought about what he wanted to say. He wasn't usually comfortable speaking to God; most of the time he didn't. People of faith—the Sunday morning regulars—never seem to have a problem talking to the Lord. They tell Him about their lives, pray for others in need, ask Him for signs and advice. Some people won't put on a pair of socks before asking Him what color they should wear that day. But Devon held a different opinion about his Creator. God could see and hear everything, so He already knew what was going on in everyone's life. Wouldn't He help when He felt it was necessary? Surely He didn't want to hear everyone's issues day in and day out. But tonight was different. Something compelled him to come here. He had a thing in his heart that he needed to let out, and the only one he could spill it out to was the here.

Devon cleared his head for a moment, then opened his heart.

TWELVE

The time had finally arrived. The clock on the nurses' station desk had hit 6:55 A.M. Lauren heard the elevator down the hall ding as the doors opened and knew the day nurses were here to relieve the night shift. This nightmare week from hell was over. She planned to punch out, drive directly home—sometimes she stopped at Valdesarie's Bakery to pick up freshly baked bread for Clay, but not today—get into bed, and not set the alarm. If Clay woke her up for any reason, he'd be a dead man.

Two hours ago, they came with a gurney and carted John Doe's dead body away. Lauren and Lisa stood at the nurses' station and watched as the orderlies wheeled him out, his body still frozen in that hideous position. They had covered him entirely over with a sheet, but there was no denying what was underneath. The image of his face frozen in terror and agony, now forever burned into her mind, like a hot branding iron on the backside of a screaming calf. She stared at the gurney as they pushed it down the hall, in anger instead of sympathy. He dropped into her world out of nowhere and made her life a living hell for four days straight. And the man never said a word or moved a muscle. *Fuck John Doe! I hope he's burning!* Lauren violently shook her head. The thought was repulsive. She'd never had those kinds of feelings before, but here they were now, front and center. She prayed that these negative thoughts and emotions were leaving with John Doe tonight, never to return.

"I see the creepy guy in 337 is gone," one of the day nurses said to Lauren. She only shook her head in response.

"If you give me a few minutes to gather my things, I'll head out with you," Lisa said.

Lauren didn't turn around to acknowledge, she was already halfway to the elevator and had no intention of stopping. As she stepped into the elevator, she thought she heard Lisa again, calling out something in the distance. She paid no attention. The doors closed after she pushed the button for the ground floor and all was quiet.

When the doors opened on the first floor, Lauren meandered out in the direction of the employee locker room. Traffic was light this morning. There were usually groups of staff members roaming the halls, coming to work, or departing as she was, but today she seemed to walk the long corridor alone. She was thankful for the solitude. There was no energy left for a polite conversation today.

A few staff members were in the locker room when she walked in, but they didn't bother to talk with her. The look on her face must have given them the hint that she didn't want to be bothered.

Lauren left the locker room after retrieving her coat and headed down the east corridor towards the door to the parking lot. As she continued her walk, she had an overwhelming feeling that she had forgotten something. She shrugged it off, thinking that nothing was more important at this moment than getting the hell out of this hospital and home to her sanctuary. But something *was* there. With the door in sight, all she had to do was continue walking the twenty remaining feet, and she would be home free. Each step suddenly became unsettling. This was more than just the feeling of forgetting something; it was becoming an urge. She now had the impulse to turn around and head back into the hospital. *No! I'm leaving right now, and I'm not coming back for a while... if ever!*

She made it to the door and pushed it open without hesitation. Icy wind—Stella—accompanied by bits of snow and freezing rain assaulted her face immediately. The sensation was brutal. Using as much energy as she could muster, Lauren gave the door a solid push with her arms, back, and legs. The door did open, but something was still wrong. Something told her to go back inside and resolve this insatiable feeling nagging at her conscience.

She gave up on the door and let the wind slam it shut in her face. *I hate this place!* Lauren turned and walked back through the corridor at a brisk pace, letting out exasperated sighs with every other step. She didn't know where she was heading, just that there was a reason for her to be back inside the hospital. Whatever seemed to direct her didn't tell her much, just that she had something left to do here.

The halls were filling up with morning staff and visitors, all of whom Lauren tried desperately to avoid. Her brisk pace and facial expressions kept them from bugging her as she strode past.

After several minutes of walking the halls of the first floor, she had reached her limit. Whatever it was compelling her to remain here was going to have to take a back seat. Lauren wanted out. Now!

As she turned to head back toward the corridor to the employee entrance, another feeling came over her, telling her without words that she was now where she was supposed to be. It was warmth, almost like an unexpected hug from a loved one. She smiled as this new feeling lightening her mood. When she looked to her left, she realized she was standing at the entrance to the hospital chapel.

It was quiet in this part of the building. The architects and builders must have placed the chapel here intentionally, away from the chaos and noise of the rest of the floor. A calmness filled the area which Lauren embraced, allowing her to clear her mind and forget about the anger that had built up in her over that last four days.

She stepped through the entrance and into the quiet room. It was dimly lit and decorated with flower arrangements and softly glowing candles. A center aisle split six rows of pews and led up to an altar with a large cross hanging in the center. On the left side of the aisle, seated in the back pew, was a younger man with blond hair wearing a paramedic's uniform. His head bowed, eyes closed, and lips moving. On the right side and one pew back from the front sat a very tall, younger-looking man in a suit. His head tilted up to the ceiling. After a few seconds of standing still in the back, Lauren heard a sniffle come from the tall man.

This made sense. Lauren had just gone through what she

would later recall as the most stressful and terrifying event of her life. The way she had perceived the world she lived in based on her twenty-eight years of existence now turned completely upside down over the last four days. Her grasp on reality now in question and her opinion of life and the afterlife more undefinable than ever. But it was intuition that guided her through the event. The Voice spoke up and held her hand as she stood face to face with unimaginable evil. The Voice led her, carried her, and protected her. Some may joke about a little voice inside their head that tells them right from wrong, but now Lauren understood that The Voice is more than a person's conscience. It is a guiding light from the other side of the veil.

As she stood in the chapel's quiet, the Voice spoke up and finally told her why she was here.

She walked over to the blond man in the paramedic uniform and touched him on the shoulder. He looked up at her and smiled as if he knew she was coming. Lauren reached out her hand, and he took it without hesitation. She led him down to the front, and they both stepped into the pew by the man in the suit. She reached for his hand. He was surprised and apprehensive at first. He didn't seem like a person who readily shared his emotions. After Lauren gave him a reassuring smile, he relented. It took her a moment, but she recalled she had met this man earlier in the evening in the ER when he wouldn't allow her to look in on Reverend Allen.

These three people, who did not know each other, sat in the quiet solitude of the Cumberland Springs Memorial Hospital chapel, with their heads bowed and their hearts open. As they sat together hand in hand, it became apparent to each of them that something brought together for a reason. They had all felt the overwhelming drive to visit this chapel. They could feel each other's pulse as they tightly held hands and realized their hearts were beating in unison. They now understood that they were *intended* to know one another. The reason wasn't apparent to them yet, but their hearts spoke, letting them know that there was a purpose for all of this.

Robert Ferencz

THIRTEEN

A faded manila folder with slightly worn brown edges rested in the center of Glen Crawford's desk. Warm light from a brass desk lamp—the same lamp that sat on this very desk since 1964—shined onto the surface of the folder, shaking off the fade of time, making it seem a much brighter shade of yellow than it actually was. Attached in the top right corner was a piece of masking tape with a handwritten name on it. The tape had been losing its grip over time and looked as if it could crumble into dust at any moment, but the name remained legible in dark blue ink. The name carried with it a flood of memories and emotions which Glen had tried desperately over the years to suppress, never fully able to accomplish the task. The name was Lucas Rolley.

For over an hour, Glen had sat silently in his office, staring at the folder which he had retrieved from the archives shortly after he'd brought Agent Ward back to the station to pick up his car. Ward said he was heading back to the hospital to watch over John Doe. Glen had planned on heading back there himself to see if his officers had any new information about the attack on Reverend Allen, but something weighed heavily enough on his mind to hold him back.

During their conversation at Mrs. Rolley's house, Agent Ward said he believed Lucas Rolley to be victim zero, the first in Hanson Parker's—John Doe—long string of child abductions. Glen didn't believe Ward's theory; in fact, it pissed him off. He was there that summer when they found Lucas. Yes, he was missing for three days, but when they finally found him and examined his body, the cause of death was natural. The boy had a heart condition that had gone undiagnosed until it was too late. Sad, but that was the fact.

Yet here Glen sat by the dim light of an old desk lamp, looking at a file from 1984 labeled Lucas Rolley.

There couldn't be anything in here that would change his mind about Lucas. He'd read through this file three or four times since becoming a Cumberland Springs police officer, and it was the same conclusion every time he reached the last page: a tragic but natural death. Why then did he sit at his desk at this late hour when he could be at home, enjoying a beautifully crafted turkey sandwich? The answer was simple: he'd never gotten over the death of his friend. Lucas meant the world to him, and over thirty years later, the shock of losing him still stabbed Glen in the heart. He'd never known pain like that before and still hasn't to this day. He imagined if something were to happen to one of his children or Vicki, the pain would be worse. But thank God they were all still safe and accounted for.

Opening this folder and reading through its fourteen pages—plus newspaper clippings—would fill his head and heart with emotions he didn't want to contend with right now. He could leave the office, stop by the hospital to check on his officers, then go home with a clear conscience. He would have completed his duty for king and country tonight with honor. Did he have to open old wounds and fill his heart with anguish, just because a person he'd only met today had a theory?

Glen switched off the desk lamp, grabbed his jacket, and left his office. The folder stayed untouched in the middle of his desk. Maybe he would open it tomorrow when he came back to work. Perhaps he would put it back in the archives where he found it and go back to living his life the way he had for the past thirty years. None of that mattered now. What he found most important at this moment was finishing his job and getting home to his family.

"No sign at all of anyone suspicious, Chief," Larry Gilmore said as Glen got off the elevator on the third floor ICU.

"Where's that FBI agent?" Glen asked.

"That fella who was following you around earlier? He stopped in for a few seconds to see a patient, but apparently, that patient was already gone."

"Gone?" Glen replied quickly.

"Well, gone yeah, I mean he died," Larry said.

Glen looked over at room 337 where John Doe had resided for the last four days. He stood in silence, thinking about the whirlwind of excitement that man had caused this week. Cumberland Springs wasn't the kind of place where excitement was appreciated, and Glen's job as police chief was to keep the excitement down to a minimum. It was a difficult task with an unidentified half-dead body showing up out of nowhere, an FBI agent hell-bent on his own agenda, and the town's most highly regarded church leader getting the shit kicked out of him by—as Reverend Allen put it—the devil himself.

"Can you handle this from here, Larry?" Glen asked as he put his hand on Larry's shoulder.

"I got this, Chief. Go on home." (Edited)

Glen did just as his officer advised, though he didn't need permission to do so.

The sun had just added a purple hue to the sky as it announced that it would arrive soon. It was already 5:30 A.M. Glen had left the warm comfort of his home and family over twelve hours ago in exchange for chaos and mayhem. It felt good to be home. No other place on God's earth could wash away his troubles like walking through the front door of his home.

There was a light on in the kitchen. As Glen opened the front door, the smell of freshly brewed coffee hit his senses and brought an enormous smile to his face. The odor was divine. His mouth watered and his heartfelt as if it could leap out of his chest.

And there she was, standing at the kitchen counter in her fluffy white robe, looking like an angel on earth. Her face radiated with a welcoming smile, a smile which she saved only for her husband. Vicki was an angel, sent down from Heaven just for Glen. He'd often wondered what he did to deserve this woman, but felt that this was the way God wanted his life to go. There was no reason to question it. The blessing of true love belonged to them both.

Vicki reached out her arms and Glen dove into her warm

embrace. She didn't speak. She knew her husband well enough to know what he needed, and right now he needed her to simply be here with him.

End of the road

ONE

The road felt chillingly familiar. He'd only spent a short period of his life in this area, which was now over thirty years ago, but it appeared the land was somehow etched like a tattoo on his soul. The trees and hills, the stream that kept pace alongside Route 31, the mailboxes, the fields… the white barn on the hill. Time had not altered this place. For whatever reason, it had left it alone, unspoiled, untarnished. Though he couldn't remember a time in his life when he actually felt good or happy —or human—something about this place filled him with warmth.

The warmth, as comforting and delightful as a pleasant summer day, unfortunately, faded before it had given him a chance to embrace it. The chilling reality of what he had done all those years ago took its place. This is where it started. The beginning of the horror that was to be his life all began here, in this tiny slice of Heaven. Well, his life had actually been shit way before he had ever even heard of Cumberland Springs, but nothing compared to the mess it would turn into afterward.

Year after horrific year, he continued on, selfishly hungering for the feelings of elation he would receive as a reward from that thing living inside of him when he did as instructed. Decent human beings could never fathom what he had done in the service of his new god. Decency: the word had no place in his life. He was a slave to depravity. Had there ever been a good side to Hanson Parker? If there was, his memory wouldn't allow the space for it.

He was here once again in south-central Pennsylvania, in the middle of picturesque rolling hills and countryside. In the middle of an untainted part of the world. It was a place of great beauty and solitude. A place where people were kind and selfless and cared deeply for one another. A place where families were happy and their children kept safe. And it was a place which he'd gashed a hideous scare into and had clearly gotten away with no one knowing what he had done.

There may have been a slight sliver of a conscience living inside of his head somewhere; it did poke through the fog occasionally and give him an inkling of a second thought about his despicable actions. *What about the families? What about the lives you've destroyed?* Those thoughts were quickly tamped down by that other thing living within him. That vile creature he'd picked up one chilly night while lying face down in an alley in Baltimore. That thing that had introduced him to a more intense pleasure than he'd imagined was possible to achieve in a human body.

Hanson didn't just dabble with drugs at a young age. He leaped freely off the springboard and did a flying somersault into a giant festering pool of them. From his first hit of weed at age twelve, he lusted after anything that would give him a rush. If it induced even the slightest amount of pleasure, his chips were all in. The old standards—coke, heroin, speed, crack—and the new synthetics; he'd take it all, and in any place he could shove it into his body. He'd thought he had done everything available. That is until Zlo came into the picture.

He had no idea how he ended up in Baltimore that night in 1984. The best he could figure was that in a drug-fueled haze he had bought a Greyhound bus ticket to anywhere, and Baltimore was where they dumped him off. Maybe he owed money to someone, which would make sense. He'd had a well-established network of drug dealers in Boston who were willing to take whatever pennies he could scrounge up or trade for anything he stole out of unlocked cars or open apartment windows. What other reason would he have to leave, other than being in trouble? Perhaps someone fronted drugs to him before he could pay and finally came looking for their compensation. Hanson's brain was so fried at this point though, he had no idea. All he knew was that he was in another large city, and in these places, drugs were easier to find than parking spaces.

Not long after arriving in Baltimore, he snatched a few purses from a couple of unsuspecting elderly women and was back in business. Old ladies always carried cash, and weren't afraid to shop alone, even at night. Maybe they thought it was still the 1950s when people respected each other. *Yeah, right!*

The combined yield from the purses came to $77.50. The going rate for a shot of heroin in Boston, which would fix him for an hour or so, was between $5 and $10. This purse grab could keep him in stock for the rest of the night and then some if he found the right dealer, which wouldn't be difficult.

It took about twenty minutes of walking around the red-light district before a strung-out hooker in cheap pink nylons and ten-inch platform boots directed him to a dealer around the corner. Niko was the guy's name. He had an Asian face and effeminate features. Niko was a crook…

"Twenty-five bucks for a one-hit? *Fuck you!*" Hanson yelled in outrage.

Niko laughed from behind a perfectly polished set of gleaming white teeth. "Fuck you too, Holmes! You want some of my shit, you pay."

"Ten bucks tops or I'm taking my business down to the next alley."

"Man, you welcome to do that, but you get yo throat cut down there," Niko laughed. "Plus, I don't know you, motherfucker. We have not yet established a *rapport.*"

"I'll take my chances down the street," Hanson said and began walking away.

Niko grabbed his arm. "Ok, man, tell you what I'm 'bout to do," he said, looking both ways cautiously. "I'll give you one hit for ten, you like the quality of my product, we'll move to twenty, and I'll keep the price stable there. Cool?"

"I'll give you ten for the first, then ten for the second, then ten for the third, and so on. You try to come off ten bucks, I'm movin' down the street."

Niko kept his bright shining teeth hidden behind a frown as he contemplated Hanson's offer. Finally, he broke out the pearly whites again and laughed. "Alright, bro, take this here for ten and come back to see me when it wears off. You'll see my product is high quality and worth the bump in price."

Hanson gave the Asian ten dollars and took his little baggie of goodness. He then headed deeper into the darkness of the alley where the transaction had just taken place, found a cool crevice between two dumpsters, and began working to locate his favorite vein. It had been well over ten hours since his last high; paradise was mere moments away.

The rush hit him fast, then worked its soothing magic as his heart pumped the chemical through his bloodstream. Maybe it was because he hadn't had a hit in a while, but this shit was no joke. Good old Niko wasn't bullshitting. All of his senses dulled as he laid back against the cold, damp wall and graciously received what he regarded as his blessing.

This shit is the sh—

Hanson fell forward in his blissful stupor and road out the rest of his buzz face down in a shallow puddle of dark, oily water. A small amount of the foul liquid dribbled in and out of his mouth as he breathed. A single drop of this rancid pothole water would have made anyone lose their stomach under normal circumstances, but Hanson was unfazed. His state of ecstasy overshadowed everything, taking him to a place far away from this cold, dreary shit hole in Baltimore.

An hour later, his eyes opened. Reality flooded back into his head. The horrible taste in his mouth made him gag, and he immediately threw up in the same pothole he had unknowingly been drinking from over the last hour. He did not wake refreshed and recharged. Quite the opposite. His head throbbed in unison with his pounding heart. His throat burned from the bile and acid he'd just expelled from his stomach. He couldn't focus. Every muscle in his body screamed out in pain.

Niko!

Hanson crawled halfway out of the alley on his hands and knees until he was finally able to get himself up into at least a stagger. *Where's Niko?*

At the edge of the alley, he stabilized himself on the side of the building where he had made his exchange with the Asian earlier. The Asian was nowhere in sight. He looked around frantically, not straying too far from the security of the wall. "Niko? Niko, where are you? *Niko!*"

Footsteps approached from his left. The distinct sound of boots on concrete. Was Niko wearing boots? He couldn't remember. It was possible. He was wearing flashy white pants with a matching sport coat and miniature fedora; boots would have gone well with that outfit.

Through the blur and fog hazing over his eyes, he made out the shape of a figure approaching. The sound of boots on concrete came with the figure.

"What you want Niko for?" A female voice snapped at him. The voice seemed strangely familiar. "You look like shit, baby! You tweakin'?"

"Where's Niko?" Hanson asked. His breath and voice were labored, and he struggled to keep himself up against the wall.

"Niko got busted, like a half-hour ago. He ain't goin' get out till tomorrow. But, um, maybe I can satisfy your needs?"

Hanson placed the voice. It was the hooker he spoke with earlier. As his eyes focused, he saw she had unbuttoned her blouse and pulled out her left breast. He wasn't necessarily repulsed by her, but his stomach still hadn't settled. Almost without warning, he blew the remaining contents of his gut at her feet.

"Yeah, fuck you, dude! You couldn't handle these titties anyway," she said and spat at his feet as she stomped away.

Harsh reality set in. Niko was gone, and Hanson had no other hook up. He was in no condition to do business with someone new, even if he could find another connection. But his body screamed for more junk. It would not relent. The pain coursing through his system howled at him like a banshee in an Irish nightmare. And along with the pain came anxiety. He couldn't decide which was worse, the aching muscles or the panic.

He slithered along the brick wall back into the darkness of the alley until his legs finally gave out and he crashed face-first into a pile of wet garbage bags. The smell of rotten eggs, sour milk, and rancid vegetables combined and undulated into his nasal cavity. Hanson didn't have the strength or desire to pick himself up off of this mattress of offal. He finally resigned that this was to be his bed for the night.

When a person hits rock bottom, usually their emotions surface as sorrow or guilt. They know they are in a terrible situation and can't seem to help themselves. Self-pity and self-loathing set in. They understand that this is not how a human being should to live, but they feel as though they deserve nothing better. Hanson Parker was different. To him, lying face down in a pile of rotten garbage was just par for the course. He didn't carry guilt, because he had no feelings or empathy for anyone but himself. He did only what he wanted, regardless of the consequences. And the only thing he cared to do was get high.

Were his parents to blame? Who knows? He'd spit in the face of all the love they tried to give him while he was flopping out of high school. They tried the best they could, but he would not accept them, no matter what. Tough love, soft love, the church… it all went in one ear and out the other. He didn't care who loved him. Love didn't matter. And not that he came from a dysfunctional family; his parents did everything possible to make him feel the love they had for him. Nothing at all mattered. *I don't know! I don't care! Leave me alone!*

"Are you here?" A voice spoke close to his ear. He felt no breath from the voice, but it sounded like it was only an inch away from his head.

Hanson's face had made a comfortable crevice in the black plastic garbage bag. He had no desire to move. "Go away," he said, his statement muffled into the bag.

"You require a repose. Perhaps I can be of service?" The voice was even closer now, almost as if it were right in front of his face, coming from inside of the bag. Its tone was light and confident with a slightly nondescript foreign accent.

Hanson gathered what little strength he could muster and pulled his face up. He'd expected to see someone squatting down in front of him. No one was there.

Instead of collapsing back into his bed of refuse, Hanson pulled himself up to a seated position, using the cold brick wall as a backrest. He thought for sure he had heard someone talking to him a moment ago. He sat still with his eyes open and surveyed the alley; the place wet and stinking. He noticed a back door to a Chinese restaurant across from where he sat, a trash dumpster stationed to the left of the doorway. This made sense now. Someone came out of the restaurant to empty trash into the dumpster, saw him lying in the garbage across the alley, and said something in his ear. They must have gone back inside before he could pull his face out of the bag.

He glanced back down at his trash bag pillow. It looked remarkably comfortable. *Fuck it*, he thought and collapsed back into the black plastic.

"That is no place for a gentleman to lie," the voice spoke.

Hanson stopped himself from falling back into the bag. There was still no one around that he could see, and the voice was so close. "Who's there? Where are you?"

"I'm with you," it said. "I'm here for you. I care about you."

"You ca…" *You care about me?*

"Yes, I care about you. Very much." The voice sounded reassuring, confident. It seemed to have its shit together and affairs in order. But where was it coming from?

Hanson tried to pull himself up and failed miserably. He hadn't eaten in several days, and the only hydration he'd given himself was the oily water he'd unknowingly sucked out of an alley pothole earlier. His body was in a terrible state of malnourishment and dehydration. Yet, it didn't matter. If he had his choice right now of a healthy gourmet dinner and freshwater or a cheap ten dollar shot of heroin, he'd choose the heroin every time.

"Unless you've got some dope, I don't give a fuck how much you care about me," Hanson said, then laughed, realizing that he was talking to the air.

Laughter came from behind him, which was impossible. The only thing behind him was a brick wall. "I can provide you with much more than any drug can, young sir. What I can give you is bliss, in its purest form."

"Are you some bible thumper trying to sell me on Jesu—"

"Ah, ah, ah... We don't use the 'J' word," the voice gently scolded him. It sounded pleasant, yet serious.

Hanson paused. This wasn't an internal monolog coming from his own imagination. There was something authentic in the way the voice responded to him. This was a conversation, back and forth. An exchange between two people, one of which was not visible. He no longer felt it funny. "I'd like to be left alone now."

"Oh? But we've just become acquainted. We have so much more to exchange, to share, to do for one another."

"I don't do anything for anybody," Hanson snapped. "So, just get the fuck out of my face!"

"That won't do," the voice said. "I can tell you have a taste for stimulus. What if I told you I can provide you with a feeling which would invigorate you more than any man-made substance ever could?"

"Drugs?" Hanson asked.

"Better."

"If there's something better than drugs, I haven't seen it." Hanson winced as he tried to move. Pain shot through every cell of his body. He was crashing hard. He'd had rough crashes in the past, but something felt different about this one. The pain was intense enough that it scared him. "What's your name?" he eek'd out.

"My name is unusual; something your words cannot pronounce. I prefer to go by the epithet of, Zlo. A name given to me by a priest—bible thumper, as you say—whom I met some years ago. Funny fellow; died tragically. You haven't given me your name?"

I can't believe I'm going along with this, talking to thin air. "Hanson Parker."

"Ah, Mr. Parker. It is my humble pleasure to make your acquaintance."

"Where are you?"

"I'm right here with you," the voice said. It seemed pleasant, like it was actually enjoying the conversation.

"Why can't I see you?" Hanson asked.

"There will come a time when you will look upon my face, however, that time is quite a long way down the road. You and I have much to do together. Experiences to share. Marvellous adventures to undertake. So much fun; you'll see!"

"I don't know what that fucking Asian dude sold me, but this is a trip!" Pain ripped through Hanson's body as he spoke. He cried out.

"Indeed, it is. Now, let us talk about what I can do for you. What I can give you to enhance your life, ease your suffering, and leave all of your burdens right here in this despicable place."

Hanson trusted the voice in a strange sort of way. The drugs and dehydration could easily have turned his brain into mush, throwing away any form of judgment or reason, but he was feeling comfortable with it. The voice actually seemed to care about him. At this point in his life, face down in an alley, suffering from horrific withdrawal, what harm could it do to go along with a pleasant voice that comes out of nowhere? He couldn't do much worse at the moment.

"Fine. What do you want to do for me?"

"I want to give you everything you've ever desired and more than you've ever imagined." The voice had become soothing and beautiful, as if it were singing as it spoke; perfect in pitch and harmony.

"Sure, great. Give it to me."

"You want this?"

"Yeah."

"You need this?"

"I guess."

"You desire this?" The voice now rose as if a choir sang behind it. The sound was hypnotic.

"Yes! Give it to me!" Hanson actually begged. "I want it! Now!" He couldn't believe it, but he was being uplifted by its sound. His heart filled with joy. He was about to receive a reward, and he could feel the honesty in the vibrations coming from the music the voice spilled out. Emotions flowed through him he'd never felt before. In some strange way, it felt like love.

Silence.

"Hello?" Hanson called out after a few quiet moments.

No reply.

"Don't do this to me! You said you were going to help me." Desperation set in. "Where are you, fucker?" Hanson cried. It had abandoned him. The thing that came to him from out of nowhere, promising him everything he could ever desire and more, had vanished into the thin air it spoke from. Pain coursed through every fiber of his tissue, both physically and emotionally.

"I am here," the voice spoke up from behind him. "I'll always be here for you if you'll let me."

Relief coursed through Hanson's veins like fresh spring water. It *was* here. It hadn't abandoned him. He felt the same insatiable hunger to have the voice with him as he felt for the drugs he'd loved so much. Joy spilled out of his mouth. "You didn't leave me!"

"I will never leave you if you make me a part of you."

Hanson internalized what the voice had just said. He imagined what it would be like to have the voice with him at all times. It soothed him. It cared for him in a way he'd never felt before. It understood him and did not judge him. The voice spoke to him from a place of understanding and compassion. And it was so beautiful! That singing. The choir that had accompanied it as it rose in excitement. What would it be like to have that in his life? It also seemed to know things. It sounded intelligent and worldly. He could talk to it, and it would converse with him and care about what he had to say. He hadn't spoken to anyone except drug dealers for as long as he could remember, and those exchanges were nothing but arguments and haggling. No one ever wanted to hear about his thoughts or feelings. But here was something that cared. So what if the thing didn't appear physically, it was here, and he could *feel* it. He thought of the few brief moments when he believed the voice had abandoned him. He cried.

"Yes," Hanson called out. "Become part of me!"

"Do you freely allow me into your life?"

"Yes!" Hanson did not hesitate.

"Do you allow me into your mind, body, and soul?"

"Yes, I do!"

"Say it," the voice gently commanded. "Say my name and welcome me."

"Zlo, I freely welcome you into my mind, body, and soul," Hanson shouted and fell back into the pile of trash bags. His head was spinning out of control, but not in a bad way. He felt like he was on a wild amusement park ride, out of control and enjoying the butterflies the ride created in his stomach. Warmth blanketed him like sunshine in mid-spring. He felt nourished and healthy and vibrant. He wanted to leap to his feet and run through the world, spinning and jumping and singing like a lunatic. There was beauty in everything, even the trash bags and dumpsters littering the alley. He loved it all. No drug in the world had ever made him feel this elation.

Suddenly, the world went black.

"Time to rise, Mr. Parker," Zlo said. This time his voice wasn't coming from behind, in front, or in his ear. Now the voice was in him. In his head. In his body, vibrating throughout his body as it spoke.

"Where am I?" Hanson asked.

"You're in an alleyway, covered in refuse."

Hanson giggled as the vibration of Zlo's voice tickled him from inside. "How long have I been here?"

"By your calendar, three days. That's all I can give you."

"Are you telling me I just rode that buzz for three days?" Hanson asked.

"You're not understanding our arrangement properly. I'll refresh. You enjoy stimulation and have ruined yourself in constant pursuit of it. I can provide you with stimulation of a quality which humanity cannot manufacture. I just gave you a dose of said stimulation. That's the most your body can handle in this form, your human form. If I were to give you more, you would perish, and I need you... alive. We're going to do great things together. Wonderful things which will fulfill both of us. Each time you give me what I require, I shall reward you with the stimulation you so desire."

"What are you going to have me do?" Hanson asked. He didn't care, though, there was nothing he wouldn't do to have another taste of what Zlo had just given him.

"We're going to do great things which give us both the stimulation we desire. You'll see."

Thirty years later, Hanson Parker could no longer handle the misery. The things that creature made him do to receive that intense pleasure went far beyond the basic description of evil. And though he'd destroyed his conscience long before he'd met Zlo, some small part of it still somehow remained. It was time to return to the place where the depravity he shared with his inner daemon began.

"Ah, a familiar road we travel today, I see, Mr. Parker," Zlo's voice echoed its usual vibration through Hanson's system. He ignored it.

TWO

Rules were rules. The terms of their twisted arrangement were clear and to the point. If Hanson wanted his reward, all he had to do was provide the one thing which Zlo desired. Done at Hanson's leisure, whenever he was in desperate need, no rush or hurry. The ball in his court. And Zlo rarely poked at him about it or goaded him to action—though he advised at first to get things rolling. Ultimately, he didn't need to; Hanson's desire to feel that intense pleasure was always insatiable enough to spark him into action. It was more important to him than anything on earth. More important than humanity itself. More important than his soul. When his hunger for it arose to its boiling point, Hanson Parker would move mountains to get it. He hated himself for what he had become, but he would not stop as long as a fix like that was within his reach.

When self-loathing and guilt crept into his thoughts, Zlo would laugh at him and say something intelligently witty, yet disturbing and demoralizing. "Don't kid yourself, Hanson, you'll never be able to stop. You don't have the will or conviction to strive for decency. And if you ever confessed to what you have done, you'd spend the rest of your miserable existence in a cold cell, assaulted day after day by those who are just as deplorable as you."

"*You* made me do this! *You* made me a monster!"

"I made nothing. I did, however, choose you. You were the perfect traveling companion and still are in some respects. Although I would prefer it if you didn't whine so much, that tends to bore," Zlo said.

Hanson was not intelligent enough to make a compelling or articulate argument. Though it wouldn't have mattered, he knew Zlo wasn't going anywhere; that was made quite clear. Hanson had asked him to leave on several occasions, and Zlo would kindly remind him—in his strangely stylish way—that their agreement was set in stone, bound until his last day above ground, until such time when he would be remanded to serve another master.

"I don't serve anyone!"

"You serve yourself and your wants and desires, don't you? In turn, you are serving me. And inadvertently, you are serving the one whom *I* serve. We can call it a Tree of Servitude." Zlo often laughed at his own wit, sending those twisted vibrations through Hanson's system.

"Who do you serve?" Hanson asked.

"Service is a virtue, as they say. We all serve another in some way, shape, or form. Have patients, Mr. Parker, in good time I shall introduce and present you to the one whom I serve. He'll enjoy you very much, I'm certain of that."

Most of the time, Hanson could ignore his traveling companion, until the hunger surfaced. He tried going back to street drugs as a substitute for Zlo's reward, but they were pointless and ineffective now. It was as if his body had become overly tolerant of the old stuff, knowing that the only high he could rely on anymore came from the thing existing within him. Zlo again would laugh.

Desire became hunger, hunger became blood lust, blood lust became action, action destroyed his soul.

As vicious cycle continued on, relentlessly, Hanson learned to justify his actions. *Everybody needs things, I just need something that destroys lives. So what! Fuck them!* And other days, he contemplated suicide. On those days, Zlo would allow just a hint of his reward, reminding Hanson that the only thing worth living for was indeed still available to him and was already within him. Beautiful and horrifying.

Something had changed in Hanson the night he invited Zlo into his life. An unusual physical transformation. He was no longer sickly. The agony that came along with being a junkie seemed to dissipate, like morning fog running from sunlight. He hadn't gained muscle or weight, just health. He became hydrated and nourished. "I feel better than I've felt in years!"

"I need to keep you around for as long as possible," Zlo replied.

"Are you doing something inside of me?"

"I am."

Hanson didn't care what was happening to his body, he felt great, and that's all that mattered. If he ate a cheap fifty cent candy bar, it nourished him as if he had just finished a marvelous dinner, full of his most favorite foods, and beverages. The smallest amount of nutrition turned into an incredibly fulfilling meal. He knew it was artificial; Zlo had done something inside of him to allow his body to function at peak levels, but that was fine. He could now go through life eating only a candy bar and a soda here and there, and his body operated without a hitch.

After Hanson came out of that first three-day high, Zlo instructed him to take the remaining $67.50 he had from the stolen purses and purchase a Greyhound Bus ticket to Kernstown, VA. "It's time to begin our *Grand Adventure*, Mr. Parker. We're going to have such fun. You'll see."

Hanson did as instructed without question. Whatever this *Grand Adventure* entailed that Zlo seemed so excited about didn't matter. He'd finally found the rush he had searched for all these years. No drug had ever provided him with the sensations he received from Zlo's reward. Three days of indescribable bliss! There was no price he wouldn't pay for it. No task he would refuse. No mountain he wouldn't climb. No life he wouldn't destroy. All that mattered now was his new god.

THREE

The bus arrived in Kernstown on a rainy Saturday afternoon, a small, out of the way place, just south of Winchester, Virginia. Hanson wore only the white t-shirt and Levis which he'd had on for longer than his memory would allow. Repulsed by his smell, the other passengers on the bus sat as far from him as possible. The stench of rotten garbage and body odor had clung to him like a deer tick, filling the entire cab and causing most of the passengers to cover their noses in tissues or inside of their clothing. There was a collective sigh of relief when the door finally swung open, and Hanson stepped off. He turned and shook two middle fingers at the passengers as he looked back at the bus. The driver quickly closed the door and sped away.

The rain was not coming down hard, but steady. Hanson stood outside of a 7-Eleven where the bus had dropped him, which appeared to be the center of town. A church across the street, a few houses in each direction, a mill of some sort in the distance behind the church, this convenience store, and a small strip mall with four or five stores. That was it. He did not know why he was here, or if there was even a plan at all. Zlo hadn't said a word during the trip, and he didn't seem to have anything to say now.

Hanson stood under the awning of the store but did not go inside. He continued to wait for instructions. Still no word from his traveling companion. *Okay,* he said to himself. *What now?*

No reply.

"*Zlo!*" He whispered.

Silence.

He became impatient. Hanson didn't do well in small towns. In a city with a large population, most people didn't think twice about seeing a transient junkie wandering the streets in filthy clothes and a ragged beard, but in small-town America, he stood out like a whore in church. Soon people would stare as they walked by into the store. They would ask the clerk questions: *"Who is* that*? Where did* he *come from? How long has* he *been standing there?"* It would only be a matter of moments before a local cop would cruise into the parking lot. He'd walk past, sizing Hanson up, then go inside to question the clerk about the unknown visitor out front. Next would be the harassment, the shakedown, possibly a night in a jail cell.

"What the fuck, Zlo? Where are you?"

And now he was talking to himself. A nonchalant glance over his shoulder into the store window revealed that the clerk was indeed leaning over the counter, looking at him. A customer had joined the staring party as well. *I don't know officer, he must have got off of that Greyhound a little while ago. But yeah, he's out there talking to himself. Looks like he's upset. We're all pretty nervous right now.*

Shit!

"You seem out of sorts, Hanson." The voice along with its vibration resonated through Hanson's body. "Is something amiss?"

"Amiss?" Hanson spoke aloud. "Yes, *you're* a miss! What the fuck am I doing here? I thought you dumped me off out here and split."

Zlo laughed, and Hanson's body shook from the vibrations. "Oh, I won't be *splitting,* as you say, anytime soon. We have so much to do. So much to share. So much to enjoy!"

"Yeah, that sounds great and everything, but I'm sticking out like a sore thumb in this shit splat town."

"Understood," Zlo said. "Follow my instructions and our operation will be up and running post-haste. Do you see that sign to your right that says, 'Civil War Marker, SR 706'?"

Hanson looked around, and his eyes fixed on a brown rectangular sign about a hundred yards from where he stood. "Yeah, I see it."

"Good. Now walk over there, turn right and follow that road to the end."

"How far?"

There was no reply.

Hanson sighed deeply, then set out to follow Zlo's instructions. The rain had picked up and as he continued to walk he became cold. Though it was the middle of July, the droplets pelting his face and body felt as though they could turn to ice at any moment. For an instant, he felt as if something was physically trying to stop him, like a force working against him to knock him off of this task his traveling companion had appointed to him. The wind pushed against him from the front. He squinted as cold rain hit his eyes and stung him deeply. What was he doing out here in the middle of nowhere? Was he actually listening to a disembodied voice that sent him on a wild goose chase? Had all these years of drug abuse led him to schizophrenia? Something in his heart lobbied for him to turn around and call this whole thing off. This trip was ridiculous! *Fuck this scavenger hunt bullshit.* "I'm done," Hanson said aloud, and he turned back toward the 7-Eleven.

"You most certainly are not," the voice resonated through his body, causing his head to throb. "You are done only when I say you are done!"

The shock to Hanson's system scared him and caused his legs to weaken. He lost his balance and dropped down to one knee. "I don't want to do this," he cried.

"Get to your feet and stop acting like a child!" Zlo scolded. "We are amid an important effort, one you'll never comprehend. And, your participation will be marked on your soul for all of eternity."

Suddenly, Hanson felt warm and strong and happy. Something was happening, and it was incredible. He wanted to run and jump and skip and sing. It was glorious. He was being rewarded. And then it was gone.

"Remember that?" Zlo said.

"Please, don't let it stop," Hanson begged. "Please give me more! I need it!"

"Yes, I imagine you do. And as you do what I need, I shall give the reward you need. Now, Mr. Parker, please proceed to the end of this road and await further instruction."

FOUR

Hanson had walked a little over a mile before the road ended in a circular cul-de-sac. Ahead of him was a wide-open field surrounded by thick trees and underbrush. The remnants of a crumbling stone wall, which looked like it had been erected centuries ago by hard labor, lay embedded to the earth and stretched on acre after acre around the field's perimeter. Its purpose merely ceremonial these days as its remaining rocks stood only a few feet high—almost nonexistent in some places. An iron sign, painted white with black letters and maintained by the National Register of Historic Places, informed one that the Battle of Kernstown had taken place on this very spot. Apparently, from the sign's sacred text, Stonewall Jackson did not have a particularly good afternoon on this date of March 23rd, 1862. Far across the field in the distance, Hanson could see a large barn accompanied by a house and several smaller outbuildings. Immediately to his left in the cul-de-sac, positioned at a slight angle, resided a small church and cemetery, encircled by a decorative rusted iron fence which had been painted and repainted countless times. There were no cars in the church parking lot. As far as Hanson could tell, no one knew he was standing out here in the middle of the day…in the middle of July…in the middle of the rain…in the middle of nowhere.

There were two semi-wet cigarettes left in the pack he'd carried with him since Baltimore. Now seemed like as good a time as any to catch a smoke. He spotted a small pavilion with four or five picnic tables under it next to the church, a nice dry spot for a break.

"Where are you going?"

He had only taken three steps toward the church before Zlo spoke up. His voice sounded urgent and disapproving. The vibration resonated with a different feeling throughout Hanson's body than it had before.

"I'm going to get out of this damn rain and have a cigarette," Hanson replied.

"Not there, you're not!" Zlo's voice demanded.

"Well, I can't smoke it here; it's raining!" Hanson laughed at the thought of himself standing in the rain, arguing with thin air.

"Then you'll not smoke it at all!"

Hanson paused for a moment as the rain intensified. A tinge of anger set in. He'd never let anyone tell him what to do and wasn't about to change policy now. *Go fuck yourself,* he thought, and began walking toward the church pavilion.

Suddenly, a shock wave hit his system from the inside, and his knees buckled, sending him to the ground face first. He hit the pavement hard and lay in a shallow puddle of water—a much cleaner puddle than the one from the alley in Baltimore. His body trembled with aftershocks and muscle aches.

"You will not proceed one step further in that direction!" The voice and vibrations yelled out. The sound terrified him. He'd had a few back and forth's with Zlo throughout their short acquaintanceship, but never an exchange as intense as this.

"Okay," Hanson said as he slowly got to his hands and knees. "I guess I won't smoke it."

The tremors subsided within a few seconds, and Hanson was able to get to his feet. He felt genuine concern. Was Zlo in control? Had he invited something into himself that could force him to do things? It certainly *stopped* him from doing something. Did that mean it had physical control over him?

"Do you see that house and barn across the field?" Zlo spoke up.

Hanson walked over to the low stone wall and surveyed the field. His legs were still weak from the shock treatment Zlo had just dealt him, but he was getting his sea legs back. At the other end of the open expanse, he saw a large red barn and an eighteenth-century brick farmhouse next to it. "I see it."

"Walk in that direction, but be discrete. Stay out of sight in the woods along the edge of the field."

Hanson did as instructed with little reluctance; not wanting to have another altercation with his internal associate, he felt it best to comply without argument. He stepped over the stone wall and headed for the tree line to the right of the field. Creeping around in the middle of a field in an unfamiliar place made him feel vulnerable, but Zlo seemed to have a plan. And after the incident at the church, he thought it best to do as he was told.

The tall grass at the edge of the field was soaking wet. Hanson's feet sloshed in pockets of water that had collected in random pools about the area. It didn't matter at this point; the rain had already soaked him to the bone. He found little relief from the rain once he entered the woods as rainwater had collected on the canopy of leaves overhead and spilled larger droplets down onto him. The dampness was part of him now and would be for the foreseeable future.

The voice had not spoken to him during his trek through the woods. Hanson had asked a few simple questions but knew even before he spoke them aloud that they wouldn't receive an answer. Zlo seemed to keep things close to the chest now, giving Hanson only bits and pieces as they traveled along. He felt there was no other choice but to follow. In the past, however, Hanson never did what he was told. In fact, he strove to do the exact opposite, even if he knew the opposite was the wrong choice. It was authority he detested. He refused to accommodate anyone for any reason. So why did he now find himself in the middle of a soaking wet field in a place he'd never dream of visiting? The answer was simple: He'd received a new sensation that no drug on earth could provide. Feelings he would do anything—absolutely anything—to feel again. Zlo had given him a drink from the well, and it restored him, replenished him, and revived him. There was nothing he wouldn't do for his new drug. He knew as he trekked farther through these soaking wet trees and bushes that it was peanuts compared to the deserts he would cross. If this is what Zlo had asked of him, so be it. He was pleased to serve with honor.

The trees opened up onto the backside of the farm. From Hanson's vantage point, concealed behind an ash tree, he could see that the lights were on in the farmhouse and there were two vehicles parked around back, an older pickup truck and a car. After standing still and observing for several minutes, he felt safe in assuming that no one was walking around the barnyard or outbuildings, though he could not see directly into the barn. "What now?"

Zlo did not answer.

"Hey," Hanson whispered. "I'm at the farm. What now?"

Still no answer.

This fucker pulls me out here in the middle of nowhere in the rain—

"Stop whining," Zlo spoke up.

"Well, I'm at the freaking farm," Hanson said.

"I'm well aware of that, Mr. Parker," Zlo said. "Now, stay here, out of sight, and wait for nightfall."

The rain had soaked him through and through, and now as evening approached, he shivered. Not as much as when he'd had withdrawals from heroin, but still enough to remind him of those days. Something in him felt as if those good old days might be over. Hanson had resolved to himself that being a junkie was to be his station in life. Nothing gave him the pleasure or satisfaction that drugs did. They were his sustenance, his nourishment, his salvation. But now a new savior had emerged. A friend, a lover... a god. The days of hustling for a hit of junk, then waking up face down in a pile of shit seemed distant to him now. All of it replaced by a new friend who cared enough to provide him with something he needed and desired. He couldn't remember ever thinking of someone as a friend. But Zlo was unique. He cared about Hanson. In some strange way, maybe they were friends. Maybe Hanson had lost his mind.

FIVE

Hanson stood shivering in the cold, still perched in his hiding spot behind a large ash tree on the edge of the wood line. It had been well over six hours, and now the sun had finally gone down. He stood in darkness. Earlier in the day, he'd witnessed a few children playing on the back porch, a boy and a girl. Neither looked to be older than ten. An attractive, middle-aged woman came out of the house at one point to call them in for supper. That's about the same time a middle-aged man and a teenaged boy came out of the barn and went into the house. None of them had come back outside since.

He continued to wait patiently. Zlo was here; he could feel it. Especially around the time when the kids were playing on the back porch. He could sense Zlo watching with him.

"Are you ready to begin, Mr. Parker?" The voice spoke up, startling Hanson.

"Sure, I guess."

"Oh, come now. Have a touch of conviction. Excitement!" Zlo said. "We're about to begin our *Grand Adventure*."

"Yeah, *Grand Adventure*. Ok."

"Good. Now, you will need to procure a few items from this place. I'm certain the items will be among the contents of these various buildings. You will need a shovel, a pickaxe, and lantern. Use the utmost discretion."

"Discretion?"

"Don't make noise. Don't get caught."

"Oh," Hanson said.

This wouldn't be a difficult task. Through all the years of being a junkie, Hanson became quite good at stealing to fund his habit. He'd made several relationships with underhanded pawnshop owners who would give him pennies on the dollar for just about anything he could steal out of someone's house, car, or backyard shed. A sleazy shop owner in Hartford once gave him

221

$11.50 for a gas weed trimmer. The thing was brand new and probably worth at least $200, but money was money; it all went for the same purpose.

He felt little apprehension about sneaking into the big red barn, or any of the other small buildings on the property. There would be a million places to hide if anyone came out of the house, and Hanson knew he could slither his skinny ass into almost any crack or crevasse.

The barn looked like the best place to check first. A shovel, a pickaxe, and a lantern. What barn wouldn't contain those things?

Hanson slowly skulked across the edge of the barnyard with a slippery grace that would have made the Grinch proud. Though the rain had turned the ground into thick mud, he could still traverse the area with little effort. For a few harrowing moments, he had to cross the space in front of the barn facing the house which was lit by two overhead floodlights hanging over a large sliding barn door. He accomplished this quickly and headed around to the other side of the structure which faced away from the house. The spot was well out of view and the best way to enter the barn unnoticed. Plus, the door was unlocked and already open a crack. Perfect... almost.

A strange noise came from inside, one Hanson thought he may have recognized from movies and TV, but not something he had never had actual contact with. He slowly opened the door and peaked in. The room was almost entirely dark. The only things visible were enormous shadows of shapes his mind could not perceive. He waited for several moments and listened for the noise to occur again. It did not. The darkness held to its silence.

After a moment of contemplation, he slid into the barn and quietly closed the door behind him. He couldn't see a thing. He reached out his hands to feel around, then realized there would be a lot to knock over in a place like this. He'd have to have light. Luckily, the cheap disposable, *Kum & Go!* lighter he'd been carrying around with the smashed pack of wet cigarettes was still in his front pocket. *I'm as prepared as a Boy Scout!* He boasted as he sparked the flint wheel with his thumb. It took four tries before the lighter finally produced a flame. The moment it did, Hanson erupted in terror as he was now face to face with a monster.

The beast was enormous and inches from his face. It stood twice his size, and its length seemed to go on forever into the darkness. Hanson yelled out in horror; the creature joined him with a shriek of its own. He lost his grip on the lighter as he fell backward and hit the ground. The room returned to darkness. Suddenly, the sound of more creatures erupted, and the entire barn was a now horrifying chorus of shrieks and whinnies. Hanson could feel the dirt floor rumble as the beasts jumped and kicked and lunged in a chaotic dance. He scurried across the ground as quickly as he could on his hands and knees and found himself in a small corner. He could feel and smell what must have been hay or straw all around him. Hanson gathered as much as he could, pulled it over his body, and lay still and cowering in the fetal position.

Without warning, harsh illumination filled the barn with a powerful glow from overhead lights, which someone must have switched on manually. Hanson scurried to cover himself with more hay as he saw how much of his body was exposed. He did the best he could with what was available but wasn't confident that it was enough. From what he could see, he realized he had crawled into some kind of stall with wooden slatted walls on each side and a sliding wooden gate that was open. He also saw the beast in full view. Majestic to some, frightening to others; the nightmare in the darkness was merely a horse. And a big fucker at that! There were a lot of other horses in the barn as well, but they were all locked in individual stalls.

"How did you get out, girl," a youthful voice asked. "I thought I put you up for the night. Come on."

Looking under the stall, Hanson could see blue jeans tucked into oversized green rubber boots heading his way. He slowed his breath the best he could, even though he was terribly nervous. It was the teenaged kid he'd seen earlier in the afternoon. He was leading the horse in Hanson's direction. *Out of all the places in this big ass barn, he's gonna put that thing in here!*

The kid entered the stall first, and the horse obediently followed. Hanson stared up at him through his improvised camouflage suit of straw and hay. The kid's foot was mere inches away from touching Hanson's knee.

"He must not discover you," Zlo's voice spoke up, startling Hanson as usual with its vibration. "You will do what is necessary to keep this situation from spreading outside of the building."

There was a foreboding sternness in Zlo's tone, and Hanson knew right away what was being implied. Zlo expected him to take out the kid. But he had no weapons. He'd have to jump him by surprise and choke him or brutally beat him unconscious... or worse.

"You must not fail here, Mr. Parker. We are merely at the precipice of our adventure. Much is at stake. You *will* do what is necessary!"

Hanson suddenly felt a touch of euphoria rush through his body, then it dissipated in an instant. Zlo had reminded him of what awaited if he followed instructions. It worked. Now he wanted to crush this kid. Jump him from behind, wrestle him to the ground and choke the life out of his smug, shit-eating little face! Fuck this little prick and this horse and this whole farm. He'd kill every one of them with pride if it meant getting another reward. A warm vibration came from within his core and shot through his entire body as he could feel Zlo laughing.

The kid stood at the other side of the stall, filling a water bucket, his back turned to Hanson. The horse seemed focused on what the kid was doing. This was the moment. A blood lust arose in Hanson that he'd never felt before. It was primal. Carnal. His prey was in sight and utterly unaware that it was about to get ripped to shreds by a fierce predator. His mouth watered and muscles flexed. Adrenaline pulsed out of Hanson's heart with every beat, pumping him full of energy and ferocity. He poised, prepared to spring. He would destroy this boy ten times over. He wanted to pound his face until every ounce of strength left his body. There would be so much blood and—

"Everything ok out here, son?" A man's voice called out. He approached the stall and joined the boy at the gate.

"Rose got out of her stall," the boy said. "I guess I didn't lock it upright. Sorry, dad."

"No problem," the man said as he rustled the boy's cap. "Come on, mom's got dessert ready." They closed the stall and left the barn.

The lights went out, and Hanson sat in the darkness under a pile of hay with the giant horse a few feet away. He wanted that kid dead. He could taste it. Zlo had told him what he needed to do and showed him the reward that awaited him if he completed the task. Now the opportunity no longer existed. *That fucking kid has my Fix!* No matter. Soon the family would be asleep, and Hanson could take care of business then. He'd take care of all of them. Zlo would be so proud that he'd have to reward him, wouldn't he?

"It's time to go now, Mr. Parker," Zlo spoke up. "We have a schedule to keep."

"What about the kid? I thought you wanted me to…"

"I wanted you to stay concealed, which you did. The boy is of no consequence now." Zlo laughed again. "You're brought to life, aren't you? Genuine life: *Power*. You felt it and relished it. Quite impressive. Quite impressive indeed."

"Can I have some more of the…" Hanson asked like a child.

"Once we get our operation up and running, you may have it any time you please. I'm preparing the way for you so you can indulge as much as you wish."

Hanson smiled and felt alive. If he could have this any time he wanted it, life would finally have a purpose. He would finally have a reason to exist.

SIX

Hanson stumbled across the dark wet field, heading back toward the woods where he'd spent most of the day. He carried with him all the items that Zlo had instructed him to find. Luckily, the farmer had fully stocked the barn with tools and equipment, and he'd had no problem locating a long-handled spade shovel, a heavy pickaxe, and two kerosene lanterns. The thing that took him the longest to retrieve in the darkness was the Kum & Go lighter he had dropped when first spooked by the horse. The lighter would be his only way of firing up the lanterns if that's what Zlo had in mind for him to do with them. Zlo had given no further instructions, only to find the items and get back into the woods.

He reached the tree line and made his way far enough into the thicket to feel safe and out of sight. By now it was probably close to midnight, and he was in the woods in the middle of nowhere, but he still felt as though someone could discover him at any moment. Years of living in the shadows of society had induced paranoia in Hanson's soul which grew more intense with each passing day.

He dropped the items on the ground and found a semi-dry spot under a pine tree. Reaching into the front pocket of his Levis, he found gold: the crumpled pack of Camel cigarettes he'd been thinking about all afternoon. There were two left. One was soaked and unusable, but the other—though bent and wrinkled—was miraculously dry enough to smoke. Hanson lit the lung dart, inhaled Turkish tobacco flavor deep into his chest, and smiled like a Cheshire cat. A moment of peace. A reward for a job well done. Another addiction to add to his list of habits. He hadn't heard from Zlo since leaving the barn and hoped he wouldn't, at least for a few more minutes. This smoke break was too enjoyable to disrupt. He wanted it to go on for hours.

It seemed like only a few seconds had passed before the

tobacco had burned down to the filter. Hanson sucked it until the last ground leaf had no more carbon to give.

"Enjoying the moment?" Zlo said.

Hanson smiled. The cigarette was gone, and the moment was over. And it was a moment which he had indeed enjoyed. "What now?"

"Pick up the equipment and head East, toward that fallen tree."

Hanson looked around and saw the tree, about a hundred yards deeper into the forest. "We're going further into the woods?"

"Much further, Mr. Parker. Continue on; you'll know when to stop," Zlo said.

"How will I know?"

Zlo didn't answer.

An hour later, Hanson was still walking through the rain-soaked, pitch dark forest with no idea where he was heading or for what purpose. The gear had become burdensome. He was tired of being wet. Zlo had given him only tiny bits of information at a time, and the info he received left him with only more questions. He couldn't help but doubt this whole *Grand Adventure* thing, as his companion liked to call it. There didn't seem to be a rhyme or reason for any of it.

But there was the reward. It existed; that he could not deny. He'd received one full dose when he first accepted Zlo and only a few tiny jolts of it since, but he was definitely sure of its existence. And if Zlo was telling him the truth, once he completed this task, he'd be able to enjoy it anytime he wanted. The hope of this reward was all he needed to carry on. It was out there waiting for him, and he was coming for it.

Out of the darkness, Hanson suddenly came upon a large monolithic structure, embedded within the weeds and underbrush of the thicket. Years of neglect and decay had overtaken the building, but somehow it remained solid. A two-story stone house, covered in a canopy of vines and forest debris. It looked as if no one had entered this place in a hundred years or more.

There were no doors or windows, only empty sockets that stared at Hanson like the black eyes of a fleshless skull.

He stood perfectly still, afraid to make a move. As the wind picked up, it seemed to breathe life into the place, transforming it from an abandoned building into a living, breathing creature, right before his eyes. It was aware of Hanson's fear and beckoned him to come inside. It wanted him. What lay beyond the open door was the stuff of nightmares. Hanson took a step backward, then another, and another.

"Are you intimidated, Mr. Parker?" Zlo said.

"Ya think?" Hanson yelled. "What the fuck am I doing out here?"

"This building is of no consequence to us. What we're here for is behind the structure. You don't have to go inside if you prefer not to."

"Yeah, I prefer not to."

He headed around to the back, which made him feel even more uneasy than he'd felt at the front side. "I can't see shit. Can I light one of these lanterns?"

"You could have done that without my permission," Zlo said.

Could have used that info an hour ago! Whatever!

Hanson got one lantern going and adjusted the flame to give as much light as possible. The flickering glow cast shadows off of everything in the area, making them dance and dart in all directions. He made the analogy that he was standing in the heart of a living ghost story, a gothic horror tale brought to life. He stood at the entrance to the old haunted house in the middle of the woods, waiting for whatever terror which lurked inside to pull him into the darkness and devour him whole. Not to mention that he'd been talking with a disembodied voice for the last few days who now lived inside of him. He waited to hear the howl of a wolf in the distance. The howl never came.

"To your left, by the large oak tree, is an overgrowth of brush. Begin by clearing it away. You'll know when to stop."

"Are you serious?" Hanson yelled. "I'm out here in the pouring rain at all hours of the night next to the creepiest house on earth, and you want me to do yard work?"

Silence.

"Know what? Fuck it! I'll do it. Got nothing else to do or lose tonight. Why not just clear out bushes? I'll plant a *goddamn* garden next and grow fucking carrots while I'm at it!"

Hanson lit the other lantern and spaced the two apart to fill the area with light. He began working on the bushes, which were thorny and rough. He'd wished he would have grabbed that pair of old leather work gloves he'd seen back in the barn next to the tools. *Wish in one hand...*

He got to work, and to his pleasant surprise, the bushes pulled out of the ground easily. The constant rain had made the ground soft and very easy to workaround. His task might not be as difficult as he had first imagined—though the task still made no sense at all.

It took about thirty minutes of work before Hanson realized what the bushes were covering. He couldn't decide if he was more afraid at the sight of the abandoned house, or what he was staring into the face of right now. His mouth hung open, and he couldn't catch his breath. His ghost story was no longer just a story, it had manifested into reality, and he stood directly at the center.

"Ah, you're getting closer, I see," Zlo said. "Look for the one that has Alice Carter carved into the face."

"These are..." Hanson had a hard time speaking. Fear had him in its frigid, icy grip and squeezed at him relentlessly.

"These are what, Mr. Parker?"

The word lodged in his throat and seemed to stick there until he finally pushed it out with a forced breath. "*Graves!*"

"You're quite astute," Zlo said. "Now, find the one with the name, Alice Carter."

Hanson remained frozen in place, crippled by fear and incapable of movement. The events of the last few days had finally sunk in. He had let something into his body, and it was calling the shots, making him do things he'd never imagined. He'd been a criminal for as long as he could remember, but he never took a life, not even the life of an animal. Earlier tonight, however, he almost killed a teenaged boy. He was even furious when the opportunity was taken away from him. The fear he felt now not only came from the idea of standing in a graveyard in the middle of the woods on a rainy night, but from the fact that this thing inside of him was calling the shots. What in the world could it make him do next?

And just like that, all fear had disappeared. Vanquished. Expelled and replaced by euphoria, which lasted for a mere second, then disappeared as well; another hint of reward released into his system to set him back on track. It worked as always, and Hanson quickly began looking for the grave of Alice Carter without reservation.

The cemetery was small, with only fifteen headstones surrounded by a two-foot-high, rusted iron fence. The faces of the grave markers were barely legible because of years of weather, but Hanson could make out that all the last names were Carter. A family plot. The oldest was Odessa Carter, born 1757, died 1831. Odessa must have been the patriarch who started the Carter family. The rest of the inhabitants were all born and died in the mid-1800s. Alice Carter's grave was in the middle row, right corner. It read: Beloved daughter of William and Audrey Carter, taken too soon, born 1848, died 1859. Her headstone was slightly smaller than the others.

Hanson cleared away all the brush and debris, fully exposing the marker and a ten-foot area around it. Zlo hadn't said it, but Hanson knew what he was here to do. One does not venture into a graveyard in the middle of the night with a shovel, a pickaxe, and a lantern to sit around and drink a few beers. He was here to dig.

To most, a situation like this would seem unimaginable at the very least—repulsive, more likely. Digging into a grave that was over one hundred and fifty years old stepped so far outside of the realm of decorum, it would no longer be visible on the spectrum of human decency. But Hanson had recently entered a new phase of his life. An awakening. True, he had done things in the past which would disgust a high percentage of the population, but now his depravity had evolved. The beacon of light ahead of him, given off by the beautiful glow of a new god, opened his heart to a world of disgusting possibilities. If Zlo told him to dig up this girl, pull her skeleton out of the earth, and dance naked with it while singing the Scandinavian National Anthem at the top of his lungs, he would do it with honor. The reward was all that mattered now, not what he had to do to get it.

"You're coming into this nicely, Hanson," Zlo said. "We are merely scratching at the surface of our *Grand Adventure*, and I can feel your ambition rising. There is so much in store. Such fun!"

"I assume you want me to dig up Alice Carter?"

"Indeed," Zlo said. "Miss Carter won't mind.".

The wind and rain had intensified and relentlessly pounded at Hanson as he dug shovel after shovel of earth—mud—out of the ground. Water poured into the hole, creating a slop filled mess that looked worse than any hog pen in rural America. As he lifted each load full of soaking wet dirt out of the grave, it felt as though a force pulled at the underside of the shovel plate, making it ten times heavier than it actually was. He struggled, aching and groaning with each clump of extracted muck.

His body urged him to stop. His heart pounded in his chest just as hard and fast as any panic attack from withdrawals had ever given him. His breath could not catch up with the demand for oxygen that his muscles requested. He gasped. He felt faint. He shook uncontrollably. Yet he continued. He would not stop until he had completed the task and received his reward, or died.

Clunk!

That wasn't a rock, he thought. He'd hit something, something hollow. Alice Carter?

"Continue, Mr. Parker," Zlo spoke up.

Hanson scraped at the object in the ground with his shovel. As he suspected, it was rectangular shaped and made of wood. He stood on top of it after he'd cleared away all the dirt and mud, thinking about what came next. He'd have to open it. But what would be inside? Alice Carter, presumably, but what would be the condition of her body? Would there even be anything left of her after one hundred and fifty-some years? He hoped not.

He didn't wait for instruction. It was time to rip the bandage off and examine the fissure underneath. Hanson grabbed one lantern and brought it into the grave with him. He also brought down the pickaxe. With the lantern in place and pickaxe in hand, he prepared to smash open the lid and expose the contents.

"Getting ahead of yourself?" Zlo asked.

"I'm getting into the box."

"Don't destroy it!" Zlo Scolded. "This coffin has been of great service over a good many years, and I expect a good many more years to come. Be gentle."

Hanson controlled his urge to break the box open, instead opting to use the flat part of the pickaxe to pry underneath the lid. It slid under with relative ease, and he could feel the top breaking free. He'd noticed several marks on the cover in various areas, which looked as though they were made at different time periods. He felt as though he hadn't been the first person to exhume Alice Carter from her final resting place.

Pausing for a moment and taking several deep breaths, Hanson mentally prepared himself for the opening. He imagined there would be an initial gaseous puff of dust, followed by a terrible sight. Alice would be nothing but bones and hair by now. She'd look up at him from the hollow sockets of her skull and grin with the eternal smile of a skinless face. *Getting my fix is definitely worth it, but if this thing reaches up and grabs me by the balls, I'm done!*

What Hanson had expected and what he'd found were farther apart than his imagination could have predicted. Alice didn't look at him. Alice didn't smile. Alice didn't reach up and grab him by the sack… Alice did nothing, because Alice wasn't there. Neither was anyone else.

It took him a moment to grasp the reality of the scene. He'd over-prepared himself for what he was certain was waiting for him under the old wooden lid, almost to the point of excitement.

He was both relieved, and a bit let down when the top came off, and the lantern light cast its glow into the box.

No body. No grotesque figure that would burn its image into his memory for the rest of his days. No eleven-year-old girl who had died in 1859. But also not an empty box.

Hanson grabbed the lantern and carefully climbed inside the coffin. Replaced by eager curiosity, his fears and repulsions about digging up an old grave on a night straight out of a horror movie no longer existed. The mystery had bealed itself into a head. He had to know—to understand—what all this was about, and what these things were that he was looking at instead of the body which he imagined would be here.

More boxes.

In the center of the coffin, neatly stacked in two rows, were ten smaller shoebox-sized boxes. Shining the lantern closer to the contents, he realized they were old wooden cigar boxes. Hanson recognized them right away. His grandfather had had a collection of these same types of boxes from all over the world, which he was very proud of. That is until the day Hanson began stealing and pawning them to buy heroin. At first, it seemed like only a few were missing or misplaced, then grandpa had to face the harsh reality that his grandson was stealing from him. As Hanson looked at the old boxes, he thought of his grandfather and how much joy it would bring him if Hanson showed up with these as a gift for him. Then he thought about how much heroin he could buy if he sold them, and the thought of grandpa's smiling face quickly faded into the air.

He lifted one box to examine it. The thing felt like it was full of lead. As he flipped the lid open, he soon found out why. The little box was loaded to the top with old coins, gold jewelry, pocket watches, rings, and various other expensive-looking trinkets. Many of the coins were misshapen and had Latin engravings on them. Hanson had been through enough pawn shops in his life to know that he had just fallen into a gold mine. There were things in this box that collectors would kill for. He wasn't any sort of expert but knew by the contents of just this one box, he'd be set for life, not to mention what was in the other nine.

"Take out fifteen of the Spanish Doubloons, the engraved pocket watch which reads: C.S.A. Thomas Jonathan Jackson, and one of the diamond rings," Zlo said. "Place the box back with the others and close everything back up."

"You want me to leave all this treasure?" Hanson pleaded. "There's a fortune here!"

"No need to overindulge, Mr. Parker. The value of what I've told you to pick out will fund our operation for years. You'll want for nothing."

The idea of putting all of this wealth back into the ground made Hanson feel weak. He couldn't imagine doing such a thing, not since he had spent so many years begging, borrowing, stealing, and hawking for pennies. It was as if he had hit the Power Ball Jackpot and then had to give it all away to charity. Heartache bubbled to the surface.

"Mr. Parker, do as I asked." Zlo's tone was authoritative and stern. The vibration this time felt more like a shock of static.

He continued with his task, though his heart ached deeper with each shovel full of dirt that hit the coffin lid.

As he finished filling in the grave, he finally developed the courage to ask: "So, what happened to the body of the girl buried here?"

"Oh, young Alice? We dug her up and threw her in a ravine a few miles from here, shortly after her funeral."

There was no need for any more questions. Hanson was happier when he knew less.

SEVEN

The short, pudgy bald man with the double chin—which flopped over his buttoned-up shirt and red bowtie—looked up at Hanson from his jeweler's eyeglass. He did not speak. It appeared he wanted to, but no words came to mind. With a slight look of frustration, he put the magnifier back up to his left eye, squinted his right, and peered intensely back at the item that Hanson had handed him moments ago. A bead of sweat formed on his high forehead, threatening to break loose and take off down the front of his face at any second.

"Where on earth did you get this?" The man finally said.

Hanson smiled. He loved it when he brought a pawn shop owner something of interest. Of course, they all tried to control their excitement, playing it cool for when the negotiations began, but this guy had a hard time keeping it down.

"Let's call it a family heirloom," Hanson said.

"This is a Spanish Doubloon from the fourteenth century," The pudgy man said with a raised voice. "No one has heirlooms like this, especially not here in Winchester, Virginia!" He looked back at the coin in his hand. "I mean… *my God!* This thing is easily worth over two hundred grand, maybe even half a million… maybe even more! I don't have that kind of cash! I couldn't even make you an offer."

"Yeah, I didn't think you'd be able to," Hanson replied. "That's why *I'm* going to make the offer to you, and you'll have no problem with it. Guaranteed."

After Hanson finished covering the grave of Alice Carter and doing his best to make it look as though the area was undisturbed, Zlo had given him another set of instructions. First, hide the tools in the abandoned house; second, proceed to the larger town of Winchester, which was a few miles to the north of Kernstown; third, find a pawnshop where he could deal for one of the coins and procure the following items: One new van without back windows, a new wardrobe, fifteen thousand dollars in cash, six cans of high ether content starting fluid, and a pistol. Further instruction would come once the items were in his possession. Zlo had also said to, "Keep the transaction discrete at all cost."

The shop owner looked at Hanson with piqued curiosity. "I'm listening."

"I know by law you people have to account for everything that goes through your store. I also know that every one of you is just as much of a crook as the customers who sell you stolen shit."

The man immediately became flustered and offended.

"Save it," Hanson said, holding up his hand. "You want this fucking coin so bad you can taste it. I can see it all over your face. Now, I have a few things I need that are way less than the value of that coin. Get me what I need—under the table—and the coin is yours. How you filter it into your inventory is your problem. But you'll probably be able to retire after you figure it out."

The man set the coin on the counter at an equal distance between Hanson and himself, a subliminal gesture saying he was interested in negotiating.

"Do you know who owns that Ford dealership across the street?" Hanson asked.

The man smiled. "Ha! My brother owns it."

"Perfect! This should be easy for you then." Hanson saw a pack of cigarettes in the pudgy man's shirt pocket. He reached across the counter, grabbed the pack out of his pocket, and shook one out. The gesture showed that he was the alpha in this exchange. "Lighter?"

The man hesitantly cracked open a silver Zippo and obliged Hanson with a flame.

"I need a new van," Hanson said. "Something fresh off the lot and indiscriminate. Put the title and registration in the name of…" He looked at the ceiling for a few moments, then smiled a devious grin. "Alice Carter." Suddenly, he felt a slight giggle from Zlo resonate through his body.

"My brother is going to flip out over this, and I could get into some serious trouble," the man said. He was nervous, yet still in the game.

"And you're going to figure it out, or the rarest coin you've ever touched in your life is going to walk out that door and make someone else rich."

Both men stared at each other. Finally, the shop owner said, "Continue."

Hanson crushed out the cigarette on the glass counter, close enough to the Doubloon to make the shop owner nervously move the coin away. The fat man was already acting like the item belonged to him.

"I need like three or four pairs of Levis," Hanson continued, "A bunch of medium T-shirts, two or three pairs of Nike shoes and socks—white please—fifteen thousand dollars in cash, six cans of high ether content starter fluid, and that Colt .45 pistol in the display case over there. Oh, and a couple boxes of ammo to go with it."

"Now hold on just a *goddamn* minute," the man shouted. "The clothes are easy, the van and fifteen grand and other shit I can probably do, but that fucking handgun is registered. How am I supposed to let that thing walk out the door still registered to me? I'll be held accountable for any kind of trouble you get into with it. And don't tell me you're just going target shooting!"

"Are you new at this business?" Hanson yelled back. "Stage a break-in. Pay a few druggies to bust out a window and knock over a few shelves. Add the gun to the list of shit stolen."

The man looked at Hanson disapprovingly.

"Oh, don't look at me like you don't know any junkies around here," Hanson said. "You buy stolen shit off of them all the time."

The shop owner walked around from behind the counter, looking down and shaking his head. He grabbed his pack of cigarettes out of Hanson's hand and put them back in his shirt pocket. "Stay here and keep out of sight," he instructed. He walked over to the door, flipped the sign to *Closed*, then walked outside, locking the door behind him.

Hanson watched through the front window as the man bobbled his way across the street toward the Ford dealer. *This might actually work.*

EIGHT

Hanson stood gawking at the oversized map which took up almost the entire East wall of the rest area. He was surprised that they had printed it on one giant piece of paper, rather than several smaller sheets fastened together. He couldn't believe they even made paper that big. An older gentleman and a teenage boy stared at the map alongside him. There was plenty of room to accommodate all three.

After several minutes of scanning over the surface, he found a little red pin that held down a small tag with the words, *YOU ARE HERE,* typed on it. Interstate 81, Rest Area #7, twenty miles north of Winchester, Virginia. The map was overly large, but focused mainly on Virginia; it showed only a few miles into each border state. His intended destination was a small town somewhere in Pennsylvania named Cumberland Springs. Zlo had not given him any more information than that, so he was shooting in the dark.

Several people of all different ages, genders, and races filtered in and out of the building to use the bathrooms and look at the various racks of travel brochures. Outside, there were stone picnic tables, and built-in charcoal grills, each of them filled with families eating and laughing and feeding their tethered dogs from the table. The smell of hotdogs and hamburgers and other summer cuisine filled the outside air and even permeated into the building.

Hanson became frustrated staring at the map, not having any luck. He went into the bathroom, took a leak in one of the self-flushing urinals, then headed back outside. Zlo was not helping at the moment. Surely if he could direct him to an abandoned house and cemetery in the middle of the woods, he could guide him to this crappy little town he wanted him to find.

"Hey buddy, want a burger?" A man's voice called out.

Hanson hadn't realized it, but while lost in thought, he had been staring at a family seated at one of the picnic tables, having a lovely afternoon lunch.

"We have a lot left over," A woman's voice added.

These people sounded nice, even sincere. Who would invite a total stranger at a rest area to sit down to dinner with them? Did people even do that these days? *Must be Bible thumpers.* But the smell of ground beef seared over charcoal activated every saliva gland in his mouth. He couldn't actually remember the last time he'd eaten. Just the idea of eating one of these delicious treats intoxicated him.

"I guess. Sure," Hanson said and walked over to the table.

"Grab a seat, friend," the man said. "I'm Tim Dorchester. This is my wife, Judy, and these two are, Andy and Alicia."

Tim looked to be somewhere in his mid to late thirties and had a pleasant smile and firm handshake. Judy was about the same age, and very well put together. The boy and girl, who had not yet reached their teenage years, sat across the table from their parents, as did a golden retriever tied to the picnic bench.

As Hanson prepared to join the family for dinner, he noticed a low growling sound coming from the dog. Its ears were down, and it had just begun to show its teeth.

"Rusty!" The boy said, scolding the dog.

The animal paid no attention and intensified its stare and growl even more.

"My goodness, Rusty," Judy said. "He's usually so friendly. I don't think I've ever heard him growl at someone before."

"Andy," Tim said. "Take ol' Rusty into the motorhome. He may have had too much sun today."

The boy did as his father instructed, but had a hard time of it. It took all of his strength to pull Rusty from the table and get him moving. Rusty was now trying to break free from young Andy, transfixed entirely on getting to Hanson. He growled and pulled and presented all of his teeth, then finally began barking ferociously.

Tim threw down his napkin onto his plastic plate, got up in haste, and grabbed the dog from his son. He then drug Rusty all the way to their motorhome—parked only a short distance away —and threw him inside. Rusty immediately jumped into the front seat where he could see through the large windshield and began relentlessly barking his head off.

"Sorry about that, buddy," Tim said as he came back to the table. "Never seen Rusty do that before." He gestured for Hanson to have a seat at the table. "Didn't catch your name?"

"Oh," Hanson said. He was at a loss. Not sure what Zlo had planned for him, he knew it wouldn't be a good idea to use his actual name. His mind Clay a blank. He had no alias prepared. He stammered for a moment, then finally blurted out, "Odell Carter."

"Odell? What a great name," Tim said. "It has such an old-fashioned ring to it. Were you named after a relative? A grandfather or great grandfather, perhaps?"

"Not sure," Hanson replied. "My parents are hippies."

Tim and Judy paused for a second and looked at each other, then everyone erupted in laughter.

"Well, Odell, please enjoy some of our food," Judy said. "We're so happy you could join us."

Judy had placed a plastic plate in front of him, and Tim handed him a platter with a few burgers left on it. The meal looked and smelled fantastic. And where did these people come from? No one was ever nice to Hanson, not that he could recall. Unless, of course, if he had paid for it. But Tim and Judy seemed genuine. He sat for a moment, vaguely aware that a smile had arisen on his face.

"We already said grace before we ate, but we're always willing to say it again," Ted said.

Before Hanson could respond, they were all holding hands and bowing their heads.

Hanson suddenly felt a shock wave of vibration pulse through his body. It came out of nowhere, abrupt and painful. His hearing muffled, and it sounded as though Tim's voice was distant and underwater. It took a second for the shock to sink in. Then he knew what was happening… Zlo had something to say.

"Look at that fucking whore and her pimp, acting like they're better than you. And the smug faces of those two little bastards across from them. Fuck these dirt people! They're laughing at you from behind those polished smiles. Get away from them, Hanson. Now! Get your ass as far away from these shit people as you can. Do it now! Right now! Don't listen to another word of their dribble, their poison, their propaganda. Get back in the van and fucking leave NOW!"

Another shock shot through Hanson's body, causing him to tense up and squeeze Tim's and Judy's hands with intense force. Judy let out a terrified gasp. Tim shook his hand loose from Hanson's grasp, then worked to pull Judy's hand free. In the motorhome, Rusty was charging the windshield over and over trying to break through the glass, leaving saliva and blood smeared all over the inside. Both Andy and Alicia screamed as they watched their father try to free their mother.

"Get in that fucking van right NOW!" Zlo commanded so loudly that Hanson's eyes throbbed.

Tim finally freed his wife from the grip of the stranger at their table. They all quickly backed away and huddled behind Tim as he herded his family away from the threat.

Hanson rushed to get up and fell backward off of the bench. He didn't hesitate while on the ground as Zlo sent wave after wave of tormenting vibrations through his system. He scrambled to his feet and ran to the van in an out-of-control sprint.

"What the fuck?" Hanson yelled as he piled into the driver's seat. "Seriously?"

"Drive now! Fast! NOW!" Zlo yelled inside his head.

Hanson did as instructed and squealed tires as he backed out of the parking space and sped down the ramp to the interstate. In the rearview mirror, he could see Tim, holding his family close and watching the van speed away.

NINE

Hanson pulled into a truck stop, ten miles further down the interstate from the rest area where Tim, Judy, and family were still recovering from the *incident*. Though slightly shaken over the whole thing himself, he'd been able to put it out of his mind and get back to focusing on the task at hand: finding Cumberland Springs.

Zlo had gone silent again. Once Hanson had the van on the highway, and out of sight of the rest area, Zlo had tapered off his ranting and retreated into the darkness. That innocent family back there had really set something off in him. Hanson didn't have the courage to ask. He didn't want Zlo sparking up and sending those painful jolts through his system anymore. He felt it better to just get back on track and avoid any contact with people for a while.

As luck would have it, a large display rack of maps and road atlas' stood facing the door just a few feet inside of the truck stop's convenience store. Hanson picked up an atlas and flipped through the pages. Every state in the union had a two-page spread with a detailed map of each city, town, and roadway that led in and out of them. Even Rhode Island had two pages of real estate.

Hanson purchased the road atlas, a 20oz Mountain Dew, and three Snicker bars, then headed out to the van to fill up the tank and get moving.

An urge crept over him, which was all too familiar: he hadn't had a hit of dope in quite a while. The hunger had boiled. He couldn't remember the last time he'd actually gone this long without shooting something into his veins. The reward had replaced all of that, except Zlo had been holding out on him. A little dose here and there would not cut it. They had an agreement, a pact. He'd receive it anytime he wanted it, as long as he did as Zlo had asked. Well, he'd done everything asked of

him so far. Where was his reward? And why the silence? He'd
only received bits and pieces of instruction since they started this
whole *Grand Adventure* bullshit. When was everything going to
be revealed? It was time for him and Zlo to have a talk. Time to
get a few things out onto the table. Time to drop the shit and
come clean.

After filling up the tank, Hanson got into the van and drove it
around to a secluded spot at the back of the truck stop, an out of
the way place where he could have a word with his traveling
companion and no one would see him talking to himself.

"I'm not going any further, Zlo," Hanson spoke aloud inside
the quiet compartment of the van. "You're going to have to give
me more than bits and pieces."

Silence.

"I mean it!" Hanson heard the trepidation in his own voice
and knew the root. He'd felt this feeling many times in his life,
for as far back as he could remember. He needed the drug. If Zlo
would not provide him with that glorious thing in his system, he
would have to resort to conventional methods. Truck stops could
be nasty places, and Hanson was adept at locating the right
element to provide him with what he desired. Plus, he sat on
fifteen grand in cash. He would not deny his hunger any longer.

"Are you seriously contemplating going back to that?" Zlo
spoke up.

Hanson jumped slightly. "Why are you keeping me in the
dark?" He demanded. "I'm driving around in circles, and you're
not telling me why."

"I've told you plenty," Zlo said.

"I want to know what you're expecting me to do. What's this
task I need to perform before I get what you promised?"

"You are so close now, Mr. Parker. Patients. Everything in
good time. Soon you will have the key to your delight, which
you may use at any moment you desire."

"That tells me nothing," Hanson said. "Give me something.
Anything! I'm flipping!"

"Indeed, you are. It's mildly impressive to see you feed from your desires. That's why I'm certain once I've given you the key, you'll use it often and we'll both get exactly what we want."

Hanson sat quiet, unsatisfied. Zlo only provided him with more talk and little action. This seemed like a snipe hunt. Although, he did lead him to a treasure buried in the woods worth more than he could have ever imagined. Plus, that indescribable feeling that undeniably existed. He'd felt it, relished it, desired it, and loved it. But Hanson was insatiable. He needed so much more than clues and brief moments of elation. He wanted it all and wanted it now!

"Give me something!" Hanson demanded.

"Alright," Zlo replied. "I'll give you one piece of information. One slice of the pie. No more, no less. Ask away."

Hanson had so many questions, all of them floating around in a clouded carousel above his head. He couldn't seem to decide. Finally, he blurted out: "What's in Cumberland Springs?" After he'd said it, he realized it was not the most crucial piece of information he'd wished to have, but it was out there now. Maybe it would give him at least a small touch of satisfaction.

"A fair question, indeed," Zlo said. "Many, many years ago, the people of this disgusting little borough did me a great disservice. One which I have never, nor will never forget. I like to begin each new *Grand Adventure* in this place as a bit of poetic justice to satisfy myself. I would have us return there repeatedly to inflict my special brand of torment upon them, but I've learned, through trial and error, to be patient and exacting. It has been quite a while since I've been there, and I feel the time is right once again. Once we reach Cumberland Springs, I will give you the last bit of information and turn you loose. The rest will be up to you. You will have every opportunity in the world after that to enjoy the stimulus which you desire so much, always at your discretion. The adventure is just about to begin, Hanson. We are about to have such *fun!*"

Hanson let out a deep sigh. He hadn't received what he wanted or needed, and his hunger seemed to grow almost out of control. But he could tell that Zlo would not provide any more.

He understood he wouldn't get any satisfaction until he reached this crappy little town his companion was so serious about. What lay ahead? He couldn't imagine, and the curiosity was almost as bad as his need for drugs.

"Where the hell is this fucking place anyway," Hanson said aloud as he grabbed the road atlas from the passenger seat and opened it to the map of Pennsylvania. After scanning it over and over, almost convinced that it didn't exist at all, it appeared. A small dot in South Central PA, nestled in the Appalachian Mountains, about fifty miles from the Maryland border and a little over a hundred miles East of Pittsburgh. "This place is tiny and in the middle of nowhere. What the hell could be out there?"

There was no use in wasting time or pondering the situation further. Zlo would not give him anything else until he found his way to this shit hole town, so why sit around any longer? He found his location on the Virginia map, planned out a route to his destination—which was only about three to four hours away—and started off.

TEN

Cumberland Springs. Honest. Quiet. Friendly. Hanson slowed the white Ford van as he approached the sign on the outskirts of town. The sign looked proud with its fresh gleaming paint and gold lettering. It boasted a credo that gave insight into the people who lived here. If they were advertising a friendly place, they must be friendly people, right? Or they were all full of shit and just as selfish and narcissistic as the inhabitants of every other town in the world. Throughout Hanson's travels, small towns and cities alike, he never came across, Honest, Quiet, or especially Friendly. People didn't welcome Hanson to their neighborhoods or invite him to backyard barbecues. There were no parties, picnics, or down-home festivities for Hanson Parker. The only thing he'd ever received in the form of a welcoming committee at a new place was a shakedown from a local cop and maybe a night or two in jail. Everywhere he went he was treated like an outcast and never welcomed with these so-called friendly open arms. Perhaps they sensed something about him. After all, he was basically nothing more than a transient junkie, roaming the earth looking for his next fix. But weren't friendly, honest people supposed to give one the benefit of the doubt? It's probably for the best that they didn't; he would have only ripped them off, anyway.

So here he was, rolling into a little town somewhere out in the sticks, being guided by a voice inside his head which he picked up in a shit hole alley while coming down from a bad trip. What could go wrong? Apparently, this *Grand Adventure* needed to kick off here, in the middle of BFE. He couldn't question his companion too much about it though. Up to this point—albeit strange and unusual—Zlo seemed to know what he was doing and where they were going. And that treasure hoard! Holy shit! Just knowing the box existed and knowing how to get to it made Hanson rest a little easier.

There was a problem in his life that he'd painfully realized. All the money in that old coffin would buy him more drugs than he could have ever dreamed of acquiring, but those substances now paled in comparison to the high he got with whatever Zlo released inside of him. He could be rich beyond belief, but Zlo would still be in control, as he was right now. Hanson had become a slave, a modern-day indentured servant. Zlo called the shots and would for as long as he wanted. The reward dangling in front of Hanson's face like a carrot on a stick, just out of his grasp but close enough to keep him motivated. Once he accomplished whatever Zlo had planned here in Cumberland Springs, he'd be able to have his carrot anytime he wanted it. The voice hadn't lied to him yet. Actually, the voice had been the only thing in his life that ever told him the truth.

As he drove past the giant welcome sign and headed toward town, the carrot felt closer than ever. Zlo was awake now, Hanson could feel the light vibration of his companion as it became excited within him.

"Ah, the homecoming," Zlo said.

"Are you from here?" Hanson asked.

"A figure of speech, Mr. Parker," Zlo replied. "It is a homecoming in the sense that I have a history with this town. I like to begin here as a sort of poetic justice. A self-indulgence, if you will."

"Ok. Sure. Poetic Justice."

"You'll need to be more enthusiastic than that, Mr. Parker," Zlo said. His voice seemed to brim with excitement. "We're about to begin. All you have ever wanted is within your grasp, waiting for you to pluck it from the vine and savor it into the very depths of your soul."

Hanson didn't always comprehend every word his companion spoke or its use of metaphor—he'd only carried a fourth-grade reading level at best—but it sounded like things were about to happen. And as long as it got him closer to his reward, he didn't care what words or phrases Zlo spit out.

"Alright, Mr. Parker, now is the time for you to use your

248

seasoned set of abilities."

"What abilities are you talking about?" Hanson replied.

"Your street smarts. Your rogue skills. You know… your cunning artistry." It seemed like Zlo was trying to motivate Hanson.

"What the hell is 'cunning artistry'?"

Zlo laughed. "You're going to need to keep a low profile. Don't draw attention to yourself. It's going to be difficult in a place like this, with these inbreds, so you'll need to be very discrete."

Hanson internalized the advice but became concerned. He still did not know what Zlo had planned for him to do here. Though he could always say no if he disagreed with anything. Or could he?

The road into town gave Hanson the impression that Cumberland Springs must be a well-manicured place. Lush foliage and old-growth trees lined each side of the blacktop, and not a single piece of litter lay anywhere, not even a stray beer can. There were also no potholes, cracks, or road bumps. The van rolled over the pavement as if it were traveling on a smooth sheet of glass.

The first business he came to before the road emptied into the central part of town was a gas station that looked like it came out of the 1950s. As with everything else he'd seen so far, the old place was well maintained and so clean that it shined in the afternoon sunlight. He glanced down at the gas gauge and saw that he was on a quarter tank. It was as good a time as any to stop for a fill-up.

As he pulled up to the pump, a bell sounded inside the garage portion of the building. Soon after, an older man emerged, wiping his hands on an oily rag. "Nice new set of wheels ya have here, son," the man said as he came around to the driver's side window. "This thing fresh off the lot?"

Hanson wasn't used to polite conversation or small talk. He began stuttering, and his lips twitched as he struggled to come up with a reply. He had no desire to talk to this old man, nor anyone else in this town. His mind seemed to close up shop, leaving his mouth empty and out in the wind on its own.

"Your van," the man said. "Is it new? The reason I ask is that my son is thinking about getting a new van for his plumbing business. I told him to find a used one, but he's set on buying something off the lot. Just wondering how much a new one might set him back."

"Lie to him," Zlo spoke up. "Makeup something and keep it short."

"I don't know," Hanson said. "I borrowed it... ah... from my sister."

"Oh, I see," the man said. "Got business here in Cumberland Springs?"

"Just here to gas up."

"Well, you came to the right place. We got plenty of that!" The old man walked to the back of the van and opened the gas cap. "Top her off?"

"Yeah, fill it." Hanson said shakily. His only social skill had come from dealing with other low-lifes and drug dealers. He didn't have the mental facilities to handle small talk while trying to remain discrete. He just wanted this guy to shut up, fill up the tank, and go the hell away.

Hanson jumped in his seat, startled as the man appeared back at his window.

He took immediate notice of Hanson's jitters. "You ok, buddy?"

"Y... y... y... yeah. I just didn't see you come back."

"Oh, well, I'm sorry I gave you a zapper there. You want the regular or hi-test? I'd recommend the good stuff if you want to get a lot of years out of this baby."

"Sure. Hi-test is fine."

"Excellent choice, my man," the attendant said and walked back to the rear of the van.

Hanson noticed three younger-looking boys on bicycles riding into the gas station lot. The oldest one couldn't have been over twelve. Each had a look of excitement about them as they laughed and joked with each other and rode their bikes too fast. They rode past the front of the van and headed for the air pump at the corner of the garage.

"What kinda trouble you boys gettin' into today?" The old man said from behind the van in a light-hearted tone.

"Hi, Mr. Ellis," one boy shouted and waved. "Didn't see you back there. We just needed to pump up the tires a little."

"Well, you're welcome to it. Want me to check the oil for ya?"

The boys all laughed, as did the old man.

Hanson felt light vibrations course through his body. Zlo was awake and active. He'd felt this same activity from his companion before when he was watching the farmhouse in Kernstown and the two children were playing on the back porch. It felt like an eagerness had arisen in him.

"We are about to begin, Mr. Parker," Zlo spoke. "Are you ready?"

"Begin what?" Hanson said. He'd become more nervous now than while talking with the gas station attendant. Something in Zlo's tone and the way the vibration of his voice felt in Hanson's body had changed. Hanson detected anticipation, hunger, even desire.

"Pay close attention to those three children over there," Zlo said.

"What are you going to do to them?"

"I am merely directing," Zlo said. "It is *you* who will take action."

"Now wait just a *goddamn* sec—"

"Ten dollars even," the old man said, standing by the driver's side window.

"*Jesus!*" Hanson yelled, and the old man jumped.

"Damn, boy, you're jumpy as hell, aren't ya?" the man said. "Something bothering you?"

"No," Hanson replied. He took a deep breath to regain composure. "You sell cigarettes here? I haven't had a smoke all day."

"Now there's your problem. You got nicotine jitters. What's your brand?"

"Camel filters."

"Just one pack?"

"I'll take a carton if you got 'em," Hanson said.

"I think I have a carton of Camels in there. Let me run in and check."

Hanson laughed to himself. This place operated like it probably did since the 1950s. Not only did someone pump your gas for you, but they'd bring you cigarettes curbside as well.

"Pay attention, Mr. Parker," Zlo said. "It's now time for you to earn your reward. Take a good look at those young boys over there, specifically the smallest of the three. Do you see?"

"Yeah, I see them," Hanson replied. "Three kids on bikes. What about them?"

"You're going to follow them," Zlo said.

"What would I do that for?"

"Because you are going to retrieve the smallest one and bring him to me tonight."

"Whoa," Hanson exclaimed. "That's taking things a little too far. I've done a lot of shit in my life, but kidnapping is way out of bounds, even for me."

"It is well within the purview of your capabilities, and you shall have no problem doing as I ask."

"What are you going to do with the kid?"

"Who are you talking to, buddy?" The old man was standing at Hanson's window, holding a carton of Camel Filters. A look of apprehension shadowed his face.

"Huh? Oh, I was just singing out loud. Some stupid song I heard earlier."

The man studied Hanson; the look on his face remained the same. "Here's your smokes. Gas and cigarettes come to $22.50."

Hanson paid the man, received his change, then started the van and pulled out onto the main road. In the rearview mirror, he could see the old man staring at him as he drove away and the three boys working on their bicycles. He had a sinking feeling in his stomach about the way the guy looked at the end of their interaction. But an even worse feeling about what Zlo had proposed for him to do. He lit a cigarette and inhaled it deeply, hoping it would calm his nerves. It didn't.

ELEVEN

Hanson drove a short distance away from the gas station until he found a dirt road pull off that led into the woods, just outside of town. He turned onto the path and drove far enough in until he felt he was out of sight from the main road.

"Ok, now it's time for you to come clean, Zlo," He said aloud. "What the *hell* is all this about?"

"I've given you your instructions, Hanson, now carry them out," Zlo replied. "Follow those young boys, single out the smallest of them, and bring him to me tonight. Is that not clear enough for you?"

"There is nothing clear about it! I'm not kidnapping a child. End of discussion!" Hanson lit another cigarette. It shook in his lips as he tried to flame the tip.

"Ah, but you will do this, not only tonight but also for the rest of our time together. And you will grow to become very good at it; an expert, perhaps even an artist. You will get to a point where you'll enjoy the thrill of the chase almost as much as the stimulation you receive from the reward. You remember the reward, don't you? That sweet rush of ecstasy you've grown so fond of."

"So that's what I have to do now to get my fix? Kidnap children?"

"Kidnap is such as strange word. You are merely bringing them to me; presenting them. After that, your work is finished and you may relax and enjoy your gift. Why does this concern you so much?"

The burning tip of the cigarette hit the filter in less than a minute as Hanson relentlessly sucked at it. He snuffed the butt into the ashtray and immediately lit another.

"I'm not a kidnapper," Hanson said. "I'll do a lot of really nasty shit and not blink an eye about it, but child abduction could land me in federal—pound you in the ass—prison! And I'm not about any of that shit. I like my asshole the size it already is."

It started slowly and graciously, like the most beautiful woman in the world looking into his eyes with a smile on her face, stroking his cheeks and running her fingers through his hair. He lost his ability to speak. Warmth and joy began flowing through his veins, emanating from his heart and filling him with peace and bliss. The feeling grew in intensity, giving him power. His mind and body energized, exploding with passion, desire, and lust. This was it, all he ever wanted to experience in life was happening right now. It was taking him to a place he'd never dreamed possible. Physical, emotional, spiritual...

And then gone.

"I HATE YOU!" Hanson screamed and pounded his fists against the steering wheel until he thought the thing would break. "Why are you torturing me?"

"Are you actually calling that torture?" Zlo replied.

"You give it, then you take it away from me after a few seconds. That's torture!"

"No, Mr. Parker, that's a reminder. When you bring me what I have requested, you will receive your reward in full, not just a dash, but all of it."

Hanson quickly realized he had no choice. The reward was now the only thing he had to live for, and not playing along would mean it could disappear from his life forever. No human life on this planet meant more to him than that eruption of glorious pleasure. As he sat staring out the windshield of the van, smoking his Camel and looking at the dirt road in front of him, he realized that this would be the moment he gave away his soul.

"Just tell me why? Why children?"

"Would you tell your plans to an ant? Would you give a second thought to a cockroach crawling into a sewer grate?"

"Oh, so I'm only as valuable as an insect?" Hanson barked back.

"Mr. Parker, my reasons are more complex and vast than your limited intellect can comprehend. Yet, if it means we can get on with our *Grand Adventure* together, I will give you a morsel of insight into my motives. Afterward, I expect you to do your work without reservation. Do you understand?"

"Yes."

"I am not here in this wretched place by choice. I was cast here before your kind were even a thought. Now I'm forced to exist here as you gravel on your knees, attempting to become innocent and righteous, while you are nothing more than a primitive breed of insects, hunting for scraps at the master's table. It is the innocence that I have grown to despise the most. I have found that the only satisfaction I can have for myself comes from causing the destruction of innocence. I feed on it. You could say it is my fix—as you so aptly put it. And it's the only thing I have found in this desperate place that brings me comfort. So you, Mr. Parker, will bring me the innocent. In turn, you may go off and enjoy your reward and I shall enjoy mine."

"What do you do with them?" Hanson asked.

"That's the amusing part. I merely show them my face. The terror that ensues when they look upon me is a treat more enjoyable than anything else the earth can provide. Their fear becomes essence and I absorb every delicate drop. I feed my desire from it. Nothing else here gives me this level of satisfaction. My master approves of it as well. He greatly approves."

"Who is this master you keep mentioning?" Hanson asked. He was angry yet intrigued.

"Be patient, Mr. Parker, you will meet him when our business has concluded. The master is very pleased by you so far and anticipates good things from you." Zlo laughed and an eerie vibration coursed through Hanson's body, which he did not feel at all comfortable with.

Hanson felt he had no choice. He needed that feeling, that euphoria, and needed it immediately. Anger came over him, causing his breathing to escalate and his heart to thump so hard that he felt it in his throat. He wasn't sure if he could get away with abducting a child; he'd attempted nothing like this before. But, he had stolen so much from so many over the years, this shouldn't be all that different. The only thing to worry about was if the merchandise tried to scream or run or fight him. He needed a plan but didn't know where to start.

TWELVE

"Hey Jimmy," Bill Ellis said as he came out of the garage to greet the Chief. He was cleaning a miscellaneous part of some old engine with an oily rag. "Thanks for stopping by."

Jim Harris had just stepped out of his police cruiser into the warm July afternoon and inhaled a deep breath of clean summer air. Cumberland Springs sat nestled in the Juniata Plateau region of the Appalachian Mountains. The air up here was refreshing and crisp. Along with the seven natural springs that surrounded the town, the air was another pleasant feature which no one around here took for granted.

"Hey there, Bill," Jim said. "How's the world treating you today?"

"Same as always, Jimmy. No complaints."

The two men shook hands, then Jim leaned back against his police car. "My office said you called in about something suspicious."

Bill fumbled with his shirt pocket, trying to get something out that seemed stuck. "Yeah, I did, Jimmy." After a few seconds, he freed the item in his pocket, a small notepad held together at the top by a spiral wire. "Probably nothin' but me being overly watchful. But I figured better safe than sorry, right?"

"Sure."

Bill fumbled through the notebook, struggling to see the writing on the pages. "I wrote down this license plate number earlier, if I can just find the damn thing." He fumbled through a few more pages. "Ah, here it is."

"What am I looking at here, Bill?" Jimmy asked as Bill handed him the notebook.

"Ya know, Jimmy, I'm a pretty friendly fellow. I try not to judge or make assumptions about people. I think you know that from all your years of knowing me."

"Well, of course, Bill. That goes without saying."

"I gotta tell ya, I had a strange feeling about a kid who stopped in here earlier for gas." Bill looked at the road in front of the gas station and shook his head. "There was something off about him. I can't put my finger on it. All I can say is I had a strange feeling about the guy."

Jim studied Bill's scribbling in the notebook. "Virginia plate?"

"Yeah, he was an out of stater."

"What kind of vehicle?"

"It was a white Ford van, like a work vehicle, no windows in the back. Looked brand new, off the lot."

Jim copied the plate number into his own notebook and the description of the vehicle. "What did this person look like?"

Bill looked up at the sky and winced as if the sunlight would help to enhance his memory. "He didn't get out of the van, so I couldn't tell you just how tall he was, but I'd guess medium height, maybe 5'8 to 5'10, no bigger than that. He had dark greasy hair and a scruffy face. Probably hadn't shaved in a few weeks. Oh, and dark brown eyes."

Jim wrote in his notebook as Bill talked. "So what made you suspicious of him?"

"Well, I was making friendly small talk while I filled up his tank, and he didn't seem to want to engage." Bill laughed and scratched his head. "Now, I know that's no reason to get suspicious. Who wants to spend the day talking to an old fart at a gas station, anyway? But most folks are polite enough to exchange at least a few pleasantries. This fella wanted no part of it. And he was real jittery. When I came up to his window, he jumped like I scared the devil out of him. That happened a few times." Bill put his hands in his pocket and looked down at the ground. His face became sullen. "Jim, I hate to make assumptions about anyone, friend or stranger…"

Jim stopped writing and studied the change in Bill's demeanor. The change in the old man gave him a sudden feeling of concern.

"When I was gassing him up," Bill continued. "The two Rolley boys and little Glen Crawford came riding in on their bikes to put some air in the tires. While they were at the air pump, I thought I heard the guy in the van talking to himself out loud. When I walked up to his window, he was lookin' at the boys... in a very suspicious manner. I don't know how to describe it other than that."

"When was this?" Jim had become very serious. The mention of a stranger taking a keen interest in three of Cumberland Springs' kids gave him a jolt of concern.

"About a half-hour ago."

"Which way did the guy in the van go?"

"He headed off towards town after I filled his tank. He also bought a carton of Camels," Bill added.

"Where did the boys go?"

"They were here for about ten more minutes after the van left, then they rode off in the same direction, towards town."

Jim handed Bill his notebook back and quickly got into the driver's seat of the cruiser. "Kim, I need you to run a plate for me," he said into the mic of the police radio.

Bill leaned into the open passenger side window. "You think this is something to worry about?"

Jim didn't answer right away, his focus seemed to be elsewhere. Finally, he said: "I imagine its nothing, but I'm going to check it out further. Plus, I'll keep an eye on those kids as well. It takes a village, right?"

"I suppose it does," Bill laughed.

"If that van happens to head back this way, call me, would you?"

"Sure thing, Chief," Bill said.

THIRTEEN

The area was clean and perfectly manicured, like a Norman Rockwell Christmas painting had come to life. The road into town had given way to a cobblestone roundabout surrounded by historic painted brick buildings and a white gazebo on a mound of grass and brightly colored flowers resting in its center. European style street lamps on black metal poles dotted the town square and surrounding sidewalks. Several people were out and about in the area, some shopping at the various stores in the square, others relaxing on benches in front of storefronts. A group of children played in and around the gazebo, chasing each other up and down the steps and over the four benches at its center. Hanson found the scene looked almost too good to be true, as if it were the set of a movie where the props department had gone above and beyond to create the perfect small town. He thought at any moment he would hear a director yell: "Cut! Where did the damn white van come from?"

He drove the van around the roundabout and found a parking space in front of one store. The sign above the large glass window read: Le Chance Hardware, Est. 1910. Two older men sat on a bench in front of the store. They took an immediate interest in Hanson as he pulled into the parking space, not leaving the comfort of their seat, but watching him with curious eyes. He quickly realized that this would not be the most inconspicuous spot for him to do his reconnaissance from. These old guys were staring him up and down like he'd already committed the crime was planning. It didn't take long for his paranoia to get the best of him. He pulled the van away from the spot and drove out of the other side of the town square. The two men watched him leave with great intent.

Several side streets surrounded the central part of town which led through neighborhoods of Cottage, Tudor, and Victorian-style houses, all of which looked as though they were built in the late nineteenth and early parts of the twentieth century, and were as well kept as the town square. In the short time Hanson had been in Cumberland Springs, he could feel that there was a great sense of pride, carried by everyone who lived here. He also realized that the people who were out in their yards and on the sidewalks as he drove by seemed to stop what they were doing and take notice of him; A highly curious bunch, all keeping a record of the big white van rolling through the neighborhood.

His feelings of insecurity rose to even higher levels. He was now sure that he'd get caught if he went took a shot at grabbing one of those kids. Everyone here was looking at him. He stood out like a sore thumb. Even if he could take the kid without getting caught, someone would be sure to come forward with a description of a strange white van cruising their streets. He imagined by now someone had to have written down his license plate number.

Hanson shook another cigarette out of the pack he'd been working on since stopping at the gas station; it was the last one. He had put away twenty coffin nails in less than an hour, definitely a new record for him. Thankfully, he'd bought the whole carton.

Pressure was overwhelming him to the point of a breakdown. He wanted out of this position but saw no path. He couldn't live without Zlo's reward, there was just no way, but could he live with what he had to do in order to get it? Hanson knew in his heart that before the night in the alley when Zlo manifested, his life would not last much longer. He could feel his demise swiftly approaching from deep within. His health had deteriorated to the point where he almost couldn't recover from a single hit of heroin, and for him, life without the drug was not an option. It was his only purpose for carrying on to the next day. But then a new purpose presented itself, one which gave life meaning that he'd never dreamed possible. But with it came a despicable price, which he was almost certain he couldn't pay.

Hanson turned through a few of the old tree-lined streets and picturesque neighborhoods until he found a road that led away from town in the opposite direction from the way he had come in. He had no idea where he was going. He drove aimlessly, thinking about how his life may be on the verge of ending soon and how it wouldn't really matter to anyone—except perhaps anyone he'd owed money to. And then it happened. As the town disappeared into the background and the road gave way to dense woods to his left and farmland to his right, with nothing or no one else around, he came upon the three boys on their bicycles who he'd seen at the gas station. The smallest of the three trailing behind the two older ones. He couldn't believe his eyes. This was the break that changed everything. It was as if they just appeared out of thin air, like bait cast into a lake right in front of a largemouth bass resting under a fallen log.

He slowed the van and kept it at a safe distance. He couldn't make his move right now, not in broad daylight, and not with all three of them together. It would be safer to follow them for a while, get a feel for their activity, make his move if or when they separated.

The road crested at a slight hilltop; on the way up, the boys slowed to a point where they had to jump off of their bikes and push. Hanson was afraid they would stop for a break and notice him at a distance, crawling slowly behind them, but as luck would have it, they kept moving without looking back.

They disappeared over the rise. Hanson crept the van up to its peak to where he could see over the incline. The boys were rolling fast now, down the hill at breakneck speed, pushing the limits of their bikes and their abilities to control them.

Hanson continued on but maintained a slow pace. Even though they were now out of sight, he still felt that he had a bead on them.

The road dipped then climbed to another crest which the boys easily rolled up and over, aided by the speed they picked up from blasting down the last hill. When Hanson had skulked up to the top of the second hill and looked over, he saw a house on the right side of the road, about a thousand yards ahead of him. The boys had laid their bikes over in the yard and were walking up the front porch steps. Hanson waited a moment and watched as they all went inside.

After a few moments, he felt it was safe to continue on past the house.

A quarter-mile up the road, another stroke of luck came his way; he couldn't believe his eyes. Pay dirt once again. An old brick farmhouse with a large stone and wooden barn behind it sat on the same side of the road as the house where the boys resided. The place looked abandoned. It rested about fifty yards off of the road. The front yard almost completely choked with tall dead grass, iron weeds, and wilting sunflowers. The roof had a large hole, the front porch sagged in the middle, and rotting boards covered over the bottom floor windows. The house looked very out of place with the pleasant theme of the rest of the town, almost like a tornado had picked it up from another state, flew it across the country, and plopped it down here in the middle of Mayberry.

He slowly pulled into the driveway, which had certainly not seen recent traffic but was legible enough for him to navigate over to the back of the house. Dead grass and briars scraped at the side of the van as he proceeded, and grasshoppers flew off in every direction, looking as if they were shocked at being disturbed.

A quick check of the perimeter gave him confidence that the place was indeed abandoned. There were no signs of life that he could see from the outside, in the house or the barn. He couldn't have imagined a better scenario.

Hanson slid the van comfortably inside the barn and closed the large double doors. They creaked loudly through the warm afternoon air. He winced at first, nervous over the loud noise, but quickly realized that he and the grasshoppers would be the only ones around to hear it.

At the back of the house, he sat down on the decaying steps of a small porch which led into what appeared to be a built-on mudroom. He lit another cigarette. The steps creaked and groaned under the thin weight of his boney ass, and the room looked as if it could fall away from the house at any minute. He wasn't sure this would be the best place for a smoke break, but it was out of sight and the sun felt good on his skin.

He hadn't been much of a day person over the years—the creeps come out at night. He'd spent most of his daylight hours sleeping off whatever binge he'd gone on the night before or lying low in case someone he'd stolen from was out looking for him. Sitting in the sun on a warm summer day in a secluded place was a new sensation, one he surprisingly embraced. But he wasn't here to sun himself like a fat lady at the beach. He had an objective to complete. There was no time to relax or reflect right now. Those kids were in that house down the road and now was his time to figure out how he was going to grab one of them.

Walking down the road in broad daylight would be trouble waiting to happen. No doubt someone would drive by and ask if he was lost or needed help. He was going to have to sneak across the extensive field that ran between the two houses and try his best to stay out of sight. Luckily, the grass seemed high enough that he could drop prone if he needed to hide and easily stay well concealed.

No time like the present, he thought, and snuffed out his Camel on the bottom of his shoe.

The dry brown grass came up to Hanson's waist as he slogged across the field, and small bugs and more grasshoppers annoyingly jumped and flew as he disturbed them with his footsteps. Some insects were enormous. He jumped several times as they startled him with their buzzing wings and chirps.

As he approached the backside of the house that the boys had gone into, he ducked down into the high grass on his hands and knees. Now was the time for stealth. If caught lurking around this open field, he had no excuse prepared, nor could he think of one at the moment. He was going to have to apply all of his street smarts to this little country place. The skills he developed over his many years of sneaking into houses and backyard tool sheds, looking for items to steal and pawn for drugs, would come in handy during this *Grand Adventure,* as Zlo liked to call it.

A large garden, fenced in with chicken wire, was about ten yards away from the back of the house. A brick-paved path cutting through the garden led up to a wooden potting shed, made of old reclaimed barn wood. The thing didn't look very sturdy, nor did it look abandoned like the farm he had just come from. The house itself was cute and well maintained from what he could see from his position. Voices leaked out from inside, both children and an adult female, as all the windows appeared to be open.

Zlo had remained silent for most of the afternoon. His silence gave Hanson a sign of how the rest of their relationship was going to go. He'd receive small pieces of information or direction, then left on his own to figure out the rest. As he sat in the tall grass, casing an unsuspecting house in the middle of the country, he made a final decision: He would complete the task Zlo asked him to perform, but if he didn't receive the right amount of reward promised, that would be the end of his relationship with Zlo. No more games, no more double-speak, no more waiting. He wanted that sensation the way he got it in that alley in Baltimore. All of it! Not a hint, not a glimmer, not a skosh. The whole fucking thing or he was out. End of discussion.

He needed to get closer, but there wasn't enough cover to conceal him once he left the high grass. His only course of action would be to get inside of that little potting shed in the back corner of the garden. From there, he would be right behind the house, and could make out what the voices from inside the house were saying.

Inside the house, coming from what could have been the kitchen window, he heard the clanking of dishes and silverware. They were having lunch. The people inside were all occupied. Now was his best chance of breaking cover and heading for the old shed.

Zlo had done something to Hanson's body when he allowed him in. He couldn't describe it, but he felt healthy. Super healthy. He had altered Hanson's body chemistry, or cell structure, or something down deep inside. He was functioning at a level he'd never know before. His muscles felt alive, his heart pumped hard and strong, and his focus was clear and precise. When he got up and ran from the cover of the tall grass, he felt like a world-class athlete. He jumped the chicken wire fence like a track and field star and landed as silently as a cat stalking its prey. These abilities amazed him; he looked forward to using them more often.

Hanson quietly ducked inside the shed and pulled the door closed, doing his best to keep it from creaking. It was open when he went in, but he didn't feel like anyone would notice it being closed now. This didn't seem like a building that saw much traffic.

With the door safely closed and enough afternoon light shining through a small dirty window next to the door, he could survey his surroundings. He'd rummaged through hundreds of these backyard sheds in his lifetime, looking for items to steal and pawn for drug money. They were always a much easier target than a house. The risk of running into a homeowner who had heard a noise in the middle of the night and pulled out his trusty .357 Magnum from the nightstand to protect himself and his family as he investigated was much lower outside of the house. And these places were a treasure chest of pawnable valuables, especially tools; that was the hot ticket item. A good old toolbox full of new drivers and wrenches that the man of the house planned on using someday, but never seemed to get around to, could bring a small fortune to a junkie at a pawnshop. The contents of this shed, at first glance estimate, could have easily brought him a $200 yield. But Zlo had taken care of his need for money; there would be no need to steal for his supper anymore.

The gardening tools and lawn care equipment were standard backyard shed fare, but there was something in this room that stood out. A handcrafted piece that caught his attention right away. Hanging on the wall at the back part of the building, about five feet up, was a sign with freshly hand-painted red letters. The lettering looked as if illustrated by a child. It read: Cumberland Springs Adventure Society. Underneath the sign sat a tall wooden crate that looked like a makeshift podium. There were other items scattered around this area of the shed that looked like kids spent time here. A football, baseball gloves, and bats, Matchbox cars…

Suddenly, there were voices outside. Hanson peaked out of the dirty window. *Shit!* All three boys were walking up the brick path through the garden and heading his way. He looked around in haste for a place to hide, but at first came up short. The shed was small, too small. He was about to be discovered. It would be over before it began. This *Grand Adventure* would never have the chance to get off the ground. First, the boys would scream, then run back into the house. They'd alert an adult who, if they didn't come out here with a gun, would certainly call the police. He'd have to sprint back across the field, hit the van, then peel off quickly.

"The tarp," Zlo spoke. The surprise vibration caused Hanson to let out a slight, yelp!

He looked around fast. "Tarp?" Hanson whispered. "Where's a fucking tarp?"

Covering a lawnmower was a small grey canvas tarp. He didn't think of it at first because it didn't appear big enough to conceal him under. But it was the last—the only—option as time ticked down to its end.

He stepped over the lawnmower, then slinked his way between it and the far back wall of the shed. The door was creaking open as he slowly and quietly slid the tarp off of the mower and pulled it over himself. Curling up into the fetal position, he was just barely able to get all of himself concealed with just the tip of his hair sticking out.

The boys barged into the shed with familiarity, laughing and cracking jokes at each other. Hanson couldn't see them, but he could tell that they had gone to the other end of the room. He slowed his breath and did his best to remain perfectly still. He had been trying to get near these kids all day to work out his plan, but never imagined he'd get this close.

FOURTEEN

"Hurry up! Get in here and close the door," Michael commanded his younger brother. "I don't want mom to hear this."

"I'm coming! I'm coming!" Lucas said. He hated being bossed around by his older brother.

"Yeah doofus," Glen added, laughing. "Hurry your ass up!"

Lucas closed the door and barred it with the makeshift bar they had fashioned out of an old 2x4 and an ax handle that held it against the door.

Michael stood behind the podium they had built out of wooden soda crates. A Grape Nehi logo, worn and faded, showed through on the left side. "Sergent at Arms, is the clubhouse secure?"

"The clubhouse is secure, sir," Lucas replied.

"Vice President, is the time of the meeting at hand?"

Glen looked at his watch. "The time is precisely 3:00 PM, sir."

"I call this meeting of the Cumberland Springs Adventure Society to order. Are there any objections?"

"Nay."

"Nay."

"Good," Michael said. "First order of business: dad said we can keep the sign hanging up in here as long as we don't make a mess or break anything. Plus, we gotta ask first before using any of his tools."

Glen and Lucas smiled. They had all worked very hard on painting the sign that would grace the back wall of their clubhouse, but created it before asking permission. Michael felt that his dad would have no choice but to allow them to hang it up after he saw all the hard work they had put in it. He was right.

"Awesome," Lucas said. "I thought for sure he was going to be mad that we used his paint without asking."

"Your dad is a cool guy," Glen said. "I knew he wouldn't care."

"Yeah, dad is pretty cool," Michael said. "Now on to the next order of business. Yesterday I was with dad at the hardware store and I saw Nicholas LaChance. His father was making him help at the store. Anyway, you know how there's a bunch of old guys that sit around in there every Saturday drinking coffee and hiding from their wives? Well, Nicholas overheard them talking about a ghost story that has to do with that old white barn that sits on Chas Martin's property. Apparently, back in the late 1800s, a drifter came into town looking for work and the Martin's gave him a job as a farmhand. A few days later, Mr. Martin's daughter claimed the man attacked her and tried to steal her virtue—whatever that means. So Mr. Martin rounded up a bunch of guys from town and they took this man into Martin's barn and hung him by the neck till he died. And now, every time there's a full moon at midnight, you can see the man's body hanging from the rafters of Chas Martin's barn. His eyes are open and his lips move. One of the old guys at LaChance's said he saw it himself with his very own eyes."

Glen and Lucas sat silently. Glen with his mouth open, looking nervous. Lucas on the edge of his seat with his eyes wide.

Although Lucas Rolley was the youngest at age ten, he was certainly the most ambitious of the three. On any of their adventures, Michael almost always had to hold him back from charging into somewhere without caution. When they were exploring the abandoned Walton Foundry, he'd saved his little brother's ass twice that day, once from falling into a twenty-foot deep grease pit—still loaded full of old grease at the bottom—and again when he climbed up to the top of a rusted out stamping machine and almost fell into a pile of sharp metal shards. There were countless other times as well, which Michael shuddered to think about, and Lucas still laughed over.

Glen Crawford, on the other hand, was the most cautious of the group. While he was up for a good adventure just as much as the other two, his approach was much more reserved and calculated. He could see the dangers in the places they had explored and did his best to point them out to keep his friends safe. He had a watchful eye and was a great protector, something the other two definitely needed, whether they knew it or not.

"We have to go out there tonight," Lucas said. "I have that NASA calendar on the wall in my room and it shows the cycles of the moon. I looked at it this morning and it showed there was a full moon tonight. This is perfect!"

"It's not perfect," Michael said. "We have to plan this out. We can't just do it on the spur of the moment."

Glen spoke up. "We need to plan this before we go. But, here's something else, guys: I was at the grocery store with my mom the other day and at the checkout I saw a National Enquirer headline that said, 'Enquirer will pay one million dollars for proof of ghosts.' Can you even imagine that?"

"A million dollars!" Lucas shouted. "We have to go! Tonight!"

"Lucas, settle down!" Michael reprimanded his brother. "Mom's gonna hear you yelling and come out here."

Glen interjected: "The only way we could do this is if I sleepover, and I can't tonight. My parents rented two movies and told me I have to be home by 7:00 PM for family night. When's the next full moon?"

"That's 29 days," Lucas said. "We can't wait that long!"

"Yes, we can wait that long, Lucas," Michael said in his *older brother knows best,* tone. "That will be August Eighteenth, plenty of time for us to plan and prepare for a Cumberland Springs Adventure Society mission."

"You love saying that," Lucas mocked. "Can't you just say 'an adventure?' Do you have to say the full name every time we talk about something we're going to explore?"

"Yes, I do," Michael said. "We're an organized body of explorers, not just a group of random wanderers."

"You spend too much time at Boy Scouts."

"Alright, guys, that's enough," Glen said. "We just can't do this tonight. It's not the right time."

Lucas bottled up and stared out the dirty window by the door. This bothered Michael. He knew how headstrong his little brother could be. Once there was an idea planted in the kid's head, hell or high water would not stop him. He could easily picture Lucas sneaking out tonight on his own with his pocket 35mm camera that aunt Janice bought him for his tenth birthday, riding out to Martin's farm in the middle of the night alone. He was going to have to babysit the little jerk tonight. There was no way around it.

"You need to get the thought out of your mind right now, Lucas," Michael said.

"Yeah, whatever, Mother Teresa."

Glen couldn't stop himself from laughing. Lucas was such a quick-witted little shit.

"Does your dad smoke?" Glen asked. "I keep smelling cigarette smoke."

"No, he doesn't," Michael replied. "Unless he sneaks out here to do it without anyone seeing him."

"Michael probably farted and you're smelling his stale ass," Lucas said.

Michael threw a baseball glove at his brother and all three boys started laughing hysterically.

"Come on," Glen said. "Let's go ride some more. I only have a few hours before I have to be home."

Lucas lifted the bar off of the door and all three filtered out. Glen paused in the doorway, looking back over his shoulder. At that moment, he didn't feel quite right. The smell of tobacco hit his nose again, but there was something else that he couldn't put his finger on. The air was strange. Bad. A chill went down his back. He suddenly felt a tinge of depression.

"Come on Glen, let's go," the other two boys yelled, almost in unison.

Glen snapped out of his trance and ran after the other two. He didn't know why, but at that moment he wanted to get as far away from the potting shed as possible.

FIFTEEN

It was 11:30 PM and Hanson was dying for a cigarette. He'd put away three packs during the day, which was a record even for him—it was just that kind of day—but he couldn't risk lighting one up right now. The kid could show up any minute, and if he smelled smoke or saw the flick of a lighter, it would be a dead giveaway and he'd surely lose his shot at grabbing the little shit.

Earlier, he had thought about sneaking into the boy's house in the middle of the night to make the grab, but that idea was way too bold. He didn't have the guts to make a play like that right off the bat, anyway. But he also knew he couldn't spend much more time stalking the kid through this shit splat little town either. These people were already becoming suspicious of the big white van cruising the neighborhood. It was only a matter of time before the local cop would be all over his ass.

The boys had given Hanson the perfect opportunity. From the gist of their conversation he'd overheard in the potting shed earlier, there was a good chance the youngest of the three was going to sneak off on his own tonight to mess around in this barn. He had a very positive feeling about it. All he had to do was hide out and jump the kid from within the darkness when the opportunity presented itself. Couldn't be more simple, except that he'd now gone two hours without a cigarette and he was ready to chew off his own foot.

He'd driven just about every backcountry road in this county for most of the day in search of a white barn or something that would allude to the name Chas Martin. It took a few hours, but finally, his lighthouse in the fog appeared. A large, decrepit white barn with the name Chas Martin painted in green letters on the side facing the road. The tin roof and siding boards may have been replaced a few times over the years, but the foundation looked original. It had the same stonework style as some historic buildings he'd seen while driving through the area. Possibly 19th century, if he had to guess. Not that it mattered.

When he cased the barn, he noticed there wasn't a house close by. There was a remnant of a foundation next to it where a house may have once existed—same style stonework as the barn —but nothing here at the present day. Inside, the barn looked like it was just being used to store old junk. He felt confident pulling the van in to keep it out of sight.

Was this really about to happen? Hanson couldn't say for sure. He'd been able to come up with a thousand reasons during the day why he shouldn't go through with it, and only one reason he should. But that one reason heavily outweighed *everything* else. He'd decided that living without Zlo's reward would not happen. If he turned his back on Zlo and didn't acquiesce to his demand, he'd have no chance at having that beautiful thing in his life. That sweet nectar that exploded joy from the very depths of his soul. Without Zlo and this glorious thing he provided, Hanson figured he had maybe two months to live at best. So it was now a matter of survival, right? The strong overtaking the weak. The herd surviving through natural selection. On a primal level, what he was about to do took place in nature every day, and had since the beginning of it all. That was the only justification he needed. It was the trigger to pull to get him through this event with a clean conscience. It was one life for another; his life. Nothing was more important than that. Purely self-preservation, nothing personal.

Hanson felt a slight vibration coming from inside his body. Zlo had not spoken, but he was stirring; becoming active. Something was about to happen.

Outside of the barn, the wind had picked up a bit. A summer rain was in the air. Leaves rustled and added a static background noise to the environment.

A flash of light. It wasn't lightning, but more like a strobe from a lightbulb. Hanson could see this through the gaps between the old barn's wooden slats. It flickered a few more times, each time closer and brighter. Someone was coming. Footsteps in the grass outside, walking along the structure.

The vibrations from within became more intense. Zlo was still silent, but engaged. Hanson felt excitement welling up inside of him as well, ready to burst out at any moment. His heart raced in anticipation of what was about to happen, and his skin now soaked with sweat. All reservations were off, he couldn't wait for this to go down now. He wanted it. Needed it.

Hanson had given a list to the pawnshop owner in Virginia of things he needed along with the van. Zlo had told him what items to procure but did not explain what he was to do with any of these things. One item was a case of *high ether content starter fluid.* He supposed it was to knock out the victim without hurting them too badly. Apparently, as far as he'd seen in movies, all he had to do was spray this stuff into a rag, hold it over the kid's face for a few seconds, and it would put the little fucker right to sleep. Simple! But he honestly did not know if it would work. Worst-case scenario, he'd have to do it the old-fashioned way and crack him over the head and hope for the best.

As the storm blew closer, creaks and moans echoed throughout the rafters as the old structure strained to stay intact against the increasing wind.

Suddenly, the door opened a crack. A beam of light from a flashlight peaked in and hesitantly searched around the room.

The moment was at hand.

Hanson had made his way into a horse stall—eerily reminiscent of the one he had hidden in at the farm in Virginia—and perched in a ready position under the cover of darkness, ether soaked rag in hand. The smell of it made him light-headed, and it was nowhere near his face. An excellent sign.

Rain began pelting the tin roof overhead, adding a passive white noise to every corner of the room. The rain droplets seemed to push the boy inside as he finally came all the way in and closed the barn door behind him.

The beam from the kid's flashlight stretched out from its source like an elongated light saber and waved around in the darkness, erratically searching and scanning. After a moment of random movements, the beam fixated on something. Hanson knew right away, the light was shining on the van. Reflections from the chrome and glass parts danced out from it and jumped around in chaotic patterns.

Would the kid notice that the van was out of place, get scared, and run off? The flashlight beam hadn't moved in almost a minute; he was clearly studying the vehicle.

Hanson's heart pounded the inside of his ribcage like a boxer training on a heavy bag.

The little boy was slowly inching closer to the van, giving it his full attention. He was now merely a few feet away from where his attacker poised to strike. This was it. Hanson began a silent countdown from five… four… three…

Suddenly, the flashlight beam was shining directly into Hanson's face, blinding him with blazing white light. He held up a hand to deflect it, immediately compromising himself. How did the kid even know to look this way? Hanson hadn't made a noise or a movement. It had to be the powerful smell from the ether rag, or maybe from the smell of cigarettes which had become Hanson's natural scent. Regardless of the reason, the time for action was here!

The brightness of the flashlight shining in Hanson's face made it impossible to see the kid, who used the beam as an illusionary shield. The only option he had was to leap at the light source itself and hope his target wasn't standing to the left or right of it. Dead center would be his best bet. Unfortunately, Hanson was dead wrong. He jumped from the stall with all the force his legs could muster, splayed his arms out in a full Super Man stretch, and landed on his chest and face, eating a giant clump of ancient dry earth from the barn floor.

Surprisingly, the kid didn't scream or run. He did, however, do something unexpected; something that Hanson had not accounted for and which terribly confused him.

Dazzling flashes of light, much brighter than the flashlight beam, began popping off one by one, accompanied by a low mechanical sound. The flashes lit up the entire room as each one exploded. They also took Hanson's sight away almost completely, leaving him with nothing but blackness and the remnants of the explosions flashing in front of his eyes. These weren't firecrackers or gunshots; there wasn't a loud accompanied bang or pop to go with the light. When another flash went off, it became clear by the low mechanical noise that followed what the boy was doing. He was taking pictures. The little shit was using a camera as a defense weapon. That also meant that he now had photos of Hanson as well.

This was going to be it. The *Grand Adventure* would either begin or end within the next few seconds. If Hanson could somehow regain his bearings long enough to get the ether soaked rag around the kid's face, he would be off and running. If the little fucker got away, and with photographic evidence, it was all over. They would plaster Hanson's face on every police board from coast to coast. The authorities took it very seriously when someone tried to abduct a child. Hell, even the FBI would be involved. It was sink or swim time.

Hanson stood up fully erect, holding his arm up to cover his eyes from the relentless barrage of flashes that seemed to pound his face. The kid would not let up the pressure.

"You're making a right, proper mess of this, Hanson," Zlo spoke up.

"Well, you're not doing anything to help me!" Hanson yelled out.

"I'm not trying to help you, asshole!" The kid said and laughed. He continued snapping off pictures as if to mock Hanson and his blindness. He was slowly stepping backward toward the door, preparing his escape as he snapped off a few more shots.

Zlo spoke: "When I give the word, you will leap your hardest, thirty degrees to your left. If you fail, you will lose the opportunity. After which I shall leave you to deal with the rest of your miserable existence on your own."

Hanson closed his eyes and stopped trying to fend off the

flashes. He stood still and waited for his command. During this time, the kid seemed to enjoy the relentless taunting with his camera, as he laughed and danced around his opponent, feeling in complete control of the situation.

"Now!" Zlo shouted, and the vibration shocked Hanson's system like never before.

He made his best estimate as to what thirty degrees to his position was and sprung into action, legs off the ground and both arms open wide. To his most pleasant surprise, he had struck pay dirt; dead center. Now he had the kid wrapped up in his arms and trapped underneath him as they both hit the ground. The concussion of hitting the dirt must have knocked the wind out of the boy because the only scream he could seem to get out was a low hissing whisper. He did struggle violently, but his little body was no match for Hanson's strength, especially now that Hanson was dealing with a renewed vigor given to him by his internal companion. Hanson still had the rag in his right hand, which he quickly brought around to cover the boy's mouth and nose. Without hesitation, the little fucker bit down on two of Hanson's fingers as hard as he could and wouldn't let go. Hanson held tight, fighting off the pain and the urge to pull his hand away. Soon, the pressure from the boy's bite lessened. His struggles slowly trickled off. The boy went limp and his hands fell away and thudded onto the dirt floor of the old wooden barn with the peeling white paint and green letters that spelled Chas Martin on the side facing the road.

The *Grand Adventure* had begun.

SIXTEEN

Scrawled into the wooden bench—perhaps by a steady hand and a cheap pocket knife—was the phrase, "Tom loves Lynn." Years of weather and changing seasons had worn the inscription down considerably, but the sentiment still held onto the wood enough to proclaim its message to the world. Somewhere out there was a man named Tom who once loved a girl named Lynn. Perhaps he still loved her? Could they have been one of those rare couples who found endearing love at a young age and held on to it like the most precious commodity on earth? Sure, why not? They could have gotten married, had a couple of kids, a dog, a house in the suburbs, shrubs in the front yard, two cars in the garage, church on Sundays, Friday movie nights with the kids, sex twice a week, and pot roast on the table every night for dinner. Couldn't they? Sometimes, life works out for people. They live, and they're happy, no further questions necessary. Hanson stared at the engraving as he sat next to it, not at all caring if Tom and Lynn had achieved happily ever after or if they were dead in a gutter somewhere. It didn't matter. Truth be told, to Hanson, nothing mattered.

Hanson had not lived a life worth living, a fact he was well aware of day after miserable day. Every decision he had made and every thought he'd ever had revolved around serving himself and his selfish desires without regard for others. He used to blame Zlo, that despicable thing that had taken up residence inside of him, but as the years went on, he came to understand that he was still the one who had committed the acts. He performed his task as instructed because he wanted the reward that came with it. The lives he helped take, the families he destroyed, and the communities he devastated meant nothing. All that mattered was getting a hit of that glory.

He'd lost track of how long it had been since he became Zlo's puppet—as he often thought of himself, suspended by strings, dancing on a small wooden stage for his master's enjoyment—it could have been decades. But even before that night in Baltimore, when it all began, he knew his life held little value. The tiny sliver of conscience he'd once possessed now burried even further into the depths of his soul with the addition of his traveling companion. The reward came from Zlo. His purpose came from Zlo, and therefore his function and only ambition was in the service of Zlo. There was not a human on earth whose life mattered to him as much as his reward, his *Fix*. He had become a slave to his inner daemon, existing only at the pleasure of his master.

But an unusual feeling surfaced within Hanson over the last few years, something he'd felt a few times in the past and had even acted upon on a couple of occasions. There were times during his journey with Zlo when the fog surrounding his conscience would lift for a moment, allowing a crack of light to peek through the darkness. Out-of-place thoughts surfaced that were restricted from his thinking by selfishness or by the ridiculing voice which vibrated within him and kept him on the dark path. At first, the feelings started as tinges of guilt, creeping into Hanson's sub-conscience in small doses at unsuspecting moments. But as the years went on, the tinges became more than just a nuisance; they evolved into full-on emotions, which he could not ignore no matter what Zlo had to say about it.

When the guilt became too strong to ignore, Hanson fell into a good old-fashioned, pass the Prozac please, I'll have seconds, depression. He had lived his life over the last thirty years in almost constant misery, but he'd always had his reward to bring him back into the fold. When the despair of his actions weighed too heavily upon him, he had the option to perform his task and receive his reward, and the reward had always set him straight. With each release of bliss, he understood more and more that this was his life and there would be no living without it. But then the guilt came. There were more moments of reflection when he looked back on his long career of depravity and allowed feelings of dread over the things he had done to rise up and drag him down into the darkest muck of his heart. Zlo would laugh and mock. The bastard not only knew what Hanson was thinking but could also hear what he was feeling. When the mocking started it only fueled Hanson's depression, but there was very little, if anything, he could do about it. Making Zlo leave would surely lead to his demise, and even though he thought of ending it all so many times, he could never quite muster up the courage to do it.

A part of Hanson had believed that his death would actually save the lives of countless innocent children. During his first suicide attempt, Zlo had—with his usual twisted wit and candor—informed Hanson that his death would not do anything to stop the vicious cycle in which he had taken part. Zlo would simply move on to another weak-minded excuse for a human being, make him the same offer, and be back in business in no time, possibly with someone more aggressive and hungrier for reward than Hanson. Hanson's effort wouldn't produce even the slightest positive ripple on the world.

During his second attempt at ending his tenure above ground, Zlo must have thought Hanson was actually going to go through with it. As he wrapped his lips around the cold barrel of the Colt .45 and felt the front site scratch the back of his throat, Zlo cut loose a dose of euphoria, bringing Hanson back in from the ledge and back onto the course of their *Grand Adventure.* It took less than a second of that wonderful sensation coursing through his body before he yanked the gun out of his mouth and thanked Zlo for the new life he had given him. All the regrets he'd faced up to that moment washed away like a spring thaw running down the side of a Colorado mountain.

Sometime later, after realizing that he'd never have the strength to take his own life, and knowing that Zlo would also never allow it, another alternative came to mind, one that would surely make this nightmare end: he would turn himself over to the police. It didn't matter that he'd be spending the rest of his life in federal butt fuck prison, or even wind up strapped to a wooden chair and pumped full of 50,000 volts, at least it would be over. Zlo laughed and even goaded him to do it, seeming to know what the outcome would be and not worrying in the least. The first attempt got him two days in a state police holding cell, then three months in a state mental hospital. Confession number two yielded the same result and a few extra months in the nuthouse. It became apparent that no one believed a lunatic with a head full of voices other than his own. Another fruit bat in search of his fifteen minutes.

"Are you prepared to get serious now, Mr. Parker?" Zlo had said. "We have so much fun left to share."

Hanson did his best now to ignore the vibrating voice. He continued staring at the names of Tom and Lynn scribed into the park bench where he rested near the Cumberland Springs town square gazebo as if they could help him block out the sound. But Zlo would never be discounted.

"Pay attention, Mr. Parker! It is time for you to center, focus, get back on point. Do you understand?" The voice vibrated through Hanson as it always had, letting him know it meant business. It would not be trifled with or ignored. It was in control. It pulled the strings and set the policy, and the policy was to be obeyed.

Zlo laughed, heartily enough to send shocks out to every one of Hanson's extremities. "I believe I have identified your intention, Mr. Parker." The voice continued, laughing. "You've returned to the place where we began our *Grand Adventure*, haven't you? Wait, don't tell me… You're looking to relive a fond memory? Perhaps revisit the scene of your first 'exercise'?" Zlo laughed harder than Hanson had ever heard or felt in the entire time they had been together. It terrified him. "Is it erotic for you, Hanson, thinking of that first young boy you took all those years ago in the white barn? Are you becoming aroused? Are you *hard?*" The laughter continued and grew more powerful.

Hanson fell to the ground because of Zlo's intensity. It shocked him worse than a bathtub full of toasters. He couldn't stand; couldn't even bring himself to his knees. All he could do was lay on the ground in the fetal position, quivering, listening to the maniacal laughter coursing throughout his body, carried on a

Robert Ferencz

field of electrified vibration. Helpless. Defenseless. Broken.

"Ok, Mr. Parker," Zlo said, finally calming slightly from his hysterical outbreak. "What are we to do here in this miserable, despicable place?"

Hanson didn't answer.

"Oh come now, don't go silent on me. You're finally becoming interesting."

Hanson remained silent. His body was having a hard time recovering from the shock of Zlo's outbreak. He also didn't want to speak. All these years of being a servant to a voice had worn deeply on him. The question had been posed to him years ago—probably by one of his favorite drug dealers—before he'd ever met Zlo. "What wouldn't you do for a buzz, Hanson?" After meeting Zlo, the answer became apparent: nothing. There was absolutely *nothing* he would not do to get high.

"Well, Hanson, since you're not in the mood to talk, and I'm just as jolly as a pig rolling in mud tonight, I'll share a brief story with you." Zlo's voice genuinely sounded happy, much unlike his usual sarcastic tone. "It's very interesting that you brought us back to this place after all this time. Very interesting indeed. You see, I begin all of my *Grand Adventures* here, and for an excellent reason: I hate this despicable piece of earth and all those who have ever inhabited it. I have for an extremely long time."

Hanson regained a tiny amount of strength, at least enough to pull himself out of the fetal position and back onto the bench. He sat slouching and looking up at the starry night and half-moon. He wanted Zlo to shut the fuck up, but knew that would never happen by his will. Zlo spoke when he wanted for as long as he wanted, and when he fell silent, it would also be for as long as he wanted.

"Yes, Mr. Parker, I am very well acquainted with this area," Zlo continued. "Years upon years ago—way before your hopeless existence was even considered—I had what I will simply call an 'incident' with some gentlefolks who settled this region. One man, in particular, a Reverend Hopewell Yoder—

284

despicable pig—comes to mind right away."

During their time together, Zlo had rarely volunteered information about himself. His stories were mainly small snippets of events, a sentence or two. But now, as the voice went on, Hanson thought he may finally get a better understanding of the thing that had taken up residence inside of him for all of these years. Hanson perked up and listened, hoping to gain an insight he'd never had before.

"The group of in-bread talking monkeys who put down roots in this hideous place all those years ago had a penchant for the 'spiritual,' so to speak. In other words, their faith in a higher power guided them. Speaking from experience, I can tell you that there certainly *is* a higher power. I'm not a fan of Him, nor does He think much of me, but He does indeed exist. And the reason you exist, Mr. Parker, is a direct result of Him. It's a long and complex chain that I care not to elaborate on at the moment—or ever for that matter.

"As I wandered in search of a new traveling companion—the marshall of a small town had arrested my previous companion and hung in the square in front of a jeering crowd (I found that scene to be quite amusing. Rodney may have been his name. I don't particularly recall)—I ended up in this part of the world. The New World was young then, and I was in search of someone with whom I could form a long-lasting partnership, such as the partnership I formed with you, Mr. Parker. And I did find that person, a young man with an addle mind named Liam. Due to his lack of mental facility, the good people of the newly founded Cumberland Springs considered Liam as somewhat of an outcast. He wasn't completely ostracized from the community but was certainly not welcomed by it either. I believe he and his mother lived together until his mother died and he was forced to fend for himself. With no family or friends to care for him and a town which provided little support, Liam openly welcomed my companionship. But he, like most, found my task for him to be a difficult chore. Immediately, as I began explaining what was required of him, the imbecile ran to the home of Reverend Yoder and reported exactly what the 'voice in his head' had asked of him. To my shocking surprise, this Reverend Yoder was much more connected to the Spirit than I had anticipated. He was able to identify my presence within young Liam and through a rather displeasing and agonizing ritual, banished me from Liam into— of all things—a goat. He then locked me away in a cave and performed a blessing on the entrance so I could not leave on my own."

Hanson felt a change in Zlo as he went on with the story. At first, he seemed amused in retelling the event, but by the end, the shift in emotion was measurable. He felt anger and disgust emanating from Zlo. He was boiling. It was the same rage he felt at the rest stop outside of Winchester, Virginia, when Zlo had lashed out, scaring Hanson so badly that he almost crashed the van.

"These people are despicable, every last worthless man, woman, and child who ever walked the surface of this horrid place!" The voice rang throughout Hanson's body. "I can feel it now as we sit here among them, their righteousness, their virtuousness collectively floating in the air like particles of holy dust. I curse these vile creatures, each of them, to the farthest pit of hell! They are all still here, living their pure existence."

"They can't still be here," Hanson replied. "What you're describing took place over two hundred years ago. They're all dead."

"These people never die, Mr. Parker. Their repugnant seed continues on, generation after generation. They breed and continue and for whatever reason, they stay here in this grease pit of land, continuing their loathsome cycle of life. I hate them, one and all."

Hanson felt a flood of emotions emanating from Zlo's vibrations, all of them negative. But beyond the rage and hatred, he also experienced something unexpected: sadness. It wasn't in the forefront of this emotional buffet, he'd reserved that spot solely for anger, but it was there, subtly bubbling in the underlying tone.

Sadness? Coming from Zlo? Hanson never imagined it possible, but it was there and unmistakable. Knowing the feeling full well from dealing with his own life and the constant stream of sorrow and grief he'd experienced on an almost daily basis, he could easily identify the feeling.

"Mr. Parker," Zlo said, seeming to calm slightly from his anger. "You've given me an idea, one that could greatly benefit the both of us." Zlo laughed for a few seconds, then quickly regained composure. "Let's destroy this place together, once and for all. We'll drop them to their knees and rip out their very souls. We will bring them so much sorrow and pain that no degree of faith will lift them out of the hell we create. They'll suffer and squirm and beg for a savior to carry them from the ashes, but a savior shall not come. There will only be us, Mr. Parker, tearing away at them strip by strip, exposing them for the worthless piles of flesh that they are. Oh, it's perfect! My retribution will finally be at hand. *Why* have I not done such a marvelous thing in the past? All this time since gaining my freedom I have only scratched the surface of vengeance, but you bringing us back here tonight has made it all so clear."

Hanson was weak and tired. Life with Zlo over the past thirty-some years had chipped away his spirit to a point where he felt like he'd never had a soul to begin with. He had become a hollow shell, empty and barren. Physically, Zlo kept him alive and healthy somehow by actually permeating into every cell of his body. He had lived on nothing more than cigarettes, candy bars, and the occasional cheeseburger which seemed to be all he'd needed. This diet would have easily killed a normal human being over all these years, but physically Hanson looked and felt fine, almost as if he'd hardly aged. It was his spirit that had deteriorated into dust. He had gone so far beyond the limits of human decency that not even a miracle could bring him back.

As he listened to Zlo talk with excitement about the sinister plan he was devising, Hanson realized that the time had come. The Grand Adventure needed to end. He didn't care about anything anymore, not even his reward. Zlo could unleash a full dose of paradise throughout his body, and it wouldn't matter. He had come to the end of the road. *Fuck Zlo* and this whole fucked up life. The only thing Hanson had ever done to the world was to make it a worse place than he'd found it. He had not committed a single voluntary act to make the world any better since he'd taken his first step on the surface. The best thing he could do now for humanity would be to leave. There would be severe consequences to pay, that he was sure of, but he accepted it. Whatever came next—if there was anything after this—he deserved.

Hanson stood up and headed for the van.

"So you like my idea, I see," Zlo said. "I love the enthusiasm! Let's jump in and get the ball rolling right away. Perfect!"

Hanson did not answer.

SEVENTEEN

He drove aimlessly without a plan or destination. It was evening now in Cumberland Springs and the late autumn sun had gone below the horizon hours ago, dropping the temperature into winter levels. The streets were void of life. Storefronts closed with hardly a light inside, and bright street lamps illuminated the emptiness of the town, making it feel desolate and deserted. Hanson did not know what the fuck he was doing here. Something internal had brought him back. It wasn't his conscience or the little voice which was supposed to guide one onto the path of righteousness compelling him tonight—Zlo and heavy drug use snuffed those things out years ago. But there was a force that almost seemed beyond his control. A push. Perhaps even a kick in the ass. Whatever it was, there was no denying its existence or the control it had over him. What else could have led him to the middle of nowhere Pennsylvania on this cold November day?

Though it had been well over thirty years since the Grand Adventure with Zlo began here, it appeared nothing at all had changed. The cars he'd seen around town were newer models, of course, but that was pretty much it. From the houses nestled throughout the tree-lined streets to the buildings and stores around the town square, it was as if not a blade of grass had changed. It was still the same perfect picture of small-town America in real life.

He'd gone through dozens of these towns over the years while hunting his victims, but Cumberland Springs stuck with him, in his craw, like phlegm. The place was ingrained in him somehow. The town itself and the memory of the night he took his first victim haunted Hanson like a relentless poltergeist, hell-bent on making his life nothing more than a private hell. The event played out in his mind at any random moment, taunting him, ridiculing him, chastising him. *Remember that night*

Hanson? Remember what you did to that kid? Do you remember how he fought you? It became an endless mockery which began as a single voice, but with the addition of each new victim grew into an angry, jeering mob. Were his victims coming back to haunt him from within? He'd never seen them manifest as an actual apparition, but the voices...

Zlo had gone relatively quiet as Hanson drove through the streets, but not silent. He stirred. Though it made no noise, Hanson knew the daemon was awake. Subtle vibrations of excitement emitted from within. He didn't care. Zlo didn't matter anymore, and neither did that almighty god he'd been forced to worship all these years. It was time for this reign of debauchery to end. Hanson had finally had enough. All he knew now was that something brought him back to Cumberland Springs, whether he could explain it or not, didn't matter.

After a few unguided turns through tree-lined streets and picket-fenced residences, Hanson found himself on a two-lane road leading into the country. The street lamps from town had faded off behind him, leaving the only light of the old van's high beams to guide him. He had driven aimlessly for hours, not knowing where to go or why he was here. All he knew was that a feeling had brought him back, a feeling with an agenda—if that was at all possible.

Suddenly, the blacktop glowed before him like a shining yellow brick road. It seemed to illuminate something ahead for him, perhaps a purpose or reason. It may have been imagination, but a newfound clarity had come over Hanson. It was undeniable. Everything looked familiar. The bumps and cracks of the road, the open fields on one side, and the dense woodlands to the other. He knew this place and knew it well.

Night faded away without warning and Hanson found himself driving in pure, gleaming daylight. Within the blink of an eye, the world around him had washed away, and it was no longer a cold, dreary night in the middle of November. Trees were full of leaves and life, and the open fields were the brightest green with a blazing hot sun shining above. He felt warmth on his face as sun rays flooded through the windshield, filling the van with nature's heat. The world of late fall had become a beautiful and glorious summer afternoon. Magic or illusion, Hanson hadn't the faintest idea, but it felt nice, even welcoming.

He shook his head vigorously, trying to gain some sort of bearing on what had just happened. The act did not affect the situation. It had actually just become summer within the blink of an eye and turned from night into day.

As Hanson drove on, absorbing the surroundings and understanding even less about his world than he did just moments ago, something in the distance caught his attention. It wasn't a memory or a trick of the mind—although nothing at the moment seemed possible or real—but a deja vu come to life. Three small figures pushing bicycles up the hill ahead. He knew right away who the figures were because he'd seen them on this very road before, in what seemed to be these exact conditions. But that had been well over thirty years ago. Never the less, the scene unfolding before him and the memory of this day from out of the past were identical, without question.

Hanson slowed the van as he made his approach. The image of these boys had permanently burned itself into his memory all those years ago, and he became certain he was now watching the event play out as it did the first time he'd rolled into Cumberland Springs. If his memory served him correctly, over the next hill was the house the boys were heading for, and just passed that the abandoned farm where he had hidden the van on the day he'd stalked his first victim. The kids paid little attention to Hanson as he drove by. Their trek up the hill had them joyfully engrossed. Now there was no doubt in his mind, these were the same boys he'd met on that fateful summer day in 1984. Hanson *was* here again, in this time and in this place, as if dropped out of the sky and into a part of his psyche.

As he expected, just over the hill on the right side of the road sat the house with the garden shed in the back. The afternoon sun cast a strong glare off of the house's white aluminum siding, bright enough to make him wince. Hanson passed by slowly, studying the place. At one window, he could make out the figure of a woman inside who appeared to be busy doing something. It was likely a kitchen window. He imagined one of the boy's mother, standing at a sink, doing dishes or preparing an afternoon lunch. She probably had on an apron, as any other perfect housewife would wear. Red and white checkers or some shit.

Behind the house, almost as if it were peaking out from behind the back wall, it stood. The garden shed. An old, ratty, beat-up looking thing. Weathered boards, a half-open door fashioned of the same wood, one window to the right of the door which probably came out of a scrap heap somewhere. In fact, the whole damn thing looked like the resurrection of a scrap heap. It looked at Hanson as he crept by, like a person he'd known from a long time ago who was timid about saying hello again. This place knew him as he knew it. His dreams—or nightmares, as he had come to realize—brought him back here night after tortured night. It was as if his mind would never allow him to forget or deny what had taken place here. The day he had committed himself to the life he'd have for the next three decades all began in this decrepit shit shack in the back of someone's yard.

"This is bullshit," he heard himself say aloud. He slapped his face and shook his head, trying to shake off this alternate reality he'd found himself in. The act was ineffective. It was still the same bright sunny day he'd somehow driven into moments ago.

He reached over into the passenger seat to grab a cigarette. No matter where he was or what shape he was in, he always had a pack of Camel Filters close at hand. His fingers found the pack, and he shook one out. Looking at the pack, he noticed that something had changed. The artwork on the pack was the old school design that he hadn't seen in years. Maybe they were doing some sort of retro ad campaign or something. Whatever logo graced the cover of the pack didn't matter, the flavor was still the same. Sweet Turkish tobacco laced with who cares what chemicals R. J. Reynolds could think up to jam in there.

With the house and garden shed now in his rearview mirror,

Hanson looked ahead to the abandoned farm he knew would be over the next hill. It was as he remembered, standing isolated in a field of overgrown brush and weeds. He pulled the van into the barn—as he did back then—and closed the giant wooden doors. He leaned his forehead against the door and stared down at his shoes. What was he doing here? Was he living this moment in time over again? He'd had vivid dreams in the past, but there was no mistaking this for reality. The warmth of the day, chirping birds and insects, the smell of tall grass carried on the breeze. This was no dream. And those damn kids! They were definitely the same boys he'd trailed on the day he made his first abduction. No, it wasn't a dream, now he was certain. He was back at the beginning, living this fateful day over again.

Hanson looked around and saw the field he'd crossed that day which led to the little white house. He headed across, this time much less nervous than before, knowing that if he made it safely the first time, his chance for success would probably be the same now. As he retraced his steps from memory, more and more details flooded back into his mind. Even those jumping grasshoppers—*God, they were so loud*—he stirred up as he waded through the tall weeds. Everything was exact.

He made his way to the backyard of the house and easily slipped into the shed unnoticed. Inside the house was a calamity of laughter and clanking dishes emanating from the open kitchen window and screen door off the back porch. The boys were inside having lunch and enjoying a perfect day of adolescence. The mother was laughing as well. Hanson took notice of how innocent the entire scene felt. An unsullied group of people without a care in the world, unaware that the predator who would destroy their world and change their lives forever was lurking only thirty feet from their back door.

Once inside the shed and out of sight, he found his original hiding place, a faded grey canvas tarp in the back corner. He carefully slid under it like a snake slithering under a rock. Almost at the exact moment he'd finished situating himself in hiding, the door swung open and three rambunctious boys filed inside. Hanson remained perfectly still and watched as this moment in time played out word for word as he recalled. They were there for no more than fifteen minutes before leaving the shed in a haste and running out into the summer afternoon to enjoy what was left of the day.

"Now what?" The voice rang out the inside of Hanson's body, shaking him with its wicked vibrations. He did not answer, because he had no answer. *Now what?* If it really was thirty years ago, the next thing to do would be to find the old white barn the boys were talking about and hide in the shadows until the youngest one showed up tonight. The rest was history. But did he have to now? He seemed to be in complete control of his actions. He wasn't just watching the events play out like a movie. He was here, in the moment, making his own decisions. Did he have to attack that little kid tonight and kick off a thirty-year reign of depravity? What if he opted out? Suddenly, he felt excitement. He was being given a second chance somehow. Every human being on the face of this planet has contimplated the question: *what if I could go back, knowing what I know now?* Would Hanson stop this at the beginning and take a different course? Even though he'd most likely continue to self implode, at least he wouldn't be responsible for the deaths of all those children.

Excitement coursed through his body. He hadn't known a feeling like this to occur in him naturally; it had always come from whatever substance he was abusing at the time. This feeling, though, was pure, like it was in him from birth; something he could produce on his own without help from drugs or alcohol or anything else that came from outside of his body. This excitement surfaced because he had an option in front of him that could change everything. He could walk away. He knew what the outcome would be if he continued down the path he started thirty years ago, but what would happen if he simply chose to head in the other direction.

"I could walk away," he muttered aloud, under his breath.

"Could you?" Zlo quickly spoke up. "Could you really turn your back on me and all I've given you?"

"Given me? What have you given me? You made me abduct children for you and you think you've given me something?"

"Mr. Parker," Zlo said with the voice of a kindergarten teacher speaking to an unruly child. "I have not made you do anything. I merely presented you with options. You, sir, took care of the rest. Your hands never forced, I can assure you of that."

Zlo laughed. "Allow me to enlighten you to what is happening at this moment. I have indulged none of you creatures in the past, but something about you, Hanson, amuses me. Watching you struggle, yet continue on day after day, failing to let go of your addiction is... *hilarious!*" He laughed again. "You primates are all the same, and the most amusing part is that you think you're above your own primal instincts. You are not. As I am about to show you now, your attempt at grace is futile. You will fail—miserably—and I will laugh and relish in the entertainment you provide. I have brought you to the beginning, the precipice of our *Grand Adventure*, as I'm sure you can tell. What will you do now?"

"Fuck you, Zlo!" Hanson said. "I'm finished with you. I choose not to—" The sensation struck him hard, harder than ever before. It coursed through every fiber, every molecule, every atom of his body. It exploded in him like a raging river full of pleasure and ecstasy. He'd never felt it like this before. A dose heavier than he'd ever imagined. Amazing to a point beyond description, beyond this world. He had somehow connected to feelings that could not have been made on earth. It came from another dimension. He saw, heard, and tasted colors. They were beautiful and delicious and sounded like angels. Everything was perfect. Everything was correct. Everything worked. Then it was gone, replaced only by the sound and vibrations of Zlo laughing.

"Now, Mr. Parker, feel free to choose," Zlo said as he continued his snickering laughter.

Hanson lay on the dirt floor in the fetal position, quivering in the remnants of euphoria. He struggled to push himself up and get to his feet, but he was too weak from pleasure. He collapsed, letting his head bounce off the dust, still in paradise, reveling in the joy of what he'd been given. He didn't have to speak. The decision was obvious and didn't need to be put into words, but he uttered them anyway. "I'll kill the little bastard myself tonight if you give me another hit of that shit!"

Zlo's laughter erupted and went on for what felt like an hour. Truly amused. The vibrations carried his twisted emotion through Hanson's body like never before. Hanson wanted it to stop, but the tremors only became stronger. Not only did this kill his buzz, but it angered Hanson. He became furious. His role as Zlo's puppet had torn his soul to pieces over the years, to a point where he believed the was nothing left. He didn't think he was even capable of emotion anymore, but the laughter, the vibrations, and the taunting struck a final chord. Somewhere from within the depths of his psyche, emotion emerged and the broken, worthless shell of Hanson Parker stood up and said, "NO!"

Zlo's laughter tapered off over a few seconds, and the vibrations fizzled. "What did you just say?" the voice said.

"I said, NO, Zlo," Hanson spoke. "No."

"No, what?"

Hanson stood and stretched his back and arms. He felt vibrant. Something clicked in him and gave him a renewed energy, and it wasn't coming from Zlo. For so long, Zlo had been his only source of vitality, but now a reborn stamina came from somewhere else. The moment the entity joined with Hanson, he felt it flood into every cell of his body. It communed with him on a molecular level, filling every microscopic fiber, keeping him alive and strong. The damage he had done to his body during the years before Zlo, and the diet of nothing but candy bars, cheeseburgers, and cigarettes he fueled himself with over the last thirty years would have killed any normal human being by this age, but here he stood, alive and well. It was Zlo. Zlo needed him alive and needed him strong enough to carry out his task. He kept him that way to perform a service, like a milk cow producing a yield for a dairy farmer. But this fresh energy came from another place. A natural place. From within.

"Mr. Parker (Hanson), you are getting so far ahead of yourself. I have not *given* you a choice. There is not a 'yes' or a 'no,' there is only what I allow. Please tell me that over the course of all these years, you have come to understand that. Yes?"

"No, Zlo," Hanson said. "I'm finished. I'm out!"

There was silence for a moment, then the entity spoke. "Alright, Mr. Parker, I'll entertain you for a moment, only because you have entertained me for the entire time we've been associates. However, there is something you should understand, which—since you primates are all intellectually deficient—I shall explain to you. In fact, there are two things. First, there is no life without me. You are only still breathing because I have kept your body alive this long. Left to your own facilities, you wouldn't have lived for a week longer than the night I found you. So, ending your association with me would indeed mean your earthly demise. And I say earthly demise because that brings me to my second point. I once told you that everyone serves a master... Everyone. You serve me and the reward I provide you for serving me, and I serve another. I also mentioned that you would one day meet the one I serve. Your introduction to my master and his associates will not be pleasant for you. In fact, it will be immeasurably worse than any description I could provide and that you would comprehend. Master is a most formidable force who has been waiting with much anticipation to meet you. I believe there are plans for you once your association with me has concluded. You will not be pleased with what is coming for Hanson Parker. I will say that the longer you can delay this meeting, the better for you. It is inevitable one day, of course, but we can still postpone this for quite some time. So you see Hanson, your options other than staying your current course are not favorable. Do you understand?"

Hanson smiled as the Grinch did the moment his heart grew three sizes bigger on that glorious Christmas morning from the realization that he no longer needed to be what he always was.

Would this be his salvation? Was this the moment when he devoted his life to helping others and doing the Lord's work? Of course not. But it was a small enough awakening in him which finally said, *I'm finished!*

"I'm done with you, Zlo," Hanson said. "Our 'association' as you like to put it is over. I want you out. Leave. Go."

"Hanson," Zlo said. "I'll give you just one more opportunity to change your mind. If I leave, I will leave you to what comes next and I will go on, finding other ventures with others such as yourself and the cycle shall continue. You will have played your part and you will move on to the same place where all of my other servants have gone, and believe me, they are very excited about having you there."

"I don't give a shit anymore, Zlo. Get out. Now!" Tears rolled down Hanson's cheeks, but not from sadness; they came purely from relief. "GET THE FUCK OUT!" he screamed and dropped to his knees. Dust clouded around his hands as they hit the ground in front of his face.

Silence. Hanson could actually hear his heart beating in his ears because of the overwhelming quiet. Zlo had gone mute. There wasn't an audible voice nor the slightest vibration coming from within, just pure black silence. Was he gone? Did Zlo actually listen to Hanson's demand? He smiled and had the strangest feeling that he was back in command of himself. He had always been responsible for his actions, but Zlo had poked and prodded him in whatever direction he wanted him to go until Hanson relented. But now, that wasn't the case. Control was restored. Hanson moved and thought without guidance. His demented internal compass had lost its magnetic grounding. The fucking thing actually left! He couldn't believe it. That connection to the inner daemon now broken. The tether had snapped. It was over.

On his knees, Hanson put his forehead to the dirt floor and cried. He inhaled old dust as his cries intensified but didn't care. He was finally rid of it, that horrible thing that came to him while he was at his lowest point in a wet alley in Baltimore and gave him a life even worse than before. That cursed thing was really gone. He spun the wheel through a litany of emotions and finally landed on excitement. It jolted throughout his heart and flowed in his veins like sunshine in a bottle. He jumped to his feet and danced. There was no discernible rhythm to his steps, just a man frolicking like an idiot in the middle of a potting shed. After several moments of reveling, he noted his surroundings. It was suddenly frigidly cold, by at least forty to fifty degrees. And the sun which had shown in beams of light through the shed's lone window had gone. Hanson stood alone in the dark, inhaling bitter cold air into his lungs as he took heavy breaths. He looked out the window and saw a bright full moon casting a blue glow over the world outside. When he entered this shack moments ago it was a hot summer day in what appeared to be 1984, but what he saw through the window now was a frost-covered, desolate night. There were no leaves on the trees, no chirping birds, no buzzing insects, just cold black darkness.

The change in light and temperature didn't matter, Hanson felt free and as light as a puff of dandelion seeds. But all of those wonderful feelings that came along with his newfound freedom were short-lived. The energy he'd experienced moments ago brutally torn from him, as if someone pulled it away like a tablecloth, leaving the place settings behind. Pain shocked him from his stomach to his head to the very tips of his fingers and toes. There was not a single part of him that did not scream out in agony. Hanson tried to moan, to cry, but there was nothing. His mouth and throat were completely void of moisture. Every muscle constricted and shriveled, causing him to fall to the ground and involuntarily curl into the fetal position. His hands warped into claws and the fingernails cracked and broke off. His teeth felt brittle and as his jaw convulsed from the pain and cold; they cracked and broke off, leaving razor-sharp shards inside his mouth. Years before he'd met Zlo there was a moment when he ran out of money and had no other options to buy drugs, so he had to go without for a week. The pain from his withdrawal was more than he'd ever imagined possible. What he was experiencing at this moment, however, made his withdrawal day look like nothing more serious than a hangnail. It was pain on a level that could not be measured.

He shook uncontrollably. The cold had seeped into every pore of his body, making what nerve endings he had left dance in an unnatural, tumultuous rhythm. Less than a foot from where he lay was the faded canvas tarp. It looked much older and frayed than moments ago when he had used to hide under, as if it had naturally aged in a matter of minutes. It didn't matter. He needed it now. The only source of warmth in this God-forsaken place. He reached for the closest corner of it and anguish tore through his body, right down to the very marrow that filled his bones. This simple act of pulling a blanket over himself for shelter would be the most arduous task he'd ever performed to this day. His first two attempts left him just short of his target, but the third grab found pay dirt. The smallest victory in his current struggle, but a victory none the less.

Hanson felt his stomach and intestines about to explode. From somewhere deep in his heart or conscience or whatever it was, he found his final shred of dignity. He would not shit himself, no matter what the cost. Enduring even more pain than when he had grabbed for the canvas, he reached down and unbuttoned his pants. While doing so, he realized he had lost a considerable amount of weight. Once the button on his waistline came undone, his pants easily slid from his lower half and down below his ankles. It was a photo finish. The second his pants were clear, his ass let go of a river of waste. It was as if his body had needed to shed years upon years of build-up. There was little relief from the release, only more pain, and suffering as the exiting material felt like it was coated in acid.

Hanson lay quivering in misery, covered under a tattered old tarp, atop a pile of his own crap. The only comfort he had now came from the shit he lay in, which was still warm. Pain, agony, complete loss of dignity—though he'd never had much of that before—and sorrow. This is what Hanson Parker's life had amounted to. A life that had never once aided or contributed to society in any way. A selfish existence, serving only his need to feel pleasure at any and all costs to others. Now he had nothing. We come into this world with nothing and leave it with nothing, but along the way, we have the opportunity to make a difference, not always on a global scale, but within the confines of our surroundings. Those who make that difference can here leave knowing that they lived a life worth living. The only mark Hanson Parker left on the world was a long trail of suffering for every other life he ever came into contact with.

"Well, I told you this would happen," the voice said. It was Zlo, but this time it wasn't coming from within. It sounded like it stood above Hanson, looking down on him. "We could have had many more experiences along our *Grand Adventure*. In fact, I could have easily kept your worthless body alive for another century, which is far beyond what your flesh is designed to handle. Yet, you have chosen another path, one which will be far worse than your primate imagination can conceive. I, on the other hand, shall introduce myself to another worthless flesh sack, such as yourself, and begin a new *Grand Adventure* with them. The cycle will continue, endlessly for eternity, and you, Mr. Parker, will fade into obscurity in just a few moments from now. Well, that is until your eternity begins. Oh, you should not look forward to this, oh no indeed." The voice laughed and faded.

Hanson only had vision left in one eye, which was blurring, but before it did, he saw the shape of a black shadow peering down at him. The shape was humanoid, but there were no discernible features. He knew it was Zlo; he could feel it. What he also felt was Zlo's indifference. This thing had lived inside of Hanson for thirty or more years, and it felt nothing for him. It looked down on him with the same concern one would have for a piss ant walking on a sidewalk. No emotion, love, or hate, only total disregard. It honestly did not care one way or the other for Hanson. Then it was gone, and Hanson was truly alone.

THE END

The large wooden sign at the edge of town has faded a bit since its dedication back in 1976, but the message remains the same: Cumberland Springs, Honest, Quiet, Friendly. A rectangular design with an overlapping oval. The oval, centered and offset to rise out of the top, houses a hand-carved illustration of the Braddock Street bridge which spans over the small waterfall at the East entrance to the town square. During periods of heavy rain in the Spring, the little waterfall makes enough noise that conversation in the area becomes impossible. People passing each other will just politely smile and wave.

In the late 1950s, a beautification grant was awarded to Cumberland Springs to turn the land around the bridge and waterfall into a quaint park and picnic area. Over the years, city officials regularly voted to increase spending on what would become Falls Park, adding to its area and facilities. The residents of Cumberland Springs take great pride in the town centerpiece. On any given sunny day, the park will brim over with activity and laughter as families gather to spend afternoons on blankets in the grass or at any of the various picnic tables, enjoying the sight and sound of the Cumberland River as it flows over its ten-foot drop which creates the falls.

One block West of the park and no more than a five-minute walk, one will find themselves in the town square. On a meticulously manicured landscape of lush grass and colorful flowers sits a lovely white gazebo with a black shingled roof, surrounded by a brick-paved roundabout. Martin's corner drugstore, a small cafe/diner named Nana's, Davis Appliance, La Chance Hardware, Julia's Flowers, Brantley's Antiques, and the Cumberland Springs Municipal Building make up the buildings and businesses which encircle the gazebo and roundabout. The town square is another focal point, bringing residents together to shop, eat, or quietly relax in the area's atmosphere.

At the left corner next to the gazebo rests a large sacred monument which was dedicated to Cumberland Springs in 1921 by the Veterans of Foreign Wars. Inscribed in granite are the names of every resident killed in the line of duty while serving in the U.S. Armed Forces for as far back as the town history has recorded, even when the British controlled this area. The first name on the list is PVT. George Robert Wilcox, Born 1756 - Died 1779. The inscriptions become more clear as the years go on until finally, the last two names gleam like fresh wounds carved into pale skin. PVT. Ryan Henderson, Born 1985 - Died 2005 and CPL. Shayne Wallace, Born 1983 - Died 2006. Both killed in Afganistan. Shayne's high school buddies get together once a year on his birthday at the monument late in the evening and drink a case of Budweiser. No one bothers them.

Old-fashioned, European style street lamps surround the outskirts of the square and four of them dot each corner of the center by the gazebo. The area is just as pleasant to walk through at night as it is during a sunny day.

Each month of the year, an event takes place in the square or the park, which brings everyone out of their homes to join together in the fellowship of the community. Festivities begin with the New Years Eve countdown then move on to Winter Fest, the giant Easter Egg hunt in Falls Park, the Spring Cleaning Mile-Long Yard Sale, Spring Fest, Memorial Day BBQ, Summer Concerts in the park, Fourth of July cookout, and fireworks, Labor Day Picnic, High School football season kick-off, Pumpkin Fest, the Christmas Tree lighting ceremony that takes place on Thanksgiving night, and finally the Christmas eggnog/cider competition that takes place a week before Christmas day —the rules state no alcohol is to be used in the eggnog recipes, but Emily Blanton gets by on a technicality: since vanilla extract contains alcohol, she can use rum liqueur (she wins every year).

There is a pride in Cumberland Springs, handed down from generation to generation. The families who live here have the understanding that this town, its traditions, and way of life are a blessing to be preserved. Kids who go off to college always make it back to celebrate these sacred events with their family and friends. Those who live here respect what was founded all the way back in 1756, when a group of families settled and formed a community where they could bond and help each other through the struggles of the New World. This pride carries value and weight with each person who lives here or was born here.

What the residents of Cumberland Springs have not been aware of all these years is that something out there despises them. It loathes their fellowship and strength and faith. It hates each one of them, young and old, and wishes nothing but pain and destruction upon them. They continue on with their lives as peaceful and happy as they always have, all while being abhorred by a force that no one knows even exists.

It has loathed them for as far back as history remembers, but within recent years its hatred has become a raging boil. It wants them to suffer and scream and writhe in agony. It will stop at nothing to bring about the destruction of their very souls. It has now decided that the time has finally come for the good people of Cumberland Springs to revel in the misery that they deserve. The moment is at hand. The cock has crowed. They will know hardship on a level that cannot be measured in human understanding. Yes, the moment has come, the price will be paid in flesh, blood, and suffering. The innocent will be consumed in the gnashing of teeth, and this land shall burn into the earth.

Author's note :

I would like to personally thank you for taking the time to come along on this journey with me. Your time is important and if you made it through to the end of this story, you have my gratitude. This is the first of three books in this series; the other two will be coming out soon. I look forward to reading your Amazon reviews, if you feel compelled to write one.

Take care and God Bless...
Robert Ferencz

Robert lives in Nashville, TN and spends most of his time writing terrifying tales, watching horror movies, and hanging out with his lovely forever, Rochelle. He enjoys a good steak, a well-crafted pizza, and two fingers/three rocks of Jameson. Life is simple if you make it that way...

Made in the USA
Monee, IL
11 April 2021